MR MIDSHIPMAN EASY

FREDERICK MARRYAT

Mr Midshipman Easy

HEART OF OAK SEA CLASSICS

Dean King, Series Editor

Foreword by

Dean King

Introduction by

Louis J. Parascandola

AN OWL BOOK

HENRY HOLT AND COMPANY   NEW YORK

Henry Holt and Company, Inc.
Publishers since 1866
115 West 18th Street
New York, New York 10011

Henry Holt ® is a registered
trademark of Henry Holt and Company, Inc.

Published in Canada by Fitzhenry & Whiteside Ltd.,
195 Allstate Parkway, Markham, Ontario L3R 4T8.

Library of Congress Cataloging-in-Publication Data
Marryat, Frederick, 1792–1848.
Mr. Midshipman Easy / Frederick Marryat : foreword by Dean King :
introduction by Louis J. Parascandola. — 1st Holt ed.
        p.   cm. — (Heart of oak sea classics series)
Includes bibliographical references.
ISBN 0-8050-5567-3 (alk. paper).
ISBN 0-8050-5988-1 (pbk.: alk. paper)
1. Napoleonic Wars, 1800–1815—Fiction.   2. Great Britain—
History, Naval—19th century—Fiction.   I. Title.   II. Series.
PR4977.M7   1998b   98-6699
823'.7—DC21

Henry Holt books are available for special promotions and premiums.
For details contact: Director, Special Markets.

First published in 1836 by Saunders & Otley.

First Owl Books Edition 1998

Designed by Kate Nichols

Printed in the United States of America
All first editions are printed on acid-free paper. ∞

1   3   5   7   9   10   8   6   4   2

HEART OF OAK

Come cheer up, my lads, 'tis to glory we steer,
To add something new to this wonderful Year:
To honour we call you, not press you like slaves,
For who are so free as the sons of the waves?

CHORUS:
Heart of Oak are our ships,
Heart of Oak are our men,
We always are ready,
Steady, boys, steady,
We'll fight and we'll conquer again and again.

We ne'er see our foes but we wish them to stay;
They never see us but they wish us away:
If they run, why we follow, and run them on shore,
For if they won't fight us, we cannot do more.

Heart of Oak, etc.

They swear they'll invade us, these terrible foes,
They'll frighten our women, and children, and beaux;
But should their flat-bottoms in darkness get o'er,
Still Britons they'll find to receive them on shore.

Heart of Oak, etc.

We'll still make them run and we'll still make them sweat,
In spite of the Devil, and Brussels Gazette:
Then cheer up, my lads, with one voice let us sing
Our soldiers, our sailors, our statesman, and King.

Heart of Oak, etc.

—DAVID GARRICK

Source: C. H. Firth, *Naval Songs and Ballads*. Publications of the Navy Records Society, vol. XXXIII (London, 1908), p. 220.

FOREWORD

STORIES OF MIDSHIPMEN hold a special place in the tradition of naval literature. The indoctrination of a young boy—whether he be willing or intractable—into the strict ways of the Navy is somehow especially intriguing. In the course of this transition from home life to life at sea, young midshipmen ("too young," Nelson once groused on hearing that a boy had seen active duty at age eleven, not unusual at the time) experienced considerable pain. Much of this came courtesy of the older midshipmen. But there were certain immediate gratifications: new sights and scenes, clear rules and punishments (many a middy had been in hot water at home or school), and the joyful sport of boys on board ship. In any case, there was little time and no privacy for wallowing in self-pity at the sudden loss of parents and the comforts of dry land.

In contemporary fiction, C. S. Forester wrote *Mr. Midshipman Hornblower*, including an account of his famous character's first command, at the age of seventeen, when the famous frigate captain Sir Edward Pellew put him in charge of a French merchant prize carrying rice. Due to the absorbent nature of the cargo, signs of a forgotten shot hole below the water line were not apparent until too late. The expanding rice burst the brig at the seams, and Hornblower

abjectly watched his first command sink from the brig's boat crowded with his prisoners.

While Patrick O'Brian writes about Captain Jack Aubrey's service
in the Royal Navy, he has spiced the Aubrey-Maturin novels with
tantalizing flashbacks. In *The Ionian Mission*, Aubrey remembers
standing up to a tyrant and taking a beating in the *Queen* as a youngster. As boys, he and his best friend, Heneage Dundas, fought a duel,
scarring Aubrey on the arm for life. But the best known lore of
Aubrey's midshipman days stemmed from his being disrated and
turned before the mast for keeping a young woman in the cable tiers
of H.M.S. *Resolution* while on the Cape Station. That crucial time of
Aubrey's life not only produced in him an authentic understanding
for the seaman before the mast but also a bastard son.

Of earlier writers, Captain Basil Hall is one notable memoirist
who as a boy served in the Royal Navy during the Napoleonic wars.
In his three-volume *Fragments of Voyages and Travels* (1831 to 1833), he
described his first voyage on board a man-of-war, on which he suffered from seasickness, a chronically aching tooth, and relentless
teasing for his Scottish patois. He was branded "Mr. Justice Gobble"
by his mischievous messmates who quickly capitalized on his complaint of not getting his fair portion of the pudding one day. Another
writer who drew great inspiration from his days as a midshipman in
the Royal Navy was, of course, Frederick Marryat (1792–1848), who
entered the service in 1806 at the age of fourteen and later became the
most celebrated naval novelist of his day.

In his sea novels, *Frank Mildmay* (1829), *Peter Simple* (1834), *Mr
Midshipman Easy* (1836), and *Percival Keene* (1842), Marryat focused
quite a bit of attention on the protagonists' early days and their expe-
riences as midshipmen. Marryat took great delight in creating his
heroes from the ground up, finding this an effective way both to start
a novel and to venerate the naval service; for what better way to cre-
ate a story than by planting youthful faults to be overcome through
life's experience, and what better proof of the Royal Navy's benevolence than its conversion of a pampered, recalcitrant youth into a
zealous sea officer?

Always with his tongue halfway in cheek, Marryat liked to set his
protagonists off on the wrong foot. Peter Simple was considered the
"greatest fool of the family," to which he credits being sacrificed to
the "prosperity and naval superiority of the country." The incorrigi-
ble Percival Keene, a love child of the Honourable Captain Delmar,

who takes great pains to conceal this relationship, earns his naval berth through ruthless pranks ashore. In *Mr Midshipman Easy*, Jack Easy is an unexpected child of parents rapidly approaching their dotage. He is suckled by an unmarried wet nurse, spoiled by his mother, and brainwashed by his father's foolish political philosophy of universal egalitarianism in all matters at all times. Not surprisingly, the pampered, headstrong boy is a nuisance and is shipped off to school at an early age.

Like Smollett before him, Marryat made great use (and fun) of despotic schoolmasters. By standing up to these capricious bullies, Marryat's budding heroes, however else lacking, demonstrate an uncompromising sense of justice. In *Percival Keene*, when Keene's sandwich-pilfering teacher demands more mustard on the sandwiches, the outraged boy lathers on the cathartic calomel instead, poisoning him for months. Later, when the schoolmaster, who beats his delinquents with a birch rod, cancels Guy Fawkes Day vacation and confiscates the boys' fireworks, Keene contrives to light the combustibles, which are stashed under the teacher's seat. The blast nearly sends both of them to Kingdom Come, burning down the school in the process.

Like Keene and Simple, Easy has many hurdles to leap on his way to redemption. "I cannot say that I have had worse, but I have almost as bad," carps Mr. Bonnycastle, the schoolmaster, after meeting the boy. "I will apply the Promethean torch, and soon vivify that rude mass," he promises. Much to Mrs. Easy's relief, however, Bonnycastle does not flog. What she doesn't know is that he considers flogging weak tea. Instead, he canes his young reprobates so fiercely that they can't sit for days.

But even the ruthless Bonnycastle, who does temporarily subdue Easy with his barbaric caning, cannot dispirit the boy, proving that Easy has the right stuff for the Royal Navy. Like Simple and Keene, he meets naval life head-on. Easy's adventures and his eventual transformation—much to the Royal Navy's credit—are all the more compelling for Marryat's exploration of his neophyte days.

My thanks once again to Marryat expert Louis Parascandola, who—as he did in the Heart of Oak edition of *Peter Simple*—adds so perceptibly to the reading pleasure of this volume through his insightful introduction and notes on the text.

—Dean King

INTRODUCTION

C APTAIN FREDERICK MARRYAT (1792–1848) first entered my
life over twenty years ago when a college professor, Kenneth
Scott, cited him as a minor but intriguing novelist and the
author of a vinegary account of his travels to America, *A Diary in
America, with Remarks on Its Institutions* (1839). Although that brief
mention piqued my interest, my next encounter with Marryat did
not occur until several years later. While reconnoitering a new neigh-
borhood, I happened upon an old bookstore that surprisingly had a
prominent display of the captain's novels in the window. My curios-
ity drove me inside. I only wanted to buy a couple of the novels, but
the bookseller convinced me to purchase them all, offering to sell
them by the pound! After dragging the volumes home (in two trips),
I began to peruse my haul. My first glance focused on *Mr Midshipman
Easy*, the only Marryat novel I had even heard of. From that moment
I was hooked, venturing upon a voyage with Marryat from which I
have yet to disembark.

Once I had fallen under the sway of Marryat's fiction, I began
investigating his life. And what an adventuresome life it was! He was
born in London, the son of a rich merchant and member of
Parliament, Joseph Marryat. After several unsuccessful attempts to

run away to sea, young Marryat was permitted to join the Royal Navy in 1806, where he sailed under Lord Thomas Cochrane on the *Impérieuse* until 1809. It was on board the *Impérieuse* that Marryat found the grist for his novels of the sea. Marryat's years in the service came at a crucial juncture in England's history. War with Napoleonic France raged until 1815, and Marryat served with distinction in the Royal Navy, participating in over fifty engagements and earning numerous commendations until he resigned his post in 1830.

On land, Marryat pursued a writing career, composing about twenty highly profitable novels for adults and children, including *Peter Simple* (1834), *Jacob Faithful* (1834), *Mr Midshipman Easy* (1836), *Masterman Ready* (1841–42), and *The Children of the New Forest* (1847). Several of his best works were first published in the *Metropolitan Magazine*, which he edited from 1832 to 1836. In addition, he became part of the literary circle of Dickens and Lady Blessington. In fact, Marryat was among the most widely read authors of the nineteenth century, one whose writings were eagerly anticipated.*

Of all Marryat's works, *Mr Midshipman Easy* has been the most popular, and the only one never to go out of print. The appeal of the book is readily apparent in its tightly woven plot (this despite the fact that the first two of its three volumes were written in twelve days). It is a bildungsroman in which the young hero, Jack Easy, undergoes a series of adventures during which he gradually realizes the folly of his father's theory of social equality.† The practical lessons Jack Easy learns at sea, particularly from the veteran sailor Jolliffe and from the fair but firm Captain Wilson, helped educate not only young Easy but also several subsequent generations on life in the Royal Navy. Marryat was, in Joseph Conrad's words, "an enslaver of youth," and his tales of heroic tars recruited more sailors than anything the Navy could devise. His lively adventures set in faraway locations were persuasive enough that, in Melville's *Typee*, boys would say they joined the American Navy because of Marryat.

---

* For fuller biographical sketches of Marryat, see the introduction to *Peter Simple* (Holt, 1998) or the works listed in the bibliography on pages xvii–xviii (particularly Lloyd and Dorling for information on his naval career).

† Marryat's criticism of social equality would continue in his *Diary in America*. He writes that when "those selected by the people to represent them are not only bound by pledges previous to their election, but ordered by the mass how to vote after their election, then the country is not ruled by the collected wisdom of the people, but of the majority, who are as often wrong as right, and then the governing principle sinks into a democracy, as it now is in America."

Although *Mr Midshipman Easy* has strong narrative charms, Marryat felt that plot was less important than vivid characterization and humor, and he attempted to construct his novels accordingly. Jack Easy, a naive, free-spirited figure with unbounded optimism who is beloved by the crew, is one of Marryat's most engaging characters. He gets into a number of scrapes, including a hilarious triangular duel. The high jinks in which he engages with his friends Mesty and Gascoigne are among Marryat's finest moments. His quest for fun and adventure seems to be his driving force. Indeed, although Jack proves himself a creditable sailor, he has little "predilection for duty."

The lively mood that permeates the novel is partly a result of its abundant humor, particularly in the first half of the book. When a woman is brought in to act as a nurse to young Jack, it is discovered that she is unmarried. Appalled, Jack's mother blurts out, "Not a married woman, and she has a child!" The woman, bowing politely, calmly declares, "If you please, ma'am, it was a very little one." Marryat's earthy humor both titillated and shocked many nineteenth-century readers.

Even in a lighthearted book such as *Mr Midshipman Easy*, however, Marryat had his serious concerns. The book was published in 1836, when England was still reeling from a series of political and social reforms, the most notable being the First Reform Bill in 1832, which greatly increased the electorate, and the Emancipation Act in 1834, which liberated slaves throughout the British empire. In his sea novels, Marryat capitalized on the nostalgia for the past age of military glory. The subject appealed greatly to an audience wearied by the fast-changing world.

Marryat himself had somewhat vacillating feelings on reform, although his views often fell on the conservative side. Jack's relationship with the African Mesty exemplifies this ambivalence. Marryat had encountered a number of Blacks aboard ship and in his voyages to the West Indies, where he held several posts and where his family owned property. Because of this contact with Blacks, Marryat frequently included them in his novels. Mesty (short for Mephistopheles) is in many ways a stereotypic figure. He has filed teeth, desires his enemies' skulls, and spends his time glaring fiercely at Jack's foes while acting deferential to our hero. Still, Mesty is a remarkable character, a former Ashanti prince who has escaped from slavery. Jack constantly turns to him for advice, and he learns from him in much the same way that Huck learns from Jim in *Huckleberry Finn.* Jack tells Mesty, "I love you as a friend—and with my will we never part again." He lives up to his word, taking Mesty wherever he goes. Certainly, their relationship is not based on equality. Marryat's message is not that everyone is equal, but that "superiors" have an obligation to aid those below them and those beneath must accept their status. The relationship between the two men works well because each fulfills his designated role in Marryat's world order.

Marryat believed not only in distinctions between the races, but in society as a whole. Although he often shows sympathy toward social climbers in his fiction (Marryat himself was a second son), it is only a small, select group that can advance, often under the benevolent guidance of a more genteel patron. In general, Marryat felt that the ideal structure, as proposed by Jack after he has discarded his father's views, is a pyramid: "based upon the many, and rising by degrees, it becomes less as wealth, talent, and rank increase in the individual, until it ends at the apex or monarch, above all." Society is endangered when someone like the common pickpocket Easthupp tries to rise above his station or, on a larger scale, when Easy's father attempts to subvert the entire social order.

This same need for structure, according to Marryat, is what drives a ship. A major focus in *Mr Midshipman Easy* is the relationship between senior officers and those below them. Marryat, in a characteristic digression, breaks in the middle of his narration to discuss the treatment of junior officers by their superiors (see page 175). Although this may appear completely out of place, the discussion—about how those in power have an obligation to those beneath them—fits in perfectly with the theme of the book. The articles of war so beloved by young Jack are "equally binding on officers and crew; but what a dead letter do they become if officers are permitted to break them with impunity!" In the hands of a Captain Wilson, modeled on Lord Cochrane as are so many of Marryat's virtuous captains, the ship becomes, in the words of the literary scholars Elliot Engel and Margaret King, a "benevolent aristocracy" functioning in perfect harmony.

Even after leaving the Navy in 1830, Marryat remained deeply concerned about the service, and it is, of course, his portrayal of it on which Marryat's esteem largely rests. *Mr Midshipman Easy* is rich in word-pictures, taken principally from the three years Marryat spent in the Mediterranean under Cochrane. The gale so vividly described in the book in chapter twenty-five, for example, is based on an early adventure aboard the *Impérieuse* (described in Captain Taprell Dorling's *Men O' War*): "The cry of terror which ran through the lower decks; the grating of the keel as she was forced in; the violence of the shocks which convulsed the frame of the vessel; the hurrying up of the ship's company without their clothes; and then the enormous waves which again bore her up, and carried her clear over the reef, will never be effaced from my memory." And under the daring Cochrane, Marryat witnessed a number of cutting-out expeditions that found a place in *Mr Midshipman Easy*. He also participated in several deadly exchanges with the French and their allies. Marryat wrote in his journal, "the day that passed without a shot being fired in anger was with us a blank day." The chilling depiction of the taking of a Russian frigate in chapter twenty-nine of this book is just one of his many portrayals of the carnage of war. These recollections, so stirringly recounted, are what give Marryat's writing its vitality.

Marryat's powerful rendering of nautical life, his warm humor and lively characterization make me grateful for that chance discovery of his books many years ago. But I am just one in a lengthy list of admirers, including such prominent authors as Coleridge, Irving, Thackeray, Stevenson, Hemingway, Ford, Woolf, Conrad, and Forester. The recent renaissance of maritime fiction augurs well for a long overdue rekindling of interest in this early master of the genre. Like *Peter Simple*, previously released in a Heart of Oak Sea Classics edition, the spirited, action-filled narrative of *Mr Midshipman Easy* proves that, in the words of Conrad, Marryat's "adventures are enthralling; the rapidity of his action fascinates. . . . His greatness is undeniable."

—Louis J. Parascandola

SELECTED BIBLIOGRAPHY

Brantlinger, Patrick. *Rule of Darkness: British Literature and Imperialism, 1830–1914*. Ithaca, NY: Cornell University Press, 1988.

Buster, Walter Alan. "The Life and Novels of Captain Marryat." Dissertation, University of Virginia, 1979.

Conrad, Joseph. *Notes on Life and Letters*. Garden City, NY: Doubleday, 1921.

Dorling, Taprell. *Men O' War*. London: Philip Allan & Co., 1929.

Engel, Elliot, and Margaret F. King. *The Victorian Novel Before Victoria: British Fiction During the Reign of William IV, 1830–37*. New York: St. Martin's, 1984.

Gautier, Maurice-Paul. *Captain Frederick Marryat: L'Homme et L' Oeuvre*. Montreal: Didier, 1973.

Hannay, David. *Life of Frederick Marryat*. London: Walter Scott, 1889.

Lloyd, Christopher. *Captain Marryat and the Old Navy*. London: Longmans, Green, 1939.

Marryat, Florence. *Life and Letters of Captain Marryat*. 2 vols. New York: Appleton & Co., 1872.

Marryat, Frederick. *A Diary in America, with Remarks on Its Institutions*. 1839. Edited by Sydney Jackman. New York: Knopf, 1962.

Parascandola, Louis J. *"Puzzled Which to Choose": Conflicting*

Sociopolitical Views in the Works of Captain Frederick Marryat. New York: Peter Lang Publishing, Inc., 1997.

Warner, Oliver. *Captain Marryat: A Rediscovery.* London: Constable, 1953.

Woolf, Virginia. *The Captain's Deathbed and Other Essays.* New York: Harcourt, Brace, Jovanovich, 1950.

ACKNOWLEDGMENTS

I WOULD LIKE TO thank the following people for their support: Professors N. John Hall, Michael Timko, and the late Wendell S. Johnson of the CUNY Graduate School; Professor Steven Gale of Kentucky State University; Professor Patrick Brantlinger of Indiana University; Professor Emeritus James D. Merritt of Brooklyn College; Dr. Marilyn Kurtz; Susan Rothchild; the late Camille E. Beazer; my friends at Mid-Manhattan Library, particularly Deborah Hirsch; my colleagues at Long Island University, especially Professor Emeritus Kenneth Scott; LIU's Research Release Time Committee and LIU's Board of Trustees; Dean King; Shondel Nero; my siblings, John, Maryann, Judy, and their families; my parents, Louis and Ann.

—L.J.P.

EDITORIAL NOTE

THE FIRST FOUR CHAPTERS of *Mr Midshipman Easy* were published in the *Metropolitan Magazine* (August 1836). Marryat, shrewd businessman that he was, hoped that his audience, anxious for more, would be sufficiently hooked to then buy the book. The first edition of the novel was published in three volumes by Saunders & Otley in London in 1836. The present edition follows the text that is generally considered the best edition, that by R. Brimley Johnson (London: J. M. Dent; New York: Little, Brown and Co., 1896), with a few minor emendations. A number of the nautical terms defined in the notes are taken from *A Sea of Words: A Lexicon and Companion for Patrick O'Brian's Seafaring Tales*, 2nd edition, by Dean King with John B. Hattendorf and J. Worth Estes (New York: Henry Holt, 1997). Thanks for permission.

—L.J.P.

MR MIDSHIPMAN EASY

CHAPTER I

Which the reader will find very easy to read.

MR NICODEMUS EASY was a gentleman who lived down in Hampshire; he was a married man, and in very easy circumstances. Most couples find it very easy to have a family, but not always quite so easy to maintain them. Mr Easy was not at all uneasy on the latter score, as he had no children; but he was anxious to have them, as most people covet what they cannot obtain. After ten years, Mr Easy gave it up as a bad job. Philosophy is said to console a man under disappointment, although Shakespeare asserts that it is no remedy for toothache;* so Mr Easy turned philosopher, the very best profession a man can take up, when he is fit for nothing else; he must be a very incapable person indeed who cannot talk nonsense. For some time, Mr Easy could not decide upon what description his nonsense should consist of; at last he fixed upon the rights of man, equality, and all that; how every person was born to inherit his share of the earth, a right at present only admitted to a certain length; that is, about six feet, for we all inherit our graves and are allowed to take possession without dispute. But no one

---

* No remedy for toothache: "For there was never yet philosopher / That could endure the toothache patiently" (*Much Ado About Nothing* 5.1.35–36).

would listen to Mr Easy's philosophy. The women would not acknowledge the rights of men, whom they declared always to be in the wrong; and, as the gentlemen who visited Mr Easy were all men of property, they could not perceive the advantages of sharing with those who had none. However, they allowed him to discuss the question, while they discussed his port wine. The wine was good, if the arguments were not, and we must take things as we find them in this world.

While Mr Easy talked philosophy, Mrs Easy played patience, and they were a very happy couple, riding side by side on their hobbies, and never interfering with each other. Mr Easy knew his wife could not understand him, and therefore did not expect her to listen very attentively; and Mrs Easy did not care how much her husband talked, provided she was not put out in her game. Mutual forbearance will always ensure domestic felicity.

There was another cause for their agreeing so well. Upon any disputed question Mr Easy invariably gave it up to Mrs Easy, telling her that she should have her own way—and this pleased his wife; but, as Mr Easy always took care, when it came to the point, to have his way, he was pleased as well. It is true that Mrs Easy had long found out that she did not have her own way long; but she was of an easy disposition, and as, in nine cases out of ten, it was of very little consequence how things were done, she was quite satisfied with his submission during the heat of the argument. Mr Easy had admitted that she was right, and if like all men he would do wrong, why, what could a poor woman do? With a lady of such a quiet disposition, it is easy to imagine that the domestic felicity of Mr Easy was not easily disturbed. But, as people have observed before, there is a mutability in human affairs. It was at the finale of the eleventh year of their marriage that Mrs Easy at first complained that she could not enjoy her breakfast. Mrs Easy had her own suspicions, everybody else considered it past doubt, all except Mr Easy; he little "thought, good easy man, that his greatness was ripening"; he had decided that to have an heir was no Easy task, and it never came into his calculations, that there could be a change in his wife's figure. You might have added to it, subtracted from it, divided it, or multiplied it, but as it was a zero, the result would be always the same. Mrs Easy also was not quite sure—she believed it might be the case, there was no saying; it might be a mistake, like that of Mrs

Trunnion's in the novel,* and, therefore, she said nothing to her husband about the matter. At last Mr Easy opened his eyes, and when, upon interrogating his wife, he found out the astounding truth, he opened his eyes still wider, and then he snapped his fingers and danced, like a bear upon hot plates, with delight, thereby proving that different causes may produce similar effects in two instances at one and the same time. The bear dances from pain, Mr Easy from pleasure; and again, when we are indifferent, or do not care for anything, we snap our fingers at it, and when we are overjoyed, and obtain what we most care for, we also snap our fingers. Two months after Mr Easy snapped his fingers, Mrs Easy felt no inclination to snap hers, either from indifference or pleasure. The fact was, that Mrs Easy's time was come, to undergo what Shakespeare pronounces "the pleasing punishment that women bear";† but Mrs Easy, like the rest of her sex, declared "that all men were liars," and most particularly poets.

But while Mrs Easy was suffering, Mr Easy was in ecstasies. He laughed at pain, as all philosophers do when it is suffered by other people, and not by themselves.

In due course of time, Mrs Easy presented her husband with a fine boy, whom we present to the public as our hero.

CHAPTER II

In which Mrs Easy, as usual, has her own way.

IT WAS the fourth day after Mrs Easy's confinement that Mr Easy, who was sitting by her bedside in an easy chair, commenced as follows: "I have been thinking, my dear Mrs Easy, about the name I shall give this child."

"Name, Mr Easy! why, what name should you give it but your own?"

---

* Mrs Trunnion's in the novel: Character in Tobias Smollett's novel *The Adventures of Peregrine Pickle* (1751). She mistakenly thought she was pregnant.
† "The pleasing punishment that women bear": *A Comedy of Errors* 1.1.46.

"Not so, my dear," replied Mr Easy; "they call all names proper names, but I think that mine is not. It is the very worst name in the calendar."

"Why, what's the matter with it, Mr Easy?"

"The matter affects me as well as the boy. Nicodemus is a long name to write at full length, and Nick is vulgar. Besides, as there will be two Nicks, they will naturally call my boy young Nick, and of course I shall be styled old Nick,* which will be diabolical."

"Well, Mr Easy, at all events then let me choose the name."

"That you shall, my dear, and it was with this view that I have mentioned the subject so early."

"I think, Mr Easy, I will call the boy after my poor father—his name shall be Robert."

"Very well, my dear, if you wish it, it shall be Robert. You shall have your own way. But I think, my dear, upon a little consideration, you will acknowledge that there is a decided objection."

"An objection, Mr Easy?"

"Yes, my dear; Robert may be very well, but you must reflect upon the consequences; he is certain to be called Bob."

"Well, my dear, and suppose they do call him Bob?"

"I cannot bear even the supposition, my dear. You forget the county in which we are residing, the downs covered with sheep."

"Why, Mr Easy, what can sheep have to do with a Christian name?"

"There it is; women never look to consequences. My dear, they have a great deal to do with the name of Bob. I will appeal to any farmer in the county, if ninety-nine shepherds' dogs out of one hundred are not called Bob. Now observe, your child is out of doors somewhere in the fields or plantations; you want and you call him. Instead of your child, what do you find? Why, a dozen curs at least, who come running up to you, all answering to the name of Bob, and wagging their stumps of tails. You see, Mrs Easy, it is a dilemma not to be got over. You level your only son to the brute creation by giving him a Christian name which, from its peculiar brevity, has been monopolised by all the dogs in the county. Any other name you please, my dear, but in this one instance you must allow me to lay my positive veto."

* Old Nick: The devil.

"Well, then, let me see—but I'll think of it, Mr Easy; my head aches very much just now."

"I will think for you, my dear. What do you say to John?"

"O no, Mr Easy, such a common name."

"A proof of its popularity, my dear. It is scriptural—we have the Apostle and the Baptist—we have a dozen Popes who were all Johns. It is royal—we have plenty of kings who were Johns—and moreover, it is short, and sounds honest and manly."

"Yes, very true, my dear; but they will call him Jack."

"Well, we have had several celebrated characters who were Jacks. There was—let me see—Jack the Giant Killer, and Jack of the Bean Stock—and Jack—Jack—"

"Jack Spratt," replied Mrs Easy.

"And Jack Cade, Mrs Easy, the great rebel—and Three-fingered Jack, Mrs Easy, the celebrated negro—and, above all, Jack Falstaff, ma'am, Jack Falstaff—honest Jack Falstaff—witty Jack Falstaff—"

"I thought, Mr Easy, that I was to be permitted to choose the name."

"Well, so you shall, my dear; I give it up to you. Do just as you please; but depend upon it that John is the right name. Is it not now, my dear?"

"It's the way you always treat me, Mr Easy; you say that you give it up, and that I shall have my own way, but I never do have it. I am sure that the child will be christened John."

"Nay, my dear, it shall be just what you please. Now I recollect it, there were several Greek emperors who were Johns; but decide for yourself, my dear."

"No, no," replied Mrs Easy, who was ill, and unable to contend any longer, "I give it up, Mr Easy. I know how it will be, as it always is: you give me my own way as people give pieces of gold to children, it's their own money, but they must not spend it. Pray call him John."

"There, my dear, did not I tell you you would be of my opinion upon reflection? I knew you would. I have given you your own way, and you tell me to call him John; so now we're both of the same mind, and that point is settled."

"I should like to go to sleep, Mr Easy; I feel far from well."

"You shall always do just as you like, my dear," replied the husband, "and have your own way in everything. It is the greatest pleasure I have when I yield to your wishes. I will walk in the garden. Good-bye, my dear."

Mrs Easy made no reply, and the philosopher quitted the room. As may easily be imagined, on the following day the boy was christened John.

CHAPTER III

In which our hero has to wait the issue of an argument.

THE READER may observe that, in general, all my first chapters are very short, and increase in length as the work advances. I mention this as a proof of my modesty and diffidence. At first, I am like a young bird just out of its mother's nest, pluming my little feathers and taking short flights. By degrees I obtain more confidence, and wing my course over hill and dale.

It is very difficult to throw any interest into a chapter on childhood. There is the same uniformity in all children until they develop. We cannot, therefore, say much relative to Jack Easy's earliest days; he sucked and threw up his milk while the nurse blessed it for a pretty dear, slept, and sucked again. He crowed in the morning like a cock, screamed when he was washed, stared at the candle, and made wry faces with the wind. Six months passed in these innocent amusements, and then he was put into shorts. But I ought here to have remarked, that Mrs Easy did not find herself equal to nursing her own infant, and it was necessary to look out for a substitute.

Now a common-place person would have been satisfied with the recommendation of the medical man, who looks but to the one thing needful, which is a sufficient and wholesome supply of nourishment for the child; but Mr Easy was a philosopher, and had latterly taken to craniology,* and he descanted very learnedly with the Doctor upon the effect of his only son obtaining his nutriment from an unknown source. "Who knows," observed Mr Easy, "but that my son may not imbibe with his milk the very worst passions of human nature."

"I have examined her," replied the Doctor, "and can safely recommend her."

---

*Craniology: The study of the size and shape of skulls for scientific purposes; now generally called phrenology.

"That examination is only preliminary to one more important," replied Mr Easy. "I must examine her."

"Examine who, Mr Easy?" exclaimed his wife, who had lain down again on the bed.

"The nurse, my dear."

"Examine what, Mr Easy?" continued the lady.

"Her head, my dear," replied the husband. "I must ascertain what her propensities are."

"I think you had better leave her alone, Mr Easy. She comes this evening, and I shall question her pretty severely. Doctor Middleton, what do you know of this young person?"

"I know, madam, that she is very healthy and strong, or I should not have selected her."

"But is her character good?"

"Really, madam, I know little about her character; but you can make any inquiries you please. But at the same time I ought to observe, that if you are too particular in that point, you will have some difficulty in providing yourself."

"Well, I shall see," replied Mrs Easy.

"And I shall feel," rejoined the husband.

This parleying was interrupted by the arrival of the very person in question, who was announced by the housemaid, and was ushered in. She was a handsome, florid, healthy-looking girl, awkward and naive in her manner, and apparently not over wise; there was more of the dove than of the serpent in her composition.

Mr Easy, who was very anxious to make his own discoveries, was the first who spoke. "Young woman, come this way, I wish to examine your head."

"Oh! dear me, sir, it's quite clean, I assure you," cried the girl, dropping a curtsey.

Doctor Middleton, who sat between the bed and Mr Easy's chair, rubbed his hands and laughed.

In the meantime, Mr Easy had untied the string and taken off the cap of the young woman, and was very busy putting his fingers through her hair, during which the face of the young woman expressed fear and astonishment.

"I am glad to perceive that you have a large portion of benevolence."

"Yes," replied the young woman, dropping a curtsey.

"And veneration also."

"Thanky, sir."

"And the organ of modesty is strongly developed."

"Yes, sir," replied the girl with a smile.

"That's quite a new organ," thought Dr Middleton.

"Philo-progenitiveness very powerful."

"If you please, sir, I don't know what that is," answered Sarah, with a curtsey.

"Nevertheless you have given us a practical illustration. Mrs Easy, I am satisfied. Have you any questions to ask? But it is quite unnecessary."

"To be sure I have, Mr Easy. Pray, young woman, what is your name?"

"Sarah, if you please, ma'am."

"How long have you been married?"

"Married, ma'am?"

"Yes, married."

"If you please, ma'am, I had a misfortune, ma'am," replied the girl, casting down her eyes.

"What, have you not been married?"

"No, ma'am, not yet."

"Good heavens! Dr Middleton, what can you mean by bringing this person here?" exclaimed Mrs Easy. "Not a married woman, and she has a child!"

"If you please, ma'am," interrupted the young woman, dropping a curtsey, "it was a very little one."

"A very little one!" exclaimed Mrs Easy.

"Yes, ma'am, very small, indeed, and died soon after it was born."

"Oh, Dr Middleton!—what could you mean, Dr Middleton?"

"My dear madam," exclaimed the Doctor, rising from his chair, "this is the only person that I could find suited to the wants of your child, and if you do not take her I cannot answer for its life. It is true, that a married woman might be procured; but married women, who have a proper feeling, will not desert their own children; and as Mr Easy asserts, and you appear to imagine, the temper and disposition of your child may be affected by the nourishment it receives, I think it more likely to be injured by the milk of a married woman who will desert her own child for the sake of gain. The misfortune which has happened to this young woman is not always a proof of a bad heart, but of strong attachment, and the overweening confidence of simplicity."

"You are correct, Doctor," replied Mr Easy, "and her head proves that she is a modest young woman, with strong religious feeling, kindness of disposition, and every other requisite."

"The head may prove it all for what I know, Mr Easy, but her conduct tells another tale."

"She is well fitted for the situation, ma'am," continued the Doctor.

"And if you please, ma'am," rejoined Sarah, "it was *such a little one.*"

"Shall I try the baby, ma'am?" said the monthly nurse, who had listened in silence. "It is fretting so, poor thing, and has its dear little fist right down its throat."

Dr Middleton gave the signal of assent, and in a few seconds Master John Easy was fixed to Sarah as tight as a leech.

"Lord love it, how hungry it is!—there, there, stop it a moment, it's choking, poor thing!"

Mrs Easy, who was lying on her bed, rose up, and went to the child. Her first feeling was that of envy, that another should have such a pleasure which was denied to herself; the next, that of delight, at the satisfaction expressed by the infant. In a few minutes the child fell back in a deep sleep. Mrs Easy was satisfied; maternal feelings conquered all others, and Sarah was duly installed.

To make short work of it, we have said that Jack Easy in six months was in shorts. He soon afterwards began to crawl and show his legs; indeed, so indecorously, that it was evident that he had imbibed no modesty with Sarah's milk, neither did he appear to have gained veneration or benevolence, for he snatched at everything, squeezed the kitten to death, scratched his mother, and pulled his father by the hair; notwithstanding all which, both his father and mother and the whole household declared him to be the finest and sweetest child in the universe. But if we were to narrate all the wonderful events of Jack's childhood from the time of his birth up to the age of seven years, as chronicled by Sarah, who continued his dry nurse after he had been weaned, it would take at least three volumes folio. Jack was brought up in the way that every only child usually is—that is, he was allowed to have his own way.

CHAPTER IV

In which the doctor prescribes going to school as a remedy for a cut finger.

HAVE YOU no idea of putting the boy to school, Mr Easy?" said Dr Middleton, who had been summoned by a groom with his horse in a foam to attend immediately at Forest Hill, the name of Mr Easy's mansion, and who, upon his arrival, had found that Master Easy had cut his thumb. One would have thought that he had cut his head off by the agitation pervading the whole household—Mr Easy walking up and down very uneasy, Mrs Easy with great difficulty prevented from syncope,* and all the maids bustling and passing round Mrs Easy's chair. Everybody appeared excited except Master Jack Easy himself, who, with a rag round his finger, and his pinafore spotted with blood, was playing at bob-cherry, and cared nothing about the matter.

"Well, what's the matter, my little man?" said Dr Middleton, on entering, addressing himself to Jack, as the most sensible of the whole party.

"Oh, Dr Middleton," interrupted Mrs Easy, "he has cut his hand; I'm sure that a nerve is divided, and then the lock-jaw—"

The Doctor made no reply, but examined the finger: Jack Easy continued to play bob-cherry with his right hand.

"Have you such a thing as a piece of sticking-plaster in the house, madam?" observed the Doctor, after examination.

"O yes:—run, Mary,—run, Sarah!" In a few seconds the maids appeared, Sarah bringing the sticking-plaster, and Mary following with the scissors.

"Make yourself quite easy, madam," said Dr Middleton, after he put on the plaster, "I will answer for no evil consequences."

"Had I not better take him upstairs, and let him lie down a little?" replied Mrs Easy, slipping a guinea into the Doctor's hand.

"It is not absolutely requisite, madam," said the Doctor; "but at all events he will be kept out of more mischief."

"Come, my dear, you hear what Dr Middleton says."

"Yes, I heard," replied Jack; "but I sha'n't go."

* Syncope: Fainting.

"My dear Johnny—come, love—now do, my dear Johnny."

Johnny played bob-cherry, and made no answer.

"Come, Master Johnny," said Sarah.

"Go away, Sarah," said Johnny, with a back-hander.

"Oh! fie, Master Johnny," said Mary.

"Johnny, my love," said Mrs Easy in a coaxing tone, "come now—will you go?"

"I'll go in the garden and get some more cherries," replied Master Johnny.

"Come, then, love, we will go into the garden."

Master Johnny jumped off his chair, and took his mamma by the hand.

"What a dear, good, obedient child it is!" exclaimed Mrs Easy; "you may lead him with a thread."

"Yes, to pick cherries," thought Dr Middleton.

Mrs Easy, and Johnny, and Sarah, and Mary, went into the garden, leaving Dr Middleton alone with Mr Easy, who had been silent during this scene. Now Dr Middleton was a clever, sensible man, who had no wish to impose upon anyone. As for his taking a guinea for putting on a piece of sticking-plaster, his conscience was very easy on that score. His time was equally valuable, whether he were employed for something or nothing; and, moreover, he attended the poor gratis. Constantly in the house, he had seen much of Mr John Easy, and perceived that he was a courageous, decided boy, of a naturally good disposition; but from the idiosyncracy of the father, and the doating folly of the mother, in a sure way of being spoiled. As soon, therefore, as the lady was out of hearing, he took a chair, and made the query at the commencement of the chapter, which we shall now repeat.

"Have you no idea of putting the boy to school, Mr Easy?"

Mr Easy crossed his legs, and clasped his hands together over his knees, as he always did when he was about to commence an argument.

"The great objection that I have to sending a boy to school, Dr Middleton, is, that I conceive that the discipline enforced is, not only contrary to the rights of man, but also in opposition to all sound sense and common judgment. Not content with punishment, which is in itself erroneous, and an infringement of social justice, they even degrade the minds of the boys still more by applying punishment to the most degraded part, adding contumely to tyranny. Of course, it is intended that a boy who is sent to school should gain by precept and example; but is he to learn benevolence by the angry look and the flourish of the vindictive birch,—or forbearance, by the cruelty of the ushers,—or patience, when the masters over him are out of all patience,—or modesty, when his nether parts are exposed to general examination? Is he not daily reading a lesson at variance with that equality which we all possess, but of which we are unjustly deprived? Why should there be a distinction between the flogger and the floggee? Are they not both fashioned alike after God's image, endowed with the same reason, having an equal right to what the world offers, and which was intended by Providence to be equally distributed? Is it not that the sacred inheritance of all, which has tyrannously and impiously been ravished from the many for the benefit of the few, and which ravishment, from long custom of iniquity and inculcation of false precepts, has too long been basely submitted to? Is it not the duty of a father to preserve his only son from imbibing these dangerous and debasing errors, which will render him only one of a vile herd who are content to suffer, provided that they live? And yet are not these very errors inculcated at school, and impressed upon their mind inversely by the birch? Do not they there receive their first lesson in slavery with the first lesson in A B C; and are not their minds thereby prostrated, so as never to rise again, but ever to bow to despotism, to cringe to rank, to think and act by the precepts of others, and to tacitly disavow that sacred equality which is our birthright? No, sir, without they can teach without resorting to such a fundamental error as flogging, my boy shall never go to school."

And Mr Easy threw himself back in his chair, imagining like all philosophers, that he had said something very clever.

Dr Middleton knew his man, and therefore patiently waited until he had exhausted his oratory.

"I will grant," said the Doctor at last, "that all you say may have great truth in it; but, Mr Easy, do you not think that by not permitting a boy to be educated, you allow him to remain more open to that very error of which you speak? It is only education which will conquer prejudice, and enable a man to break through the trammels of custom. Now, allowing that the birch is used, yet it is at a period when the young mind is so elastic as to soon become indifferent; and after he has attained the usual rudiments of education, you will then find him prepared to receive those lessons which you can yourself instil."

"I will teach him everything myself," replied Mr Easy, folding his arms consequentially and determinedly.

"I do not doubt your capability, Mr Easy; but unfortunately you will always have a difficulty which you never can get over. Excuse me, I know what you are capable of, and the boy would indeed be happy with such a preceptor, but—if I must speak plain—you must be aware as well as I am, that the maternal fondness of Mrs Easy will always be a bar to your intention. He is already so spoiled by her, that he will not obey; and without obedience you cannot inculcate."

"I grant, my dear sir, that there is a difficulty on that point; but maternal weakness must then be overcome by paternal severity."

"May I ask how, Mr Easy? for it appears to me impossible."

"Impossible! By heavens, I'll make him obey, or I'll—" —Here Mr Easy stopped before the word flog was fairly out of his mouth,—"I'll know the reason why, Dr Middleton."

Dr Middleton checked his inclination to laugh, and replied, "That you would hit upon some scheme, by which you would obtain the necessary power over him, I have no doubt; but what will be the consequence? The boy will consider his mother as a protector, and you as a tyrant. He will have an aversion to you, and with that aversion he will never pay respect and attention to your valuable precepts when he arrives at an age to understand them. Now it appears to me that this difficulty which you have raised may be got over. I know a very worthy clergyman who does not use the birch; but I will write, and put the direct question to him; and then if your boy is removed from the danger arising from Mrs Easy's overindulgence, in a short time he will be ready for your more important tuition."

"I think," replied Mr Easy, after a pause, "that what you say merits consideration. I acknowledge that in consequence of Mrs Easy's nonsensical indulgence, the boy is unruly, and will not obey me at present; and if your friend does not apply the rod, I will think seriously of sending my son John to him to learn the elements."

The Doctor had gained his point by flattering the philosopher.

In a day he returned with a letter from the pedagogue in answer to one supposed to be sent to him, in which the use of the birch was indignantly disclaimed, and Mr Easy announced to his wife, when they met that day at tea-time, his intentions with regard to his son John.

"To school, Mr Easy? what, send Johnny to school! a mere infant to school!"

"Surely, my dear, you must be aware that at nine years it is high time that he learnt to read."

"Why he almost reads already, Mr Easy; surely I can teach him that. Does he not, Sarah?"

"Lord bless him, yes, ma'am, he was saying his letters yesterday."

"Oh, Mr Easy, what can have put this in your head? Johnny, dear, come here—tell me now what's the letter A? You were singing it in the garden this morning."

"I want some sugar," replied Johnny, stretching his arm over the table to the sugar-basin, which was out of his reach.

"Well, my love, you shall have a great lump if you will tell me what's the letter A."

"A was an archer, and shot at a frog," replied Johnny in a surly tone.

"There now, Mr Easy; and he can go through the whole alphabet—can't he, Sarah?"

"That he can, the dear—can't you, Johnny dear?"

"No," replied Johnny.

"Yes, you can, my love; you know what's the letter B. Now don't you?"

"Yes," replied Johnny.

"There, Mr Easy, you see what the boy knows, and how obedient he is too. Come, Johnny dear, tell us what was B?"

"No, I won't," replied Johnny, "I want some more sugar"; and Johnny, who had climbed on a chair, spread himself over the table to reach it.

"Mercy! Sarah, pull him off—he'll upset the urn," screamed Mrs Easy. Sarah caught hold of Johnny by the loins to pull him back, but Johnny, resisting the interference, turned round on his back as he lay on the table, and kicked Sarah in the face, just as she made another desperate grasp at him. The rebound from the kick, given as he lay on a smooth mahogany table, brought Johnny's head in contact with the urn, which was upset in the opposite direction, and, notwithstanding a rapid movement on the part of Mr Easy, he received a sufficient portion of boiling liquid on his legs to scald him severely, and induce him to stamp and swear in a very unphilosophical way. In the meantime Sarah and Mrs Easy had caught up Johnny, and were both holding him at the same time, exclaiming and lamenting. The pain of the scald, and the indifference shown towards him, were too much for Mr Easy's temper to put up with. He snatched Johnny out of their arms, and, quite forgetting his equality and rights of man, belaboured him without mercy. Sarah flew into interfere, and received a blow which not only made her see a thousand stars, but sent her reeling on the floor. Mrs Easy went off into hysterics, and Johnny howled so as to be heard at a quarter of a mile.

How long Mr Easy would have continued it is impossible to say; but the door opened, and Mr Easy looked up while still administering the punishment, and perceived Dr Middleton in mute astonishment. He had promised to come in to tea, and enforce Mr Easy's arguments, if it were necessary; but it certainly appeared to him, that in the argument which Mr Easy was then enforcing, he required no assistance. However, at the entrance of Dr Middleton, Johnny was dropped, and lay roaring on the floor; Sarah, too, remained where she had been floored, Mrs Easy had rolled on the floor, the urn was also on the floor, and Mr Easy, although not floored, had not a leg to stand upon.

Never did a medical man look in more opportunely. Mr Easy at first was not certainly of that opinion, but his legs became so painful that he soon became a convert.

Dr Middleton, as in duty bound, first picked up Mrs Easy, and laid her on the sofa. Sarah rose, picked up Johnny, and carried him, kicking and roaring, out of the room; in return for which attention she received sundry bites. The footman, who had announced the doctor, picked up the urn, that being all that was in his department. Mr Easy threw himself panting in agony on the other sofa, and Dr Middleton was excessively embarrassed how to act: he perceived that Mr Easy required his assistance, and that Mrs Easy could do without it; but how to leave a lady, who was half really and half pretendedly in hysterics, was difficult; for if he attempted to leave her, she kicked and flounced, and burst out the more. At last Dr Middleton rang the bell, which brought the footman, who summoned all the maids, who carried Mrs Easy upstairs, and then the Doctor was able to attend to the only patient who really required his assistance. Mr Easy explained the affair in few words, broken into ejaculations from pain, as the Doctor removed his stockings. From the applications of Dr Middleton, Mr Easy soon obtained bodily relief; but what annoyed him still more than his scalded legs, was the Doctor having been a witness to his infringement of the equality and rights of man. Dr Middleton perceived this, and he knew also how to pour balm into that wound.

"My dear Mr Easy, I am very sorry that you have had this accident, for which you are indebted to Mrs Easy's foolish indulgence of the boy; but I am glad to perceive that you have taken up those parental duties which are inculcated by the Scriptures. Solomon says, 'that he who spares the rod, spoils the child,' thereby implying that it is the duty of a father to correct his children, and in a father, the so doing does not interfere with the rights of man, or any natural equality, for the son being a part or portion of the father, he is only correcting his own self; and the proof of it is, that a father, in punishing his own son, feels as much pain in so doing as if he were himself punished. It is, therefore, nothing but self-discipline, which is strictly enjoined us by the Scriptures."

"That is exactly my opinion," replied Mr Easy, comforted at the Doctor having so logically got him out of the scrape. "But—he shall go to school to-morrow, that I'm determined on."

"He will have to thank Mrs Easy for that," replied the Doctor.

"Exactly," replied Mr Easy. "Doctor, my legs are getting very hot again."

"Continue to bathe them with the vinegar and water, Mr Easy, until I send you an embrocation, which will give you immediate relief. I will call to-morrow. By-the-bye, I am to see a little patient at Mr Bonnycastle's: if it is any accommodation, I will take your son with me."

"It will be a great accommodation, Doctor," replied Mr Easy.

"Then, my dear sir, I will just go up and see how Mrs Easy is, and to-morrow I will call at ten. I can wait an hour. Good-night."

"Good-night, Doctor."

The doctor had his game to play with Mrs Easy. He magnified her husband's accident—he magnified his wrath, and advised her by no means to say one word, until he was well and more pacified. The next day he repeated this dose, and, in spite of the ejaculations of Sarah, and the tears of Mrs Easy, who dared not venture to plead her cause, and the violent resistance of Master Johnny, who appeared to have a presentiment of what was to come, our hero was put into Dr Middleton's chariot, and with the exception of one plate of glass, which he kicked out of the window with his feet, and for which feat the Doctor, now that he had him all to himself, boxed his ears till he was nearly blind, he was, without any further eventful occurrence, carried by the Doctor's footman into the parlour of Mr Bonnycastle.

CHAPTER V

Jack Easy is sent to a school at which there is no flogging.

MASTER JACK had been plumped down in a chair by the Doctor's servant, who, as he quitted him, first looked at his own hands, from which the blood was drawn in several parts, and then at Master Jack, with his teeth closed, and lips compressed, as much as to say, "If I only dared, would not I, that's all!" and then walked out of the room, repaired to the carriage at the front door, when he showed his hands to the coachman, who looked down from his box in great commiseration, at the same time fully sharing his fellow-servant's indignation. But we must repair to the parlour. Dr Middleton ran over a newspaper, while Johnny sat on the chair all of a heap, looking like a lump of sulks, with his feet on the upper front bar, and his knees almost up to his nose. He was a promising pupil, Jack.

Mr Bonnycastle made his appearance—a tall, well-built, hand-some, fair man, with a fine powdered head, dressed in solemn black, and knee buckles; his linen beautifully clean, and with a peculiar bland expression of countenance. When he smiled he showed a row of teeth white as ivory, and his mild blue eye was the *ne plus ultra** of beneficence. He was the beau-ideal of a precep-tor, and it was impossible to see him and hear his mild pleasing voice, without wishing that all your sons were under his protection. He was a ripe scholar, and a good one, and at the time we speak of, had the care of upwards of one hundred boys. He was celebrated for turning them out well, and many of his pupils were rising fast in the senate, as well as distinguishing themselves in the higher professions.

Dr Middleton, who was on intimate terms with Bonnycastle, rose as he entered the room, and they shook hands. Middleton then turned to where Jack sat, and pointing to him, said, "Look there."

Bonnycastle smiled. "I cannot say that I have had worse, but I

---

* *Ne plus ultra*: Perfection.

have almost as bad. I will apply the Promethean torch,* and soon vivify that rude mass. Come, sit down, Middleton."

"But," said the Doctor, as he resumed his chair, "tell me, Bonnycastle, how you will possibly manage to lick such a cub into shape, when you do not resort to flogging?"

"I have no opinion of flogging, and therefore I do not resort to it. The fact is, I was at Harrow myself, and was rather a pickle. I was called up as often as most boys in the school, and I perfectly recollect, that eventually I cared nothing for a flogging. I had become case-hardened. It is the least effective part that you can touch a boy upon. It leaves nothing behind to refresh their memories."

"I should have thought otherwise."

"My dear Middleton, I can produce more effect by one caning than twenty floggings. Observe, you flog upon a part the most quiescent; but you cane upon all parts, from the head to the heels. Now, when once the first sting of the birch is over, then a dull sensation comes over the part, and the pain after that is nothing; whereas a good sound caning leaves sores and bruises in every part, and on all the parts which are required for muscular action. After a flogging, a boy may run out in the hours of recreation, and join his playmates as well as ever, but a good caning tells a very different tale; he cannot move one part of his body without being reminded for days by the pain of the punishment he has undergone, and he is very careful how he is called up again."

"My dear sir, I really had an idea that you were excessively lenient," replied Middleton, laughing; "I am glad that I am under a mistake."

"Look at that cub, Doctor, sitting there more like a brute than a reasonable being; do you imagine that I could ever lick it into shape without strong measures? At the same time, allow me to say, that I consider my system by far the best. At the public schools, punishment is no check; it is so trifling that it is derided: with me punishment is punishment in the true sense of the word, and the consequence is, that it is much more seldom resorted to."

"You are a terrorist, Bonnycastle."

"The two strongest impulses in our nature are fear and love. In

* Promethean torch: Prometheus was a Titan punished by Zeus for giving mankind fire. Zeus punished him by chaining him to a rock where an eagle ate his liver each day only to have it grow back every night. According to some Greek mythological stories, Prometheus created man, fashioning him out of mud.

theory, acting upon the latter is very beautiful; but in practice, I never found it to answer,—and for the best of reasons, our self-love is stronger than our love for others. Now I never yet found fear to fail, for the very same reason that the other does, because with fear we act upon self-love, and nothing else."

"And yet we have many now who would introduce a system of schooling without correction; and who maintain that the present system is degrading."

"There are a great many fools in this world, Doctor."

"That reminds me of this boy's father," replied Dr Middleton; who then detailed to the pedagogue the idiosyncracy of Mr Easy, and all the circumstances attending Jack being sent to his school.

"There is no time to be lost then, Doctor. I must conquer this young gentleman before his parents call to see him. Depend upon it, in a week I will have him obedient and well broke in."

Dr Middleton wished Jack good-bye, and told him to be a good boy. Jack did not vouchsafe to answer. "Never mind, Doctor, he will be more polished next time you call here, depend upon it." And the Doctor departed.

Although Mr Bonnycastle was severe, he was very judicious. Mischief of all kinds was visited but by slender punishment, such as being kept in at play hours, &c.; and he seldom interfered with the boys for fighting, although he checked decided oppression. The great "*sine qua non*"* with him was attention to their studies. He soon discovered the capabilities of his pupils, and he forced them accordingly; but the idle boy, the bird who "could sing and wou'dn't sing," received no mercy. The consequence was, that he turned out the cleverest boys, and his conduct was so uniform and unvarying in its tenor, that if he was feared when they were under his control, he was invariably liked by those whom he had instructed, and they continued his friends in after-life.

Mr Bonnycastle at once perceived that it was no use coaxing our hero, and that fear was the only attribute by which he could be controlled. So, as soon as Dr Middleton had quitted the room, he addressed him in a commanding tone, "Now, boy, what is your name?"

Jack started; he looked up at his master, perceived his eye fixed upon him, and a countenance not to be played with. Jack was no fool,

* "*Sine qua non*": Something indispensible.

and somehow or another, the discipline he had received from his father had given him some intimation of what was to come. All this put together induced Jack to condescend to answer, with his forefinger between his teeth, "Johnny."

"And what is your other name, sir?"

Jack, who appeared to repent his condescension, did not at first answer, but he looked again in Mr Bonnycastle's face, and then round the room: there was no one to help him, and he could not help himself, so he replied "Easy."

"Do you know why you are sent to school?"

"Scalding father."

"No; you are sent to learn to read and write."

"But I won't read and write," replied Jack, sulkily.

"Yes, you will; and you are going to read your letters now directly."

Jack made no answer. Mr Bonnycastle opened a sort of bookcase, and displayed to John's astonished view a series of canes, ranged up and down like billiard cues, and continued, "Do you know what those are for?"

Jack eyed them wistfully; he had some faint idea that he was sure to be better acquainted with them, but he made no answer.

"They are to teach little boys to read and write, and now I am going to teach you. You'll soon learn. Look now here," continued Mr Bonnycastle, opening a book with large type, and taking a capital at the head of a chapter, about half an inch long. "Do you see that letter?"

"Yes," replied Johnny, turning his eyes away, and picking his fingers.

"Well, that is the letter B. Do you see it? look at it, so that you may know it again. That's the letter B. Now tell me what letter that is?"

Jack now determined to resist, so he made no answer.

"So you cannot tell; well, then, we will try what one of these little fellows will do," said Mr Bonnycastle, taking down a cane. "Observe, Johnny, that's the letter B. Now, what letter is that? Answer me directly."

"I won't learn to read and write."

Whack came the cane on Johnny's shoulders, who burst out into a roar as he writhed with pain.

Mr Bonnycastle waited a few seconds. "That's the letter B. Now tell me, sir, directly, what that letter is?"

"I'll tell my *mar.*" Whack! "O law! O law!"

"What letter is that?"

Johnny, with his mouth open, panting, and the tears on his cheeks, answered, indignantly, "Stop till I tell Sarah."

Whack came the cane again, and a fresh burst from Johnny.

"What letter's that?"

"I won't tell," roared Johnny; "I won't tell—that I won't."

Whack—whack—whack, and a pause. "I told you before, that's the letter B. What letter is that? Tell me directly."

Johnny, by way of reply, made a snatch at the cane. Whack—he caught it, certainly, but not exactly as he would have wished. Johnny then snatched up the book, and dashed it to the corner of the room. Whack, whack. Johnny attempted to seize Mr Bonnycastle with his teeth. Whack, whack, whack, whack; and Johnny fell on the carpet, and roared with pain. Mr Bonnycastle then left him for a little while, to recover himself, and sat down.

At last Johnny's exclamations settled down in deep sobs, and then Mr Bonnycastle said to him, "Now, Johnny, you perceive that you must do as you are bid, or else you will have more beating. Get up immediately. Do you hear, sir?"

Somehow or another, Johnny, without intending it, stood upon his feet.

"That's a good boy; now you see, by getting up as you were bid, you have not been beaten. Now, Johnny, you must go and bring the book from where you threw it down. Do you hear, sir? bring it directly!"

Johnny looked at Mr Bonnycastle and the cane. With every intention to refuse, Johnny picked up the book and laid it on the table.

"That's a good boy; now we will find the letter B. Here it is: now, Johnny, tell me what that letter is?"

Johnny made no answer.

"Tell me directly, sir," said Mr Bonnycastle, raising his cane up in the air. The appeal was too powerful. Johnny eyed the cane; it moved, it was coming. Breathlessly he shrieked out, "B!"

"Very well indeed, Johnny—very well. Now your first lesson is over, and you shall go to bed. You have learnt more than you think for. To-morrow we will begin again. Now we'll put the cane by."

Mr Bonnycastle rang the bell, and desired Master Johnny to be put to bed, in a room by himself, and not to give him any supper, as hunger would, the next morning, much facilitate his studies. Pain and hunger alone will tame brutes, and the same remedy must be applied to conquer those passions in man which assimilate him with brutes. Johnny was conducted to bed, although it was but six o'clock. He was not only in pain, but his ideas were confused; and no wonder, after all his life having been humoured and indulged—never punished until the day before. After all the caresses of his mother and Sarah, which he never knew the value of—after stuffing himself all day long, and being tempted to eat till he turned away in satiety, to find himself without his mother, without Sarah, without supper—covered with wheals, and, what was worse than all, without his own way. No wonder Johnny was confused; at the same time that he was subdued; and, as Mr Bonnycastle had truly told him, he had learnt more than he had any idea of. And what would Mrs Easy have said, had she known all this—and Sarah, too? And Mr Easy, with his rights of man? At the very time that Johnny was having the devil driven out of him, they were consoling themselves with the idea, that, at all events, there was no birch used at Mr Bonnycastle's, quite losing sight of the fact, that as there are more ways of killing a dog besides hanging him, so are there more ways of teaching than *a posteriori*.* Happy in their ignorance, they all went fast asleep, little dreaming that Johnny was already so far advanced in knowledge, as to have a tolerable comprehension of the *mystery of cane*. As for Johnny, he had cried himself to sleep, at least six hours before them.

CHAPTER VI

In which Jack makes essay of his father's sublime philosophy, and arrives very near to truth at last.

THE NEXT MORNING Master Jack Easy was not only very sore, but very hungry, and as Mr Bonnycastle informed him that he would not only have plenty of cane, but also no breakfast, if he did not learn his letters, Johnny had wisdom enough to say the whole alphabet, for which he received a great deal of praise, the which, if he did not duly appreciate, he at all events infinitely preferred to beating. Mr Bonnycastle perceived that he had conquered the boy by one

---

* *A posteriori*: Inductive reasoning, relying on one's own experience.

hour's well-timed severity. He therefore handed him over to the ushers in the school, and as they were equally empowered to administer the needful impulse, Johnny very soon became a very tractable boy.

It may be imagined that the absence of Johnny was severely felt at home, but such was not the case. In the first place, Dr Middleton had pointed out to Mrs Easy that there was no flogging at the school, and that the punishment received by Johnny from his father would very likely be repeated—and in the next, although Mrs Easy thought that she never could have survived the parting with her own son, she soon found out that she was much happier without him. A spoilt child is always a source of anxiety and worry, and after Johnny's departure Mrs Easy found a quiet and repose much more suited to her disposition. Gradually she weaned herself from him, and, satisfied with seeing him occasionally, and hearing the reports of Dr Middleton, she, at last, was quite reconciled to his being at school, and not coming back except during the holidays. John Easy made great progress; he had good natural abilities, and Mr Easy rubbed his hands when he saw the Doctor, saying, "Yes, let them have him for a year or two longer, and then I'll finish him myself." Each vacation he had attempted to instil into Johnny's mind the equal rights of man. Johnny appeared to pay but little attention to his father's discourses, but evidently showed that they were not altogether thrown away, as he helped himself to everything he wanted, without asking leave. And thus was our hero educated until he arrived at the age of sixteen, when he was a stout, good-looking boy, with plenty to say for himself,—indeed, when it suited his purpose, he could out-talk his father.

Nothing pleased Mr Easy so much as Jack's loquacity. "That's right; argue the point, Jack—argue the point, boy," would he say, as Jack disputed with his mother. And then he would turn to the Doctor, rubbing his hands, and observe, "Depend upon it, Jack will be a great, a very great man." And then he would call Jack and give him a guinea for his cleverness; and at last Jack thought it a very clever thing to argue. He never would attempt to argue with Mr Bonnycastle, because he was aware that Mr Bonnycastle's arguments were too strong for him, but he argued with all the boys until it ended in a fight, which decided the point; and he sometimes argued with the ushers. In short, at the time we now speak of, which was at the breaking up of the Midsummer holidays, Jack was as full of argument as he was fond of it. He would argue the point to the point of a needle, and he would divide that point into as many as there were days of the year, and argue upon each. In short, there was no end to Jack's arguing the point, although there seldom was point to his argument.

Jack had been fishing in the river, without any success, for a whole morning, and observed a large pond which had the appearance of being well stocked—he cleared the park palings, and threw in his line. He had pulled up several fine fish, when he was accosted by the proprietor, accompanied by a couple of keepers.

"May I request the pleasure of your name, young gentleman?" said the proprietor to Jack.

Now Jack was always urbane and polite.

"Certainly, sir; my name is Easy, very much at your service."

"And you appear to me to be taking it very easy," replied the gentleman. "Pray, sir, may I enquire whether you are aware that you are trespassing?"

"The word trespass, my dear sir," replied Jack, "will admit of much argument, and I will divide it into three heads. It implies, according to the conventional meaning, coming without permission upon the land or property of another. Now, sir, the question may all be resolved in the following. Was not the world made for all? and has any one, or any portion of its inhabitants, an exclusive right to claim any part of it, as his property? If you please, I have laid down the proposition, and we will now argue the point."

The gentleman who accosted Jack had heard of Mr Easy and his arguments; he was a humorist, and more inclined to laugh than to be angry; at the same time that he considered it necessary to show Jack that under existing circumstances they were not tenable.

"But, Mr Easy, allowing the trespass on the property to be venial, surely you do not mean to say that you are justified in taking my fish; I bought the fish, and stocked the pond, and have fed them ever since. You cannot deny but that they are private property, and that to take them is a theft?"

"That will again admit of much ratiocination, my dear sir," replied Jack; "but,—I beg your pardon, I have a fish." Jack pulled up a large carp, much to the indignation of the keepers, and to the amusement of their master, unhooked it, placed it in his basket, renewed his bait with the greatest *sang froid*, and then throwing in his line, resumed his discourse. "As I was observing, my dear sir," continued Jack, "that will admit of much ratiocination. All the creatures of the earth were given to man for his use—man means mankind—

they were never intended to be made a monopoly of. Water is also the gift of heaven, and meant for the use of all. We now come to the question how far the fish are your property. If the fish only bred on purpose to please you, and make you a present of their stock, it might then require a different line of argument; but as in breeding they only acted in obedience to an instinct with which they are endowed on purpose that they may supply man, I submit to you that you cannot prove these fish to be yours more than mine. As for feeding with the idea that they were your own, that is not an unusual case in this world, even when a man is giving bread and butter to his children. Further—but I have another bite—I beg your pardon, my dear sir—ah! he's off again—"

"Then, Mr Easy, you mean to say that the world and its contents are made for all."

"Exactly, sir; that is my father's opinion, who is a very great philosopher."

"How then does your father account for some possessing property and others being without it?"

"Because those who are the strongest have deprived those who are weaker."

"But would not that be always the case even if we were in that state of general inheritance which you have supposed? For instance, allowing two men to chase the same animal, and both to come up to it at the same time, would not the strongest bear it off?"

"I grant that, sir."

"Well, then, where is your equality?"

"That does not disprove that men were not intended to be equal; it only proves that they are not so. Neither does it disprove that everything was not made for the benefit of all; it only proves that the strong will take advantage of the weak, which is very natural."

"Oh! you grant that to be very natural. Well, Mr Easy, I am glad to perceive that we are of one mind, and I trust we shall continue so. You'll observe that I and my keepers being three, we are the strong party in this instance, and admitting your argument, that the fish are as much yours as mine, still I take advantage of my strength to repossess myself of them, which is, as you say, very natural—James, take those fish."

"If you please," interrupted Jack, "we will argue that point—"

"Not at all; I will act according to your own arguments—I have the fish, but I now mean to have more—that fishing-rod is as much mine as yours, and being the stronger party I will take possession of it. James, William, take that fishing-rod,—it is ours."

"I presume you will first allow me to observe," replied Jack, "that although I have expressed my opinion that the earth and the animals on it were made for us all, that I never yet have asserted, that what a man creates by himself, or has created for him for a consideration, is not his own property."

"I beg your pardon; the trees that that rod was made from were made for us all, and if you, or any one for you, have thought proper to make it into a rod, it is no more my fault than it is that I have been feeding the fish, with the supposition that they were my own. Everything being common, and it being but natural that the strong should take advantage of the weak, I must take that rod as my property, until I am dispossessed by one more powerful. Moreover, being the stronger party, and having possession of this land, which you say does not belong to me more than to you—I also shall direct my keepers to see you off this property. James, take the rod—see Mr Easy over the park palings. Mr Easy, I wish you a good morning."

"Sir, I beg your pardon, you have not yet heard all my arguments," replied Jack, who did not approve of the conclusions drawn.

"I have no time to hear more, Mr Easy; I wish you a good morning." And the proprietor departed, leaving Jack in company with the keepers.

"I'll trouble you for that rod, master," said William. James was very busy stringing the fish through the gills upon a piece of osier.

"At all events *you* will hear reason," said Jack: "I have arguments——"

"I never heard no good arguments in favour of poaching," interrupted the keeper.

"You're an insolent fellow," replied Jack. "It is by paying such vagabonds as you that people are able to be guilty of injustice."

"It's by paying us that the land an't poached—and if there be some excuse for a poor devil who is out of work, there be none for you, who call yourself a gentleman."

"According to his 'count, as we be all equal, he be no more a gentleman than we be."

"Silence, you blackguard, I shall not condescend to argue with such as you: if I did, I could prove that you are a set of base slaves, who have just as much right to this property as your master or I have."

"As you have, I dare say, master."

"As I have, you scoundrel; this pond is as much my property, and so are the fish in it, as they are of your master, who has usurped the right."

"I say, James, what do you say, shall we put the young gentleman in possession of his property?" said William, winking to the other.

James took the hint, they seized Jack by the arms and legs, and soused him into the pond. Jack arose after a deep submersion, and floundered on shore blowing and spluttering. But in the meantime the keepers had walked away, carrying with them the rod and line, fish, and tin can of bait, laughing loudly at the practical joke which they had played our hero.

"Well," thought Jack, "either there must be some mistake in my father's philosophy, or else this is a very wicked world. I shall submit this case to my father."

And Jack received this reply—"I have told you before, Jack, that these important truths will not at present be admitted—but it does not the less follow that they are true. This is the age of iron, in which might has become right—but the time will come when these truths will be admitted, and your father's name will be more celebrated than that of any philosopher of ancient days. Recollect, Jack, that although in preaching against wrong and advocating the rights of man, you will be treated as a martyr, it is still your duty to persevere; and if you are dragged through all the horse-ponds in the kingdom, never give up your argument."

"That I never will, sir," replied Jack; "but the next time I argue it shall be, if possible, with power on my side, and, at all events, not quite so near a pond."

"I think," said Mrs Easy, who had been a silent listener, "that Jack had better fish in the river, and then, if he catches no fish, at all events he will not be soused in the water, and spoil his clothes."

But Mrs Easy was no philosopher.

A few days afterwards, Jack discovered, one fine morning, on the other side of a hedge, a summer apple-tree bearing tempting fruit, and he immediately broke through the hedge, and climbing the tree, as our first mother did before him, he culled the fairest and did eat.

"I say, you sir, what are you doing there?" cried a rough voice.

Jack looked down, and perceived a stout, thickset personage in grey coat and red waistcoat, standing underneath him.

"Don't you see what I'm about," replied Jack, "I'm eating apples—shall I throw you down a few?"

"Thank you kindly—the fewer that are pulled the better; perhaps, as you are so free to give them to others as well as to help yourself, you may think that they are your own property!"

"Not a bit more my property than they are yours, my good man."

"I guess that's something like the truth; but you are not quite at the truth yet, my lad; those apples are mine, and I'll trouble you to come down as fast as you please; when you're down we can then settle our accounts; and," continued the man, shaking his cudgel, "depend upon it you shall have your receipt in full."

Jack did not much like the appearance of things.

"My good man," said he, "it is quite a prejudice on your part to imagine that apples were not given, as well as all other fruit, for the benefit of us all—they are common property, believe me."

"That's a matter of opinion, my lad, and I may be allowed to have my own."

"You'll find it in the Bible," says Jack.

"I never did yet, and I've read it through and through all, bating the 'Pocryfar.'"*

"Then," said Jack, "go home and fetch the Bible, and I'll prove it to you."

"I suspect you'll not wait till I come back again. No, no; I have lost plenty of apples, and have long wanted to find the robbers out; now I've caught one I'll take care that he don't 'scape without apple sauce, at all events—so come down, you young thief, come down directly—or it will be all the worse for you."

"Thank you," said Jack, "but I am very well here. I will, if you please, argue the point from where I am."

"I've no time to argue the point, my lad; I've plenty to do, but do not think I'll let you off. If you don't choose to come down, why then you may stay there, and I'll answer for it, as soon as work is done I shall find you safe enough."

"What can be done," thought Jack, "with a man who will not listen to argument? What a world is this!—however, he'll not find me here when he comes back, I've a notion."

But in this Jack was mistaken. The farmer walked to the hedge, and called to a boy, who took his orders and ran to the farm-house. In a minute or two a large bull-dog was seen bounding along the

---

* The 'Pocryfar: The Apocrypha, those books not accepted as canonical works of the Bible by Protestants.

orchard to his master. "Mark him, Cæsar," said the farmer to the dog, "mark him." The dog crouched down on the grass with his head up, and eyes glaring at Jack, showing a range of teeth that drove all our hero's philosophy out of his head.

"I can't wait here, but Cæsar can, and I will tell you, as a friend, that if he gets hold of you, he'll not leave a limb of you together,— when work's done I'll come back"; so saying, the farmer walked off, leaving Jack and the dog to argue the point, if so inclined. What a sad jade must philosophy be, to put her votaries in such predicaments!

After a while the dog laid his head down and closed his eyes, as if asleep, but Jack observed that at the least movement on his part one eye was seen partially to unclose; so Jack, like a prudent man, resolved to remain where he was. He picked a few more apples, for it was his dinner-time, and as he chewed he ruminated.

Jack had been but a few minutes ruminating before he was interrupted by another ruminating animal, no less a personage than a bull, who had been turned out with full possession of the orchard, and who now advanced, bellowing occasionally, and tossing his head at the sight of Cæsar, whom he considered as much a trespasser as his master had our hero. Cæsar started on his legs and faced the bull, who advanced pawing, with his tail up in the air. When within a few yards the bull made a rush at the dog, who evaded him and attacked him in return, and thus did the warfare continue until the opponents were already at some distance from the apple-tree. Jack prepared for immediate flight, but unfortunately the combat was carried on by the side of the hedge at which Jack had gained admission. Never mind, thought Jack, there are two sides to every field and although the other hedge joined on to the garden near to the farm-house, there was no option. "At all events," said Jack, "I'll try it." Jack was slipping down the trunk, when he heard a tremendous roar; the bull-dog had been tossed by the bull; he was then high in the air, and Jack saw him fall on the other side of the hedge; and the bull was thus celebrating his victory with a flourish of trumpets. Upon which Jack, perceiving that he was relieved from his sentry, slipped down the rest of the tree and took to his heels. Unfortunately for Jack, the bull saw him, and, flushed with victory, he immediately set up another roar, and bounded after Jack. Jack perceived his danger, and fear gave him wings; he not only flew over the orchard, but he flew over the hedge, which was about five feet high, just as the bull drove his head into it. Look before you leap, is an old proverb. Had Jack done so, he would have done better; but as there were cogent reasons to be offered in extenuation of our philosopher, we shall say no more, but merely state that Jack, when he got to the other side of the hedge, found that he had pitched into a small apiary, and had upset two hives of bees who resented the intrusion; and Jack had hardly time to get upon his legs before he found them very busy stinging him in all quarters. All that Jack could do was to run for it, but the bees flew faster than he could run, and Jack was mad with pain, when he stumbled, half-blinded, over the brickwork of a well. Jack could not stop his pitching into the well, but he seized the iron chain as it struck him across the face. Down went Jack, and round went the windlass, and after a rapid descent of forty feet our hero found himself under water, and no longer troubled with the bees, who, whether they had lost scent of their prey from his rapid descent, or being notoriously clever insects, acknowledged the truth of the adage, "leave well alone," had certainly left Jack with no other companion than Truth. Jack rose from his immersion, and seized the rope to which the chain of the bucket was made fast—it had all of it been unwound from the windlass, and therefore it enabled Jack to keep his head above water. After a few seconds Jack felt something against his legs, it was the bucket, about two feet under the water; Jack put his feet into it and found himself pretty comfortable, for the water, after the sting of the bees and the heat he had been put into by the race with the bull, was quite cool and refreshing.

"At all events," thought Jack, "if it had not been for the bull, I should have been watched by the dog, and then thrashed by the farmer; but then again, if it had not been for the bull, I should not have tumbled among the bees; and if it had not been for the bees, I should not have tumbled into the well; and if it had not been for the chain, I should have been drowned. Such has been the chain of events, all because I wanted to eat an apple.

"However, I have got rid of the farmer, and the dog, and the bull, and the bees—all's well that ends well; but how the devil am I to get out of the well?—All creation appear to have conspired against the rights of man. As my father said, this is an iron age,* and here I am swinging to an iron chain."

We have given the whole of Jack's soliloquy, as it will prove that Jack was no fool, although he was a bit of a philosopher; and a man

* Iron age: Thought of in classical mythology as the most morally depraved age of the world.

who could reason so well upon cause and effect, at the bottom of a well, up to his neck in water, showed a good deal of presence of mind. But if Jack's mind had been a little twisted by his father's philosophy, it had still sufficient strength and elasticity to recover itself in due time. Had Jack been a common personage, we should never have selected him for our hero.

CHAPTER VII

In which Jack makes some very sage reflections, and comes to a very unwise decision.

AFTER ALL, it must be acknowledged that although there are cases of distress in which a well may become a place of refuge, a well is not at all calculated for a prolonged residence—so thought Jack. After he had been there some fifteen minutes, his teeth chattered, and his limbs trembled; he felt a numbness all over, and he thought it high time to call for assistance, which at first he would not, as he was afraid he should be pulled up to encounter the indignation of the farmer and his family. Jack was arranging his jaws for a halloo, when he felt the chain pulled up, and he slowly emerged from the water. At first he heard complaints of the weight of the bucket, at which Jack was not surprised; then he heard a tittering and laughing between two parties; and soon afterwards he mounted up gaily. At last his head appeared above the low wall, and he was about to extend his arms so as to secure a position on it, when those who were working at the windlass beheld him. It was a heavy farming man and a maid-servant.

"Thank you," said Jack.

One never should be too quick in returning thanks; the girl screamed and let go the winch, the man, frightened, did not hold it fast; it slipped from his grasp, whirled round, struck him under the chin, and threw him over it headlong, and before the "Thank you" was fairly out of Jack's lips, down he went again like lightning to the bottom. Fortunately for Jack, he had not yet let go the chain, or he might have struck the sides and have been killed; as it was, he was merely soused a second time, and in a minute or two regained his former position.

"This is mighty pleasant," thought Jack, as he clapped his wet hat once more on his head; "at all events, they can't now plead ignorance, they must know that I'm here."

In the meantime the girl ran into the kitchen, threw herself down on a stool, from which she reeled off in a fit upon sundry heaps of dough waiting to be baked in the oven, which were laid to rise on the floor before the fire.

"Mercy on me, what is the matter with Susan?" exclaimed the farmer's wife. "Here—where's Mary—where's John—Deary me, if the bread won't all be turned to pancakes."

John soon followed, holding his under-jaw in his hand, looking very dismal and very frightened, for two reasons; one, because he thought that his jaw was broken, and the other, because he thought he had seen the devil.

"Mercy on us, what is the matter?" exclaimed the farmer's wife again. "Mary, Mary, Mary!" screamed she, beginning to be frightened herself, for with all her efforts she could not remove Susan from the bed of dough, where she lay senseless and heavy as lead. Mary answered to her mistress's loud appeal, and with her assistance they raised up Susan; but as for the bread, there was no hopes of it ever rising again. "Why don't you come here and help Susan, John?" cried Mary.

"Aw-yaw-aw!" was all the reply of John, who had had enough quite of helping Susan, and who continued to hold his head, as it were, in his hand.

"What's the matter here, missus?" exclaimed the farmer, coming in. "Highty-tighty, what ails Susan? and what ails you?" continued the farmer, turning to John. "Dang it, but everything seems to go wrong, this blessed day. First, there be all the apples stolen—then there be all the hives turned topsy-turvy in the garden—then there be Cæsar with his flank opened by the bull—then there be the bull broken through the hedge and tumbled into the saw-pit—and now I come to get more help to drag him out, I find one woman dead like, and John looks as if he had seen the devil."

"Aw-yaw-aw!" replied John, nodding his head very significantly.

"One would think that the devil had broke loose to-day. What is it, John? Have you seen him, and has Susan seen him?"

"Aw-yaw."

"He's stopped your jaw, then, at all events, and I thought the devil himself wouldn't have done that—we shall get nothing of you. Is that wench coming to her senses?"

"Yes, yes, she's better now,—Susan, what's the matter?"

"Oh, oh, ma'am! the well, the well——"

"The well! Something wrong there, I suppose: well, I will go and see."

The farmer trotted off to the well; he perceived the bucket was at the bottom and all the rope out; he looked about him, and then he looked into the well. Jack, who had become very impatient, had been looking up some time for the assistance which he expected would have come sooner; the round face of the farmer occasioned a partial eclipse of the round disk which bounded his view, just as one of the satelites of Jupiter sometimes obscures the face of the planet round which he revolves.

"Here I am," cried Jack; "get me up quick, or I shall be dead"; and what Jack said was true, for he was quite done up by having been so long down, although his courage had not failed him.

"Dang it, but there be somebody fallen into the well," cried the farmer; "no end to mishaps this day. Well, we must get a Christian out of a well afore we get a bull out of a saw-pit, so I'll go and call the men."

In a very short time the men who were assembled round the saw-pit were brought to the well.

"Down below there, hold on now."

"Never fear," cried Jack.

Away went the winch, and once more Jack had an extended horizon to survey. As soon as he was at the top, the men hauled him over the bricks and laid him down upon the ground, for Jack's strength had failed him.

"Dang it, if it bean't that chap who was on my apple-tree," cried the farmer—"howsomever, he must not die for stealing a few apples; lift him up, lads, and take him in—he is dead with cold—no wonder."

The farmer led the way, and the men carried Jack into the house, when the farmer gave him a glass of brandy; this restored Jack's circulation, and in a short time he was all right again.

After some previous conversation, in which Jack narrated all that had happened, "What may be your name?" inquired the farmer.

"My name is Easy," replied Jack.

"What! be you the son of Mr Easy, of Forest Hill?"

"Yes."

"Dang it, he be my landlord, and a right good landlord too—why didn't you say so when you were up in the apple-tree? You might have picked the whole orchard and welcome."

"My dear sir," replied Jack, who had taken a second glass of brandy, and was quite talkative again, "let this be a warning to you, and when a man proposes to argue the point, always, in future, listen. Had you waited, I would have proved to you most incontestibly that you had no more right to the apples than I had; but you would not listen to argument, and without discussion we can never arrive at truth. You send for your dog, who is ripped up by the bull—the bull breaks his leg in a saw-pit—the bee-hives are overturned, and you lose all your honey—your man John breaks his jaw—your maid Susan spoils all the bread—and why? because you would not allow me to argue the point."

"Well, Mr Easy, it be all true that all these mishaps have happened because I would not allow you to argue the point, perhaps, although, as I rent the orchard from your father, I cannot imagine how you could prove to me that the apples were not mine; but now, let's take your side of the question, and I don't see how you be much better off: you get up in a tree for a few apples, with plenty of money to buy them if you like—you are kept there by a dog—you are nearly gored by a bull—you are stung by the bees, and you tumble souse into a well, and are nearly killed a dozen times, and all for a few apples not worth twopence."

"All very true, my good man," replied Jack; "but you forget that I, as a philosopher, was defending the rights of man."

"Well, I never knew before that a lad who stole apples was called a philosopher—we calls it petty larceny in the indictments: and as for your rights of man, I cannot see how they can be defended by doing what's wrong."

"You do not comprehend the matter, farmer."

"No, I don't—and I be too old to learn, Master Easy. All I have to say is this, you are welcome to all the apples in the orchard if you please, and if you prefers, as it seems you do, to steal them, instead of asking for them, which I only can account for by the reason that they say, that 'stolen fruit be sweetest,' I've only to say that I shall give orders that you be not interfered with. My chaise be at the door, Master Easy, and the man will drive you to your father's—make my compliments to him, and say, that I'm very sorry that you tumbled into our well."

As Jack was much more inclined for bed than argument, he wished the farmer good-night, and allowed himself to be driven home.

The pain from the sting of the bees, now that his circulation had fully returned, was so great, that he was not sorry to find Dr Middleton taking his tea with his father and mother. Jack merely said that he had been so unfortunate as to upset a hive, and had been severely stung. He deferred the whole story till another opportunity. Dr Middleton prescribed for Jack, but on taking his hand found that he was in a high fever, which, after the events of the day, was not to be wondered at. Jack was bled, and kept his bed for a week, by which time he was restored; but, during that time, Jack had been thinking very seriously, and had made up his mind.

But we must explain a circumstance which had occurred, which was probably the cause of Jack's decision. When Jack returned on the evening in question, he found seated with his father and Dr Middleton a Captain Wilson, a sort of cousin to the family, who but occasionally paid them a visit, for he lived at some distance; and having a wife and large family, with nothing but his half-pay for their support, he could not afford to expend even shoe-leather in compliments. The object of this visit on the part of Captain Wilson was to request the aid of Mr Easy. He had succeeded in obtaining his appointment to a sloop of war (for he was in the king's service), but was without the means of fitting himself out, without leaving his wife and family penniless. He therefore came to request Mr Easy to lend him a few hundred pounds, until he should be able, by his prize-money,* to repay them. Mr Easy was not a man to refuse such a request, and always having plenty of spare cash at his banker's, he drew a cheque for a thousand pounds, which he gave to Captain Wilson, requesting that he would only repay it at his convenience. Captain Wilson wrote an acknowledgment of the debt, promising to pay upon his first prize-money, which receipt, however binding it may be to a man of honour, was, in point of law, about as valuable as if he had agreed to pay as soon "as the cows came home." The affair had been just concluded, and Captain Wilson had returned into the parlour with Mr Easy, when Jack returned from his expedition.

---

* Prize-money: Profits accruing from the sale of a prize (an enemy vessel and its cargo captured at sea). The money was divided up between officers, crew, and the Crown.

Jack greeted Captain Wilson, whom he had long known; but, as we before observed, he suffered so much pain, that he soon retired with Dr Middleton, and went to bed.

During a week there is room for much reflection, even in a lad of fourteen, although at that age we are not much inclined to think. But Jack was in bed; his eyes were so swollen with the stings of the bees that he could neither read nor otherwise amuse himself; and he preferred his own thoughts to the gabble of Sarah, who attended him; so Jack thought, and the result of his cogitations we shall soon bring forward.

It was on the eighth day that Jack left his bed and came down into the drawing-room. He then detailed to his father the adventures which had taken place, which had obliged him to take to his bed.

"You see, Jack," replied his father, "it's just what I told you: the world is so utterly demoralised by what is called social compact, and the phalanx supporting it, by contributing a portion of their unjust possessions for the security of the remainder, is so powerful, that any one who opposes it must expect to pass the life of a martyr; but martyrs are always required previous to any truth, however sublime, being received, and, like Abraham, whom I have always considered as a great philosopher, I am willing to sacrifice my only son in so noble a cause."

"That's all very good on your part, father, but we must argue the point a little. If you are as great a philosopher as Abraham, I am not quite so dutiful a son as Isaac, whose blind obedience, in my opinion, is very contrary to your rights of man: but the fact, in few words, is simply this. In promulgating your philosophy, in the short space of two days, I have been robbed of the fish I caught, and my rod and line—I have been soused into a fish-pond—I have been frightened out of my wits by a bull-dog—been nearly killed by a bull—been stung to death by bees, and twice tumbled into a well. Now, if all that happens in two days, what must I expect to suffer in a whole year? It appears to be very unwise to attempt making further converts, for people on shore seem determined not to listen to reason or argument. But it has occurred to me, that although the whole earth has been so nefariously divided among the few, that the waters at least are the property of all. No man claims his share of the sea—every one may there plough as he pleases, without being taken up for a trespasser. Even war makes no difference; every one may go on as he pleases,

and if they meet, it is nothing but a neutral ground on which the parties contend. It is, then, only upon the ocean that I am likely to find
that equality and rights of man, which we are so anxious to establish
on shore; and therefore I have resolved not to go to school again,
which I detest, but to go to sea, and propagate our opinions as much
as I can."

"I cannot listen to that, Jack. In the first place, you must return to
school; in the next place, you shall not go to sea."

"Then, father, all I have to say is, that I swear by the rights of man
I will not go back to school, and that I will go to sea. Who and what
is to prevent me? Was not I born my own master?—has any one a
right to dictate to me as if I were not his equal? Have I not as much
right to my share of the sea as any other mortal? I stand upon perfect
equality," continued Jack, stamping his right foot on the floor.

What had Mr Easy to offer in reply? He must either, as a philosopher, have sacrificed his hypothesis, or, as a father, have sacrificed his
son. Like all philosophers, he preferred what he considered as the
less important of the two, he sacrificed his *son;* but—we will do him
justice—he did it with a sigh.

"Jack, you shall, if you wish it, go to sea."

"That, of course," replied Jack, with the air of a conqueror; "but
the question is, with whom? Now it has occurred to me, that Captain
Wilson has just been appointed to a ship, and I should like to sail
with him."

"I will write to him," said Mr Easy, mournfully, "but I should
have liked to have felt his head first"; and thus was the matter
arranged.

The answer from Captain Wilson was, of course, in the affirmative, and he promised that he would treat Jack as his own son.

Our hero mounted his father's horse, and rode off to Mr
Bonnycastle.

"I am going to sea, Mr Bonnycastle."

"The very best thing for you," replied Mr Bonnycastle.

Our hero met Dr Middleton.

"I am going to sea, Dr Middleton."

"The very best thing for you," replied the Doctor.

"I am going to sea, mother," said John.

"To sea, John, to sea? no, no, dear John, you are not going to sea,"
replied Mrs Easy, with horror.

"Yes, I am; father has agreed, and says he will obtain your consent."

"My consent! Oh, my dear, dear boy!"—and Mrs Easy wept bitterly, as Rachel mourning for her children.*

CHAPTER VIII

In which Mr Easy has his first lesson as to zeal in his Majesty's service.

As THERE WAS no time to lose, our hero very soon bade adieu to his paternal roof, as the phrase is, and found his way down to Portsmouth. As Jack had plenty of money, and was very much pleased at finding himself his own master, he was in no hurry to join his ship, and five or six companions, not very creditable, whom either Jack had picked up, or had picked up Jack, and who lived upon him, strongly advised him to put it off until the very last moment. As this advice happened to coincide with Jack's opinion, our hero was three weeks at Portsmouth before any one knew of his arrival, but at last Captain Wilson received a letter from Mr Easy, by which he found that Jack had left home at the period we have mentioned, and he desired the first lieutenant to make inquiries, as he was afraid that some accident might have happened to him. As Mr Sawbridge, the first lieutenant, happened to be going on shore on the same evening for the last time previous to the ship's sailing, he looked into the Blue Posts, George, and Fountain Inns, to inquire if there was such a person arrived as Mr Easy. "O yes," replied the waiter at the Fountain,—"Mr Easy has been here these three weeks."

"The devil he has," roared Mr Sawbridge, with all the indignation of a first lieutenant defrauded three weeks of a midshipman; "where is he; in the coffee-room?"

"Oh dear no, sir," replied the waiter, "Mr Easy has the front apartments on the first floor."

"Well, then, show me up to the first floor."

---

* Rachel: Rachel, in the Old Testament, was childless for many years before bearing Joseph and Benjamin. Marryat is alluding to the biblical passage in which she believed both of her sons to be dead: " . . . Rachel weeping for her children. She refused to be comforted for her children, because they were not" (Jeremiah 31:15).

"May I request the pleasure of your name, sir?" said the waiter.

"First lieutenants don't send up their names to midshipmen," replied Mr Sawbridge; "he shall soon know who I am."

At this reply, the waiter walked upstairs, followed by Mr Sawbridge, and threw open the door.

"A gentleman wishes to see you, sir," said the waiter.

"Desire him to walk in," said Jack: "and, waiter, mind that the punch is a little better than it was yesterday; I have asked two more gentlemen to dine here."

In the meantime, Mr Sawbridge, who was not in his uniform, had entered, and perceived Jack alone, with the dinner table laid out in the best style for eight, a considerable show of plate for even the Fountain Inn, and everything, as well as the apartment itself, according to Mr Sawbridge's opinion, much more fit for a commander-in-chief than a midshipman of a sloop of war.

Now Mr Sawbridge was a good officer, one who had really worked his way up to the present rank, that is to say, that he had served seven-and-twenty years, and had nothing but his pay. He was a little soured in the service, and certainly had an aversion to the young men of family who were now fast crowding into it—and with some grounds, as he perceived his own chance of promotion decrease in the same ratio as the numbers increased. He considered that in proportion as midshipmen assumed a cleaner and more gentlemanly appearance, so did they become more useless, and it may therefore be easily imagined that his bile was raised by this parade and display in a lad, who was very shortly to be, and ought three weeks before to have been, shrinking from his frown. Nevertheless, Sawbridge was a good-hearted man, although a little envious of luxury, which he could not pretend to indulge in himself.

"May I beg to ask," said Jack, who was always remarkably polite and gentlemanly in his address, "in what manner I may be of service to you?"

"Yes, sir, you may—by joining your ship immediately. And may I beg to ask in return, sir, what is the reason you have stayed on shore three weeks without joining her?"

Hereupon Jack, who did not much admire the peremptory tone of Mr Sawbridge, and who during the answer had taken a seat, crossed his legs, and played with the gold chain to which his watch was secured, after a pause very coolly replied—

"And pray, who are you?"

"Who am I, sir?" replied Sawbridge, jumping out of his chair—"my name is Sawbridge, sir, and I am the first lieutenant of the *Harpy*. Now, sir, you have your answer."

Mr Sawbridge, who imagined that the name of the first lieutenant would strike terror to a culprit midshipman, threw himself back in the chair, and assumed an air of importance.

"Really, sir," replied Jack, "what may be your exact situation on board, my ignorance of the service will not allow me to guess, but if I may judge from your behaviour, you have no small opinion of yourself."

"Look ye, young man, you may not know what a first lieutenant is, and I take it for granted that you do not, by your behaviour; but depend upon it, I'll let you know very soon. In the meantime, sir, I insist upon it, that you go immediately on board."

"I'm sorry that I cannot comply with your very moderate request," replied Jack, coolly. "I shall go on board when it suits my convenience, and I beg that you will give yourself no further trouble on my account."

Jack then rang the bell; the waiter, who had been listening outside, immediately entered, and before Mr Sawbridge, who was dumb with astonishment at Jack's impertinence, could have time to reply—

"Waiter," said Jack, "show this gentleman downstairs."

"By the god of war!" exclaimed the first lieutenant, "but I'll soon show you down to the boat, my young bantam; and when once I get you safe on board, I'll make you know the difference between a midshipman and a first lieutenant."

"I can only admit of *equality*, sir," replied Jack; "we are all born equal—I trust you'll allow that."

"Equality—damn it, I suppose you'll take the command of the ship. However, sir, your ignorance will be a little enlightened by-and-bye. I shall now go and report your conduct to Captain Wilson; and I tell you plainly, that if you are not on board this evening, to-morrow morning, at daylight, I shall send a sergeant and a file of marines to fetch you."

"You may depend upon it, sir," replied Jack, "that I also shall not fail to mention to Captain Wilson, that I consider you a very quarrelsome, impertinent fellow, and recommend him not to allow you to remain on board. It will be quite uncomfortable to be in the same ship with such an ungentlemanly bear."

"He must be mad—quite mad," exclaimed Sawbridge, whose

astonishment even mastered his indignation. "Mad as a march hare—by God."

"No, sir," replied Jack, "I am not mad, but I am a philosopher."

"A *what?*" exclaimed Sawbridge, "damme, what next?—well, my joker, all the better for you, I shall put your philosophy to the proof."

"It is for that very reason, sir," replied Jack, "that I have decided upon going to sea; and if you do remain on board, I hope to argue the point with you, and make you a convert to the truth of equality and the rights of man."

"By the Lord that made us both, I'll soon make you a convert to the thirty-six articles of war*—that is, if you remain on board; but I shall now go to the captain, and report your conduct, sir, and leave you to your dinner with what appetite you may."

"Sir, I am infinitely obliged to you; but you need not be afraid of my appetite; I am only sorry, as you happen to belong to the same ship, that I cannot, in justice to the gentlemanly young men whom I expect, ask you to join them. I wish you a very good morning, sir."

"Twenty years have I been in the service," roared Sawbridge, "and damme—but he's mad—downright, stark, staring mad," and the first lieutenant bounced out of the room.

Jack was a little astonished himself. Had Mr Sawbridge made his appearance in uniform it might have been different; but that a plain-looking man, with black whiskers, shaggy hair, and old blue frock coat and yellow cassimere waistcoat, should venture to address him in such a manner, was quite incomprehensible;—he calls me mad, thought Jack, I shall tell Captain Wilson what is my opinion about his lieutenant. Shortly afterwards the company arrived, and Jack soon forgot all about it.

In the meantime Sawbridge called at the captain's lodgings, and found him at home. He made a very faithful report of all that had happened, and concluded his report by demanding, in great wrath, either an instant dismissal or a court-martial on our hero, Jack.

"Stop, Sawbridge," replied Captain Wilson, "take a chair: as Mr Easy says, we must argue the point, and then I will leave it to your better feelings. As for the court-martial, it will not hold good, for Mr Easy, in the first place, has not yet joined the ship, and in the next

---

* Thirty-six articles of war: Regulations of the Royal Navy concerning the actions of officers and seamen. They first appeared in 1652 and were revised several times. They were supposed to be posted on board each ship of the Royal Navy and read to the crew once a month.

place, could not be supposed to know that you were the first lieutenant, or even an officer, for you went to him out of uniform."

"Very true, sir," replied Sawbridge, "I had forgotten that."

"Then, as for his dismissal, or rather, not allowing him to join, Mr
Easy has been brought up in the country, and has never seen anything aquatic larger than a fish-pond, perhaps, in his life; and as for
the service, or the nature of it, I believe he is as ignorant of it as a
child not a year old—I doubt whether he knows the rank of a lieutenant, certainly, he can have no idea of the power of a first lieutenant, by his treatment of you."

"I should think not," replied Sawbridge, drily.

"I do not think, therefore, that conduct which must have proceeded from sheer ignorance should be so severely punished—I
appeal to you, Sawbridge."

"Well, sir, perhaps you are right—but still he told me he was a
philosopher, and talked about equality and rights of man. Told me
that he could only admit of equality between us, and begged to argue
the point. Now, sir, if a midshipman is to argue the point every time
that an order is given, the service will come to a pretty pass."

"That is all very true, Sawbridge; and now you remind me of
what never occurred to me at the time that I promised to take Mr
Easy in the ship. I now recollect that his father, who is a distant relation of mine, has some very wild notions in his head, just like what
have been repeated by his son on your interview with him. I have
occasionally dined there, and Mr Easy has always been upholding
the principles of natural equality and of the rights of man, much to
the amusement of his guests, and I confess, at the time, of mine also.
I recollect telling him that I trusted he would never be able to dis-
seminate his opinions in the service to which I belonged, as we
should have an end of all discipline. I little thought, at the time, that
his only son, who has no more occasion to go to sea than the
Archbishop of Canterbury, for his father has a very handsome property—I believe seven or eight thousand a year—would ever have
sailed with me, and have brought these opinions with him into any
ship that I commanded. It is a pity, a great pity—"

"He never could have brought his pigs to a worse market,"
observed Sawbridge.

"I agree with you, and, as a father myself, I cannot but help feeling how careful we should be, how we inculcate anything like
abstract and philosophical ideas to youth. Allowing them to be in

themselves correct, still they are dangerous as sharp instruments are in the hands of a child;—allowing them to be erroneous, they are seized upon with an avidity by young and ardent minds, and are not to be eradicated without the greatest difficulty, and very often not until they have accomplished their ruin."

"Then you think, sir, that these ideas have taken deep root in this young man, and we shall not easily rid him of them?"

"I do not say so; but still, recollect they have been instilled, perhaps, from the earliest period, by one from whom they must have been received with all confidence—from a father to a son; and that son has never yet been sufficiently in the world to have proved their fallacy."

"Well, sir," replied Sawbridge, "if I may venture to offer an opinion on the subject—and in so doing I assure you that I only shall from a feeling for the service—if, as you say, these opinions will not easily be eradicated, as the young man is independent, would it not be both better for himself, as well as for the service, that he is sent home again? As an officer he will never do any good for himself, and he may do much harm to others. I submit this to you, Captain Wilson, with all respect; but as your first lieutenant, I feel very jealous at any chance of the discipline of the ship being interfered with by the introduction of this young man, to whom it appears that a profession is no object."

"My dear Sawbridge," replied Captain Wilson, after taking one or two turns up and down the room, "we entered the service together, we were messmates for many years, and you must be aware that it is not only long friendship, but an intimate knowledge of your unrewarded merit, which has induced me to request you to come with me as my first lieutenant. Now, I will put a case to you, and you shall then decide the question—and moreover, I will abide by your decision.

"Suppose that you were a commander like myself, with a wife and seven children, and that, struggling for many years to support them, you found yourself, notwithstanding the utmost parsimony, gradually running into debt. That, after many long applications, you had at last succeeded in obtaining employment by an appointment to a fine sloop, and there was every prospect, by prize-money and increased pay, of recovering yourself from your difficulties, if not realising a sufficient provision for your family. Then suppose that all this prospect and all these hopes were likely to be dashed to the ground by the fact of having no means of fitting yourself out, no credit, no means of paying debts you have contracted, for which you would have been arrested, or anything sufficient to leave for the support of your family during your absence, your agent only consenting to advance one-half of what you require. Now, suppose, in this awkward dilemma, without anyone in this world upon whom you have any legitimate claim, as a last resource you were to apply to one with whom you have but a distant connection, and but an occasional acquaintance—and that when you had made your request for the loan of two or three hundred pounds, fully anticipating a refusal (from the feeling that he who goes a-borrowing goes a-sorrowing),— I say, suppose, to your astonishment, that this generous person was to present you with a cheque on his banker for one thousand pounds, demanding no interest, no legal security, and requests you only to pay it at your convenience,—I ask you, Sawbridge, what would be your feelings towards such a man?"

"I would die for him," replied Sawbridge, with emotion.

"And suppose that, by the merest chance, or from a whim of the moment, the son of that man was to be placed under your protection?"

"I would be a father to him," replied Sawbridge.

"But we must proceed a little further: suppose that you were to find the lad was not all that you could wish—that he had imbibed erroneous doctrines, which would probably, if not eradicated, be attended with consequences fatal to his welfare and happiness, would you therefore, on that account, withdraw your protection, and leave him to the mercy of others, who had no claims of gratitude to sway them in his favour?"

"Most certainly not, sir," replied Sawbridge; "on the contrary, I would never part with the son until, by precept or otherwise, I had set him right again, and thus had, as far as it was possible, paid the debt of gratitude due to the generous father."

"I hardly need say to you, Sawbridge, after what has passed, that this lad you have just come from, is the son, and that Mr Easy of Forest Hill is the father."

"Then, sir, I can only say, that not only to please you, but also from respect to a man who has shown such goodwill towards one of our cloth, I shall most cheerfully forgive all that has passed between the lad and me, and all that may probably take place before we make him what he ought to be."

"Thank you, Sawbridge; I expected as much, and am not disappointed in my opinion of you."

"And now, Captain Wilson, pray what is to be done?"

"We must get him on board, but not with a file of marines,—that will do more harm than good. I will send a note, requesting him to breakfast with me to-morrow morning, and have a little conversation with him. I do not wish to frighten him; he would not scruple to run back to Forest Hill—now I wish to keep him if I possibly can."

"You are right, sir; his father appears his greatest enemy. What a pity that a man with so good a heart should be so weak in the head! Then, sir, I shall take no notice of this at present, but leave the whole affair in your hands."

"Do, Sawbridge; you have obliged me very much by your kindness in this business."

Mr Sawbridge then took his leave, and Captain Wilson despatched a note to our hero, requesting the pleasure of his company to breakfast at nine o'clock the ensuing morning. The answer was in the affirmative, but verbal, for Jack had drunk too much champagne to trust his pen to paper.

CHAPTER IX

In which Mr Easy finds himself on the other side of the Bay of Biscay.

THE NEXT MORNING Jack Easy would have forgotten all about his engagement with the captain, had it not been for the waiter, who thought that, after the reception which our hero had given the first lieutenant, it would be just as well that he should not be disrespectful to the captain. Now Jack had not, hitherto, put on his uniform, and he thought this a fitting occasion, particularly as the waiter suggested the propriety of his appearance in it. Whether it was from a presentiment of what he was to suffer, Jack was not at all pleased, as most lads are, with the change in his dress. It appeared to him that he was sacrificing his independence; however, he did not follow his first impulse, which was to take it off again, but took his hat, which the waiter had brushed and handed to him, and then set off for the captain's lodgings. Captain Wilson received him as if he had not been aware of his delay in joining his ship, or his interview with his first lieutenant, but before breakfast was over, Jack himself narrated the affair in a few words. Captain Wilson then entered into a detail of the duties and rank of every person on board of the ship, pointing out to Jack, that where discipline was required, it was impossible, when duty was carried on, that more than one could command; and that that one was the captain, who represented the king in person, who represented the country; and that, as the orders were transmitted from the captain through the lieutenant, and from the lieutenant to the midshipmen, who, in their turn, communicated them to the whole ship's company, in fact, it was the captain alone who gave the orders, and that everyone was *equally* obliged to obey. Indeed, as the captain himself had to obey the orders of his superiors, the admiral and the admiralty; *all* on board might be said to be *equally* obliged to obey. Captain Wilson laid a strong emphasis on the word *equally,* as he cautiously administered his first dose; indeed, in the whole of his address, he made use of special pleading, which would have done credit to the bar; for at the same time that he was explaining to Jack that he was entering a service in which *equality* could never for a moment exist, if the service was to exist, he contrived to show that all the grades were levelled, by all being equally bound to do their duty to their country, and that, in fact, whether a seaman obeyed *his* orders, or he obeyed the orders of *his* superior officer, they were in reality only obeying the orders of the country, which were administered through their channels.

Jack did not altogether dislike this view of the subject, and the captain took care not to dwell too long upon it. He then entered upon other details, which he was aware would be more agreeable to Jack. He pointed out that the articles of war were the rules by which the service was to be guided, and that everybody, from the captain to the least boy in the ship, was *equally* bound to adhere to them— that a certain allowance of provisions and wine were allowed to each person on board, and that this allowance was the same to all; the same to the captain as to the boy; the same in quantity as in quality; everyone *equally* entitled to his allowance;—that, although there were, of necessity, various grades necessary in the service, and the captain's orders were obliged to be passed and obeyed by all, yet still, whatever was the grade of the officer, they were *equally* considered as gentlemen. In short, Captain Wilson, who told the truth, and nothing but the truth, without telling the whole truth, actually made Jack fancy that he had at last found out that equality he had been seeking for in vain on shore, when, at last, he recollected the language used by Mr Sawbridge the evening before, and asked the captain why that personage had so conducted himself. Now, as the language of Mr Sawbridge was very much at variance with equality, Captain Wilson was not a little puzzled. However, he first pointed out that the first lieutenant was, at the time being, the captain, as he was the senior officer on board, as would Jack himself be if he were the senior officer on board; and that, as he before observed, the captain or senior officer represented the country. That in the articles of war, everybody who absented himself from the ship, committed an error, or breach of those articles; and if any error or breach of those articles was committed by anyone belonging to the ship, if the senior officer did not take notice of it, he then himself committed a breach of those articles, and was liable himself to be punished, if he could not prove that he had noticed it; it was therefore to save himself that he was obliged to point out the error; and if he did it in strong language, it only proved his *zeal* for his country.

"Upon my honour, then," replied Jack, "there can be no doubt of his zeal; for if the whole country had been at stake, he could not have put himself in a greater passion."

"Then he did his duty; but depend upon it it was not a pleasant one to him: and I'll answer for it, when you meet him on board, he will be as friendly with you as if nothing had happened."

"He told me that he'd soon make me know what a first lieutenant was: what did he mean by that?" inquired Jack.

"All zeal."

"Yes, but he said, that as soon as he got on board, he'd show me the difference between a first lieutenant and a midshipman."

"All zeal."

"He said my ignorance should be a little enlightened by-and-bye."

"All zeal."

"And that he'd send a sergeant and marines to fetch me."

"All zeal."

"That he would put my philosophy to the proof."

"All zeal, Mr Easy. Zeal will break out in this way; but we should do nothing in the service without it. Recollect that I hope and trust one day to see you also a zealous officer."

Here Jack cogitated considerably, and gave no answer.

"You will, I am sure," continued Captain Wilson, "find Mr Sawbridge one of your best friends."

"Perhaps so," replied Jack, "but I did not much admire our first acquaintance."

"It will perhaps be your unpleasant duty to find as much fault yourself; we are all equally bound to do our duty to our country. But, Mr Easy, I sent for you to say that we shall sail to-morrow; and, as I shall send my things off this afternoon by the launch, you had better send yours off also. At eight o'clock I shall go on board, and we can both go in the same boat."

To this Jack made no sort of objection, and having paid his bill at the Fountain, he sent his chest down to the boat by some of the crew who came up for it, and attended the summons of the captain to embark. By nine o'clock that evening, Mr Jack Easy was safe on board his Majesty's sloop *Harpy.*

When Jack arrived on board, it was dark, and he did not know what to do with himself. The captain was received by the officers on deck, who took off their hats to salute him. The captain returned the salute, and so did Jack very politely, after which, the captain entered into conversation with the first lieutenant, and for a while Jack was left to himself. It was too dark to distinguish faces, and to one who had never been on board of a ship, too dark to move, so Jack stood where he was, which was not far from the main bitts;* but he did not stay long; the boat had been hooked on to the quarter davits,† and the boatswain had called out—"Set taut, my lads!"

And then with the shrill whistle, and "Away with her!" forward came galloping and bounding along, the men with the tackles; and in the dark Jack was upset, and half a dozen marines fell upon him; the men, who had no idea that an officer was floored among the others, were pleased at the joke, and continued to dance over those who were down, until they rolled themselves out of the way. Jack, who did not understand this, fared badly, and it was not till the calls piped belay,‡ that he could recover his legs, after having been trampled upon by half the starboard watch, and the breath completely jammed out of his body, Jack reeled to a carronade§ slide, when the officers who had been laughing at the lark as well as the men, perceived his situation—among others, Mr Sawbridge, the first lieutenant.

* Bitts: A bitt is a strong pair of oak posts used to secure items.
† Davits: A davit is a curved piece of iron or timber used to lift the anchor.
‡ Piped belay: The boatswain (or bos'n) often conveyed commands by whistling on a silver pipe. Belay meant to disregard or stop, allowing the men a chance to rest.
§ Carronade: A short-barreled lightweight gun.

"Are you hurt, Mr Easy?" said he, kindly.

"A little," replied Jack, catching his breath.

"You've had but a rough welcome," replied the first lieutenant, "but at certain times, on board ship, it is every man for himself, and God for us all. Harpur," continued the first lieutenant to the doctor, "take Mr Easy down in the gun-room with you, and I will be down myself as soon as I can. Where is Mr Jolliffe?"

"Here, sir," replied Mr Jolliffe, a master's mate, coming aft from the booms.*

"There is a youngster come on board with the captain. Order one of the quarter-masters to get a hammock slung."

In the meantime Jack went down into the gun-room, where a glass of wine somewhat recovered him. He did not stay there long, nor did he venture to talk much. As soon as his hammock was ready, Jack was glad to go to bed—and as he was much bruised he was not disturbed the next morning till past nine o'clock. He then dressed himself, went on deck, found that the sloop was just clear of the Needles,† that he felt very queer, then very sick, and was conducted by a marine down below, put into his hammock, where he remained during a gale of wind of three days, bewildered, confused, puzzled, and every minute knocking his head against the beams with the pitching and tossing of the sloop.

"And this is going to sea," thought Jack; "no wonder that no one interferes with another here, or talks about a trespass; for I'm sure anyone is welcome to my share of the ocean; and if I once get on shore again, the devil may have my portion if he chooses."

Captain Wilson and Mr Sawbridge had both allowed Jack more leisure than most midshipmen, during his illness. By the time that the gale was over, the sloop was off Cape Finisterre.‡ The next morning the sea was nearly down, and there was but a slight breeze on the waters. The comparative quiet of the night before had very much recovered our hero, and when the hammocks were piped up, he was accosted by Mr Jolliffe, the master's mate, who asked, "whether he intended to rouse and bit,§ or whether he intended to sail to Gibraltar between his blankets."

---

* Aft from the booms: Aft (or abaft) means toward the rear of the ship; booms were poles used to extend a particular sail. In this case, they're stacked for future use.
† The Needles: The three chalk stacks at the western end of the Isle of Wight.
‡ Cape Finisterre: The westernmost point of Spain.
§ Rouse and bit: Rise and shine.

Jack, who felt himself quite another person, turned out of his hammock and dressed himself. A marine had, by the captain's orders, attended Jack during his illness, and this man came to his assistance, opened his chest, and brought him all he required, or Jack would have been in a sad dilemma.

Jack then inquired where he was to go, for he had not been in the midshipmen's berth, although five days on board. The marine pointed it out to him, and Jack, who felt excessively hungry, crawled over and between chests, until he found himself fairly in a hole infinitely inferior to the dog-kennels which received his father's pointers.

"I'd not only give up the ocean," thought Jack, "and my share of it, but also my share of the *Harpy*, unto anyone who fancies it. Equality enough here! for everyone appears equally miserably off."

As he thus gave vent to his thoughts, he perceived that there was another person in the berth—Mr Jolliffe, the master's mate, who had fixed his eye upon Jack, and to whom Jack returned the compliment. The first thing that Jack observed was, that Mr Jolliffe was very deeply pockmarked, and that he had but one eye, and that was a piercer; it appeared like a little ball of fire, and as if it reflected more light from the solitary candle than the candle gave.

"I don't like your looks," thought Jack—"we shall never be friends."

But here Jack fell into the common error of judging by appearances, as will be proved hereafter.

"I'm glad to see you up again, youngster," said Jolliffe; "you've been on your beam ends longer than usual, but those who are strongest suffer most—you made your mind up but late to come to sea. However, they say, 'better late than never.' "

"I feel very much inclined to argue the truth of that saying," replied Jack; "but it's no use just now. I'm terribly hungry—when shall I get some breakfast?"

"To-morrow morning at half-past eight," replied Mr Jolliffe. "Breakfast for to-day has been over these two hours."

"But must I then go without?"

"No, I do not say that, as we must make allowances for your illness; but it will not be breakfast."

"Call it what you please," replied Jack, "only pray desire the servants to give me something to eat. Dry toast or muffins—anything will do, but I should prefer coffee."

"You forget that you are off Finisterre, in a midshipman's berth:

coffee we have none—muffins we never see,—dry toast cannot be made, as we have no soft bread; but a cup of tea, and ship's biscuit and butter, I can desire the steward to get ready for you."

"Well then," replied Jack, "I will thank you to procure me that."

"Marine," cried Jolliffe, "call Mesty."

"Pass the word for Mesty," cried the marine—and the two syllables were handed forward until lost in the forepart of the vessel.

The person so named must be introduced to the reader. He was a curious anomaly—a black man who had been brought to America as a slave, and there sold.

He was a very tall, spare-built, yet muscular form, and had a face by no means common with his race. His head was long and narrow, high cheek-bones, from whence his face descended down to almost a point at the chin; his nose was very small, but it was straight and almost Roman; his mouth also was unusually small; and his lips thin for an African; his teeth very white, and filed to sharp points. He claimed the rank of prince in his own country, with what truth could not of course be substantiated. His master had settled at New York, and there Mesty had learned English, if it could be so-called: the fact is, that all the emigrant labourers at New York being Irishmen, he had learned English with the strong brogue and peculiar phraseology of the sister kingdom dashed with a little Yankeeism.

Having been told that there was no slavery in England, Mesty had concealed himself on board an English merchant vessel, and escaped. On his arrival in England he had entered on board of a man-of-war. Having no name, it was necessary to christen him on the ship's books, and the first lieutenant, who had entered him, struck with his remarkable expression of countenance, and being a German scholar, had named him Mephistopheles Faust, from whence his Christian name had been razéed to Mesty. Mesty in other points was an eccentric character; at one moment, when he remembered his lineage, he was proud to excess, at others he was grave and almost sullen—but when nothing either in daily occurrences or in his mind ran contrary, he exhibited the drollery so often found in his nation, with a spice of Irish humour, as if he had caught up the latter with his Irish brogue.

Mesty was soon seen coming aft, but almost double as he couched under the beams, and taking large strides with his naked feet.

"By the powers, Massa Yolliffe, but it is not seasonable at all to send for me just now, anyhow, seeing how the praters are in the copper, and so many blackguard 'palpeens* all ready to change net for net, and better themselves by the same mistake, 'dam um.' "

"Mesty, you know I never send for you myself, or allow others to do so, unless it is necessary," replied Jolliffe; "but this poor lad has eaten nothing since he has been on board, and is very hungry—you must get him a little tea."

"Is it tay you mane, sir?—I guess, to make tay, in the first place I must ab water, and in the next must ab room in the galley to put the kettle on—and 'pose you wanted to burn the tip of your little finger just now, it's not in the galley that you find a berth for it—and den the water before seven bells. I've a notion it's just impassible."

"But he must have something, Mesty."

"Never mind the tea, then," replied Jack, "I'll take some milk."

"Is it milk massa manes, and the bumboat† woman on the oder side of the bay?"

"We have no milk, Mr Easy; you forget that we are on blue water," replied Jolliffe, "and I really am afraid that you'll have to wait till dinner-time. Mesty tells the truth."

"I tell you what, Massa Yolliffe, it just seven bells, and if the young gentleman would, instead of tay, try a little out of the copper, it might keep him asy. It but a little difference, *tay* soup and *pay* soup. Now a bowl of that, with some nuts and a flourish of pepper, will do him good, anyhow."

"Perhaps the best thing he can take, Mesty; get it as fast as you can."

In a few minutes the black brought down a bowl of soup and whole peas swimming in it, put before our hero a tin bread-basket full of small biscuit, called midshipmen's nuts, and the pepper-castor. Jack's visions of tea, coffee, muffins, dry toast, and milk, vanished as he perceived the mess; but he was very hungry, and he found it much better than he expected; and he moreover found himself much the better after he had swallowed it. It struck seven bells, and he accompanied Mr Jolliffe on deck.

---

* 'Palpeens: Spalpeens, rascals.
† Bumboat: A boat carrying provisions for sale to ships.

CHAPTER X

Showing how Jack transgresses against his own philosophy.

WHEN JACK EASY had gained the deck, he found the sun shining gaily, a soft air blowing from the shore, and the whole of the rigging and every part of the ship loaded with the shirts, trousers, and jackets of the seamen, which had been wetted during the heavy gale, and were now hanging up to dry; all the wet sails were also spread on the booms or triced up in the rigging, and the ship was slowly forging through the blue water. The captain and first lieutenant were standing on the gangway in converse, and the majority of the officers were with their quadrants and sextants ascertaining the latitude at noon. The decks were white and clean, the sweepers had just laid by their brooms, and the men were busy coiling down the ropes. It was a scene of cheerfulness, activity, and order, which lightened his heart after the four days of suffering, close air, and confinement, from which he had just emerged.

The captain, who perceived him, beckoned to him, asked him kindly how he felt: the first lieutenant also smiled upon him, and many of the officers, as well as his messmates, congratulated him upon his recovery.

The captain's steward came up to him, touched his hat, and requested the pleasure of his company to dinner in the cabin. Jack was the essence of politeness, took off his hat, and accepted the invitation. Jack was standing on a rope which a seaman was coiling down; the man touched his hat and requested he would be so kind as to take his foot off. Jack took his hat off his head in return, and his foot off the rope. The master touched his hat, and reported twelve o'clock to the first lieutenant,—the first lieutenant touched his hat, and reported twelve o'clock to the captain,—the captain touched his hat, and told the first lieutenant to make it so. The officer of the watch touched his hat, and asked the captain whether they should pipe to dinner,—the captain touched his hat, and said,—"If you please."

The midshipman received his orders, and touched his hat, which he gave to the head boatswain's mate, who touched his hat, and then the calls whistled cheerily.

"Well," thought Jack, "politeness seems to be the order of the day, and everyone has an equal respect for the other." Jack stayed on deck; he peeped through the ports, which were open, and looked down into the deep blue wave; he cast his eyes aloft, and watched the tall spars sweeping and tracing with their points, as it were, a small portion of the clear sky, as they acted in obedience to the motion of the vessel; he looked forward at the range of carronades which lined the sides of the deck, and then he proceeded to climb one of the carronades, and lean over the hammocks to gaze on the distant land.

"Young gentleman, get off those hammocks," cried the master, who was officer of the watch, in a surly tone.

Jack looked round.

"Do you hear me, sir? I'm speaking to you," said the master again.

Jack felt very indignant, and he thought that politeness was not quite so general as he supposed.

It happened that Captain Wilson was upon deck.

"Come here, Mr Easy," said the captain; "it is a rule in the service, that no one gets on the hammocks, unless in case of emergency—I never do—nor the first lieutenant—nor any of the officers or men,— therefore, upon the principle of equality, you must not do it either."

"Certainly not, sir," replied Jack, "but still I do not see why that officer in the shining hat should be so angry, and not speak to me as if I were a gentleman, as well as himself."

"I have already explained that to you, Mr Easy."

"O yes, I recollect now, it's zeal: but this zeal appears to me to be the only unpleasant thing in the service. It's a pity, as you said, that the service cannot do without it."

Captain Wilson laughed, and walked away; and shortly afterwards, as he turned up and down the deck with the master, he hinted to him, that he should not speak so sharply to a lad who had committed such a trifling error through ignorance. Now Mr Smallsole, the master, who was a surly sort of a personage, and did not like even a hint of disapprobation of his conduct, although very regardless of the feeling of others, determined to pay this off on Jack, the very first convenient opportunity. Jack dined in the cabin, and was very much pleased to find that everyone drank wine with him, and that everybody at the captain's table appeared to be on an equality. Before the dessert had been on the table five minutes, Jack became loquacious on his favourite topic; all the company stared with surprise at such an unheard-of doctrine being broached on board of a man-of-war; the captain argued the point, so as to controvert, without too much

offending, Jack's notions, laughing the whole time that the conversation was carried on.

It will be observed, that this day may be considered as the first in
which Jack really made his appearance on board, and it also was on
this first day that Jack made known, at the captain's table, his very
peculiar notions. If the company at the captain's table, which consisted of the second lieutenant, purser, Mr Jolliffe, and one of the
midshipmen, were astonished at such heterodox opinions being
stated in the presence of the captain, they were equally astonished at
the cool, good-humoured ridicule with which they were received by
Captain Wilson. The report of Jack's boldness, and every word and
opinion that he had uttered (of course much magnified) was circu-
lated that evening through the whole ship; it was canvassed in the
gun-room by the officers; it was descanted upon by the midshipmen
as they walked the deck; the captain's steward held a levee abreast of
the ship's funnel, in which he narrated this new doctrine. The
sergeant of marines gave his opinion in his berth, that it was
damnable. The boatswain talked over the matter with the other warrant officers, till the grog was all gone, and then dismissed it as too
dry a subject: and it was the general opinion of the ship's company,
that as soon as they arrived at Gibraltar Bay, our hero would bid
adieu to the service, either by being sentenced to death by a court-
martial, or by being dismissed, and towed on shore on a grating.
Others, who had more of the wisdom of the serpent, and who had
been informed by Mr Sawbridge that our hero was a lad who would
inherit a large property, argued differently, and considered that
Captain Wilson had very good reason for being so lenient—and
among them was the second lieutenant. There were but four who
were well inclined towards Jack,—to wit, the captain, the first lieutenant, Mr Jolliffe, the one-eyed master's mate, and Mephistopheles,
the black, who, having heard that Jack had uttered such sentiments,
loved him with all his heart and soul.

We have referred to the second lieutenant, Mr Asper. This young
man had a very high respect for birth, and particularly for money, of
which he had very little. He was the son of an eminent merchant who,
during the time that he was a midshipman, had allowed him a much
larger sum for his expenses than was necessary or proper; and, during his career, he found that his full pocket procured him consequence, not only among his own messmates, but also with many of
the officers of the ships that he sailed in. A man who is able and

willing to pay a large tavern bill will always find followers—that is, to the tavern; and lieutenants did not disdain to dine, walk arm-in-arm, and be "hail fellow well met" with a midshipman, at whose expense they lived during the time they were on shore. Mr Asper had just received his commission and appointment, when his father became a bankrupt, and the fountain was dried up from which he had drawn such liberal supplies. Since that, Mr Asper had felt that his consequence was gone: he could no longer talk about the service being a bore, or that he should give it up; he could no longer obtain that deference paid to his purse, and not to himself; and he had contracted very expensive habits, without having any longer the means of gratifying them. It was therefore no wonder that he imbibed a great respect for money; and, as he could no longer find the means himself, he was glad to pick up anybody else at whose cost he could indulge in that extravagance and expense to which he had been so long accustomed, and still sighed for. Now, Mr Asper knew that our hero was well supplied with money, as he had obtained from the waiter the amount of the bill paid at the Fountain, and he had been waiting for Jack's appearance on deck to become his very dearest and most intimate friend. The conversation in the cabin made him feel assured that Jack would require and be grateful for support, and he had taken the opportunity of a walk with Mr Sawbridge, to offer to take Jack in his watch. Whether it was that Mr Sawbridge saw through the design of Mr Asper, or whether he imagined that our hero would be better pleased with him than with the master, considering his harshness of deportment; or with himself, who could not, as first lieutenant, overlook any remission of duty, the offer was accepted, and Jack Easy was ordered, as he now entered upon his duties, to keep watch under Lieutenant Asper.

But not only was this the first day that Jack may be said to have appeared in the service, but it was the first day in which he had entered the midshipman's berth, and was made acquainted with his messmates.

We have already mentioned Mr Jolliffe, the master's mate, but we must introduce him more particularly. Nature is sometimes extremely arbitrary, and never did she show herself more so than in insisting that Mr Jolliffe should have the most sinister expression of countenance that ever had been looked upon.

He had suffered martyrdom with the small-pox, which probably had contracted his lineaments: his face was not only deeply pitted, but scarred with this cruel disorder. One eye had been lost, and all eyebrows had disappeared—and the contrast between the dull, sight-less, opaque orb on one side of his face, and the brilliant, piercing little ball on the other, was almost terrifying. His nose had been eaten away by the disease till it formed a sharp but irregular point; part of the muscles of the chin were contracted, and it was drawn in with unnat-ural seams and puckers. He was tall, gaunt, and thin, seldom smiled, and when he did, the smile produced a still further distortion.

Mr Jolliffe was the son of a warrant officer. He did not contract this disease until he had been sent out to the West Indies, where it swept away hundreds. He had now been long in the service, with little or no chance of promotion. He had suffered from indigence, from reflections upon his humble birth, from sarcasms on his appear-ance. Every contumely had been heaped upon him at one time or another, in the ships in which he served; among a crowd he had found himself desolate—and now, although no one dared treat him to his face with disrespect, he was only respected in the service from a knowledge of his utility and exemplary performance of his duties—he had no friends or even companions. For many years he had retired within himself, he had improved by reading and study, had felt all the philanthropy of a Christian, and extended it towards others. Silent and reserved, he seldom spoke in the berth, unless his authority, as caterer, was called for; all respected Mr Jolliffe, but no one liked, as a companion, one at whose appearance the very dogs would bark. At the same time every one acknowledged his correct behaviour in every point, his sense of justice, his forbearance, his kindness, and his good sense. With him life was indeed a pilgrimage, and he wended his way in all Christian charity and all Christian zeal.

In all societies, however small they may be, provided that they do but amount to half-a-dozen, you will invariably meet with a bully. And it is also generally the case that you will find one of that society who is more or less the butt. You will discover this even in occasional meetings, such as a dinner-party, the major part of which have never met before.

Previous to the removal of the cloth, the bully will have shown himself by his dictatorial manner, and will also have selected the one upon whom he imagines that he can best practise. In a midshipman's berth, this fact has become almost proverbial, although now perhaps it is not attended with that disagreeable despotism which was per-mitted at the time that our hero entered the service.

The bully of the midshipman's berth of H.M. sloop *Harpy* was a young man about seventeen, with light, curly hair, and florid countenance, the son of the clerk in the dockyard at Plymouth, and his name was Vigors.

The butt was a pudding-faced Tartar-physiognomied boy of fifteen, whose intellects, with fostering, if not great, might at least have been respectable, had he not lost all confidence in his own powers from the constant jeers and mockeries of those who had a greater fluency of speech without perhaps so much real power of mind. Although slow, what he learnt he invariably retained. This lad's name was Gossett. His father was a wealthy yeoman of Lynn, in Norfolk. There were at the time but three other midshipmen in the ship, of whom it can only be said that they were like midshipmen in general, with little appetite for learning, but good appetites for dinner, hating everything like work, fond of everything like fun, fighting *"à l'outrance"** one minute, and sworn friends the next—with general principles of honour and justice, but which were occasionally warped according to circumstances; with all the virtues and vices so heterogeneously jumbled and heaped together, that it was almost impossible to ascribe any action to its true motive, and to ascertain to what point their vice was softened down into almost a virtue, and their virtues from mere excess degenerated into vice. Their names were O'Connor, Mills, and Gascoigne. The other shipmates of our hero it will be better to introduce as they appear on the stage.

After Jack had dined in the cabin, he followed his messmates Jolliffe and Gascoigne down into the midshipmen's berth.

"I say, Easy," observed Gascoigne, "you are a devilish free and easy sort of a fellow, to tell the captain that you considered yourself as great a man as he was."

"I beg your pardon," replied Jack, "I did not argue individually, but generally, upon the principles of the rights of man."

"Well," replied Gascoigne, "it's the first time I ever heard a middy do such a bold thing; take care your rights of man don't get you in the wrong box—there's no arguing on board of a man-of-war. The captain took it amazingly easy, but you'd better not broach that subject too often."

"Gascoigne gives you very good advice, Mr Easy," observed Jolliffe; "allowing that your ideas are correct, which it appears to me

---

* *"À l'outrance"*: Heavily, excessively.

they are not, or at least impossible to be acted upon, there is such a thing as prudence, and however much this question may be canvassed on shore, in his Majesty's service it is not only dangerous in itself, but will be very prejudicial to you."

"Man is a free agent," replied Easy.

"I'll be shot if a midshipman is," replied Gascoigne, laughing, "and that you'll soon find."

"And yet it was in the expectation of finding that equality that I was induced to come to sea."

"On the first of April, I presume," replied Gascoigne. "But are you really serious?"

Hereupon Jack entered into a long argument, to which Jolliffe and Gascoigne listened without interruption, and Mesty with admiration; at the end of it, Gascoigne laughed heartily, and Jolliffe sighed.

"From whence did you learn all this?" inquired Jolliffe.

"From my father, who is a great philosopher, and has constantly upheld these opinions."

"And did your father wish you to go to sea?"

"No, he was opposed to it," replied Jack, "but of course he could not combat my right and free-will."

"Mr Easy, as a friend," replied Jolliffe, "I request that you would as much as possible keep your opinions to yourself. I shall have an opportunity of talking to you on the subject and will then explain to you my reasons."

As soon as Mr Jolliffe had ceased, down came Mr Vigors and O'Connor, who had heard the news of Jack's heresy.

"You do not know Mr Vigors and Mr O'Connor," said Jolliffe to Easy.

Jack, who was the essence of politeness, rose and bowed, at which the others took their seats, without returning the salutation. Vigors had, from what he had heard and now seen of Easy, thought he had somebody else to play upon, and without ceremony he commenced.

"So, my chap, you are come on board to raise a mutiny here with your equality—you came off scot free at the captain's table; but it won't do, I can tell you, even in the midshipman's berth: some must knock under, and you are one of them."

"If, sir," replied Easy, "you mean by knock under, that I must submit, I can assure you that you are mistaken. Upon the same principle that I would never play the tyrant to those weaker than myself, so will I resent oppression if attempted."

"Damme, but he's a regular sea lawyer already: however, my boy, we'll soon put your mettle to the proof."

"Am I then to infer that I am not on an equality with my messmates?" replied Jack, looking at Jolliffe. The latter was about to answer him, but Vigors interrupted.

"Yes, you are on an equality as far as this,—that you have an equal right to the berth, if you are not knocked out of it for insolence to your masters; that you have an equal share to pay for the things purchased for the mess, and an equal right to have your share, provided you can get it; you have an equal right to talk, provided you are not told to hold your tongue. The fact is, you have an equal right with everyone else to do as you can, get what you can, and say what you can, always provided that you can do it; for here the weakest goes to the wall, and that is midshipman's berth equality. Now, do you understand all that; or will you wait for a practical illustration?"

"I am then to infer that the equality here is as much destroyed as it even will be among savages, where the strong oppress the weak, and the only law is club law—in fact, much the same as it is at a public or large school, on shore?"

"I suspect you are right for once. You were at a public school: how did they treat you there?"

"As you propose treating people here,—'the weakest went to the wall.' "

"Well, then, a nod's as good as a wink to a blind horse, that's all, my hearty," said Vigors.

But the hands being turned up, "Shorten sail" put an end to the altercation for the present.

As our hero had not yet received orders to go to his duty, he remained below with Mesty.

"By de powers, Massa Easy, but I lub you with my hole soul," said Mesty. "By Jasus, you really tark fine, Massa Easy; dat Mr Vigor—nebber care for him, wouldn't you lik him—and sure you would," continued the black, feeling the muscle of Jack's arm. "By the soul of my fader, I'd bet my week's allowance on you anyhow. Nebber be 'fraid, Massa Easy."

"I am not afraid," replied Jack; "I've thrashed bigger fellows than he"; and Jack's assertion was true. Mr Bonnycastle never interfered in a fair fight, and took no notice of black eyes, provided the lessons were well said. Jack had fought and fought again, until he was a very good bruiser, and although not so tall as Vigors, he was much better built for fighting. A knowing Westminster boy would have bet his half-crown upon Jack had he seen him and his anticipated adversary.

The constant battles which Jack was obliged to fight at school had been brought forward by Jack against his father's arguments in favour of equality, but they had been overruled by Mr Easy's pointing out that the combats of *boys* had nothing to do with the rights of man.

As soon as the watch was called, Vigors, O'Connor, Gossett, and Gascoigne came down into the berth. Vigors, who was the strongest in the berth, except Jolliffe, had successively had his superiority acknowledged, and, when on deck, he had talked of Easy's impertinence, and his intention of bringing him to his senses. The others, therefore, came down to see the fun.

"Well, Mr Easy," observed Vigors, as he came into the berth, "you take after your name, at all events; I suppose you intend to eat the king's provision, and do nothing."

Jack's mettle was already up.

"You will oblige me, sir, by minding your own business," replied Jack.

"You impudent blackguard, if you say another word, I'll give you a good thrashing, and knock some of your equality out of you."

"Indeed," replied Jack, who almost fancied himself back at Mr Bonnycastle's; "we'll try that."

Whereupon Jack very coolly divested himself of his upper garments, neckerchief, and shirt, much to the surprise of Mr Vigors, who little contemplated such a proof of decision and confidence, and still more to the delight of the other midshipmen, who would have forfeited a week's allowance to see Vigors well thrashed. Vigors, however, knew that he had gone too far to retreat; he therefore prepared for action; and, when ready, the whole party went out into the steerage to settle the business.

Vigors had gained his assumed authority more by bullying than fighting; others had submitted to him without a sufficient trial; Jack, on the contrary, had won his way up in school by hard and scientific combat; the result, therefore, may easily be imagined. In less than a quarter of an hour Vigors, beaten dead, with his eyes closed, and three teeth out, gave in: while Jack, after a basin of water, looked as fresh as ever, with the exception of a few trifling scratches.

The news of this victory was soon through the ship; and before Jack had resumed his clothes it had been told confidentially by Sawbridge to the captain.

"So soon!" said Captain Wilson, laughing; "I expected that a midshipman's berth would do wonders; but I did not expect this yet awhile. This victory is the first severe blow to Mr Easy's equality, and will be more valuable than twenty defeats. Let him now go to his duty, he will soon find his level."

CHAPTER XI

In which our hero proves that all on board should equally sacrifice decency to duty.

THE SUCCESS of any young man in a profession very much depends upon the occurrences at the commencement of his career, as from those is his character judged, and he is treated accordingly. Jack had chosen to enter the service at a much later period than most lads; he was tall and manly for his age, and his countenance, if not strictly handsome, wore that expression of honesty and boldness which is sure to please. His spirit in not submitting to, and meeting, Vigors when he had hardly recovered from his severe prostration of sea-sickness, had gained him with the many respect, and with all, except his antagonist and Mr Smallsole, good-will. Instead of being laughed at by his messmates, he was played with; for Jolliffe smiled at his absurdities, and attempted to reason him out of them, and the others liked Jack for himself and his generosity, and moreover, because they looked up to him as a protector against Vigors, who had persecuted them all; for Jack had declared, that as might was right in a midshipman's berth, he would so far restore equality, that if he could not put down those who were the strongest, at all events he would protect the weak, and, let who would come into the berth, they must be his master before they should tyrannise over those weaker than he.

Thus did Jack Easy make the best use that he could of his strength, and become, as it were, the champion and security of those who, although much longer at sea and more experienced than he was, were glad to shelter themselves under his courage and skill, the latter of which had excited the admiration of the butcher of the ship, who had been a pugilist by profession. Thus did Jack at once take the rank of an oldster, and soon became the leader of all the mischief. We particularly observe this, because, had it so happened that our hero had succumbed to Vigors, the case would have been the very reverse. He then would have had to go through the ordeal to which most who enter the naval service are exposed, which cannot be better explained than by comparing it to the fagging carried to such an iniquitous extent in public schools.

Mr Asper, for his own reasons, made him his companion: they walked the night watch together, and he listened to all Jack's nonsense about the rights of man. And here Mr Asper did good without intending it, for, at the same time that he appeared to agree with Jack, to secure his favour, he cautioned him, and pointed out why this equality could not exist altogether on board of a man-of-war.

As for himself, he said, he saw no difference between a lieutenant, or even a captain, and a midshipman, provided they were gentlemen: he should choose his friends where he liked, and despised that power of annoyance which the service permitted. Of course, Jack and Mr Asper were good friends, especially as, when half the watch was over, to conciliate his good-will and to get rid of his eternal arguing, Mr Asper would send Jack down to bed.

They were now entering the Straits, and expected to anchor the next day at Gibraltar, and Jack was forward on the forecastle,* talking with Mesty, with whom he had contracted a great friendship, for there was nothing that Mesty would not have done for Jack, although he had not been three weeks in the ship; but a little reflection will show that it was natural.

Mesty had been a great man in his own country; he had suffered all the horrors of a passage in a slave ship; he had been sold as a slave twice; he had escaped—but he found that the universal feeling was strong against his colour, and that on board of a man-of-war he was condemned, although free, to the humblest of offices.

He had never heard anyone utter the sentiments, which *now* beat in his own heart, of liberty and equality—we say *now*, for when he was in his own country before his captivity, he had no ideas of equality; no one has who is in power: but he had been schooled; and although people talked of liberty and equality at New York, he found that what they preached for themselves, they did not practise towards others, and that, in the midst of liberty and equality, he and thousands more were enslaved and degraded beings.

---

* Forecastle (or fo'c'sle): A short raised deck near the bow of a vessel.

Escaping to England, he had regained his liberty, but not his equality; his colour had prevented the latter, and in that feeling all the world appeared to conspire together against him, until, to his astonishment, he heard those sentiments boldly expressed from the lips of Jack, and that in a service where it was almost tantamount to mutiny. Mesty, whose character is not yet developed, immediately took a fondness for our hero, and in a hundred ways showed his attachment. Jack also liked Mesty, and was fond of talking with him, and every evening, since the combat with Vigors, they had generally met in the forecastle to discuss the principles of equality and the rights of man.

The boatswain, whose name was Biggs, was a slight, dapper, active little man, who, as captain of the foretop, had shown an uncommon degree of courage in a hurricane, so much so, as to recommend him to the admiral for promotion. It was given to him; and after the ship to which he had been appointed was paid off, he had been ordered to join H.M. sloop *Harpy*. Jack's conversation with Mesty was interrupted by the voice of the boatswain, who was haranguing his boy. "It's now ten minutes, sir, by my repeater," said the boatswain, "that I have sent for you"; and Mr Biggs pulled out a huge silver watch, almost as big as a Norfolk turnip. A Jew had sold him the watch;* the boatswain had heard of repeaters, and wished to have one. Moses had only shown him watches with the hour and minute hands; he now produced one with a second hand, telling him it was a repeater.

"What makes it a repeater?" inquired the boatswain.

"Common watches," said the cunning Jew, "only tell the minutes and hours; but all repeaters tell the seconds."

The boatswain was satisfied—bought the watch, and, although many had told him it was no repeater, he insisted that it was, and would call it so.

"I swear," continued the boatswain, "it's ten minutes and twenty seconds by my repeater."

"If you please, sir," said the boy, "I was changing my trousers when you sent for me, and then I had to stow away my bag again."

"Silence, sir; I'd have you to know that when you are sent for by your officer, trousers or no trousers, it is your duty to come up directly."

---

* A Jew had sold him the watch: Unfortunately, Marryat often employed some of the common stereotypes of the age regarding Jews.

"Without trousers, sir?" replied the boy.

"Yes, sir, without trousers; if the captain required me, I should come without my shirt. Duty before decency." So saying, the boatswain lays hold of the boy.

"Surely, Mr Biggs," said Jack, "you are not going to punish that boy for not coming up without his trousers?"

"Yes, Mr Easy, I am—I must teach him a lesson. We are bound, now that new-fangled ideas are brought into the ship, to uphold the dignity of the service; and the orders of an officer are not to be delayed ten minutes and twenty seconds because a boy has no trousers on." Whereupon the boatswain administered several smart cuts with his rattan upon the boy, proving that it was quite as well that he had put on his trousers before he came on deck. "There," said Mr Biggs, "is a lesson for you, you scamp—and, Mr Easy, it is a lesson for you also," continued the boatswain, walking away with a most consequential air.

"Murder Irish!" said Mesty—"how him cut caper. De oder day he hawl out de weather ear-ring, and touch him hat to a midshipman. Sure enough, make um cat laugh."

The next day the *Harpy* was at anchor in Gibraltar Bay; the captain went on shore, directing the gig* to be sent for him before nine o'clock; after which hour the sally-port† is only opened by special permission. There happened to be a ball given by the officers of the garrison on that evening, and a polite invitation was sent to the officers of H.M. sloop *Harpy*. As those who accepted the invitation would be detained late, it was not possible for them to come off that night. And as their services were required for the next day, Captain Wilson allowed them to remain on shore until seven o'clock the next morning, at which hour, as there was a large party, there would be two boats sent for them.

Mr Asper obtained leave, and asked permission to take our hero with him; to which Mr Sawbridge consented. Many other officers obtained leave, and, among others, the boatswain, who, aware that his services would be in request as soon as the equipment commenced, asked permission for this evening. And Mr Sawbridge, feeling that he could be better spared at this than at any other time, consented. Asper and Jack went to an inn, dined, bespoke beds, and

---

* Gig: A light, narrow boat.
† Sally-port: The opening on a ship's side used for entry.

then dressed themselves for the ball, which was very brilliant, and, from the company of the officers, very pleasant. Captain Wilson looked on at the commencement, and then returned on board. Jack behaved with his usual politeness, danced till two o'clock, and then, as the ball thinned, Asper proposed that they should retire. Having once more applied to the refreshment-room, they had procured their hats, and were about to depart, when one of the officers of the garrison asked Jack if he would like to see a baboon, which had just been brought down from the rock; and, taking some of the cakes, they repaired to the court where the animal was chained down to a small tank. Jack fed the brute till all the cakes were gone, and then, because he had no more to give him, the baboon flew at Jack, who, in making his retreat fell back into the tank, which was about two feet deep. This was a joke, and having laughed heartily, they wished the officer goodnight, and went to the inn.

Now, what with the number of officers of the *Harpy* on shore, who had all put up at the same inn, and other occupants, the landlord was obliged to put his company into double and treble-bedded rooms; but this was of little consequence. Jack was shown into a double-bedded room, and proceeded to undress; the other was evidently occupied, by the heavy breathing which saluted Jack's ear.

As Jack undressed, he recollected that his trousers were wet through, and to dry them he opened the window, hung them out, and then jammed down the window again upon them, to hold them in their position, after which he turned in and fell fast asleep. At six o'clock he was called, as he had requested, and proceeded to dress, but to his astonishment found the window thrown open and his trousers missing. It was evident, that his partner in the room had thrown the window open during the night, and that his trousers, having fallen down into the street, had been walked off with by somebody or another. Jack looked out of the window once more, and perceived that whoever had thrown open the window had been unwell during the night. A nice drunken companion I have had, thought Jack; but what's to be done? And in saying this, he walked up to the other bed, and perceived that it was tenanted by the boatswain. Well, thought Jack, as Mr Biggs has thought proper to lose my trousers, I think I have a right to take his, or at least the wear of them to go on board. It was but last night he declared that decency must give way to duty, and that the orders of a superior officer were to be obeyed, with or without garments. I know he is obliged to be on board, and now he shall try how he likes to obey orders in his shirt tails. So cogitating, Jack took the trousers of the boatswain, who still snored, although he had been called, and putting them on, completed the rest of his dress, and quitted the room. He went to that of Mr Asper, where he found him just ready, and, having paid the bill—for Asper had forgotten his purse—they proceeded down to the sally-port, where they found other officers waiting, sufficient to load the first boat, which shoved off, and they went on board. As soon as he was down below, Jack hastened to change his trousers, and, unobserved by anyone, threw those belonging to Mr Biggs on a chair in his cabin, and, having made a confidant of Mesty, who was delighted, he went on deck, and waited the issue of the affair.

Before Jack left the hotel, he had told the waiter that there was the boatswain still fast asleep, and that he must be roused up immediately; and this injunction was obeyed. The boatswain, who had drunk too much the night before, and, as Jack had truly imagined, had opened the window because he was unwell, was wakened up, and hearing how late it was, hastened to dress himself. Not finding his trousers, he rang the bell, supposing that they had been taken down to be brushed, and, in the meantime, put on everything else, that he might lose no time: the waiter who answered the bell, denied having taken the trousers out of the room, and poor Mr Biggs was in a sad quandary. What had become of them, he could not tell: he had no recollection of having gone to bed the night before; he inquired of the waiter, who said that he knew nothing about them—that he was very tipsy when he came home, and that when he called him, he had found the window open, and it appeared that he had been unwell—he supposed that he had thrown his trousers out of the window. Time flew, and the boatswain was in despair. "Could they lend him a pair?"

"He would call his master."

The master of the inn knew very well the difference of rank between officers, and those whom he could trust and those whom he could not. He sent up the bill by the waiter, and stated that, for a deposit, the gentleman might have a pair of trousers. The boatswain felt in his pockets and remembered that all his money was in his trousers' pocket. He could not only not leave a deposit, but could not pay his bill. The landlord was inexorable. It was bad enough to lose his money, but he could not lose more.

"I shall be tried by a court-martial, by heavens!" exclaimed the boatswain. "It's not far from the sally-port: I'll make a run for it, and I can slip into one of the boats and get another pair of trousers before I report myself as having come on board"; so making up his mind, the boatswain took to his heels, and with his check shirt tails streaming in the wind, ran as hard as he could to where the boat was waiting to receive him. He was encountered by many, but he only ran the faster the more they jeered, and, at last, arrived breathless at his goal, flew down the steps, jumped into the boat, and squatted on the stern sheets, much to the surprise of the officers and men, who thought him mad. He stated in a few words that somebody had stolen his trousers during the night; and as it was already late, the boat shoved off, the men as well as officers convulsed with laughter.

"Have any of you a pea-jacket?" inquired the boatswain of the men—but the weather was so warm that none of them had brought a pea-jacket. The boatswain looked round; he perceived that the officers were sitting on a boat-cloak.*

"Whose boat-cloak is that?" inquired the boatswain.

"Mine," replied Gascoigne.

"I trust, Mr Gascoigne, you will have the kindness to lend it to me to go up the side with."

"Indeed I will not," replied Gascoigne, who would sooner have thrown it overboard and have lost it, than not beheld the anticipated fun: "recollect I asked you for a fishing-line, when we were becalmed off Cape St Vincent, and you sent word that you'd see me d——d first. Now I'll just see you the same before you have my boat-cloak."

"Oh, Mr Gascoigne, I'll give you three lines, directly I get on board."

"I dare say you will, but that won't do now. 'Tit for tat,' Mr Boatswain, and hang all favours," replied Gascoigne, who was steering the boat, having been sent on shore for the others. "In bow—rowed of all." The boat was laid alongside—the relentless Gascoigne caught up his boat-cloak as the other officers rose to go on board, and rolling it up, in spite of the earnest entreaties of Mr Biggs, tossed it into the main chains, to the man who had thrown the stern fast; and to make the situation of Mr Biggs still more deplorable, the first lieutenant was standing looking into the boat, and Captain Wilson walking the quarter-deck.

"Come, Mr Biggs, I expected you off in the first boat," cried Mr

---

* Boat-cloak: A large cloak used by officers.

Sawbridge; "be as smart as you please, for the yards are not yet squared."

"Shall I go ahead in this boat, and square them, sir?"

"That boat! no; let her drop astern, jump up here and lower down the dingey. What the devil do you sit there for, Mr Biggs?— you'll oblige me by showing a little more activity, or, by Jove, you may save yourself the trouble of asking to go on shore again. Are you sober, sir?"

The last observation decided Mr Biggs. He sprung up from the boat just as he was, and touched his hat as he passed the first lieutenant.

"Perfectly sober, sir, but I've lost my trousers."

"So it appears, sir," replied Mr Sawbridge, as Mr Biggs stood on the planeshear* of the sloop where the hammock netting divides for an entrance, with his shirt tails fluttering in the sea breeze; but Mr Sawbridge could not contain himself any longer; he ran down the ship ladder which led on the quarter-deck, choked with laughter. Mr Biggs could not descend until after Mr Sawbridge, and the conversation had attracted the notice of all, and every eye in the ship was on him.

"What's all this?" said Captain Wilson, coming to the gangway.

"Duty before decency," replied Jack, who stood by enjoying the joke.

Mr Biggs recollected the day before—he cast a furious look at Jack, as he touched his hat to the captain, and then dived down to the lower deck.

If anything could add to the indignation of the boatswain, it was to find that his trousers had come on board before him. He now felt that a trick had been played him, and also that our hero must have been the party, but he could prove nothing; he could not say who slept in the same room, for he was fast asleep when Jack went to bed, and fast asleep when Jack quitted the room.

The truth of the story soon became known to all the ship, and "duty before decency" became a bye-word. All that the boatswain could do he did, which was to revenge himself upon the poor boy— and Gascoigne and Jack never got any fishing-tackle. The boatswain was as obnoxious to the men as Vigors, and in consequence of Jack's

---

* Planeshear (or planksheer): Continuous planking covering the timberheads on a wooden ship.

known opinions upon the rights of man, and his having floored their two greatest enemies, he became a great favourite with the seamen, and as all favourites are honoured by them with a *soubriquet*, our hero obtained that of *Equality Jack*.

⟨⟨⟩⟩

CHAPTER XII

In which our hero prefers going down to going up; a choice, it is to be hoped, he will reverse upon a more important occasion.

THE NEXT DAY being Sunday, the hands were turned up to divisions, and the weather not being favourable, instead of the service the articles of war were read with all due respect shown to the same, the captain, officers, and crew, with their hats off in a mizzling rain. Jack, who had been told by the captain that these articles of war were the rules and regulations of the service, by which the captain, officers, and men, were equally bound, listened to them as they were read by the clerk with the greatest attention. He little thought that there were about five hundred orders from the admiralty tacked on to them, which, like the numerous codicils of some wills, contained the most important matter, and to a certain degree make the will nugatory.

Jack listened very attentively, and, as each article was propounded, felt that he was not likely to commit himself in that point, and, although he was rather astonished to find such a positive injunction against swearing considered quite a dead letter in the ship, he thought that, altogether, he saw his way very clear. But to make certain of it, as soon as the hands had been piped down he begged the clerk to let him have a copy of the articles.

Now the clerk had three, being the allowance of the ship, or at least all that he had in his possession, and made some demur at parting with one; but at last he proposed—"some rascal," as he said, having stolen his tooth-brush—that if Jack would give him one he would give him one of the copies of the articles of war. Jack replied that the one he had in use was very much worn, and that unfortunately he had but one new one, which he could not spare. Thereupon the clerk, who was a very clean personage, and could not bear that his teeth should be dirty, agreed to accept the one in use, as Jack could not part with the other. The exchange was made, and Jack read the articles of war over and over again, till he thought he was fully master of them.

"Now," says Jack, "I know what I am to do, and what I am to expect, and these articles of war I will carry in my pocket as long as I'm in the service; that is to say, if they last so long: and provided they do not, I am able to replace them with another old tooth-brush, which appears to be the value attached to them."

The *Harpy* remained a fortnight in Gibraltar Bay, and Jack had occasionally a run on shore, and Mr Asper invariably went with him to keep him out of mischief; that is to say, he allowed him to throw his money away on no one more worthless than himself.

One morning Jack went down in the berth, and found young Gossett blubbering.

"What's the matter, my dear Mr Gossett?" inquired Jack, who was just as polite to the youngster as he was to anybody else.

"Vigors has been thrashing me with a rope's end," replied Gossett, rubbing his arm and shoulders.

"What for?" inquired Jack.

"Because he says the service is going to hell—(I'm sure it's no fault of mine)—and that now all subordination is destroyed, and that upstarts join the ship who, because they have a five-pound note in their pocket, are allowed to do just as they please. He said he was determined to uphold the service, and then he knocked me down—and when I got up again he told me that I could stand a little more—and then he took out his colt, and said he was determined to ride the high horse—and that there should be no Equality Jack in future."

"Well," replied Jack.

"And then he colted me for half an hour, and that's all."

"By de soul of my fader, but it all for true, Massa Easy—he larrup um, sure enough—all for noteing, bad luck to him—I tink," continued Mesty, "he hab debelish bad memory—and he want a little more of Equality Jack."

"And he shall have it too," replied our hero; "why it's against the articles of war, 'all quarrelling, fighting, &c.' I say, Mr Gossett, have you got the spirit of a louse?"

"Yes," replied Gossett.

"Well, then, will you do what I tell you next time, and trust to me for protection?"

"I don't care what I do," replied the boy, "if you will back me against the cowardly tyrant?"

"Do you refer to me?" cried Vigors, who had stopped at the door of the berth.

"Say yes," said Jack.

"Yes, I do," cried Gossett.

"You do, do you?—well, then, my chick, I must trouble you with a little more of this," said Vigors, drawing out his colt.

"I think that you had better not, Mr Vigors," observed Jack.

"Mind your own business, if you please," returned Vigors, not much liking the interference. "I am not addressing my conversation to you, and I will thank you never to interfere with me. I presume I have a right to choose my own acquaintance, and, depend upon it, it will not be that of a leveller."

"All that is at your pleasure, Mr Vigors," replied Jack; "you have a right to choose your own acquaintance, and so have I a right to choose my own friends, and, further, to support them. That lad is my friend, Mr Vigors."

"Then," replied Vigors, who could not help bullying even at the risk of another combat which he probably intended to stand, "I shall take the liberty of giving your friend a thrashing"; and he suited the action to the word.

"Then I shall take the liberty to defend my friend," replied Jack; "and as you call me a leveller, I'll try if I may not deserve the name"—whereupon Jack placed a blow so well under the ear, that Mr Vigors dropped on the deck, and was not in a condition to come to the scratch, even if he had been inclined. "And now, youngster," said Jack, wresting the colt out of Vigors' hand, "do as I bid you— give him a good colting—if you don't I'll thrash you."

Gossett required no second threat;—the pleasure of thrashing his enemy, if only for once, was quite enough—and he laid well on. Jack with his fists doubled ready to protect him if there was a show of resistance, but Vigors was half stupefied with the blow under the ear, and quite cowed; he took his thrashing in the most pensive manner.

"That will do," said Jack; "and now do not be afraid, Gossett; the very first time he offers to strike you when I am not present, I will pay him off for it as soon as you tell me. I won't be called Equality Jack for nothing."

When Jolliffe, who heard of this, met our hero alone, he said to him, "Take my advice, boy, and do not in future fight the battles of

others, you'll find very soon that you will have enough to do to fight
your own."

Whereupon Jack argued the point for half an hour, and then they
separated. But Mr Jolliffe was right. Jack began to find himself constantly in hot water, and the captain and first lieutenant, although
they did not really withdraw their protection, thought it high time
that Jack should find out that, on board a man-of-war, everybody and
everything must find its level.

There was on board of his Majesty's sloop *Harpy*, a man of the
name of Easthupp, who did the duty of purser's steward; this was
the second ship that he had served in: in the former he had been sent
with a draft of men from the Tender lying off the Tower. How he had
come into the service was not known in the present ship; but the fact
was, that he had been one of the swell mob—and had been sent on
board the Tender with a letter of recommendation from the magis-
trates to Captain Crouch. He was a cockney by birth, for he had been
left at the work-house of St Mary Axe, where he had been taught to
read and write, and had afterwards made his escape. He joined the
juvenile thieves of the metropolis, had been sent to Bridewell,
obtained his liberty, and by degrees had risen from petty thieving of
goods exposed outside of the shops and market-stalls, to the higher
class of gentleman pickpockets. His appearance was somewhat genteel, with a bullying sort of an impudent air, which is mistaken for
fashion by those who know no better. A remarkable neat dresser, for
that was part of his profession; a very plausible manner and address;
a great fluency of language, although he clipped the king's English;
and, as he had suffered more than once by the law, it is not to be wondered at, that he was, as he called himself, a *hout-and-hout* radical.
During the latter part of his service, in his last ship, he had been
employed under the purser's steward, and having offered himself in
this capacity to the purser of H.M. sloop *Harpy*, with one or two
forged certificates, he had been accepted.

Now, when Mr Easthupp heard of Jack's opinion, he wished to
cultivate his acquaintance, and with a bow and a flourish, introduced himself before they arrived at Gibraltar; but our hero took an
immediate dislike to this fellow from his excessive and impertinent
familiarity.

Jack knew a gentleman when he met one, and did not choose to
be a companion to a man beneath him in every way, but who, upon
the strength of Jack's liberal opinions, presumed to be his equal.

Jack's equality did not go so far as that; in theory it was all very well, but in practice it was only when it suited his own purpose.

But the purser's steward was not to be checked—a man who has belonged to the swell mob is not easily repulsed; and, although Jack would plainly show him that his company was not agreeable, Easthupp would constantly accost him familiarly on the forecastle and lower deck, with his arms folded, and with an air almost amounting to familiarity. At last, Jack told him to go about his business and not presume to talk to him; whereupon Easthupp rejoined, and after an exchange of hard words, it ended by Jack kicking Mr Easthupp, as he called himself, down the after-lower-deck hatchway. This was but a sorry specimen of Jack's equality—and Mr Easthupp, who considered that his honour had been compromised, went up to the captain on the quarter-deck and lodged his complaint—whereupon Captain Wilson desired that Mr Easy might be summoned.

As soon as Jack made his appearance, Captain Wilson called to Easthupp. "Now, purser's steward, what is this you have to say?"

"If you please, Captain Vilson, I am wery sorry to be obliged to make hany complaint of hany hofficer, but this Mr Heasy thought proper to make use of language quite hunbecoming of a gentleman, and then to kick me as I vent down the atchvay."

"Well, Mr Easy, is this true?"

"Yes, sir," replied Jack; "I have several times told the fellow not to address himself to me, and he will. I did tell him he was a radical blackguard, and I did kick him down the hatchway."

"You told him he was a radical blackguard, Mr Easy?"

"Yes, sir, he comes bothering me about his republic, and asserting that we have no want of a king and aristocracy."

Captain Wilson looked significantly at Mr Sawbridge.

"I certainly did hoffer my political opinions, Captain Vilson; but you must be avare that ve hall ave an hequal stake in the country—and it's a Hinglishman's birthright."

"I'm not aware what your stake in the country may be, Mr Easthupp," observed Captain Wilson, "but I think that, if you used such expressions, Mr Easy was fully warranted in telling you his opinion."

"I ham villing, Captain Vilson, to make hany hallowance for the eat of political discussion—but that is not hall that I ave to complain hof. Mr Heasy thought proper to say that I was a swindler and a liar."

"Did you make use of those expressions, Mr Easy?"

"Yes, sir, he did," continued the steward; "and, moreover, told me not to cheat the men, and not to cheat my master, the purser. Now, Captain Vilson, is it not true that I am in a wery hostensible sitevation? but I flatter myself that I ave been vell edecated, and vos wonce moving in a wery different society—misfortains vill appin to us hall, and I feel my character has been severely injured by such impertations"; whereupon Mr Easthupp took out his handkerchief, flourished, and blew his nose. "I told Mr Heasy, that I considered myself quite as much of a gentleman as himself, and at hall hewents did not keep company with a black feller (Mr Heasy will hunderstand the insinevation); vereupon Mr Heasy, as I before said, your vorship, I mean you, Captain Vilson, thought proper to kick me down the atchvay."

"Very well, steward, I have heard your complaint, and now you may go."

Mr Easthupp took his hat off with an air, made his bow, and went down the main ladder.

"Mr Easy," said Captain Wilson, "you must be aware that by the regulations of the service by which we are all equally bound, it is not permitted that any officer shall take the law into his own hands. Now, although I do not consider it necessary to make any remark as to your calling the man a radical blackguard, for I consider his impertinent intrusion of his opinions deserved it, still you have no right to attack any man's character without grounds—and as that man is in an office of trust, you were not at all warranted in asserting that he was a cheat. Will you explain to me why you made use of such language?"

Now our hero had no proofs against the man; he had nothing to offer in extenuation, until he recollected, all at once, the reason assigned by the captain for the language used by Mr Sawbridge. Jack had the wit to perceive that it would hit home, so he replied, very quietly and respectfully:

"If you please, Captain Wilson, that was all zeal."

"Zeal, Mr Easy? I think it but a bad excuse. But pray, then, why did you kick the man down the hatchway?—you must have known that that was contrary to the rules of the service."

"Yes, sir," replied Jack, demurely; "but that was all zeal, too."

"Then allow me to say," replied Captain Wilson, biting his lips, "that I think that your zeal has in this instance been very much misplaced, and I trust you will not show so much again."

"And yet, sir," replied Jack, aware that he was giving the captain a hard hit, and therefore looked proportionally humble, "we should do nothing in the service without it—and I trust one day, as you told me, to become a very zealous officer."

"I trust so, too, Mr Easy," replied the captain. "There, you may go now, and let me hear no more of kicking people down the hatchway. That sort of zeal is misplaced."

"More than my foot was, at all events," muttered Jack, as he walked off.

Captain Wilson, as soon as our hero disappeared, laughed heartily, and told Mr Sawbridge, "he had ascribed his language to our hero as all zeal. He has very cleverly given me it all back again; and really, Sawbridge, as it proves how weak was my defence of you, you may gain from this lesson."

Sawbridge thought so, too—but both agreed that Jack's rights of man were in considerable danger.

The day before the ship sailed, the captain and Mr Asper dined with the governor; and as there was little more to do, Mr Sawbridge, who had not quitted the ship since she had been in port, and had some few purchases to make, left her in the afternoon in the charge of Mr Smallsole, the master. Now, as we have observed, he was Jack's inveterate enemy—indeed Jack had already made three, Mr Smallsole, Mr Biggs, the boatswain, and Easthupp, the purser's steward. Mr Smallsole was glad to be left in command, as he hoped to have an opportunity of punishing our hero, who certainly laid himself not a little open to it.

Like all those who are seldom in command, the master was proportionally tyrannical and abusive—he swore at the men, made them do the duty twice and thrice over, on the pretence that it was not smartly done, and found fault with every officer remaining on board.

"Mr Biggs—by God, sir, you seem to be all asleep forward. I suppose you think that you are to do nothing now the first lieutenant is out of the ship? How long will it be, sir, before you are ready to sway away?"

"By de holy poker, I tink he sway away finely, Massy Easy," observed Mesty, who was in converse with our hero on the forecastle.

Mr Smallsole's violence made Mr Biggs violent, which made the boatswain's mate violent—and the captain of the forecastle violent also; all which is practically exemplified by philosophy in the laws of motion, communicated from one body to another; and as Mr

Smallsole swore, so did the boatswain swear. Also the boatswain's mate, the captain of the forecastle, and all the men—showing the force of example.

Mr Smallsole came forward.

"Damnation, Mr Biggs, what the devil are you about? Can't you move here?"

"As much as we can, sir," replied the boatswain, "lumbered as the forecastle is with idlers." And here Mr Biggs looked at our hero and Mesty, who were standing against the bulwark.

"What are you doing here, sir?" cried Mr Smallsole to our hero.

"Nothing at all, sir?" replied Jack.

"Then I'll give you something to do, sir. Go up to the mast-head,* and wait there till I call you down. Come, sir, I'll show you the way," continued the master, walking aft. Jack followed till they were on the quarter-deck.

"Now, sir, up to the main-top gallant mast-head; perch yourself upon the cross-trees—up with you."

"What am I to go up there for, sir?" inquired Jack.

"For punishment, sir," replied the master.

"What have I done, sir?"

"No reply, sir—up with you."

"If you please, sir," replied Jack, "I should wish to argue this point a little."

"Argue the point!" roared Mr Smallsole—"By Jove, I'll teach you to argue the point—away with you, sir."

"If you please, sir," continued Jack, "the captain told me that the articles of war were the rules and regulations by which everyone in the service was to be guided. Now, sir," said Jack, "I have read them over till I know them by heart, and there is not one word of mast-heading in the whole of them." Here Jack took the articles out of his pocket, and unfolded them.

"Will you go to the mast-head, sir, or will you not?" said Mr Smallsole.

"Will you show me the mast-head in the articles of war, sir?" replied Jack; "here they are."

"I tell you, sir, to go to the mast-head: if not, I'll be d——d if I don't hoist you up in a bread-bag."

---

* The mast-head: The highest point of the mast (a vertical pole carrying a vessel's sails). It was used for observation or as a place of solitary confinement for punishment.

"There's nothing about bread-bags in the articles of war, sir," replied Jack; "but I'll tell you what there is, sir"; and Jack commenced reading,—

"All flag-officers, and all persons in or belonging to his Majesty's ships or vessels of war, being guilty of profane oaths, execrations, drunkenness, uncleanness, or other scandalous actions, in derogation of God's honour and corruption of good manners, shall incur such punishment as—"

"Damnation," cried the master, who was mad with rage, hearing that the whole ship's company were laughing.

"No, sir, not damnation," replied Jack, "that's when he's tried above; but according to the nature and degree of the offence."

"Will you go to the mast-head, sir, or will you not?"

"If you please," replied Jack, "I'd rather not."

"Then, sir, consider yourself under an arrest—I'll try you by a court-martial, by God. Go down below, sir."

"With the greatest pleasure, sir," replied Jack, "that's all right and according to the articles of war, which are to guide us all." Jack folded up his articles of war, put them into his pocket, and went down into the berth.

Soon after Jack had gone down, Jolliffe, who had heard the whole of the altercation, followed him: "My lad," said Jolliffe, "I'm sorry for all this; you should have gone to the mast-head."

"I should like to argue that point a little," replied Jack.

"Yes, so would everybody; but if that were permitted, the service would be at a stand-still—that would not do;—you must obey an order first, and then complain afterwards, if the order is unjust."

"It is not so in the articles of war."

"But it is so in the service."

"The captain told me that the articles of war were the guides of the service, and we were all equally bound to obey them."

"Well, but allowing that, I do not think your articles of war will bear you out. You observe, they say any officer, mariner, &c., guilty of disobedience to any lawful command. Now are you not guilty under that article?"

"That remains to be argued still," replied Jack. "A lawful command means an order established by law; now where is that law?— besides, the captain told me when I kicked that blackguard down the hatchway, that there was only the captain who could punish, and that officers could not take the law into their own hands; why then has the master?"

"His doing wrong as superior officer is no reason why you as an inferior should disobey him. If that were permitted,—if every order were to be cavilled at, and argued upon, as just or unjust, there would be an end of all discipline. Besides, recollect that in the service there is custom, which is the same as law."

"That admits of a little argument," replied Jack.

"The service will admit of none, my dear boy: recollect that, even on shore, we have two laws, that which is written, and the '*lex non scripta,*'* which is custom; of course we have it in the service, for the articles of war cannot provide for everything."

"They provide a court-martial for everything though," replied Jack.

"Yes, with death or dismissal from the service—neither of which would be very agreeable. You have got yourself into a scrape, and although the captain is evidently your friend, he cannot overlook it: fortunately, it is with the master, which is of less consequence than with the other officers; but still you will have to submit, for the captain cannot overlook it."

"I'll tell you what, Jolliffe," replied Jack, "my eyes now begin to be opened to a great many things. The captain tells me, when I am astonished at bad language, that it is all zeal, and then I found out that what is all zeal in a superior to an inferior, is insolence when reversed. He tells me, that the articles of war are made to equally guide us all—the master breaks what is positively mentioned in the second article twenty times over, and goes scot free, while I am to be punished because I do not comply with what the articles do not mention. How was I to know that I ought to go to the mast-head for punishment? particularly when the captain tells me that he alone is to punish in the ship. If I obey an order in opposition to the captain's order, is not that as bad as disobeying the captain? I think that I have made out a very strong case, and my arguments are not to be confuted."

"I am afraid that the master will make out a very strong case, and that your arguments will never be heard."

"That will be contrary to all the rules of justice."

"But according to all the rules of service."

* "*Lex non scripta*": Common law.

"I do believe that I am a great fool," observed Jack, after a pause. "What do you imagine made me come to sea, Jolliffe?"

"Because you did not know when you were well off," replied the mate, drily.

"That's true enough; but my reason was, because I thought I should find that equality here that I could not find on shore."

Jolliffe stared.

"My dear boy, I heard you say that you obtained those opinions from your father; I mean no disrespect to him, but he must be either mad or foolish, if at his age he has not discovered, that there is no such thing in existence."

"I begin to think so," replied Jack; "but that does not prove that there ought not to be."

"I beg your pardon; the very non-existence proves that it ought not to be—'whatever is, is right,'*—you might as well expect to find perfect happiness or perfection in the individual. Your father must be a visionary."

"The best thing that I can do is to go home again."

"No, my dear Easy, the best thing that you can do is, to stay in the service, for it will soon put an end to all such nonsensical ideas; and it will make you a clever, sensible fellow. The service is a rough, but a good school, where everybody finds his level,—not the level of equality, but the level which his natural talent and acquirements will rise or sink him to, in proportion as they are plus or minus. It is a noble service, but has its imperfections, as everything in this world must have. I have little reason to speak in its favour, as far as I am concerned, for it has been hard bread to me; but there must be exceptions in every rule. Do not think of quitting the service until you have given it a fair trial. I am aware that you are an only son, and your father is a man of property, and, therefore, in the common parlance of the world, you are independent; but, believe me, no man, however rich, is independent, unless he has a profession, and you will find no better than this, notwithstanding—"

"What?"

"That you will be, most certainly, sent to the mast-head to-morrow."

"We'll argue that point," replied Jack; "at all events, I will go and turn in to-night."

* "Whatever is, is right": From Alexander Pope's poem "An Essay on Man" (1733–34).

CHAPTER XIII

In which our hero begins to act and think for himself.

WHATEVER MAY have been Jack's thoughts, at all events they did not spoil his rest. He possessed in himself all the materials of a true philosopher, but there was a great deal of weeding still required. Jolliffe's arguments, sensible as they were, had very little effect upon him; for, strange to say, it is much more easy to shake a man's opinions when he is wrong, than when he is right; proving that we are all of a very perverse nature. "Well," thought Jack, "if I am to go to the mast-head, I am, that's all; but it does not prove that my arguments are not good, only that they will not be listened to"; and then Jack shut his eyes, and in a few minutes was fast asleep.

The master had reported to the first lieutenant, and the first lieutenant to the captain, when he came on board the next morning, the conduct of Mr Easy, who was sent for in the cabin, to hear if he had anything to offer in extenuation of his offence. Jack made an oration, which lasted more than half an hour, in which all the arguments he had brought forward to Jolliffe in the preceding chapter were entered fully into. Mr Jolliffe was then examined, and also Mr Smallsole was interrogated: after which the captain and the first lieutenant were left alone.

"Sawbridge," said Captain Wilson, "How true it is that any deviation from what is right invariably leads us into a scrape. I have done wrong: wishing to get this boy out of his father's hands, and fearful that he would not join the ship, and imagining him to be by no means the shrewd fellow that he is in reality, I represented the service in a much more favourable light than I should have done; all that he says I told him I did tell him, and it is I who really led the boy into error. Mr Smallsole has behaved tyrannically and unjustly; he punished the lad for no crime; so that between the master and me, I am now on the horns of a dilemma. If I punish the boy, I feel that I am punishing him more for my own fault and the fault of others, than his own. If I do not punish him, I allow a flagrant and open violation of discipline to pass uncensured, which will be injurious to the service."

"He must be punished, sir," replied Sawbridge.

"Send for him," said the captain.

Jack made his appearance, with a very polite bow.

"Mr Easy, as you suppose that the articles of war contained all the rules and regulations of the service, I take it for granted that you have erred through ignorance. But recollect, that although you have erred through ignorance, such a violation of discipline, if passed unnoticed, will have a very injurious effect with the men, whose obedience is enforced by the example shown to them by the officers. I feel so convinced of your zeal, which you showed the other day in the case of Easthupp, that I am sure you will see the propriety of my proving to the men, by punishing you, that discipline must be enforced, and I shall therefore send for you on the quarter-deck, and order you to go to the mast-head in presence of the ship's company, as it was in presence of the ship's company that you refused."

"With the greatest pleasure, Captain Wilson," replied Jack.

"And in future, Mr Easy, although I shall ever set my face against it, recollect that if any officer punishes you, and you imagine that you are unfairly treated, you will submit to the punishment, and then apply to me for redress."

"Certainly, sir," replied Jack, "now that I am aware of your wishes."

"You will oblige me, Mr Easy, by going on the quarter-deck, and wait there till I come up."

Jack made his best bow, and exit.

"Old Jolliffe told me that I should have to go," said Jack to himself, "and he was right, so far; but hang me if I hadn't the best of the argument, and that's all I care about."

Captain Wilson sent for the master, and reprimanded him for his oppression, as it was evident that there was no ground for punishment, and he forbade him ever to mast-head another midshipman, but to report his conduct to the first lieutenant or himself. He then proceeded to the quarter-deck, and, calling for Mr Easy, gave him what appeared to be a very severe reprimand, which Jack looked upon very quietly, because it was all *zeal* on the captain's part to give it, and all *zeal* on his own to take it. Our hero was then ordered up to the mast-head.

Jack took off his hat, and took three or four steps, in obedience to the order—and then returned and made his best bow—inquired of Captain Wilson whether he wished him to go to the fore or to the main-mast head.

"To the main, Mr Easy," replied the captain, biting his lips.

Jack ascended three spokes of the Jacob's ladder, when he again stopped, and took off his hat.

"I beg your pardon, Captain Wilson—you have not informed me whether it was your wish that I should go to the topmast, or the top-gallant cross-trees."

"To the top-gallant cross-trees, Mr Easy," replied the captain.

Jack ascended, taking it very easy; he stopped at the main-top for breath; at the main-topmast head, to look about him; and, at last, gained the spot agreed upon, where he seated himself, and, taking out the articles of war, commenced them again to ascertain whether he could not have strengthened his arguments. He had not, however, read through the seventh article before the hands were turned up— "Up anchor!" and Mr Sawbridge called, "All hands down from aloft!" Jack took the hint, folded up his documents, and came down as leisurely as he went up. Jack was a much better philosopher than his father.

The *Harpy* was soon under way, and made all sail, steering for Cape de Gatte, where Captain Wilson hoped to pick up a Spanish vessel or two, on his way to Toulon to receive orders of the admiral.

A succession of light breezes and calms rendered the passage very tedious; but the boats were constantly out, chasing the vessels along shore, and Jack usually asked to be employed on this service; indeed, although so short a time afloat, he was, from his age and strength, one of the most effective midshipmen, and to be trusted, provided a whim did not come into his head; but hitherto Jack had always been under orders, and had always acquitted himself very well.

When the *Harpy* was at Tarragona, it so happened that there were several cases of dysentery in the ship, and Mr Asper and Mr Jolliffe were two of those who were suffering. This reduced the number of officers; and, at the same time, they had received information from the men of a fishing-boat, who, to obtain their own release, had given the intelligence, that a small convoy was coming down from Rosas as soon as the wind was fair, under the protection of two gun-boats.

Captain Wilson kept well off-shore until the wind changed, and then, allowing for the time that the vessels would take to run down the distance between Tarragona and Rosas, steered in the night to intercept them; but it again fell calm, and the boats were therefore hoisted out, with directions to proceed along the shore, as it was sup-posed that the vessels could not now be far distant. Mr Sawbridge

had the command of the expedition in the pinnace;* the first cutter
was in charge of the gunner, Mr Minus; and, as the other officers
were sick, Mr Sawbridge, who liked Jack more and more every day,
at his particular request gave him the command of the second cutter.
As soon as he heard of it, Mesty declared to our hero that he would
go with him; but without permission that was not possible. Jack
obtained leave for Mesty to go in lieu of a marine; there were many
men sick of the dysentery, and Mr Sawbridge was not sorry to take
an idler out of the ship instead of a working man, especially as Mesty
was known to be a good hand.

It was ten o'clock at night when the boats quitted the ship; and, as
it was possible that they might not return till late the next day, one
day's biscuit and rum were put on board each, that the crews might
not suffer from exhaustion. The boats pulled in-shore, and then
coasted for three hours without seeing anything: the night was fine
overhead, but there was no moon. It still continued calm, and the
men began to feel fatigued, when, just as they were within a mile of
a low point, they perceived the convoy over the land, coming down
with their sails squared, before a light breeze.

Mr Sawbridge immediately ordered the boats to lie upon their
oars, awaiting their coming, and arranging for the attack.

The white lateen sails† of the gun-boat in advance were now
plainly distinguishable from the rest, which were all huddled together in her wake. Down she came like a beautiful swan in the
water, her sails just filled with the wind, and running about three
knots an hour. Mr Sawbridge kept her three masts in one, that they
might not be perceived, and winded the boats with their heads the
same way, so that they might dash on board of her with a few strokes
of the oars. So favourable was the course of the gun-boat, that she
stood right between the launch on one bow, and the two cutters on
the other; and they were not perceived until they were actually
alongside; the resistance was trifling, but some muskets and pistols
had been fired, and the alarm was given. Mr Sawbridge took possession, with the crew of the launch, and brought the vessel to the wind,
as he perceived that at the alarm all the convoy had done the same,
directing the cutters to board the largest vessels, and secure as many
as they could, while he would do the same with the launch, as he

* Pinnace: A small boat, usually with eight oars.
† Lateen sails: Triangular sails at an angle of about forty-five degrees to the mast.

brought them to: but the other gun-boat, which had not yet been seen, and had been forgotten, now made her appearance, and came down in a gallant manner to the support of her comrade.

Mr Sawbridge threw half his men into the launch, as she carried a heavy carronade, and sent her to assist the cutters, which had made right for the gun-boat. A smart firing of round and grape was opened upon the boats, which continued to advance upon her; but the officer commanding that gun-boat, finding that he had no support from his consort, and concluding that she had been captured, hauled his wind again, and stood out in the offing. Our hero pulled after her, although he could not see the other boats; but the breeze had freshened, and all pursuit was useless: he therefore directed his course to the convoy, and after a hard pull, contrived to get on board of a one-masted xebeque,* of about fifty tons. Mesty, who had eyes as sharp as a needle, had observed that, when the alarm was given, several of the convoy had not rounded the point, and he therefore proposed, as this vessel was very light, that they should make short tacks with her, to weather the point, as if they were escaping, and by that means be able, particularly if it fell calm again, to capture some others. Jack thought this advice good. The convoy who had rounded the point had all stood out to seaward with the gun-boat, and had now a fresh breeze. To chase them was therefore useless; and the only chance was to do as Mesty had proposed. He therefore stood out into the breeze, and, after half an hour, tacked in-shore, and fetched well to windward of the low point; but, finding no vessels, he stood out again. Thus had he made three or four tacks, and had gained, perhaps, six or seven miles, when he perceived signals of recall made to leeward,† enforced with guns.

"Mr Sawbridge wants us to come back, Mesty."

"Mr Sawbridge mind him own business," replied Mesty, "we nebber take all dis trubble to ply to windward for noting."

"But, Mesty, we must obey orders."

"Yes, sar, when he have him thumb upon you; but now, must do what tink most proper. By de powers, he catch me 'fore I go back."

"But we shall lose the ship."

"Find her again, by-and-bye, Massa Easy."

---

* Xebeque (or xebec): A small, fast three-masted vessel carrying up to four hundred men and mounting up to twenty-four guns.
† Leeward: The side of the vessel sheltered from the wind.

"But they will think that we are lost."

"So much the better, nebba look after us, Massa Easy; I guess we have a fine cruise anyhow. Morrow we take large vessel—make sail, take more, den we go to Toulon."

"But I don't know my way to Toulon; I know it lies up this way, and that's all."

"Dat enough, what you want more? Massa Easy, 'pose you not find fleet, fleet soon find you. By God, nobody nebba lost here. Now, Massa Easy, let um go 'bout 'gain. Somebody else burn buscuit and boil kettle to-morrow for de gentlemen. Murder Irish! only tink, Massa Easy—I boil kettle, and prince in my own country!"

Easy was very much of a mind with Mesty; "for," argued Jack, "if I go back now, I only bring a small vessel half-full of beans, and I shall be ashamed to show my face. Now it is true, that they may suppose that we have been sunk by the fire of the gun-boat. Well, what then? they have a gun-boat to show for their night's work, and it will appear that there was harder fighting than there has been, and Mr Sawbridge may benefit by it." (Jack was a very knowing fellow to have learnt so much about the service already.) "Well, and when they discover that we are not lost, how glad they will be to find us, especially if we bring some prizes—which I will do, or I'll not go back again. It's not often that one gets a command before being two months at sea, and, hang me, now I've got it if I won't keep it; and Mr Smallsole may mast-head whom he pleases. I'm sorry for poor Gossett, though; if Vigors supposes me dead, how he will murder the poor little fellow—however, it is all for the good of the service, and I'll revenge him when I come back. Hang me if I won't take a cruise."

"I talk to the men, they say they all tick to you like leech. Now dat job settled, I tink we better go 'bout again."

A short time after this decision on the part of our hero, the day broke: Jack first looked to leeward, and perceived the gun-boat and convoy standing in for the shore about ten miles distant, followed by the *Harpy*, under all sail. He could also perceive the captured gun-boat lying-to in-shore to prevent their escape.

"*Harpy* hab um all, by Gosh!" cried Mesty; "I ab notion dat she soon settle um hash."

They were so busy looking at the *Harpy* and the convoy that, for some time, they quite forgot to look to windward. At last Mesty turned his eyes that way.

"Dam um, I see right last night; look, Massa Easy—one chip, one brig tree lateen—dem for us. By de power, but we make *bon* prize to-night."

The vessels found out by Mesty were not above three miles to windward; they were under all sail, beating up for the protection of a battery, not far distant.

"Now, Massa, suppose they see our boat, dey tink something; keep boat alongside, and shift her when we go 'bout every time: better not sail so fast now—keep further off till they drop anchor for de night; and den, when it dark, we take 'em."

All Mesty's advice was good, with the exception perhaps of advising our hero how to disobey orders and take a cruise. To prevent the vessel from approaching too near the others, and at the same time to let her have the appearance of doing her best, a sail was towed overboard under the bows, and after that they watched the motions of the *Harpy*.

The distance was too great to distinguish very clearly, but Mesty shinned up the mast of the vessel, and reported progress.

"By Jesus, dare one gun—two gun—go it, *Harpy*. Won't she ab um, sure enough. Now gun-boat fire—dat our gun-boat—no, dat not ours. Now our gun-boat fire—dat pretty—fire away. Ah, now de *Harpy* cum up. All 'mung 'em. Bung, bung, bung—rattle de grape, by gosh. I ab notion de Spaniard is very pretty considerable trouble just now, anyhow. All hove-to, so help me gosh—not more firing; *Harpy* take um all—dare gun-boat hove-to, she strike um colours. By all powers, but suppose dey tink we no share prize-money—they find it not little mistake. Now, my lads, it all over, and," continued Mesty, sliding down the mast, "I tink you better not show yourself too much; only two men stay on deck, and dem two take off um jackets."

Mesty's report was correct; the *Harpy* had captured the other gun-boat, and the whole convoy. The only drawback to their good fortune was the disappearance of Mr Easy and the cutter: it was supposed that a shot from the gun-boat must have sunk her, and that the whole crew were drowned. Captain Wilson and Mr Sawbridge seriously regretted the loss of our hero, as they thought that he would have turned out a shining character as soon as he had sown his wild oats; so did Mr Asper, because our hero's purse went with him; so did Jolliffe, because he had taken an affection for him; so did little Gossett, because he anticipated no mercy from Vigors. On the other hand, there were some who were glad that he was gone; and as for the ship's company in general, they lamented the loss of the poor cutter's crew for twenty-four hours, which, in a man-of-war, is a very long while, and then they thought no more about them. We must leave the *Harpy* to make the best of her way to Toulon, and now follow our hero.

The cutter's crew knew very well that Jack was acting contrary to orders, but anything was to them a change from the monotony of a man-of-war, and they, as well as Mesty, highly approved of a holiday.

It was, however, necessary that they should soon proceed to business, for they had but their allowance of bread and grog for one day, and in the vessel they found nothing except a few heads of garlic, for the Spaniards coasting down shore had purchased their provisions as they required them. There were only three prisoners on board, and they had been put down in the hold among the beans; a bag of which had been roused on deck, and a part put into the kettle to make soup. Jack did not much admire the fare of the first day—it was bean-soup for breakfast, bean-soup for dinner, and if you felt hungry during the intervals it was still bean-soup, and nothing else.

One of the men could speak a little Lingua Franca,* and the prisoners were interrogated as to the vessels to windward. The ship was stated to be valuable, and also one of the brigs. The ship carried guns, and that was all that they knew about them. As the sun went down the vessels dropped their anchors off the battery. The breeze continued light, and the vessel which contained Jack and his fortunes was about four miles to leeward. As for the *Harpy*, they had long lost sight of her, and it was now time to proceed to some arrangement. As soon as it was dark, Jack turned his hands up, and made a very long speech. He pointed out to the men that his zeal had induced him not to return to the ship until he had brought something with him worth having—that they had had nothing but beans to eat during the whole day, which was anything but agreeable, and that, therefore, it was absolutely necessary that they should better their condition: that there was a large ship not four miles off, and that he intended to take her; and as soon as he had taken her he intended to take some more; that he trusted to their zeal to support him on this occasion, and that he expected to do a great deal during the cruise. He pointed out to them, that they must consider themselves as on board of a man-of-war, and be guided by the articles of war, which were written for

---

* Lingua Franca: A means of communication combining elements of several languages, including Italian, Spanish, and Arabic, and spoken in some Mediterranean areas.

them all—and that in case they forgot them, he had a copy in his pocket, which he would read to them to-morrow morning, as soon as they were comfortably settled on board of the ship. He then appointed Mesty as first lieutenant; the marine as sergeant; the coxswain as boatswain; two men as midshipmen to keep watch; two others as boatswain's mates, leaving two more for the ship's company, who were divided into the larboard* and starboard watch. The cutter's crew were perfectly content with Jack's speech, and their brevet rank,† and after that, they commenced a more important topic, which was, how they were to take the ship. After some discussion, Mesty's advice was approved of; which was, that they should anchor not far ahead of the ship, and wait till about two o'clock in the morning, when they would drop silently down upon her in the cutter, and take possession.

About nine o'clock the vessel was anchored as they proposed, and Jack was a little astonished to find that the ship was much larger than he had any idea of; for, although polacca-rigged,‡ she was nearly the same tonnage as the *Harpy*. The Spanish prisoners were first tied hand and foot, and laid upon the beans, that they might give no alarm, the sails were furled and all was kept quiet.On board of the ship, on the contrary, there was noise and revelry; and about half-past ten a boat was seen to leave her and pull for the shore; after which, the noise gradually ceased, the lights one by one disappeared, and then all was silent.

"What do you think, Mesty?" said Jack; "do you think we shall take her?"

"It is take her you mane; sure enough we'll take her: stop a bit—wait till um all fast asleep."

About twelve o'clock there came on a mizzling heavy rain, which was very favourable for our hero's operations. But as it promised soon to clear up, by Mesty's advice they did not delay any longer. They crept softly into the boat, and with two oars to steer her, dropped under the bows of the vessel, climbed up the fore chains, and found the deck empty. "Take care not fire pistol," said Mesty to the men, as they came up, putting his finger to their lips to impress them with the necessity of silence, for Mesty had been an African

---

* Larboard: The port, or left, side.
† Brevet rank: An officer's commission entitling him to a higher rank but without higher pay.
‡ Polacca-rigged: A polacca, or polacre, is a type of three-masted vessel that was common in the Mediterranean at the time.

warrior, and knew the advantage of surprise. All the men being on deck, and the boat made fast, Jack and Mesty led the way aft; not a soul was to be seen: indeed, it was too dark to see anybody unless they were walking the deck. The companion-hatch was secured, and the gratings laid on the after-hatchways, and then they went aft to the binnacle* again, where there was a light burning. Mesty ordered two of the men to go forward to secure the hatches, and then to remain there on guard—and then the rest of the men and our hero consulted at the wheel.

"By the power we ab the ship!" said Mesty, "but must manage plenty yet. I tink der some d——n lazy rascal sleep 'tween the guns. A lilly while it no rain, and den we see better. Now keep all quiet."

"There must be a great many men in this ship," replied our hero; "she is very large, and has twelve or fourteen guns—how shall we manage to secure them?"

"All right," replied Mesty, "manage all dat by-and-bye. Don't care how soon daylight come."

"It has left off raining already," observed Easy; "there is a candle in the binnacle,—suppose we light it, and look round the decks."

"Yes," replied Mesty, "one man sentry over cabin-hatch, and another over after-hatch. Now den we light candle, and all the rest go round the deck. Mind you leave all your pistols on capstern."†

Jack lighted the candle, and they proceeded round the decks: they had not walked far, when, between two of the guns, they discovered a heap covered with gregos.‡ "There de *watch*," whispered Mesty; "all fast—not ready for dem yet."

Mesty blew out the candle, and they all retreated to the binnacle, where Mesty took out a coil of the ropes about the mizen-mast,§ and cutting it into lengths, gave them to the other men to unlay. In a few minutes they had prepared a great many seizings to tie the men with.

"Now den we light candle again, and make sure of them lazy hounds," said Mesty; "very much oblige to dem all de same, they let us take de ship—mind now, wake one at a time, and shut him mouth."

---

* Binnacle: A box housing the compass.
† Capstern (or capstan): A revolving mechanism, arranged vertically and fitted with bars that were pushed by the seaman in weighing the anchor.
‡ Gregos (or griegos): Coarse, hooded jackets.
§ Mizen-mast (or mizzenmast): The aftermost mast of a three-masted vessel.

"But suppose they get their mouths free and cry out?" replied Jack.

"Den, Mr Easy," replied Mesty, changing his countenance to an expression almost demoniacal—"there no help for it,"—and Mesty showed his knife which he held in his right hand.

"Oh no! do not let us murder them."

"No, massa—suppose can help it, but suppose they get upper hand—what become of us? Spaniards hab knives, and use dem too, by de power!"

The observation of Mesty was correct, and the expression of his countenance when he showed his knife proved what a relentless enemy he could be, if his blood was once roused—but Mesty had figured in the Ashantee wars in former days, and after that the reader need not be surprised. They proceeded cautiously to where the Spaniards lay. The arrangements of Mesty were very good. There were two men to gag them while the others were to tie their limbs. Mesty and Easy were to kneel by them with the candle, with raised knives to awe them into silence, or to strike home, if their own safety required it.

The gregos were removed off the first man, who opened his eyes at the sight of the candle, but the coxswain's hand was on his mouth—he was secured in silence. The other two men were awaked, and threw off their coverings, but they were also secured without there being occasion to resort to bloodshed.

"What shall we do now, Mesty?"

"Now, sar," said Mesty, "open the after-hatch and watch—suppose more men come up, we make them fast; suppose no more come up, we wait till daylight—and see what take place."

Mesty then went forward to see if the men were watchful on the forecastle; and having again gone round the whole of the deck to see if there were any more men on it, he blew out the candle, and took his station with the others at the after-hatchway.

It was just at break of day that the Spaniards who had to keep the morning watch having woke up, as people generally do at that hour at which they expect to be called, dressed themselves and came on deck, imagining, and very truly, that those of the middle watch had fallen asleep, but little imagining that the deck was in possession of Englishmen. Mesty and the others retreated, to allow them all to come up before they could perceive them, and fortunately this was accomplished. Four men came on the deck, looked round them, and tried to make out in the dark where their shipmates might be. The grating was slapped on again by Jack, and before they could well gain their eyesight, they were seized and secured, not however without a scuffle and some noise.

By the time that these men were secured and laid between the guns it was daylight, and they now perceived what a fine vessel they had fairly taken possession of—but there was much to be done yet. There was, of course, a number of men in the ship, and moreover they were not a mile from a battery of ten guns. Mesty, who was foremost in everything, left four men abaft, and went forward on the forecastle, examined the cable, which was *coir* rope, and therefore easily divided, and then directed the two men forward to coil a hawser upon the fore-grating, the weight of which would make all safe in that quarter, and afterwards to join them on the quarter-deck.

"Now, Mr Easy, the great ting will be to get hold of captain; we must get him on deck. Open cabin-hatch now, and keep the after-hatch fast. Two men stay there, the others all come aft."

"Yes," replied Jack, "It will be a great point to secure the captain—but how are we to get him up?"

"You no know how to get captain up? By de holy, I know very well."

And Mesty took up the coils of rope about the mizen-mast, and threw them upon deck, one after another, making all the noise possible. In a short time, there was a violent pull of a bell at the cabin-door, and in a minute afterwards a man in his shirt came up the cabin-hatchway, who was immediately secured.

"Dis de captain's servant," said Mesty, "he come say no make such d——d noise. Stop a little—captain get in passion, and come up himself."

And Mesty renewed the noise with the ropes over the cabin. Mesty was right; in a few minutes the captain himself came up, boiling with indignation. At the sound of the cabin-door opening, the seamen and our hero concealed themselves behind the companion-hatch, which was very high, so as to give the captain time to get fairly on deck. The men already secured had been covered over with the gregos. The captain was a most powerful man, and it was with difficulty that he was pinioned, and then not without his giving the alarm, had there been anyone to assist him; but as yet no one had turned out of his hammock.

"Now we all right," said Mesty, "and soon ab de ship; but I must make him 'fraid."

The captain was seated down on the deck against one of the guns, and Mesty, putting on the look of a demon, extended above him his long nervous arm, with the sharp knife clutched, as if ready every instant to strike it into his heart. The Spanish captain felt his situation anything but pleasant. He was then interrogated as to the number of men in the ship, officers, &c., to all which questions he answered truly; he cast his eyes at the firm and relentless countenance of Mesty, who appeared but to wait the signal.

"I tink all pretty safe now," said Mesty. "Mr Easy, we now go down below and beat all men into the hold."

Our hero approved of this suggestion. Taking their pistols from the capstern, they rushed down with their cutlasses, and leaving two men to guard the cabin-door, they were soon among the crew, who were all naked in their hammocks: the resistance, although the numbers were more than double of the English, was of course trifling. In a few minutes, the Spaniards were all thrown down into the hold of the vessel, and the hatches placed over them. Every part of the ship was now in their possession, except the cabin, and to that they all repaired. Our hero tried the door, and found it fast; they beat it open, and were received with loud screams from one side of the cabin, and the discharge of two pistols from the other, fortunately without injury: those who had fired the pistols were an elderly man and a lad about the age of our hero. They were thrown down and secured; the cabin was searched, and nobody else found in it but three women; one old and shrivelled, the other two, although with their countenances distorted with terror, were lovely as houris.* So thought Jack, as he took off his hat, and made them a very low bow with his usual politeness, as they crouched, half-dressed, in a corner. He told them in English that they had nothing to fear, and begged that they would attend to their toilets. The ladies made no reply, because, in the first place, they did not know what Jack said, and, in the next, they could not speak English.

Mesty interrupted Jack in his attentions, by pointing out that they must all go upon deck—so Jack again took off his hat and bowed, and then followed his men, who led away the two prisoners taken in the cabin. It was now five o'clock in the morning, and there was movement on board of the other vessels, which laid not far from the ship.

"Now, then," said Jack, "what shall we do with the prisoners?—

---

* Houris: A houri is a beautiful woman, a nymph promised as a wife in Moslem paradise.

could we not send the boat and bring our own vessel alongside, and put them all in, tied as they are? We should then get rid of them."

"Massa Easy, you be one very fine officer one of these days. Dat d——n good idea, anyhow;—but suppose we send our own boat, what they *tink* on board of de oder vessel? Lower down lilly boat from stern, put in four men, and drop vessel 'longside—dat it."

This was done; the cutter was on the seaward side of the ship, and, as the ship was the outermost vessel, was concealed from the view of the Spaniards on board of the other vessels, and in the battery on shore. As soon as the lateen vessel was alongside, the men who had already been secured on deck, amounting to seven, were lowered into her, and laid upon the beans in the hold; all except the captain, the two cabin-prisoners, and the captain's servant. They then went down below, took off one part of the hatches, and ordered the Spaniards up from the hold: as they came on deck they were made fast and treated in the same manner. Mesty and the men went down to examine if there were any left concealed, and finding that they were all out, returned on deck. The men who had been beaten down in the hold were twenty-two in number, making the whole complement of thirty. As soon as they had all been put into the xebeque, she was again hauled off and anchored outside, and Jack found himself in possession of a fine ship of fourteen guns, with three prisoners male and three prisoners female.

When the men returned in the boat from the vessel in which the prisoners had been confined (the hatches having been secured over them, by way of further precaution), by the advice of Mesty they put on the jackets and caps of the Spanish seamen, of which there was a plentiful supply below.

"Now, what's to be done, Mesty?" inquired Jack.

"Now, sar, we send some of the men aloft to get sails all ready, and while they do that I cast loose this fellow," pointing to the captain's servant, "and make him get some breakfast, for he know where to find it."

"Capital idea of yours, Mesty, for I'm tired of bean-soup already, and I will go down and pay my respects to the ladies."

Mesty looked over the counter.

"Yes, and be quick too, Massa Easy; d——m the women, they toss their handkerchief in the air to people in the battery—quick, Massa Easy."

Mesty was right—the Spanish girls were waving their handkerchiefs for assistance; it was all that they could do, poor things. Jack hastened into the cabin, laid hold of the two young ladies, very politely pulled them out of the quarter gallery, and begged that they would not give themselves so much trouble. The young ladies looked very much confused, and as they could no longer wave their handkerchiefs, they put them up to their eyes and began to weep, while the elderly lady went on her knees, and held her hands up for mercy. Jack raised her up, and very politely handed her to one of the cabin lockers.

In the meantime Mesty, with his gleaming knife and expressive look, had done wonders with the captain's steward, for such the man was: and a breakfast of chocolate, salt meat, hams and sausages, white biscuit and red wine, had been spread on the quarter-deck. The men had come from aloft, and Jack was summoned on deck. Jack offered his hand to the two young ladies, and beckoned the old one to follow: the old lady did not think it advisable to refuse his courtesy, so they accompanied him.

As soon as the females came on deck, and found the two cabin prisoners bound, they ran to them and embraced them with tears. Jack's heart melted, and as there was now no fear, he asked Mesty for his knife, and cut loose the two Spaniards, pointing to the breakfast, and requesting that they would join them. The Spaniards made a bow, and the ladies thanked Jack with a sweet smile; and the captain of the vessel, who still lay pinioned against the gun, looked, as much as to say, Why the devil don't you ask me? but the fact was, they had had such trouble to secure him, that Jack did not much like the idea of letting him loose again. Jack and the seamen commenced their breakfast, and as the ladies and prisoners did not appear inclined to eat, they ate their share and their own too; during which, the elderly man inquired of Jack if he could speak French.

Jack, with his mouth full of sausage, replied, that he could; and then commenced a conversation, from which Jack learnt as follows:—

The elderly gentleman was a passenger with the young man, who was his son, and the ladies, who were his wife and his two daughters, and they were proceeding to Tarragona. Whereupon Jack made a bow and thanked him; and then the gentleman, whose name was Don Cordova de Rimarosa, wished to know what Jack intended to do with them, hoping, as a gentleman, he would put them on shore with their effects, as they were non-combatants. Jack explained all this to Mesty and the men, and then finished his sausage. The men, who were a little elevated with the wine which they had been drinking, proposed that they should take the ladies a cruise, and Jack at first did not dislike the idea, but he said nothing. Mesty, however, opposed this, saying, that ladies only made a row in a ship, and the coxswain sided with him, saying, that they should all be at daggers drawn. Whereupon Jack pulled out the "articles of war," and informed the men, that there was no provision in them for women, and therefore the thing was impossible.

The next question was, as to the propriety of allowing them to take their effects; and it was agreed, at last, that they might take them. Jack desired the steward to feed his master the captain, and then told the Spanish Don the result of the consultation, further informing him, that as soon as it was dark, he intended to put them all on board the small vessel, when they would cast loose the men and do as they pleased. The Don and the ladies returned thanks, and went down to pack up their baggage; Mesty ordering two men to help them, but with a caution, that they were not to encumber themselves with any of the money, if there should happen to be any on board.

The crew were busy during the day making preparations for sailing. The coxswain had examined the provender in the ship, and found that there was enough for at least three months, of water, wine, and provisions, independent of luxuries for the cabin. All thoughts of taking any more of the vessels were abandoned, for their crew was but weak to manage the one which they had possession of. A fine breeze sprang up, and they dropped their fore-topsails, just as a boat was shoving off from the shore; but seeing the fore-topsails loosed, it put back again. This was fortunate, or all would have been discovered. The other vessels also loosed their sails, and the crews were heard weighing the anchors.

But the *Nostra Senora del Carmen,* which was Jack's prize, did not move. At last the sun went down, the baggage was placed in the cutter, the ladies and passengers went into the boat, thanking Jack for his kindness, who put his hand to his heart and bowed to the deck; and the captain was lowered down after them. Four men well armed pulled them alongside of the xebeque, put them and their trunks on deck, and returned to the ship. The cutter was then hoisted up, and as the anchor was too heavy to weigh, they cut the cable, and made sail. The other vessels followed their example.

Mesty and the seamen cast longing eyes upon them, but it was of no use; so they sailed in company for about an hour, and then Jack hauled his wind for a cruise.

CHAPTER XIV

In which our hero finds that disagreeable occurrences will take place on a cruise.

A S SOON as the ship had been hauled to the wind, Jack's ship's company seemed to think that there was nothing to do except to make merry; so they brought up some earthen jars full of wine, and emptied them so fast that they were soon fast asleep on the deck, with the exception of the man at the helm, who, instead of thirty-two, could clearly make out sixty-four points in the compass, and of course was able to steer to a much greater nicety. Fortunately, the weather was fine, for when the man at the helm had steered till he could see no more, and requested to be released, he found that his shipmates were so overpowered with fatigue, that it was impossible to wake them. He kicked them one by one most unmercifully in the ribs, but it was of no use: under these circumstances, he did as they did, that is, lay down with them, and in ten minutes it would have taken as much kicking to awake him as he gave his shipmates.

In the meantime the ship had it all her own way, and not knowing where she was to go, she went round and round the compass during the best part of the night. Mesty had arranged the watches, Jack had made a speech, and the men had promised everything, but the wine had got into their heads, and memory had taken that opportunity to take a stroll. Mesty had been down with Jack, examining the cabin, and in the captain's state-room they had found fourteen thousand dollars in bags. Of this they determined not to tell the men, but locked up the money and everything else of value, and took out the key. They then sat down at the cabin table, and after some conversation, it was no matter of surprise, after having been up all the night before, that Jack laid his head on the table and fell fast asleep. Mesty kept his eyes open for some time, but at last his head sank down upon his chest, and he also slumbered. Thus, about one o'clock in the morning, there was not a very good watch kept on board of the *Nostra Senora del Carmen.*

About four o'clock in the morning, Mesty tumbled forward, and he hit his head against the table, which roused him up.

"By de mass, I tink I almost fall asleep," cried he, and he went to the cabin window, which had been left open, and found that there was a strong breeze blowing in. "By de Lord, de wind ab come more aft," said Mesty, "why they not tell me?" So saying, he went on deck, where he found no one at the helm; everyone drunk, and the ship with her yards braced up running before the wind, just by way of a change. Mesty growled, but there was no time to lose; the topsails only were set,—these he lowered down, and then put the helm a-lee,* and lashed it, while he went down to call our hero to his assistance. Jack roused up, and went on deck.

"This nebber do, Massa Easy; we all go to devil together—together—dam drunken dogs—I freshen um up anyhow." So Mesty drew some buckets of water, with which he soused the ship's company, who then appeared to be recovering their senses.

"By heavens!" says Jack, "but this is contrary to the articles of war; I shall read them to them to-morrow morning."

"I tell what better ting, Massa Easy: we go lock up all de wine, and sarve out so much, and no more. I go do it at once, 'fore they wake up."

Mesty went down, leaving Jack on deck to his meditations.

"I am not sure," thought Jack, "that I have done a very wise thing. Here I am with a parcel of fellows who have no respect for the articles of war, and who get as drunk as David's sow. I have a large ship, but I have very few hands; and if it comes on bad weather, what shall I do?—for I know very little—hardly how to take in a sail. Then—as for where to steer, or how to steer, I know not—nor do any of my men; but, however, as it was very narrow when we came into the Mediterranean through the straits, it is hardly possible to get out of them without perceiving it; besides, I should know the rock of Gibraltar again if I saw it. I must talk to Mesty."

Mesty soon returned with the keys of the provision-room tied to his bandana.

"Now," says he, "they not get drunk again in a hurry."

A few more buckets of water soon brought the men to their

---

* A-lee (or alee): Away from the wind. Lashing the helm a-lee brings the bow into the wind.

senses: they again stood on their legs, and gradually recovered themselves. Daylight broke, and they found that the vessel had made an attempt for the Spanish coast, being within a mile of the beach, and facing a large battery *à fleur d'eau;* fortunately they had time to square the yards, and steer the ship along shore under the topsails, before they were perceived. Had they been seen at daylight in the position that they were in during the night, the suspicions of the Spaniards would have been awakened; and had a boat been sent off, while they were all drunk, they must have been recaptured.

The men, who perceived what danger they had been in, listened very penitently to Jack's remonstrances; and our hero, to impress them more strongly on their minds, took out the articles of war, read that on drunkenness from beginning to end; but the men had heard it read so often at the gangway, that it did not make a due impression. As Mesty said, his plan was better, and so it proved; for as soon as Jack had done, the men went down to get another jug of wine, and found, to their disappointment, that it was all under lock and key.

In the meantime, Jack called Mesty aft, and asked him if he knew the way to Toulon. Mesty declared that he knew nothing about it.

"Then Mesty, it appears to me that we have a better chance of finding our way back to Gibraltar; for you know the land was on our left side all the way coming up the Mediterranean; and if we keep it, as it is now, on our right, we shall get back again along the coast."

Mesty agreed with Jack that this was the *ne plus ultra* of navigation; and that old Smallsole could not do better with his "pig-yoke" and compasses. So they shook a reef out of the topsails, set topgallant sails, and ran directly down the coast from point to point, keeping about five miles distant. The men prepared a good dinner; Mesty gave them their allowance of wine, which was just double what they had on board the *Harpy*—so they soon appeared to be content. One man, indeed, talked very big and very mutinously, swearing that if the others would join him they would soon have liquor enough; but Mesty gave him his look, opened his knife, and swore that he would settle him, and Jack knocked him down with a handspike; so that, what with the punishment received, and that which was promised, the fellow thought he might as well say no more about it. The fact is, that had it not been from fear of Mesty, the whole of the men would, in all probability, have behaved equally as bad; nevertheless, they were a little staggered, it must be owned, at seeing Jack play so good a stick with the handspike.

After this night Jack and Mesty kept watch and watch, and everything went on very well until they were nearly abreast of Carthagena,* when a gale came on from the northward, and drove them out of sight of land. Sail after sail was reduced with difficulty from their having so few hands, and the gale blew for three days with great fury. The men were tired out and discontented. It was Jack's misfortune that he had but one good man with him: even the coxswain of the boat, although a fine-looking man, was worth nothing. Mesty was Jack's sheet-anchor. The fourth day the gale moderated, but they had no idea where they were: they knew that they had been blown off, but how far they could not tell, and Jack now began to discover that a cruise at sea without knowledge of navigation was a more nervous thing than he had contemplated. However, there was no help for it. At night they wore the ship† and stood on the other tack, and at daylight they perceived that they were close to some small islands, and much closer to some large rocks, against which the sea beat high, although the wind had subsided. Again was the helm put up, and they narrowly escaped. As soon as the sails were trimmed the men came aft and proposed that if they could find anchorage they should run into it, for they were quite tired out. This was true, and Jack consulted with Mesty, who thought it advisable to agree to the proposal. That the islands were not inhabited was very evident. The only point to ascertain was, if there were good anchorage. The coxswain offered to go in the boat and examine; and, with four men, he set off, and in about an hour returned, stating that there was plenty of water, and that it was as smooth as a mill-pond, being land-locked on every side. As they could not weigh the bower-anchor they bent the kedge, and running in without accident, came to in a small bay, between the islands, in seven fathoms water. The sails were furled, and everything put in order by the seamen, who then took the boat and pulled on shore. "They might as well have asked leave," thought Jack. In an hour they returned, and, after a short discussion, came aft to our hero in a body.

The coxswain was spokesman. He said that they had had hard work, and required now to have some rest—that there were provisions on board for three months, so that there could not be any hurry, and that they had found they could pitch a tent very well on shore,

---

* Carthagena: Cartagena, an important Spanish naval base at the time.
† They wore the ship: To wear is to come around by turning the head away from the wind.

and live there for a short time; and that, as there was no harm in getting drunk on shore, they expected that they might be allowed to take provisions and plenty of wine with them, and that the men had desired him to ask leave, because they were determined to go whether or no. Jack was about to answer with the handspike, but perceiving that the men had all put on their cutlasses, and had their pistols at their belts, he thought proper to consult Mesty, who, perceiving that resistance was useless, advised Jack to submit, observing, that the sooner all the wine was gone the better, as there would be nothing done while it lasted. Jack, therefore, very graciously told them that they should have their own way, and he would stay there as long as they pleased. Mesty gave them the keys of the provision-hatch, and told them, with a grin, to help themselves. The men then informed Jack that he and Mesty should stay on board and take care of the ship for them, and that they would take the Spaniard on shore to cook their victuals. But to this Jack observed that if he had not two hands he could not obey their orders, in case they wished him to come on shore for them. The men thought there was good argument in that observation, and therefore allowed Jack to retain the Spaniard, that he might be more prompt to their call from the beach. They then wished him good day, and begged that he would amuse himself with the "articles of war."

As soon as they had thrown a spare sail into the boat, with some spars to make a tent, and some bedding, they went down below, hoisted up two pipes of wine out of the three, a bag or two of biscuit, arms and ammunition, and as much of the salt provisions as they thought they might require. The boat being full, they shoved off with three cheers of derision. Jack was sensible to the compliment: he stood at the gangway, took off his hat, and made them a polite bow.

As soon as they were gone, Mesty grinned with his sharp-filed teeth, and looking at our hero, said—

"I tink I make um pay for all dis—stop a little; by de piper as played before Moses, but our turn come by-and-bye."

As for Jack, he said nothing, but he thought the more. In about an hour the men returned in the boat: they had forgotten many things they wanted—wood to make a fire, and several utensils; they helped themselves freely, and having now everything that they could think of, they again went on shore.

"How d——n lucky, we nebber tell dem about the dollars," said Mesty, as Jack and he were watching the motions of the men.

"It is, indeed," replied Jack; "not that they could spend them here."

"No, Massa Easy, but suppose they find all that money, they take boat and go away with it. Now, I hab them in my clutch—stop a little."

A narrow piece of salt pork had been left at the gangway: Jack, without knowing why, tossed it overboard; being almost all fat, it sank very gradually: Jack watched it as it disappeared, so did Mesty, both full of thought, when they perceived a dark object rising under it: it was a ground shark, who took it into his maw, sank down, and disappeared.

"What was that?" said Jack.

"That ground shark, Massa Easy—worst shark of all; you nebber see him till you feel him"; and Mesty's eyes sparkled with pleasure. "By de powers, they soon stop de mutiny; now I hab 'em."

Jack shuddered and walked away.

During the day, the men on shore were seen to work hard, and make all the preparations before they abandoned themselves to the sensual gratification of intemperance. The tent was pitched, the fire was lighted, and all the articles taken on shore rolled up and stowed away in their places; they were seen to sit down and dine, for they were within hail of the ship, and then one of the casks of wine was spiled.* In the meantime the Spaniard, who was a quiet lad, had prepared the dinner for Easy and his now only companion. The evening closed, and all was noise and revelry on shore; and as they danced, and sung, and tossed off the cans of wine by the light of the fire, as they hallooed and screamed, and became more and more intoxicated, Mesty turned to Jack with his bitter smile, and only said—

"Stop a little."

At last the noise grew fainter, the fire died away, and gradually all was silent. Jack was still hanging over the gangway when Mesty came up to him. The new moon had just risen, and Jack's eyes were fixed upon it.

"Now, Massa Easy, please you come aft and lower down little boat; take your pistols, and then we go on shore and bring off the cutter; they all asleep now."

"But why should we leave them without a boat, Mesty?" for Jack thought of the sharks, and the probability of the men attempting to swim off.

---

* Spiled: A spile is a spigot.

"I tell you, sar, this night they get drunk, to-morrow they get drunk again, but drunken men never keep quiet,—suppose one man say to others, 'Let's go board and kill officer, and then we do as we please,' they all say yes, and they all come and do it. No, sar—must have boat—if not for your sake, I must hab it, save my own life anyhow, for they hate me and kill me first; by de powers, stop a little."

Jack felt the truth of Mesty's observation; he went aft with him, lowered down the small boat, and they hauled it alongside. Jack went down with Mesty into the cabin and fetched his pistols. "And the Spaniard, Mesty, can we leave him on board alone?"

"Yes, sar, he no got arms, and he see dat me have—but suppose he find arms he never dare do anything—I know de man."

Our hero and Mesty went into the boat and shoved off, pulling gently on shore; the men were in a state of intoxication, so as not to be able to move, much less hear. They cast off the cutter, towed her on board, and made her fast with the other boat astern.

"Now, sar, we may go to bed; to-morrow morning you will see."

"They have everything they require on shore," replied Easy, "all they could want with the cutter would be to molest us."

"Stop a little," replied Mesty.

Jack and Mesty went to bed, and as a precaution against the Spaniard, which was hardly necessary, Mesty locked the cabin-door—but Mesty never forgot anything.

Jack slept little that night—had melancholy forebodings which he could not shake off; indeed, Jack had reflected so much since he had left the ship, he had had his eyes so much opened, and had felt what a responsibility he had taken by indulging himself in a whim of the moment, that it might be almost said, that in the course of one fortnight he had at once from a boy sprung up into a man. He was mortified and angry, but he was chiefly so with himself.

Mesty was up at daylight, and Jack soon followed him: they watched the party on shore, who had not yet left the tent. At last, just as Jack had finished his breakfast, one or two made their appearance; the men looked about them as if they were searching for something, and then walked down to the beach, to where the boat had been made fast. Jack looked at Mesty, who grinned, and answered with the words so often repeated,—

"Stop a little."

The men then walked along the rocks until they were abreast of the ship.

"Ship ahoy!"

"Halloo," replied Mesty.

"Bring the boat ashore directly, with a beaker of water."

"I knew dat," cried Mesty, rubbing his hands with delight. "Massa Easy, you must tell them No."

"But why should I not give them water, Mesty?"

"Because, sar, den they take boat."

"Very true," replied Easy.

"Do you hear on board?" cried the coxswain, who was the man who hailed—"send the boat immediately, or we'll cut the throats of every mother's son of you, by God!"

"I shall not send the boat," replied Jack, who now thought Mesty was right.

"You won't—won't you?—then your doom's sealed," replied the man, walking up to the tent with the other. In a short time all the seamen turned out of the tent, bringing with them four muskets, which they had taken on shore with them.

"Good heavens! they are not, surely, going to fire at us, Mesty."

"Stop a little."

The men then came down abreast of the ship, and the coxswain again hailed, and asked if they would bring the boat on shore.

"You must say, No, sar," replied Mesty.

"I feel I must," replied Jack; and then he answered the coxswain, "No."

The plan of the mutineers had been foreseen by the wily negro—it was to swim off to the boats which were riding astern, and to fire at him or Jack, if they attempted to haul them up alongside and defend them. To get into the boats, especially the smaller one, from out of the water was easy enough. Some of the men examined their priming and held the muskets at their hips all ready, with the muzzles towards the ship, while the coxswain and two men were throwing off their clothes.

"Stop, for God's sake, stop!" cried Jack. "The harbour is full of ground sharks,—it is, upon my soul!"

"Do you think to frighten us with ground sharks?" replied the coxswain; "keep under cover, my lad; Jack, give him a shot to prove we are in earnest, and every time he or that nigger show their heads, give them another, my lads."

"For God's sake, don't attempt to swim," said Jack, in an agony; "I will try some means to give you water."

"Too late now—you're doomed"; and the coxswain sprang off the rock into the sea, and was followed by two other men: at the same moment a musket was discharged, and the bullet whistled close to our hero's ear.

Mesty dragged Jack from the gangway, who was nearly fainting from agonising feelings. He sank on the deck for a moment, and then sprang up and ran to the port to look at the men in the water. He was just in time to see the coxswain raise himself with a loud yell out of the sea, and then disappear in a vortex, which was crimsoned with his blood.

Mesty threw down his musket in his hand, of which he had several already loaded, in case the men should have gained the boats.

"By the powers, dat no use now!"

Jack had covered his face with his hands. But the tragedy was not complete: the other men, who were in the water, had immediately turned and made for the shore; but before they could reach it, two more of these voracious monsters, attracted by the blood of the coxswain, had flown to the spot, and there was a contention for the fragments of their bodies.

Mesty, who had seen this catastrophe, turned towards our hero, who still hid his face.

"I'm glad he no see dat, anyhow," muttered Mesty.

"See what!" exclaimed Jack.

"Shark eat em all."

"Oh, horrid! horrid!" groaned our hero.

"Yes, sar, very horrid," replied Mesty, "and dat bullet at your head very horrid. Suppose the sharks no take them, what then? They kill us and the sharks have our body. I think that more horrid still."

"Mesty," replied Jack, seizing the negro convulsively by the arm, "it was not the sharks—it was I,—I who have murdered these men."

Mesty looked at Jack with surprise.

"How dat possible?"

"If I had not disobeyed orders," replied our hero, panting for breath, "if I had not shown them the example of disobedience, this would not have happened. How could I expect submission from them? It's all my fault—I see it now—and, O God! when will the sight be blotted from my memory?"

"Massa Easy, I not understand that," replied Mesty: "I think you talk foolish—might as well say, suppose Ashantee men not make war, this not happen; for suppose Ashantee not make war, I not slave,

I not run away,—I not come board *Harpy*—I not go in boat with you—I not hinder men from getting drunk—and dat why they make mutiny—and the mutiny why the shark take um?"

Jack made no reply, but he felt some consolation from the counter-argument of the negro.

The dreadful death of the three mutineers appeared to have had a sensible effect upon their companions, who walked away from the beach with their heads down and with measured steps. They were now seen to be perambulating the island, probably in search of that water which they required. At noon, they returned to their tent, and soon afterwards were in a state of intoxication, hallooing and shouting as the day before. Towards the evening they came down to the beach abreast of the ship, each with a vessel in their hands, and perceiving that they had attracted the notice of our hero and Mesty, tossed the contents of the vessels up in the air to show that they had found water, and hooting and deriding, went back, dancing, leaping, and kicking up their heels, to renew their orgies, which continued till after midnight, when they were all stupefied as before.

The next day Jack had recovered from the first shock which the catastrophe had given him, and he called Mesty into the cabin to hold a consultation.

"Mesty, how is this to end?"

"How you mean, sar?—end here, or end on board of the *Harpy*?"

"The *Harpy*,—there appears little chance of our seeing her again—we are on a desolate island, or what is the same thing; but we will hope that it will be so: but how is this mutiny to end?"

"Massa Easy, suppose I please, I make it end very soon, but I not in a hurry."

"How do you mean, Mesty, not in a hurry?"

"Look, Massa Easy; you wish take a cruise, and I wish the same ting: now because mutiny you want to go back—but by all de powers, you tink that I, a prince in my own country, feel wish to go back and boil kettle for de young gentlemen. No, Massa Easy, gib me mutiny—gib me anyting—but—once I was prince," replied Mesty, lowering his voice at the last few emphatic words.

"You must one of these days tell me your history," replied Jack; "but just now let us argue the point in question. How could you put an end to this mutiny?"

"By putting an end to all wine. Suppose I go shore after they all drunk, I spile the casks in three or four places, and in the morning all wine gone—den dey ab get sober, and beg pardon—we take dem on board, put away all arms, 'cept yours and mine, and I like to see the mutiny after dat. Blood and 'ounds—but I settle um, anyhow."

"The idea is very good, Mesty,—why should we not do so?"

"Because I not like run de risk to go ashore—all for what? to go back, boil de kettle for all gentlemans—I very happy here, Massa," replied Mesty, carelessly.

"And I am very miserable," replied Jack; "but, however, I am completely in your power, Mesty, and I must, I suppose, submit."

"What you say, Massa Easy—submit to me?—no sar, when you are on board *Harpy* as officer, you talk with me as friend, and not treat me as negro servant. Massa Easy, I feel—I feel what I am," continued Mesty, striking his bosom, "I feel it here—for all first time since I leave my country, I feel that I am someting; but, Massa Easy, I love my friend as much as I hate my enemy—and you nebber submit to me—I too proud to allow dat, 'cause, Massa Easy—I am a man— and once, I was a prince."

Although Mesty did not perhaps explain by words half so well as he did by his countenance the full tide of feeling which was overflowing in his heart, Jack fully understood and felt it. He extended his hand to Mesty, and said—

"Mesty,—that you have been a prince, I care little about, although I doubt it not, because you are incapable of a lie; but you are a man, and I respect you, nay, I love you as a friend—and with my will we never part again."

Mesty took the hand offered by Jack. It was the first peace-offering ever extended to him since he had been torn away from his native land—the first compliment, the first tribute, the first acknowledgment, perhaps, that he was not an inferior being; he pressed it in silence, for he could not speak; but could the feelings which were suffocating the negro but have been laid before sceptics, they must have acknowledged that at that moment they were all and only such as could do honour, not only to the prince, but even to the Christian. So much was Mesty affected with what had happened, that when he dropped the hand of our hero, he went down into the cabin, finding it impossible to continue the conversation, which was not renewed until the next morning.

"What is your opinion, Mesty? Tell me, and I will be governed by it."

"Den, sar, I tell you I tink it right that they first come and ask to

come on board before you take them—and, sar, I tink it also right as
we are but two and they are five, dat dey first eat all their provisions.
Let 'em starve plenty, and den dey come on board tame enough."

"At all events," replied Jack, "the first overtures of some kind or
another must come from them. I wish I had something to do—I do
not much like this cooping up on board ship."

"Massa, why you no talk with Pedro?"

"Because I cannot speak Spanish."

"I know dat, and dat why I ask de question. You very sorry when
you meet the two pretty women in the ship, you not able to talk with
them, I guess that."

"I was very sorry, I grant," replied Jack.

"Well, Massa Easy, by-and-bye we see more Spanish girl. Why not
talk all day with Pedro, and den you able to talk with dem."

"Upon my word, Mesty, I never had an idea of your value. I will
learn all the Spanish that I can," replied Jack, who was glad to have
employment found for him, and was quite disgusted with the articles
of war.

As for the men on shore, they continued the same course as
before, one day succeeded another, and without variety. It was, however, to be observed that the fire was now seldomer lighted, which
proved their fuel scarce, and the weather was not so warm as it had
been, for it was now October. Jack learnt Spanish from Pedro for a
month, during which there was no appearance of submission on the
part of the mutineers, who, for the first fortnight, when intoxicated,
used to come down and fire at Jack or Mesty when they made their
appearance. Fortunately drunken men are not good marksmen; but
latterly this had been discontinued, because they had expended their
ammunition, and they appeared to have almost forgotten that the
ship was there, for they took no notice of her whatever.

On the other hand, Jack had decided that if he waited there a year
the overtures should come from them who had mutinied; and now,
having an occupation, he passed his time very quietly, and the days
flew so fast that two months had actually been run off the calendar
before he had an idea of it.

One evening as they were down in the cabin, for the evenings had
now become very cold, Jack asked Mesty whether he had any objection to give him a history of his life. Mesty replied that if he wished
he was ready to talk, and at a nod from our hero Mesty commenced
as follows.

CHAPTER XV

In which mutiny, like fire, is quenched for want of fuel and no want of water.

ALTHOUGH WE have made the African negro hitherto talk in his own mixed jargon, yet, as we consider that, in a long narration, it will be tedious to the reader, we shall now translate the narrative part into good English, merely leaving the conversation with which it may be broken, in its peculiar dialect.

"The first thing I recollect," said Mesty, "is, that I was carried on the shoulders of a man with my legs hanging down before, and holding on by his head.

"Everyone used to look at me and get out of the way, as I rode through the town and market-place, so loaded with heavy gold ornaments that I could not bear them, and was glad when the women took them off; but as I grew older I became proud of them, because I knew that I was the son of a king. I lived happy. I did nothing but shoot my arrows, and I had a little sword which I was taught to handle, and the great captains who were about my father showed me how to kill my enemies. Sometimes I laid under the shady trees, sometimes I was with the women belonging to my father; sometimes I was with him and played with the skulls, and repeated the names of those to whom they had belonged, for in our country, when we kill our enemies, we keep their skulls as trophies.

"As I grew older, I did as I pleased; I beat the women and the slaves; I think I killed some of the latter—I know I did one, to try whether I could strike well with my two-handed sword made of hard and heavy wood,—but that is nothing in our country. I longed to be a great captain, and I thought of nothing else but war and fighting, and how many skulls I should have in my possession when I had a house and wives of my own, and I was no longer a boy. I went out in the woods to hunt, and I stayed for weeks. And one day I saw a panther basking in the sun, waving his graceful tail. I crept up softly till I was behind a rock within three yards of it, and drawing my arrow to the head, I pierced him through the body. The animal bounded up in the air, saw me, roared and made a spring, but I dropped behind the rock, and he passed over me. He turned again to me, but I had my knife ready, and, as he fixed his talons into my shoulder and breast, I pierced him to the heart. This was the happiest day of my life; I had killed a panther without assistance, and I had the wounds to show. Although I was severely hurt, I thought nothing of it. I took off the skin as my blood dropped down and mixed with that of the beast—but I rejoiced in it. Proudly did I go into the town dripping with gore and smarting with pain. Everyone extolled the feat, called me a hero and a great captain. I filed my teeth, and I became a man.

"From that day I ranked among the warriors, and, as soon as my wounds were healed, I went out to battle. In three fights I had gained five skulls, and when I returned they weighed me out gold. I then had a house and wives, and my father appointed me a Caboceer.* I wore the plume of eagle and ostrich feathers, my dress was covered with fetishes, I pulled on the boots with bells, and with my bow and arrows slung on my back, my spear and blunderbuss, my knives and my double-handed sword, I led the men to battle and brought back skulls and slaves. Everyone trembled at my name, and, if my father threatened to send me out, gold-dust covered the floor of his hall of council—Now, I boil the kettle for the young gentlemen!

"There was one man I liked. He was not a warrior, or I should have hated him, but he was brought up with me in my father's house, and was a near relative. I was grave and full of pride, he was gay and fond of music; and although there was no music to me equal to the tom-tom, yet I did not always wish for excitement. I often was melancholy, and then I liked to lay my head in the lap of one of my wives, under the shady forest behind my house, and listen to his soft music. At last he went to a town near us where his father lived, and as he departed I gave him gold-dust. He had been sent to my father to be formed into a warrior, but he had no strength of body, and he had no soul; still I loved him, because he was not like myself. There was a girl in the town who was beautiful; many asked for her as their wife, but her father had long promised her to my friend; he refused even the greatest warrior of the place, who went away in wrath to the fetishman, and throwing him his gold armlets asked for a fetish against his rival. It was given, and two days before he was to be married my friend died. His mother came to me, and it was enough. I put on my war dress, I seized my weapons, sat for a whole day with my skulls before me, working up my revenge, called out my men, and that night set off for the town where the warrior resided, killed two of his relatives and

* Caboceer: The leader in some West African villages.

carried off ten of his slaves. When he heard what I had done, he trembled and sent gold; but I knew that he had taken the girl home as his wife, and I would not listen to the old man who sought to pacify me. Again I collected a larger force and attacked him in the night: we fought, for he was prepared with his men, but after a struggle he was beaten back. I fired his house, wasted his provision ground, and taking away more slaves, I returned home with my men, intending soon to assault him again. The next day there came more messengers, who knelt in vain; so they went to my father, and many warriors begged him to interfere. My father sent for me, but I would not listen; the warriors spoke, and I turned my back: my father was wroth and threatened, the warriors brandished their two-handed swords—they dared to do it; I looked over my shoulder with contempt, and I returned to my house. I took down my skulls, and I planned. It was evening, and I was alone, when a woman covered up to the eyes approached; she fell down before me as she exposed her face.

" 'I am the girl who was promised to your relation, and I am now the wife of your enemy. I shall be a mother. I could not love your relation, for he was no warrior. It is not true that my husband asked for a fetish—it was I who bought it, for I would not wed him. Kill me and be satisfied.'

"She was very beautiful, and I wondered not that my enemy loved her—and she was with child—it was his child, and she had fetished my friend to death. I raised my sword to strike, and she did not shrink: it saved her life. 'Thou art fit to be the mother of warriors,' said I, as I dropped my sword, 'and thou shalt be my wife, but first his child shall be born, and I will have thy husband's skull.'

" 'No, no,' replied she, 'I will be the mother of no warriors but by my present husband, whom I love; if you keep me as your slave I will die.'

"I told her she said foolish things, and sent her to the women's apartment, with orders to be watched—but she hardly had been locked up before she drew her knife, plunged it into her heart, and died.

"When the king my father heard this he sent me a message—'Be satisfied with the blood that has been shed, it is enough'; but I turned away, for I wished for mine enemy's skull. That night I attacked him again, and met him hand to hand; I killed him, and carried home his skull, and I was appeased.

"But all the great warriors were wroth, and my father could not restrain them. They called out their men, and I called out my men, and I had a large body, for my name was terrible. But the force raised against me was twice that of mine, and I retreated to the bush—after awhile we met and fought, and I killed many, but my men were too few, and were overpowered—the fetish had been sent out against me, and their hearts melted; at last I sank down with my wounds, for I bled at every pore, and I told my men who were about me to take off my feathers, and my dress and boots, that my enemies might not have my skull: they did so, and I crawled into the bush to die. But I was not to die; I was recovering, when I was discovered by those who steal men to sell them: I was bound, and fastened to a chain with many more. I, a prince and a warrior, who could show the white skulls of his enemies—I offered to procure gold, but they derided me; they dragged me down to the coast, and sold me to the Whites. Little did I think, in my pride, that I should be a slave. I knew that I was to die, and hoped to die in battle: my skull would have been more prized than all the gold in the earth, and my skin would have been stuffed and hung up in a fetish-house—instead of which, I now boil the kettle for the young gentlemen!"

"Well," replied Jack, "that's better than being killed and stuffed."

"Mayhap it is," replied Mesty, "I tink very different now dan I tink den—but still, it women's work and not suit me.

"They put me with others into a cave until the ship came, and then we were sent on board, put in irons, and down in the hold, where you could not sit upright—I wanted to die, but could not: others died every day, but I lived—I was landed in America, all bone, and I fetched very little money—they laughed at me, as they bid their dollars: at last a man took me away, and I was on a plantation with hundreds more, but too ill to work, and not intending to work. The other slaves asked me if I was a fetish man; I said yes, and I would fetish any man that I did not like: one man laughed, and I held up my finger; I was too weak to get up, for my blood had long boiled with fever, and I said to him *'you shall die'*; for I meant to have killed him as soon as I was well. He went away, and in three days he was dead. I don't know how, but all the slaves feared me, and my master feared me, for he had seen the man die, and he, although he was a white man, believed in fetish, and he wished to sell me again, but no one would buy a fetish man, so he made friends with me; for I told him if I was beat he should die, and he believed me. He took me into his house, and I was his chief man, and I would not let the other slaves steal and he was content. He took me with him to New York, and there, after two years, when I had learnt English, I ran away, and got on board of an English ship—and they told me to cook. I left the ship as soon as I came to England, and offered myself to another, and they said they did not want a cook; and I went to another, and they asked me if I was a good cook: everybody seemed to think that a black man must be a cook, and nothing else. At last I starve, and I go on board a man-of-war, and here I am, after having been a warrior and a prince, cook, steward and everyting else, boiling kettle for de young gentlemen."

"Well," replied Jack, "at all events that is better than being a slave."

Mesty made no reply: anyone who knows the life of a midshipman's servant will not be surprised at his silence.

"Now, tell me, do you think you were right in being so revengeful, when you were in your own country?" inquired Jack.

"I tink so den, Massa Easy; sometimes when my blood boil, I tink so now—oder time, I no know what to tink—but when a man love very much, he hate very much."

"But you are now a Christian, Mesty."

"I hear all that your people say," replied the negro, "and it make me tink—I no longer believe in fetish, anyhow."

"Our religion tells us to love our enemies."

"Yes, I heard parson say dat—but den what we do with our friends, Massa Easy?"

"Love them too."

"I no understand dat, Massa Easy—I love you, because you good, and treat me well—Mr Vigors, he bully, and treat me ill—how possible to love him? By de power, I hate him, and wish I had him *skull*. You tink little Massa Gossitt love him?"

"No," replied Jack, laughing, "I'm afraid that he would like to have his skull as well as you, Mesty—but at all events we must try and forgive those who injure us."

"Then, Massa Easy, I tink so too—too much revenge very bad—it very easy to hate, but not very easy to forgive—so I tink that if a man forgive, he hab *more soul* in him, he more of a *man*."

"After all," thought Jack, "Mesty is about as good a Christian as most people."

"What that?" cried Mesty, looking out of the cabin window— "Ah! d——n drunken dogs—they set fire to tent."

Jack looked, and perceived that the tent on shore was in flames.

"I tink these cold nights cool their courage, anyhow," observed Mesty—"Massa Easy, you see they soon ask permission to come on board."

Jack thought so too, and was most anxious to be off; for, on looking into the lockers in the state-room, he had found a chart of the Mediterranean, which he had studied very attentively—he had found out the rock of Gibraltar, and had traced the *Harpy's* course up to Cape de Gatte, and thence to Tarragona—and, after a while, had summoned Mesty to a cabinet council.

"See, Mesty," said Jack, "I begin to make it out, here is Gibraltar, and Cape de Gatte, and Tarragona—it was hereabout we were when we took the ship, and, if you recollect, we had passed Cape de Gatte two days before we were blown off from the land, so that we had gone about twelve inches, and had only four more to go."

"Yes, Massa Easy, I see all dat."

"Well, then, we were blown off shore by the wind, and must of course have come down this way; and here you see are three little islands, called Zaffarine Islands, and with no names of towns upon them, and therefore uninhabited; and you see they lie just like the islands we are anchored among now—we must be at the Zaffarine Islands*—and only six inches from Gibraltar."

"I see, Massa Easy, dat all right—but six debbelish long inches."

"Now, Mesty, you know the compass on deck has a flourishing thing for the north point—and here is a compass with a north point also. Now the north point from the Zaffarine Islands leads out to the Spanish coast again, and Gibraltar lies five or six points of the compass to this side of it—if we steer that way we shall get to Gibraltar."

"All right, Massa Easy," replied Mesty, and Jack was right, with the exception of the variation, which he knew nothing about.

To make sure, Jack brought one of the compasses down from deck, and compared them. He then lifted off the glass, counted the points of the compass to the westward, and marked the corresponding one on the binnacle compass with his pen.

"There," said he, "that is the way to Gibraltar, and as soon as the mutiny is quelled, and the wind is fair, I'll be off."

* Zaffarine Islands: Islas Chafarinas, three small islands belonging to Spain off the Moroccan coast.

CHAPTER XVI

In which Jack's cruise is ended, and he regains the Harpy.

A FEW more days passed, and, as was expected, the mutineers could hold out no longer. In the first place, they had put in the spile of the second cask of wine so loosely when they were tipsy that it dropped out, and all the wine ran out, so that there had been none left for three or four days; in the next their fuel had long been expended, and they had latterly eaten their meat raw: the loss of their tent, which had been fired by their carelessness, had been followed by four days and nights of continual rain. Everything they had had been soaked through and through, and they were worn out, shivering with cold, and starving. Hanging they thought better than dying by inches from starvation; and yielding to the imperious demands of hunger, they came down to the beach, abreast of the ship, and dropped down on their knees.

"I tell you so, Massa Easy," said Mesty: "d——n rascals, they forget they come down fire musket at us every day: by all de powers, Mesty not forget it."

"Ship ahoy!" cried one of the men on shore.

"What do you want?" replied Jack.

"Have pity on us, sir—mercy!" exclaimed the other men, "we will return to our duty."

"Debble doubt 'em!"

"What shall I say, Mesty?"

"Tell 'em no, first, Massa Easy—tell 'em to starve and be d——d."

"I cannot take mutineers on board," replied Jack.

"Well, then, our blood be on your hands, Mr Easy," replied the first man who had spoken. "If we are to die, it must not be by inches—if you will not take us, the sharks shall—it is but a crunch, and all is over. What do you say, my lads? let's all rush in together: good-bye, Mr Easy, I hope you'll forgive us when we're dead: it was all that rascal Johnson, the coxswain, who persuaded us. Come, my lads, it's no use thinking of it, the sooner done the better—let us shake hands, and then make one run of it."

It appeared that the poor fellows had already made up their minds to do this, if our hero, persuaded by Mesty, had refused to take them on board; they shook hands all round, and then walking a few yards from the beach, stood in a line while the man gave the signal— one—two—

"Stop," cried Jack, who had not forgotten the dreadful scene which had already taken place,—"stop."

The men paused.

"What will you promise if I take you on board?"

"To do our duty cheerfully till we join the ship, and then be hung as an example to all mutineers," replied the men.

"Dat very fair," replied Mesty; "take dem at their word, Massa Easy."

"Very well," replied Jack, "I accept your conditions; and we will come for you."

Jack and Mesty hauled up the boat, stuck their pistols in their belts, and pulled to the shore. The men, as they stepped in, touched their hats respectfully to our hero, but said nothing. On their arrival on board, Jack read that part of the articles of war relative to mutiny, by which the men were reminded of the very satisfactory fact, "that they were to suffer death"; and then made a speech which, to men who were starving, appeared to be interminable. However, there is an end to everything in this world, and so there was to Jack's harangue; after which Mesty gave them some biscuit, which they devoured in thankfulness, until they could get something better. The next morning the wind was fair, they weighed their kedge with some difficulty, and ran out of the harbour: the men appeared very contrite, worked well, but in silence, for they had no very pleasant anticipations; but hope always remains with us; and each of the men, although he had no doubt but that the others would be hung, hoped that he would escape with a sound flogging. The wind, however, did not allow them to steer their course long; before night it was contrary, and they fell off three points to the northward. "However," as Jack observed, "at all events we shall make the Spanish coast, and then we must run down it to Gibraltar: I don't care—I understand navigation much better than I did." The next morning they found themselves with a very light breeze, under a high cape, and, as the sun rose, they observed a large vessel in-shore, about two miles to the westward of them, and another outside, about four miles off. Mesty took the glass and examined the one outside, which, on a sudden, had let fall all her canvas, and was now running for the shore, steering for the cape under which Jack's vessel lay. Mesty put down the glass.

"Massa Easy—I tink dat de *Harpy*."

One of the seamen took the glass and examined her, while the others who stood by showed great agitation.

"Yes, it is the *Harpy*," said the seaman. "Oh! Mr Easy, will you forgive us?" continued the man, and he and the others fell on their knees. "Do not tell all, for God's sake, Mr Easy."

Jack's heart melted; he looked at Mesty.

"I tink," said Mesty, apart to our hero, "dat with what them hab suffer already, suppose they get *seven dozen a-piece*, dat quite enough."

Jack thought that even half that punishment would suffice; so he told the men, that although he must state what had occurred, he would not tell all, and would contrive to get them off as well as he could. He was about to make a long speech, but a gun from the *Harpy*, which had now come up within range, made him defer it till a more convenient opportunity. At the same time the vessel in-shore hoisted Spanish colours and fired a gun.

"By de powers but we got in the middle of it," cried Mesty; "*Harpy* tink us Spaniard. Now, my lads, get all gun ready, bring up powder and shot. Massa, now us fire at Spaniard—*Harpy* not fire at us—no ab English colours on board—dat all we must do."

The men set to with a will; the guns were all loaded, and were soon cast loose and primed, during which operations it fell calm, and the sails of all three vessels flapped against their masts. The *Harpy* was then about two miles from Jack's vessel, and the Spaniard about a mile from him, with all her boats ahead of her, towing towards him; Mesty examined the Spanish vessel.

"Dat man-of-war, Massa Easy,—what de debbel we do for colour? must hoist something."

Mesty ran down below; he recollected that there was a very gay petticoat, which had been left by the old lady who was in the vessel when they captured her. It was of green silk, with yellow and blue flowers, but very faded, having probably been in the Don's family for a century. Mesty had found it under the mattress of one of the beds, and had put it into his bag, intending probably to cut it up into waistcoats. He soon appeared with this under his arm, made it fast to the peak halyards* and hoisted it up.

"Dere, Massa, dat do very well—dat what you call *'all nation*

* Halyards (or halliards): Ropes used for lowering or raising a sail.

colour.' Everybody strike him flag to dat—men nebber pull it down,"
said Mesty, "anyhow. Now den, ab hoist colour, we fire away—mind
you only fire one gun at a time, and point um well, den ab time to
load again."

"She's hoisted her colours, sir," said Sawbridge, on board of the
Harpy; "but they do not show out clear, and it's impossible to distinguish them; but there's a gun."

"It's not at us, sir," said Gascoigne, the midshipman; "it's at the
Spanish vessel—I saw the shot fall ahead of her."

"It must be a privateer,"* said Captain Wilson; "at all events, it is
very fortunate, for the corvette† would otherwise have towed into
Carthagena. Another gun, round and grape, and well pointed too;
she carries heavy metal, that craft: she must be a Maltese privateer."

"That's as much as to say that she's a pirate," replied Sawbridge;
"I can make nothing of her colours—they appear to me to be green—
she must be a Turk. Another gun—and devilish well aimed; it has hit
the boats."

"Yes, they are all in confusion: we will have her now, if we can
only get a trifle of wind. That is a breeze coming up in the offing.
Trim the sails, Mr Sawbridge."

The yards were squared, and the *Harpy* soon had steerage-way. In
the meantime Jack and his few men had kept up a steady, well-
directed, although slow, fire with their larboard guns upon the
Spanish corvette; and two of her boats had been disabled. The *Harpy*
brought the breeze up with her, and was soon within range; she
steered to cut off the corvette, firing only on her bow-chasers.‡

"We ab her now," cried Mesty; "fire away,—men, take good aim.
Breeze come now; one man go to helm. By de power what dat?"

The exclamation of Mesty was occasioned by a shot hulling the
ship on the starboard side. Jack and he ran over, and perceived that
three Spanish gun-boats had just made their appearance round the
point, and had attacked them. The fact was, that on the other side of
the cape was the port and town of Carthagena, and these gun-boats
had been sent out to the assistance of the corvette. The ship had now
caught the breeze, fortunately for Jack, or he would probably have
been taken into Carthagena; and the corvette, finding herself cut off

---

* Privateer: A privately owned vessel of war authorized to cruise against the enemy.
† Corvette: A small warship with a single tier of guns.
‡ Bow-chasers: Long guns used especially when chasing an enemy vessel to damage her sails
and rigging.

by both the *Harpy* and Jack's vessel, as soon as the breeze came up to her, put her head the other way, and tried to escape by running westward along the coast close in-shore. Another shot, and then another, pierced the hull of the ship, and wounded two of Jack's men; but as the corvette had turned, and the *Harpy* followed her, of course Jack did the same, and in ten minutes he was clear of the gun-boats, who did not venture to make sail and stand after him. The wind now freshened fast, and blew out the green petticoat, but the *Harpy* was exchanging broadsides with the corvette, and too busy to look after Jack's ensign. The Spaniard defended himself well, and had the assistance of the batteries as he passed, but there was no anchorage until he had run many miles further. About noon, the wind died away, and at one o'clock it again fell nearly calm; but the *Harpy* had neared her distance, and was now within three cables' length of her antagonist, engaging her and a battery of four guns. Jack came up again, for he had the last of the breeze, and was about half a mile from the corvette when it fell calm. By the advice of Mesty, he did not fire anymore, as otherwise the *Harpy* would not obtain so much credit, and it was evident that the fire of the Spaniard slackened fast. At three o'clock the Spanish colours were hauled down, and the *Harpy,* sending a boat on board and taking possession, directed her whole fire upon the battery, which was soon silenced.

The calm continued, and the *Harpy* was busy enough with the prize, shifting the prisoners and refitting both vessels, which had very much suffered in the sails and rigging. There was an occasional wonder on board the *Harpy* what that strange vessel might be, who had turned the corvette and enabled them to capture her, but when people are all very busy, there is not much time for surmise.

Jack's crew, with himself, consisted but of eight, one of which was a Spaniard, and two were wounded. It therefore left him but four, and he had also something to do, which was to assist his wounded men, and secure his guns. Moreover, Mesty did not think it prudent to leave the vessel a mile from the *Harpy* with only two on board; besides, as Jack said, he had had no dinner, and was not quite sure that he should find anything to eat when he went into the midshipmen's berth; he would therefore have some dinner cooked, and eat it before he went on board; in the meantime, they would try and close with her. Jack took things always very easy, and he said he should report himself at sunset. There were other reasons which made Jack in no very great hurry to go on board; he wanted to have time to consider a little, what he should say to excuse himself, and also how he should plead for the men. His natural correctness of feeling decided him, in the first place, to tell the whole truth; and in the next, his kind feelings determined him to tell only part of it. Jack need not have given himself this trouble, for, as far as regarded himself, he had fourteen thousand good excuses in the bags that lay in the state-room; and as for the men, after an action with the enemy, if they behave well, even mutiny is forgiven. At last, Jack, who was tired with excitement and the hard work of the day, thought and thought until he fell fast asleep, and instead of waking at sunset, did not wake till two hours afterwards; and Mesty did not call him, because he was in no hurry himself to go on board "and *boil de kettle for de young gentlemen.*"

When Jack woke up, he was astonished to find that he had slept so long; he went on deck; it was dark and still calm, but he could easily perceive that the *Harpy* and corvette were still hove-to, repairing damages. He ordered the men to lower down the small boat, and leaving Mesty in charge, with two oars he pulled to the *Harpy*. What with wounded men, with prisoners, and boats going and coming between the vessels, everyone on board the *Harpy* were well employed; and in the dark, Jack's little boat came alongside without notice. This should not have been the case, but it was, and there was some excuse for it. Jack ascended the side, and pushed his way through the prisoners, who were being mustered to be victualled. He was wrapped up in one of the gregos, and many of the prisoners wore the same.

Jack was amused at not being recognized; he slipped down the main ladder, and had to stoop under the hammocks of the wounded men, and was about to go aft to the captain's cabin to report himself, when he heard young Gossett crying out, and the sound of the rope. "Hang me, if that brute Vigors ain't thrashing young Gossett," thought Jack. "I dare say the poor fellow has had plenty of it since I have been away; I'll save him this time, at least." Jack, wrapped up in his grego, went to the window of the berth, looked in, and found it was as he expected. He cried out in an angry voice, *Mr Vigors, I'll thank you to leave Gossett alone.* At the sound of the voice, Vigors turned round with his colt in his hand, saw Jack's face at the window, and, impressed with the idea that the re-appearance was supernatural, uttered a yell and fell down in a fit—little Gossett also, trembling in every limb, stared with his mouth open. Jack was satisfied, and immediately disappeared. He then went aft to the cabin, pushed by the servant, who was giving some orders from the captain to the officer on deck, and entering the cabin, where the captain was seated with two Spanish officers, took off his hat and said,—

"Come on board, Captain Wilson."

Captain Wilson did not fall down in a fit, but he jumped up, and upset the glass before him.

"Merciful God, Mr Easy, where did you come from?"

"From that ship astern, sir," replied Jack.

"That ship astern! what is she?—where have you been so long?"

"It's a long story, sir," replied Jack.

Captain Wilson extended his hand and shook Jack's heartily.

"At all events, I'm delighted to see you, boy: now sit down and tell me your story in a few words; we will have it in detail by-and-bye."

"If you please, sir," said Jack, "we captured that ship with the cutter the night after we went away—I'm not a first-rate navigator, and I was blown to the Zaffarine Islands, where I remained two months for want of hands: as soon as I procured them I made sail again—I have lost three men by sharks, and I have two wounded in to-day's fight—the ship mounts twelve guns, is half laden with lead and cotton prints, has fourteen thousand dollars in the cabin, and three shot-holes right through her—and the sooner you send some people on board of her the better."

This was not very intelligible, but that there were fourteen thousand dollars and that she required hands sent on board, was very satisfactorily explained. Captain Wilson rang the bell, sent for Mr Asper, who started back at the sight of our hero—desired him to order Mr Jolliffe to go on board with one of the cutters, send the wounded men on board, and take charge of the vessel, and then told Jack to accompany Mr Jolliffe, and to give him every information: telling him that he would hear his story to-morrow, when they were not so very busy.

CHAPTER XVII

In which our hero finds out that Trigonometry is not only necessary to navigation, but may be required in settling affairs of honour.

A S CAPTAIN WILSON truly said, he was too busy even to hear Jack's story that night, for they were anxious to have both vessels ready to make sail as soon as a breeze should spring up, for the Spaniards had vessels of war at Carthagena, which was not ten miles off, and had known the result of the action: it was therefore necessary to change their position as soon as possible. Mr Sawbridge was on board the prize, which was a corvette mounting two guns more than the *Harpy,* and called the *Cacafuogo.*

She had escaped from Cadiz, run through the straits in the night, and was three miles from Carthagena when she was captured, which she certainly never would have been, but for Jack's fortunately blundering against the cape with his armed vessel, so that Captain Wilson and Mr Sawbridge (both of whom were promoted, the first to the rank of post-captain, the second to that of commander) may be said to be indebted to Jack for their good fortune. The *Harpy* had lost nineteen men, killed and wounded, and the Spanish corvette forty-seven. Altogether, it was a very creditable affair.

At two o'clock in the morning, the vessels were ready, everything had been done that could be done in so short a time, and they stood under easy sail during the night for Gibraltar, the *Nostra Signora del Carmen,* under the charge of Jolliffe, keeping company. Jolliffe had the advantage over his shipmates, of first hearing Jack's adventures, with which he was much astonished as well as amused—even Captain Wilson was not more happy to see Jack than was the worthy master's mate. About nine o'clock the *Harpy* hove-to,* and sent a boat on board for our hero and the men who had been so long with him in the prize, and then hoisted out the pinnace to fetch on board the dollars, which were of more importance. Jack, as he bade adieu to Jolliffe, took out of his pocket, and presented him with the *articles of war,* which, as they had been so useful to him, he thought Jolliffe could not do without, and then went down the side: the men were

---

* Hove-to: To come to a standstill without anchoring.

already in the boat, casting imploring looks upon Jack, to raise feelings of compassion, and Mesty took his seat by our hero in a very sulky humour, probably because he did not like the idea of having again "to boil de kettle for de young gentlemen." Even Jack felt a little melancholy at resigning his command, and he looked back at the green petticoat, which blew out gracefully from the mast, for Jolliffe had determined that he would not haul down the colours under which Jack had fought so gallant an action.

Jack's narration, as may be imagined, occupied a large part of the forenoon; and although Jack did not attempt to deny that he had seen the recall signal of Mr Sawbridge, yet, as his account went on, the captain became so interested, that at the end of it he quite forgot to point out to Jack the impropriety of not obeying orders. He gave Jack great credit for his conduct, and was also much pleased with that of Mesty. Jack took the opportunity of stating Mesty's aversion to his present employment, and his recommendation was graciously received. Jack also succeeded in obtaining the pardon of the men, in consideration of their subsequent good behaviour; but notwithstanding this promise on the part of Captain Wilson, they were ordered to be put in irons for the present. However, Jack told Mesty, and Mesty told the men, that they would be released with a reprimand when they arrived at Gibraltar, so that all the men cared for was a fair wind.

Captain Wilson informed Jack, that after his joining the admiral he had been sent to Malta with the prizes, and that, supposing the cutter to have been sunk, he had written to his father, acquainting him with his son's death, at which our hero was much grieved, for he knew what sorrow it would occasion, particularly to his poor mother. "But," thought Jack, "if she is unhappy for three months, she will be overjoyed for three more when she hears that I am alive, so it will be all square at the end of the six; and as soon as I arrive at Gibraltar I will write, and as the wind is fair, that will be to-morrow or next day."

After a long conversation Jack was graciously dismissed, Captain Wilson being satisfied from what he had heard that Jack would turn out a very good officer, and had already forgotten all about equality and the rights of man; but there Captain Wilson was mistaken—tares* sown in infancy are not so soon rooted out.

* Tares: Climbing plants; also the seeds of such plants.

Jack went on deck as soon as the captain had dismissed him, and found the captain and officers of the Spanish corvette standing aft, looking very seriously at the *Nostra Signora del Carmen*. When they saw our hero, whom Captain Wilson had told them was the young officer who had barred their entrance into Carthagena, they turned their eyes upon him, not quite so graciously as they might have done.

Jack, with his usual politeness, took off his hat to the Spanish captain, and, glad to have an opportunity of sporting his Spanish, expressed the usual wish, that he might live a thousand years. The Spanish captain, who had reason to wish that Jack had gone to the devil at least twenty-four hours before, was equally complimentary, and then begged to be informed what the colours were that Jack had hoisted during the action. Jack replied that they were colours to which every Spanish gentleman considered it no disgrace to surrender, although always ready to engage, and frequently attempting to board. Upon which the Spanish captain was very much puzzled. Captain Wilson, who understood a little Spanish, then interrupted by observing—

"By-the-bye, Mr Easy, what colours did you hoist up? We could not make them out. I see Mr Jolliffe still keeps them up at the peak."

"Yes, sir," replied Jack, rather puzzled what to call them, but at last he replied, "that it was the banner of equality and the rights of man."

Captain Wilson frowned, and Jack, perceiving that he was displeased, then told him the whole story, whereupon Captain Wilson laughed, and Jack then also explained, in Spanish, to the officers of the corvette, who replied, "that it was not the first time, and would not be the last, that men had got into a scrape through a petticoat."

The Spanish captain complimented Jack on his Spanish, which was really very good (for in two months, with nothing else in the world to do, he had made great progress), and asked him where he had learnt it.

Jack replied, "At the Zaffarine Islands."

"Zaffarine Isles," replied the Spanish captain; "they are not inhabited."

"Plenty of ground-sharks," replied Jack.

The Spanish captain thought our hero a very strange fellow, to fight under a green silk petticoat, and to take lessons in Spanish from the ground-sharks. However, being quite as polite as Jack, he did not contradict him, but took a huge pinch of snuff, wishing from the bottom of his heart that the ground-sharks had taken Jack before he had hoisted that confounded green petticoat.

However, Jack was in high favour with the captain, and all the ship's company, with the exception of his four enemies—the master, Vigors, the boatswain, and the purser's steward. As for Mr Vigors, he had come to his senses again, and had put his colt in his chest until Jack should take another cruise. Little Gossett, at any insulting remark made by Vigors, pointed to the window of the berth and grinned; and the very recollection made Vigors turn pale, and awed him into silence.

In two days they arrived at Gibraltar—Mr Sawbridge rejoined the ship—so did Mr Jolliffe—they remained there a fortnight, during which Jack was permitted to be continually on shore—Mr Asper accompanied him, and Jack drew a heavy bill to prove to his father that he was still alive. Mr Sawbridge made our hero relate to him all his adventures, and was so pleased with the conduct of Mesty that he appointed him to a situation which was particularly suited to him,—that of ship's corporal. Mr Sawbridge knew that it was an office of trust, and provided that he could find a man fit for it, he was very indifferent about his colour. Mesty walked and strutted about at least three inches taller than he was before. He was always clean, did his duty conscientiously, and seldom used his cane.

"I think, Mr Easy," said the first lieutenant, "that as you are so particularly fond of taking a cruise,"—for Jack had told the whole truth,—"it might be as well that you improve your navigation."

"I do think myself, sir," replied Jack, with great modesty, "that I am not yet quite perfect."

"Well, then, Mr Jolliffe will teach you; he is the most competent in this ship: the sooner you ask him the better, and if you learn it as fast as you have Spanish, it will not give you much trouble."

Jack thought the advice good; the next day he was very busy with his friend Jolliffe, and made the important discovery that two parallel lines continued to infinity would never meet.

It must not be supposed that Captain Wilson and Mr Sawbridge received their promotion instanter. Promotion is always attended with delay, as there is a certain routine in the service which must not be departed from. Captain Wilson had orders to return to Malta after his cruise. He therefore carried his own despatches away from England—from Malta the despatches had to be forwarded to Toulon to the admiral, and then the admiral had to send to England to the admiralty, whose reply had to come out again. All this, with the delays arising from vessels not sailing immediately, occupied an interval of between five and six months—during which time there was no alteration in the officers and crew of his Majesty's sloop *Harpy*.

There had, however, been one alteration; the gunner, Mr Minus, who had charge of the first cutter in the night action in which our hero was separated from his ship, carelessly loading his musket, had found himself minus his right hand, which, upon the musket going off as he rammed down, had gone off too. He was invalided and sent home during Jack's absence, and another had been appointed, whose name was Tallboys. Mr Tallboys was a stout dumpy man, with red face, and still redder hands; he had red hair and red whiskers, and he had read a great deal—for Mr Tallboys considered that the gunner was the most important personage in the ship. He had once been a captain's clerk, and having distinguished himself very much in cutting-out service, had applied for and received his warrant as a gunner. He had studied the "Art of Gunnery," a part of which he understood, but the remainder was above his comprehension: he continued, however, to read it as before, thinking that by constant reading he should understand it at last. He had gone through the work from the title-page to the finis at least forty times, and had just commenced it over again. He never came on deck without the gunner's *vade mecum** in his pocket, with his hand always upon it to refer to it in a moment.

But Mr Tallboys had, as we observed before, a great idea of the importance of a gunner, and, among other qualifications, he considered it absolutely necessary that he should be a navigator. He had at least ten instances to bring forward of bloody actions, in which the captain and all the commissioned officers had been killed or wounded and the command of the ship had devolved upon the gunner.

"Now, sir," would he say, "if the gunner is no navigator, he is not fit to take charge of his Majesty's ships. The boatswain and carpenter are merely practical men; but the gunner, sir, is, or ought to be, scientific. Gunnery, sir, is a science—we have our own disparts† and our lines of sight—our windage, and our parabolas, and projectile forces—and our point blank, and our reduction of powder upon a graduated scale. Now, sir, there's no excuse for a gunner not being a

---

* *Vade mecum*: A handbook or manual.
† Disparts: A dispart sight is a gun used for point-blank or horizontal firing.

navigator; for knowing his duty as a gunner, he has the same mathematical tools to work with." Upon this principle, Mr Tallboys had added John Hamilton Moore* to his library, and had advanced about as far into navigation as he had in gunnery, that is, to the threshold, where he stuck fast, with all his mathematical tools, which he did not know how to use. To do him justice, he studied for two or three hours every day, and it was not his fault if he did not advance—but his head was confused with technical terms; he mixed all up together, and disparts, sines and cosines, parabolas, tangents, windage, seconds, lines of sight, logarithms, projectiles, and traverse sailing, quadrature, and Gunter's scales,† were all crowded together, in a brain which had not capacity to receive the rule of three. "Too much learning," said Festus to the apostle, "hath made thee mad."‡ Mr Tallboys had not wit enough to go mad, but his learning lay like lead upon his brain: the more he read, the less he understood, at the same time that he became more satisfied with his supposed acquirements, and could not speak but in "mathematical parables.""I understand, Mr Easy," said the gunner to him one day, after they had sailed for Malta, "that you have entered into the science of navigation—at your age it was high time."

"Yes," replied Jack, "I can raise a perpendicular, at all events, and box the compass."

"Yes, but you have not yet arrived at the dispart of the compass."

"Not come to that yet," replied Jack.

"Are you aware that a ship sailing describes a parabola round the globe?"

"Not come to that yet," replied Jack.

"And that any propelled body striking against another flies off at a tangent?"

"Very likely," replied Jack; "that is a *'sine'* that he don't like it."

"You have not yet entered into *'acute'* trigonometry?"

"Not come to that yet," replied Jack.

"That will require very sharp attention."

"I should think so," replied Jack.

"You will then find out how your parallels of longitude and latitude meet."

* John Hamilton Moore: In 1770 Moore published the *New Practical Navigator,* which became a standard navigational handbook reprinted in many editions.

† Gunter's scales: A marked-up flat rule used for solving surveying and navigation problems.

‡ "Too much learning," said Festus to the apostle, "hath made thee mad": In Acts 26:24, Festus says to Saint Paul, "much learning doth make thee mad."

"Two parallel lines, if continued to infinity will never meet," replied Jack.

"I beg your pardon," said the gunner.

"I beg yours," said Jack.

Whereupon Mr Tallboys brought up a small map of the world, and showed Jack that all the parallels of latitude met at a point at the top and the bottom.

"Parallel lines never meet," replied Jack, producing Hamilton Moore.

Whereupon Jack and the gunner argued the point, until it was agreed to refer the case to Mr Jolliffe, who asserted, with a smile, "That those lines were parallels, and not parallels."

As both were right, both were satisfied.

It was fortunate that Jack would argue in this instance: had he believed all the confused assertions of the gunner, he would have been as puzzled as the gunner himself. They never met without an argument and a reference, and as Jack was put right in the end, he only learnt the faster. By the time that he did know something about navigation, he discovered that his antagonist knew nothing. Before they arrived at Malta, Jack could fudge a day's work.

But at Malta Jack got into another scrape. Although Mr Smallsole could not injure him, he was still Jack's enemy; the more so as Jack had become very popular: Vigors also submitted, planning revenge; but the parties in this instance were the boatswain and purser's steward. Jack still continued his forecastle conversations with Mesty: and the boatswain and purser's steward, probably from their respective ill-will towards our hero, had become great allies. Mr Easthupp now put on his best jacket to walk the dog-watches with Mr Biggs, and they took every opportunity to talk at our hero.

"It's my peculiar hopinion," said Mr Easthupp, one evening, pulling at the frill of his shirt, "that a gentleman should behave as a gentleman, and that if a gentleman professes opinions of hequality and such liberal sentiments, that he is bound as a gentleman to hact up to them."

"Very true, Mr Easthupp; he is bound to act up to them; and not because a person, who was a gentleman as well as himself, happens not to be on the quarter-deck, to insult him because he only has professed opinions like his own."

Hereupon Mr Biggs struck his rattan against the funnel, and looked at our hero.

"Yes," continued the purser's steward, "I should like to see the fellow who would have done so on shore; however, the time will come when I can hagain pull on my plain coat, and then the insult shall be vashed out in blood, Mr Biggs."

"And I'll be cursed if I don't some day teach a lesson to the blackguard who stole my trousers."

"Vas hall your money right, Mr Biggs?" inquired the purser's steward.

"I didn't count," replied the boatswain magnificently.

"No—gentlemen are habove that," replied Easthupp; "but there are many light-fingered gentry about. The quantity of vatches and harticles of value vich were lost ven I valked Bond Street in former times is incredible."

"I can say this, at all events," replied the boatswain, "that I should be always ready to give satisfaction to any person beneath me in rank, after I had insulted him. I don't stand upon my rank, although I don't talk about equality, damme—no, nor consort with niggers."

All this was too plain for our hero not to understand, so Jack walked up to the boatswain, and taking his hat off, with the utmost politeness, said to him—

"If I mistake not, Mr Biggs, your conversation refers to me."

"Very likely it does," replied the boatswain. "Listeners hear no good of themselves."

"It appears that gentlemen can't converse without being vatched," continued Mr Easthupp, pulling up his shirt collar.

"It is not the first time that you have thought proper to make very offensive remarks, Mr Biggs; and as you appear to consider yourself ill-treated in the affair of the trousers—for I tell you at once that it was I who brought them on board—I can only say," continued our hero, with a very polite bow, "that I shall be most happy to give you satisfaction."

"I am your superior officer, Mr Easy," replied the boatswain.

"Yes, by the rules of the service; but you just now asserted that you would waive your rank—indeed, I dispute it on this occasion; I am on the quarter-deck, and you are not."

"This is the gentleman whom you have insulted, Mr Easy," replied the boatswain, pointing to the purser's steward.

"Yes, Mr Heasy, quite as good a gentleman as yourself although I av ad misfortunes—I ham of as old a family as hany in the country," replied Mr Easthupp, now backed by the boatswain; "many the year did I valk Bond Street, and I ave as good blood in my weins as you, Mr Heasy, halthough I have been misfortunate—I've had hadmirals in my family."

"You have grossly insulted this gentleman," said Mr Biggs, in continuation; "and notwithstanding all your talk of equality, you are afraid to give him satisfaction—you shelter yourself under your quarter-deck."

"Mr Biggs," replied our hero, who was now very wroth, "I shall go on shore directly we arrive at Malta. Let you and this fellow put on plain clothes, and I will meet you both—and then I'll show you whether I am afraid to give satisfaction."

"One at a time," said the boatswain.

"No, sir, not one at a time, but both at the same time—I will fight both, or none. If you are my superior officer, you must *descend*," replied Jack, with an ironical sneer, "to meet me, or I will not descend to meet that fellow, whom I believe to have been little better than a pickpocket."

This accidental hit of Jack's made the purser's steward turn pale as a sheet, and then equally red. He raved and foamed amazingly, although he could not meet Jack's indignant look, who then turned round again.

"Now, Mr Biggs, is this to be understood, or do you shelter yourself under your *forecastle*?"

"I'm no dodger," replied the boatswain, "and we will settle the affair at Malta."

At which reply Jack returned to Mesty.

"Massa Easy, I look at um face, dat fellow Eastop, he no like it. I go shore wid you, see fair play, anyhow—suppose I can?"

Mr Biggs having declared that he would fight, of course had to look out for a second, and he fixed upon Mr Tallboys, the gunner, and requested him to be his friend. Mr Tallboys, who had been latterly very much annoyed by Jack's victories over him in the science of navigation, and therefore felt ill-will towards him, consented; but he was very much puzzled how to arrange that *three* were to fight at the same time, for he had no idea of there being two duels; so he went to his cabin and commenced reading. Jack, on the other hand, dared not say a word to Jolliffe on the subject; indeed there was no one in the ship to whom he could confide but Gascoigne: he therefore went to him, and although Gascoigne thought it was excessively *'infra dig.'** of Jack to meet even the boatswain, as the challenge had been given there was no retracting: he therefore consented, like all midshipmen, anticipating fun, and quite thoughtless of the consequences.

The second day after they had been anchored in Valette Harbour, the boatswain and gunner, Jack and Gascoigne, obtained permission to go on shore. Mr Easthupp, the purser's steward, dressed in his best blue coat, with brass buttons and velvet collar, the very one in which he had been taken up when he had been vowing and protesting that he was a gentleman, at the very time that his hand was abstracting a pocket-book, went up on the quarter-deck, and requested the same indulgence, but Mr Sawbridge refused, as he required him to return staves and hoops at the cooperage. Mesty also, much to his mortification, was not to be spared.

This was awkward, but it was got over by proposing that the meeting should take place behind the cooperage at a certain hour, on which Mr Easthupp might slip out, and borrow a portion of the time appropriated to his duty, to heal the breach in his wounded honour. So the parties all went on shore, and put up at one of the small inns to make the necessary arrangements.

Mr Tallboys then addressed Mr Gascoigne, taking him apart while the boatswain amused himself with a glass of grog, and our hero sat outside teasing a monkey.

"Mr Gascoigne," said the gunner, "I have been very much puzzled how this duel should be fought, but I have at last found it out. You see that there are *three* parties to fight; had there been two or four there would have been no difficulty, as the right line or square might guide us in that instance; but we must arrange it upon the *triangle* in this."

Gascoigne stared; he could not imagine what was coming.

"Are you aware, Mr Gascoigne, of the properties of an equilateral triangle?"

"Yes," replied the midshipman, "that it has three equal sides—but what the devil has that to do with the duel?"

"Everything, Mr Gascoigne," replied the gunner; "it has resolved the great difficulty: indeed, the duel between three can only be fought upon that principle. You observe," said the gunner, taking a piece of chalk out of his pocket, and making a triangle on the table, "in this figure we have three points, each equidistant from each other: and we

---

* *"Infra dig.":* Short for *infra dignitatem,* meaning beneath one's dignity.

have three combatants—so that, placing one at each point, it is all fair play for the three: Mr Easy, for instance, stands here, the boatswain here, and the purser's steward at the third corner. Now, if the distance is fairly measured, it will be all right."

"But then," replied Gascoigne, delighted at the idea, "how are they to fire?"

"It certainly is not of much consequence," replied the gunner, "but still, as sailors, it appears to me that they should fire with the sun; that is, Mr Easy fires at Mr Biggs, Mr Biggs fires at Mr Easthupp, and Mr Easthupp fires at Mr Easy; so that you perceive that each party has his shot at one, and at the same time receives the fire of another."

Gascoigne was in ecstacies at the novelty of the proceeding, the more so as he perceived that Easy obtained every advantage by the arrangement.

"Upon my word, Mr Tallboys, I give you great credit; you have a profound mathematical head, and I am delighted with your arrangement. Of course, in these affairs, the principals are bound to comply with the arrangements of the seconds, and I shall insist upon Mr Easy consenting to your excellent and scientific proposal."

Gascoigne went out, and pulling Jack away from the monkey, told him what the gunner had proposed, at which Jack laughed heartily.

The gunner also explained it to the boatswain, who did not very well comprehend, but replied—

"I dare say it's all right—shot for shot, and d——n all favours."

The parties then repaired to the spot with two pairs of ship's pistols, which Mr Tallboys had smuggled on shore; and, as soon as they were on the ground, the gunner called Mr Easthupp out of the cooperage. In the meantime, Gascoigne had been measuring an equilateral triangle of twelve paces—and marked it out. Mr Tallboys, on his return with the purser's steward, went over the ground, and finding that it was "equal angles subtended by equal sides," declared that it was all right. Easy took his station, the boatswain was put into his, and Mr Easthupp, who was quite in a mystery, was led by the gunner to the third position.

"But, Mr Tallboys," said the purser's steward, "I don't understand this. Mr Easy will first fight Mr Biggs, will he not?"

"No," replied the gunner, "this is a duel of three. You will fire at Mr Easy, Mr Easy will fire at Mr Biggs, and Mr Biggs will fire at you. It is all arranged, Mr Easthupp."

"But," said Mr Easthupp, "I do not understand it. Why is Mr Biggs to fire at me? I have no quarrel with Mr Biggs."

"Because Mr Easy fires at Mr Biggs, and Mr Biggs must have his shot as well."

"If you have ever been in the company of gentlemen, Mr Easthupp," observed Gascoigne, "you must know something about duelling."

"Yes, yes, I've kept the best company, Mr Gascoigne, and I can give a gentleman satisfaction; but—"

"Then, sir, if that is the case, you must know that your honour is in the hands of your second, and that no gentleman appeals."

"Yes, yes, I know that, Mr Gascoigne; but still I've no quarrel with Mr Biggs, and therefore, Mr Biggs, of course you will not aim at me."

"Why you don't think that I am going to be fired at for nothing," replied the boatswain; "no, no, I'll have my shot anyhow."

"But at your friend, Mr Biggs?"

"All the same, I shall fire at somebody; shot for shot, and hit the luckiest."

"Vel, gentlemen, I purtest against these proceedings," replied Mr Easthupp; "I came here to have satisfaction from Mr Easy, and not to be fired at by Mr Biggs."

"Don't you have satisfaction when you fire at Mr Easy?" replied the gunner; "what more would you have?"

"I purtest against Mr Biggs firing at me."

"So you would have a shot without receiving one," cried Gascoigne: "the fact is that this fellow's a confounded coward, and ought to be kicked into the cooperage again."

At this affront Mr Easthupp rallied, and accepted the pistol offered by the gunner.

"You ear those words, Mr Biggs; pretty language to use to a gentleman. You shall ear from me, sir, as soon as the ship is paid off. I purtest no longer, Mr Tallboys; death before dishonour. I'm a gentleman, damme!"

At all events, the swell was not a very courageous gentleman, for he trembled most exceedingly as he pointed his pistol.

The gunner gave the word, as if he were exercising the great guns on board ship.

"Cock your locks!"—"Take good aim at the object!" "Fire!"—"Stop your vents!"

The only one of the combatants who appeared to comply with the latter supplementary order was Mr Easthupp, who clapped his hand to his trousers behind, gave a loud yell, and then dropped down; the bullet having passed clean through his seat of honour, from his having presented his broadside as a target to the boatswain as he faced towards our hero. Jack's shot had also taken effect, having passed through both the boatswain's cheeks, without further mischief than extracting two of his best upper double teeth, and forcing through the hole of the further cheek the boatswain's own quid of tobacco. As for Mr Easthupp's ball, as he was very unsettled, and shut his eyes before he fired, it had gone the Lord knows where.

The purser's steward lay on the ground and screamed—the boatswain spit his double teeth and two or three mouthfuls of blood out, and then threw down his pistols in a rage.

"A pretty business, by God," sputtered he; "he's put my pipe out. How the devil am I to pipe to dinner when I'm ordered, all my wind 'scaping through the cheeks?"

In the meantime, the others had gone to the assistance of the purser's steward, who continued his vociferations. They examined him, and considered a wound in that part not to be dangerous.

"Hold your confounded bawling," cried the gunner, "or you'll have the guard down here: you're not hurt."

"Han't hi?" roared the steward: "Oh, let me die, let me die; don't move me!"

"Nonsense," cried the gunner, "you must get up and walk down to the boat; if you don't we'll leave you—hold your tongue, confound you. You won't? then I'll give you something to halloo for."

Whereupon Mr Tallboys commenced cuffing the poor wretch right and left, who received so many swinging boxes of the ear that he was soon reduced to merely pitiful plaints of "Oh dear!—such inhumanity—I purtest—oh dear! must I get up? I can't, indeed."

"I do not think he can move, Mr Tallboys," said Gascoigne; "I should think the best plan would be to call up two of the men from the cooperage, and let them take him at once to the hospital."

The gunner went down to the cooperage to call the men. Mr Biggs, who had bound up his face as if he had a toothache, for the bleeding had been very slight, came up to the purser's steward.

"What the hell are you making such a howling about? Look at me, with two shot-holes through my figure head, while you have only got one in your stern: I wish I could change with you, by heavens, for I could use my whistle then—now if I attempt to pipe, there will be such a wasteful expenditure of his Majesty's stores of wind, that I never shall get out a note. A wicked shot of yours, Mr Easy."

"I really am very sorry," replied Jack, with a polite bow, "and I beg to offer my best apology."

During this conversation, the purser's steward felt very faint, and thought he was going to die.

"Oh dear! oh dear! what a fool I was; I never was a gentleman— only a swell: I shall die; I never will pick a pocket again—never— never—God forgive me!"

"Why, confound the fellow," cried Gascoigne, "so you were a pickpocket, were you?"

"I never will again," replied the fellow in a faint voice. "Hi'll hamend and lead a good life—a drop of water—oh! lagged* at last!"

Then the poor wretch fainted away: and Mr Tallboys coming up with the men, he was taken on their shoulders and walked off to the hospital, attended by the gunner and also the boatswain, who thought he might as well have a little medical advice before he went on board.

"Well, Easy," said Gascoigne, collecting the pistols and tying them up in his handkerchief, "I'll be shot but we're in a pretty scrape; there's no hushing this up. I'll be hanged if I care, it's the best piece of fun I ever met with." And at the remembrance of it Gascoigne laughed till the tears ran down his cheeks. Jack's mirth was not quite so excessive, as he was afraid that the purser's steward was severely hurt, and expressed his fears.

"At all events, you did not hit him," replied Gascoigne: "all you have to answer for is the boatswain's mug,—I think you've stopped his jaw for the future."

"I'm afraid that our leave will be stopped for the future," replied Jack.

"That we may take our oaths of," replied Gascoigne.

"Then look you, Ned," said Easy; "I've lots of dollars—we may as well be hanged for a sheep as a lamb, as the saying is, I vote that we do not go on board."

"Sawbridge will send and fetch us," replied Ned; "but he must find us first."

"That won't take long, for the soldiers will soon have our description and rout us out. We shall be pinned in a couple of days."

"Confound it, and they say that the ship is to be hove down, and

* Lagged: Arrested; sentenced to penal servitude.

that we shall be here six weeks at least, cooped up on board in a broiling sun, and nothing to do but to watch the pilot fish playing round the rudder and munch bad apricots. I won't go on board. Look ye, Jack," said Gascoigne, "have you plenty of money?"

"I have twenty doubloons, besides dollars," replied Jack.

"Well, then, we will pretend to be so much alarmed at the result of this duel that we dare not show ourselves lest we should be hung. I will write a note and send it to Jolliffe, to say that we have hid ourselves until the affair is blown over, and beg him to intercede with the captain and first lieutenant. I will tell him all the particulars, and refer to the gunner for the truth of it; and then I know that, although we should be punished, they will only laugh. But I will pretend that Easthupp is killed, and we are frightened out of our lives. That will be it, and then let's get on board one of the speronares* which come with fruit from Sicily, sail in the night for Palermo, and then we'll have a cruise for a fortnight, and when the money is all gone we'll come back."

"That's a capital idea, Ned, and the sooner we do it the better. I will write to the captain, begging him to get me off from being hung, and telling him where we have fled to, and that letter shall be given after we have sailed."

They were two very nice lads—our hero and Gascoigne.

CHAPTER XVIII

In which our hero sets off on another cruise, in which he is not blown off shore.

GASCOIGNE and our hero were neither of them in uniform, and they hastened to Nix Mangare stairs, where they soon picked up the padrone of a speronare. They went with him into a wine shop, and with the assistance of a little English from a Maltese boy, whose shirt hung out of his trousers, they made a bargain, by which it was agreed that, for the consideration of two doubloons, he would sail that evening and land them at Gergenti† or some other town in Sicily,

---

* Speronares: Large rowing and sailing boats, equipped with a lateen sail.
† Gergenti: The town of Agrigento in southern Sicily.

providing them with something to eat and gregos to sleep upon. Our two midshipmen then went back to the tavern from which they had set off to fight the duel, and ordering a good dinner to be served in a back room, they amused themselves with killing flies, as they talked over the events of the day and waited for their dinner.

As Mr Tallboys did not himself think proper to go on board till the evening, and Mr Biggs also wished it to be dark before he went up the ship's side, the events of the duel did not transpire till the next morning. Even then it was not known from the boatswain or gunner, but by a hospital mate coming on board to inform the surgeon that there was one of their men wounded under their charge, but that he was doing very well.

Mr Biggs had ascended the side with his face bound up.

"Confound that Jack Easy," said he, "I have only been on leave twice since I sailed from Portsmouth. Once I was obliged to come up the side without my trousers, and show my bare stern to the whole ship's company, and now I am coming up, and dare not show my figure head." He reported himself to the officer of the watch, and hastening to his cabin went to bed and lay the whole night awake from pain, thinking what excuse he could possibly make for not coming on deck next morning to his duty.

He was, however, saved this trouble, for Mr Jolliffe brought the letter of Gascoigne up to Mr Sawbridge, and the captain had received that of our hero.

Captain Wilson came on board and found that Mr Sawbridge could communicate all the particulars of which he had not been acquainted by Jack; and after they had read over Gascoigne's letter in the cabin, and interrogated Mr Tallboys, who was sent down under an arrest, they gave free vent to their mirth.

"Upon my soul, there's no end to Mr Easy's adventures," said the captain. "I could laugh at the duel, for after all it is nothing—and he would have been let off with a severe reprimand. But the foolish boys have set off in a speronare to Sicily, and how the devil are we to get them back again?"

"They'll come back, sir," replied Sawbridge, "when all their money's gone."

"Yes, if they do not get into any more scrapes. That young scamp Gascoigne is as bad as Easy, and now they are together there's no saying what may happen. I dine at the governor's to-day; how he will laugh when I tell him of this new way of fighting a duel!"

"Yes, sir, it is just the thing that will tickle old Tom."

"We must find out if they have got off the island, Sawbridge, which may not be the case."

But it was the case. Jack and Gascoigne had eaten a very good dinner, sent for the monkey to amuse them till it was dark, and there had waited till the padrone came to them.

"What shall we do with the pistols, Easy?"

"Take them with us, and load them before we go—we may want them. Who knows but there may be a mutiny on board of the speronare? I wish we had Mesty with us."

They loaded the pistols, took a pair each and put them in their waists, concealed under their clothes, divided the ammunition between them, and soon afterwards the padrone came to tell them all was ready.

Whereupon Messrs Gascoigne and Easy paid their bill and rose to depart, but the padrone informed them that he should like to see the colour of their money before they went on board. Jack, very indignant at the insinuation that he had not sufficient cash, pulled out a handful of doubloons, and tossing two to the padrone, asked him if he was satisfied.

The padrone untied his sash, put in the money, and with many thanks and protestations of service, begged our young gentlemen to accompany him; they did so, and in a few minutes were clear of Nix Mangare stairs, and, passing close to his Majesty's ship *Harpy*, were soon out of the harbour of Valette.

Of all the varieties of vessels which float upon the wave, there is not, perhaps, one that bounds over the water so gracefully or so lightly as a speronare, or any one so picturesque and beautiful to the eye of those who watch its progress.

The night was clear, and the stars shone out brilliantly as the light craft skimmed over the water, and a fragment of a descending and waning moon threw its soft beams upon the snow-white sail. The vessel, which had no deck, was full of baskets, which had contained grapes and various fruits brought from the ancient granary of Rome, still as fertile and as luxuriant as ever. The crew consisted of the padrone, two men and a boy; the three latter, with their gregos, or night great-coats with hoods, sitting forward before the sail, with their eyes fixed on the land as they flew past point after point, thinking perhaps of their wives, or perhaps of their sweethearts, or perhaps not thinking at all.

The padrone remained aft at the helm, offering every politeness to our two young gentlemen, who only wished to be left alone. At last they requested the padrone to give them gregos to lie down upon, as they wished to go to sleep. He called the boy to take the helm, procured them all they required, and then went forward. And our two midshipmen laid down looking at the stars above them for some minutes, without exchanging a word. At last Jack commenced—

"I have been thinking, Gascoigne, that this is very delightful. My heart bounds with the vessel, and it almost appears to me as if the vessel herself was rejoicing in her liberty. Here she is capering over the waves instead of being tied by the nose with a cable and anchor."

"That's a touch of the sentimental, Jack," replied Gascoigne; "but she is no more free than she was when at anchor, for she now is forced to act in obedience to her steersman, and go just where he pleases. You may just as well say that a horse, if taken out of the stable, is free, with the curb, and his rider on his back."

"That's a touch of the rational, Ned, which destroys the illusion. Never mind, we are free, at all events. What machines we are on board of a man-of-war! we walk, talk, eat, drink, sleep, and get up, just like clock-work; we are wound up to go the twenty-four hours, and then wound up again; just like old Smallsole does the chronometers."

"Very true, Jack; but it does not appear to me, that hitherto you have kept very good time; you require a little more regulating," said Gascoigne.

"How can you expect any piece of machinery to go well, so damnably knocked about as a midshipman is?" replied our hero.

"Very true, Jack; but sometimes you don't keep any time, for you don't keep any watch. Mr Asper don't wind you up. You don't go at all."

"No; because he allows me to *go down;* but still I do go, Ned."

"Yes, to your hammock—it's *no go* with old Smallsole, if I want a bit of *caulk.* But, Jack, what do you say—shall we keep watch tonight?"

"Why, to tell you the truth, I have been thinking the same thing— I don't much like the looks of the padrone—he squints."

"That's no proof of anything, Jack, except that his eyes are not straight: but if you do not like the look of him, I can tell you that he very much liked the look of your doubloons—I saw him start, and his eyes twinkled, and I thought at the time it was a pity you had not paid him in dollars."

"It was very foolish in me, but at all events he has not seen all. He saw quite enough, Ned."

"Very true, but you should have let him see the pistols, and not have let him see the doubloons."

"Well, if he wishes to take what he has seen, he shall receive what he has not seen—why, there are only four of them."

"Oh, I have no fear of them, only it may be as well to sleep with one eye open."

"When shall we make the land?"

"To-morrow evening with this wind, and it appears to be steady. Suppose we keep watch and watch, and have our pistols out ready, with the great-coats just turned over them, to keep them out of sight?"

"Agreed—it's about twelve o'clock now—who shall keep the middle watch?"

"I will, Jack, if you like it."

"Well, then, mind you kick me hard, for I sleep devilish sound. Good-night, and keep a sharp look-out."

Jack was fast asleep in less than ten minutes; and Gascoigne, with his pistols lying by him all ready for each hand, sat up at the bottom of the boat.

There certainly is a peculiar providence in favour of midshipmen compared with the rest of mankind; they have more lives than a cat—always in the greatest danger, but always escaping from it.

The padrone of the vessel had been captivated with the doubloons which Jack had so foolishly exposed to his view, and he had, moreover, resolved to obtain them. At the very time that our two lads were conversing aft, the padrone was talking the matter over with his two men forward, and it was agreed that they should murder, rifle, and then throw them overboard.

About two o'clock in the morning, the padrone came aft to see if they were asleep, but found Gascoigne watching. He returned aft again and again, but found the young man still sitting up. Tired of waiting, anxious to possess the money, and not supposing that the lads were armed, he went once more forward and spoke to the men. Gascoigne had watched his motions; he thought it singular that, with three men in the vessel, the helm should be confided to the boy—and at last he saw them draw their knives. He pushed our hero, who woke immediately. Gascoigne put his hand over Jack's mouth, that he might not speak, and then whispered his suspicions. Jack seized his pistols—they both cocked them without noise, and then waited in silence, Jack still lying down, while Gascoigne continued to sit up at the bottom of the boat. At last Gascoigne saw the three men coming aft—he dropped one of his pistols for a second to give Jack a squeeze of the hand, which was returned, and as Gascoigne watched them making their way through the piles of empty baskets he leaned back as if he was slumbering. The padrone, followed by the two men, was at last aft,—they paused a moment before they stepped over the strengthening plank, which ran from side to side of the boat between them and the midshipmen, and as neither of them stirred, they imagined that both were asleep—advanced and raised their knives, when Gascoigne and Jack, almost at the same moment, each discharged their pistols into the breast of the padrone and one of the men, who was with him in advance, who both fell with the send aft of the boat, so as to encumber the midshipmen with the weight of their bodies. The third man started back. Jack, who could not rise, from the padrone lying across his legs, took a steady aim with his second pistol, and the third man fell. The boy at the helm, who, it appeared, either was aware of what was to be done, or seeing the men advance with their knives, had acted upon what he saw, also drew his knife and struck at Gascoigne from behind; the knife fortunately, after slightly wounding Gascoigne on the shoulder, had shut on the boy's hand—Gascoigne sprang up with his other pistol—the boy started back at the sight of it, lost his balance, and fell overboard.

Our two midshipmen took a few seconds to breathe.

"I say, Jack," said Gascoigne at last, "did you ever—"

"No, I never—" replied Jack.

"What's to be done now?"

"Why, as we've got possession, Ned, we had better put a man at the helm—for the speronare is having it all her own way."

"Very true," replied Gascoigne, "and as I can steer better than you, I suppose it must be me."

Gascoigne went to the helm, brought the boat up to the wind, and then they resumed their conversation.

"That rascal of a boy gave me a devil of a lick on the shoulder; I don't know whether he has hurt me—at all events it's my left shoulder, so I can steer just as well. I wonder whether the fellows are dead."

"The padrone is, at all events," replied Jack. "It was as much as I could do to get my legs from under him—but we'll wait till daylight before we see to that—in the meantime, I'll load the pistols again."

"The day is breaking now—it will be light in half an hour or less. What a devil of a spree, Jack!"

"Yes, but how can one help it? We ran away because two men are wounded—and now we are obliged to kill four in self-defence."

"Yes, but that is not the end of it; when we get to Sicily what are we to do? we shall be imprisoned by the authorities—perhaps hung."

"We'll argue that point with them," replied Jack.

"We had better argue the point between ourselves, Jack, and see what will be the best plan to get out of our scrape."

"I think that we just *have* got out of it—never fear but we'll get out of the next. Do you know, Gascoigne, it appears to me very odd, but I can do nothing but there's a bobbery* at the bottom of it."

"You certainly have a great talent that way, Jack. Don't I hear one of those poor fellows groan?"

"I should think that not impossible."

"What shall we do with them?"

"We will argue that point, Ned—we must either keep their bodies, or we must throw them overboard. Either tell the whole story, or say nothing about it."

"That's very evident; in short, we must do something, for your argument goes no further. But now let us take up one of your propositions."

"Well, then, suppose we keep the bodies on board, run into a seaport, go to the authorities, and state all the facts, what then?"

"We shall prove, beyond all doubt, that we have killed three men, if not four; but we shall not prove that we were obliged so to do, Jack. And then we are heretics—we shall be put in prison till they are satisfied of our innocence, which we never can prove, and there we shall remain until we have written to Malta, and a man-of-war comes to redeem us, if we are not stabbed or something else in the meantime."

"That will not be a very pleasant cruise," replied Jack. "Now let's argue the point on the other side."

"There is some difficulty there—suppose we throw their bodies overboard, toss the baskets after them, wash the boat clean, and make for the first port. We may chance to hit upon the very spot from which they sailed, and then there will be a pack of wives and chil-

---

* Bobbery: An argument.

dren, and a populace with knives, asking us what has become of the men of the boat!"

"I don't much like the idea of that," said Jack.

"And if we don't have such bad luck, still we shall be interrogated as to who we are, and how we were adrift by ourselves."

"There will be a difficulty about that again—we must swear that it is a party of pleasure, and that we are gentlemen yachting."

"Without a crew or provisions—yachts don't sail with a clean-swept hold, or gentlemen without a spare shirt—we have nothing but two gallons of water and two pairs of pistols."

"I have it," said Jack—"we are two young gentlemen in our own boat who went out to Gozo with pistols to shoot sea-mews,* were caught in a gale, and blown down to Sicily—that will excite interest."

"That's the best idea yet, as it will account for our having nothing in the boat. Well, then, at all events, we will get rid of the bodies; but suppose they are not dead—we cannot throw them overboard alive,—that will be murder."

"Very true," replied Jack, "then we must shoot them first, and toss them overboard afterwards."

"Upon my soul, Easy, you are an odd fellow: however, go and examine the men, and we'll decide that point by-and-bye: you had better keep your pistol ready cocked, for they may be shamming."

"Devil a bit of sham here, anyhow," replied Jack, pulling at the body of the padrone, "and as for this fellow you shot, you might put your fist into his chest. Now for the third," continued Jack, stepping over the strengthening piece—"he's all among the baskets. I say, my cock, are you dead?" and Jack enforced his question with a kick in the ribs. The man groaned. "That's unlucky, Gascoigne, but however, I'll soon settle him," said Jack, pointing his pistol.

"Stop, Jack," cried Gascoigne, "it really will be murder."

"No such thing, Ned; I'll just blow his brains out, and then I'll come aft and argue the point with you."

"Now do oblige me by coming aft and arguing the point first. Do, Jack, I beg of you—I entreat you."

"With all my heart," replied Jack, resuming his seat by Gascoigne; "I assert, that in this instance killing's no murder. You will observe, Ned, that by the laws of society, any one who attempts the life of another has forfeited his own; at the same time, as it is

* Sea-mews: Seagulls.

necessary that the fact should be clearly proved, and justice be duly administered, the parties are tried, convicted, and then are sentenced to the punishment."

"I grant all that."

"In this instance the attempt has been clearly proved; we are the witnesses, and are the judges and jury, and society in general, for the best of all possible reasons, because there is nobody else. These men's lives, being therefore forfeited to society, belong to us; and it does not follow because they were not all killed in the attempt, that therefore they are not now to be brought out for punishment. And as there is no common hangman here, we, of course, must do this duty as well as every other. I have now clearly proved that I am justified in what I am about to do. But the argument does not stop there—self-preservation is the first law of nature, and if we do not get rid of this man, what is the consequence?—that we shall have to account for his being wounded, and then, instead of judges, we shall immediately be placed in the position of culprits, and have to defend ourselves without witnesses. We therefore risk our lives from a misplaced lenity towards a wretch unworthy to live."

"Your last argument is strong, Easy, but I cannot consent to your doing what may occasion you uneasiness hereafter when you think of it."

"Pooh! nonsense—I am a philospher."

"Of what school, Jack? Oh, I presume you are a disciple of Mesty's. I do not mean to say that you are wrong, but still hear my proposition. Let us lower down the sail, and then I can leave the helm to assist you. We will clear the vessel of everything except the man who is still alive. At all events we may wait a little, and if at last there is no help for it, I will then agree with you to launch him overboard, even if he is not quite dead."

"Agreed; even by your own making out, it will be no great sin. He is half dead already—I only do *half* the work of tossing him over, so it will be only *quarter* murder on my part, and he would have shown no quarter on his." Here Jack left off arguing and punning, and went forward and lowered down the sail. "I've half a mind to take my doubloons back," said Jack, as they launched over the body of the padrone, "but he may have them—I wonder whether they'll ever turn up again."

"Not in our time, Jack," replied Gascoigne.

The other body, and all the basket lumber, &c., were then tossed over, and the boat was cleared of all but the man who was not yet dead.

"Now let's examine the fellow, and see if he has any chance of recovery," said Gascoigne.

The man lay on his side; Gascoigne turned him over and found that he was dead.

"Over with him, quick," said Jack, "before he comes to life again."

The body disappeared under the wave—they again hoisted the sail. Gascoigne took the helm, and our hero proceeded to draw water and wash away the stains of blood; he then cleared the boat of vine-leaves and rubbish, with which it was strewed, swept it clean fore and aft, and resumed his seat by his comrade.

"There," said Jack, "now we've swept the decks, we may pipe to dinner. I wonder whether there is anything to eat in the locker."

Jack opened it, and found some bread, garlic, sausages, a bottle of aquadente, and a jar of wine.

"So the padrone did keep his promise, after all."

"Yes, and had you not tempted him with the sight of so much gold, might now have been alive."

"To which I reply, that if you had not advised our going off in a speronare, he would now have been alive."

"And if you had not fought a duel, I should not have given the advice."

"And if the boatswain had not been obliged to come on board without his trousers at Gibraltar, I should not have fought a duel."

"And if you had not joined the ship, the boatswain would have had his trousers on."

"And if my father had not been a philosopher, I should not have gone to sea; so that it is all my father's fault, and he has killed four men off the coast of Sicily without knowing it—cause and effect. After all, there's nothing like argument; so, having settled that point, let us go to dinner."

Having finished their meal, Jack went forward and observed the land ahead; they steered the same course for three or four hours.

"We must haul our wind more," said Gascoigne; "it will not do to put into any small town; we have now to choose whether we shall land on the coast and sink the speronare, or land at some large town."

"We must argue that point," replied Jack.

"In the meantime, do you take the helm, for my arm is quite

tired," replied Gascoigne: "you can steer well enough: by-the-bye, I may as well look at my shoulder, for it is quite stiff." Gascoigne pulled off his coat, and found his shirt bloody and sticking to the wound, which, as we before observed, was slight. He again took the helm, while Jack washed it clean, and then bathed it with aquadente.

"Now take the helm again," said Gascoigne; "I'm on the sick list."

"And as surgeon—I'm an idler," replied Jack; "but what shall we do?" continued he; "abandon the speronare at night and sink her, or run in for a town?"

"We shall fall in with plenty of boats and vessels if we coast it up to Palermo, and they may overhaul us."

"We shall fall in with plenty of people if we go on shore, and they will overhaul us."

"Do you know, Jack, that I wish we were back and alongside of the *Harpy;* I've had cruising enough."

"My cruises are so unfortunate," replied Jack; "they are too full of adventure; but then I have never yet had a cruise on shore. Now, if we could only get to Palermo, we should be out of all our difficulties."

"The breeze freshens, Jack," replied Gascoigne; "and it begins to look very dirty to windward. I think we shall have a gale."

"Pleasant—I know what it is to be short-handed in a gale; however, there's one comfort, we shall not be blown *off-shore* this time."

"No, but we may be wrecked on a lee shore. She cannot carry her whole sail, Easy; we must lower it down, and take in a reef; the sooner the better, for it will be dark in an hour. Go forward and lower it down, and then I'll help you."

Jack did so, but the sail went into the water, and he could not drag it in.

"Avast heaving," said Gascoigne, "till I throw her up and take the wind out of it."

This was done: they reefed the sail, but could not hoist it up: if Gascoigne left the helm to help Jack, the sail filled; if he went to the helm and took the wind out of the sail, Jack was not strong enough to hoist it. The wind increased rapidly, and the sea got up; the sun went down, and with the sail half hoisted, they could not keep to the wind, but were obliged to run right for the land. The speronare flew, rising on the crest of the waves with half her keel clear of the water: the moon was already up, and gave them light enough to perceive that they were not five miles from the coast, which was lined with foam.

"At all events they can't accuse us of running away with the boat," observed Jack; "for she's running away with us."

"Yes," replied Gascoigne, dragging at the tiller with all his strength; "she has taken the bit between her teeth."

"I wouldn't care if I had a bit between mine," replied Jack; "for I feel devilish hungry again. What do you say, Ned?"

"With all my heart," replied Gascoigne; "but, do you know, Easy, it may be the last meal we ever make."

"Then I vote it's a good one—but why so, Ned?"

"In half an hour, or thereabouts, we shall be on shore."

"Well, that's where we want to go."

"Yes, but the sea runs high, and the boat may be dashed to pieces on the rocks."

"Then we shall be asked no questions about her or the men."

"Very true, but a lee shore is no joke; we may be knocked to pieces as well as the boat—even swimming may not help us. If we could find a cove or sandy beach, we might perhaps manage to get on shore."

"Well," replied Jack, "I have not been long at sea, and, of course, cannot know much about these things. I have been blown off shore, but I never have been blown on. It may be as you say, but I do not see the great danger—let's run her right up on the beach at once."

"That's what I shall try to do," replied Gascoigne, who had been four years at sea, and knew very well what he was about.

Jack handed him a huge piece of bread and sausage.

"Thank ye, I cannot eat."

"I can," replied Jack, with his mouth full.

Jack ate while Gascoigne steered; and the rapidity with which the speronare rushed to the beach was almost frightful. She darted like an arrow from wave to wave, and appeared as if mocking their attempts as they curled their summits almost over her narrow stern. They were within a mile of the beach, when Jack, who had finished his supper, and was looking at the foam boiling on the coast, exclaimed—

"That's very fine—very beautiful, upon my soul!"

"He cares for nothing," thought Gascoigne; "he appears to have no idea of danger."

"Now, my dear fellow," said Gascoigne, "in a few minutes we shall be on the rocks. I must continue at the helm, for the higher she

is forced up the better chance for us; but we may not meet again, so
if we do not, good-bye and God bless you."

"Gascoigne," said Jack, "you are hurt, and I am not; your shoulder is stiff, and you can hardly move your left arm. Now I can steer
for the rocks as well as you. Do you go to the bow, and there you will
have a better chance—By-the-bye," continued he, picking up his pistols, and sticking them into his waist, "I won't leave them, they've
served us too good a turn already. Gascoigne, give me the helm."

"No, no, Easy."

"I say yes," replied Jack, in a loud, authoritative tone, "and what's
more, I will be obeyed, Gascoigne. I have nerve, if I haven't knowledge, and at all events I can steer for the beach. I tell you, give me the
helm. Well, then, if you won't, I must take it."

Easy wrested the tiller from Gascoigne's hand, and gave him a
shove forward.

"Now do you look out ahead, and tell me how to steer."

Whatever may have been Gascoigne's feelings at this behaviour
of our hero's, it immediately occurred to him that he could not do
better than to run the speronare to the safest point, and that therefore
he was probably more advantageously employed than if he were at
the helm. He went forward and looked at the rocks, covered at one
moment with the tumultuous waters, and then pouring down cas-
cades from their sides as the waves recoiled. He perceived a chasm
right ahead, and he thought if the boat was steered for that, she must
be thrown up so as to enable them to get clear of her, for, at every
other part, escape appeared impossible.

"Starboard a little—that'll do. Steady—port it is—port.—Steer
small, for your life, Easy. Steady now—mind the yard don't hit your
head—hold on."

The speronare was at this moment thrown into a large cleft in a
rock, the sides of which were nearly perpendicular; nothing else
could have saved them, as, had they struck the rock outside, the boat
would have been dashed to pieces, and its fragments have disappeared in the undertow. As it was, the cleft was not four feet more
than the width of the boat, and as the waves hurled her up into it, the
yard of the speronare was thrown fore and aft with great violence,
and had not Jack been warned, he would have been struck overboard
without a chance of being saved; but he crouched down and it passed
over him. As the water receded, the boat struck, and was nearly dry
between the rocks, but another wave followed, dashing the boat fur-

ther up, but, at the same time, filling it with water. The bow of the boat was now several feet higher than the stern, where Jack held on; and the weight of the water in her, with the force of the returning waves, separated her right across abaft the mast. Jack perceived that the after part of the boat was going out again with the wave; he caught hold of the yard which had swung fore and aft, and as he clung to it, the part of the boat on which he had stood disappeared from under him, and was swept away by the returning current.

Jack required the utmost of his strength to maintain his position until another wave floated him, and dashed him higher up: but he knew his life depended on holding on to the yard, which he did, although under water, and advanced several feet. When the wave receded, he found footing on the rock, and still clinging, he walked till he had gained the fore part of the boat, which was wedged firmly into a narrow part of the cleft. The next wave was not very large, and he had gained so much that it did not throw him off his legs. He reached the rock, and as he climbed up the side of the chasm to gain the ledge above, he perceived Gascoigne standing above him, and holding out his hand to his assistance.

"Well," says Jack, shaking himself to get rid of the water, "here we are ashore, at last—I had no idea of anything like this. The rush back of the water was so strong that it has almost torn my arms out of their sockets. How very lucky I sent you forward with your disabled shoulder! By-the-bye, now that it's all over, and you must see that I was right, I beg to apologise for my rudeness."

"There needs no apology for saving my life, Easy," replied Gascoigne, trembling with the cold; "and no one but you would ever have thought of making one at such a moment."

"I wonder whether the ammunition's dry," said Jack; "I put it all in my hat."

Jack took off his hat, and found the cartridges had not suffered.

"Now, then, Gascoigne, what shall we do?"

"I hardly know," replied Gascoigne.

"Suppose then, we sit down and argue the point."

"No, I thank you, there will be too much cold water thrown upon our arguments—I'm half dead; let us walk on."

"With all my heart," said Jack, "it's devilish steep, but I can argue up hill or down hill, wet or dry—I'm used to it—for, as I told you before, Ned, my father is a philosopher, and so am I."

"By the Lord! *you are*," replied Gascoigne, as he walked on.

CHAPTER XIX

In which our hero follows his destiny and forms a tableau.

O UR HERO and his comrade climbed the precipice, and, after
some minutes' severe toil, arrived at the summit, when they sat
down to recover themselves. The sky was clear, although the gale
blew strong. They had an extensive view of the coast, lashed by the
angry waves.

"It's my opinion, Ned," said Jack, as he surveyed the expanse of
troubled water, "that we're just as well out of that."

"I agree with you, Jack; but it's also my opinion that we should be
just as well out of this, for the wind blows through one. Suppose we
go a little further inland, where we may find some shelter till the
morning."

"It's rather dark to find anything," rejoined our hero; "but however, a westerly gale on the top of a mountain with wet clothes
in the middle of the night, with nothing to eat or drink, is not the
most comfortable position in the world, and we may change for
the better."

They proceeded over a flat of a hundred yards, and then descended—the change in the atmosphere was immediate. As they continued their march inland, they came to a high road, which appeared
to run along the shore, and they turned into it; for, as Jack said very
truly, a road must lead to something. After a quarter of an hour's
walk, they again heard the rolling of the surf, and perceived the
white walls of houses.

"Here we are at last," said Jack. "I wonder if any one will turn out
to take us in, or shall we stow away for the night in one of those vessels hauled up on the beach?"

"Recollect this time, Easy," said Gascoigne, "not to show your
money; that is, show only a dollar, and say you have no more; or
promise to pay when we arrive at Palermo; and if they will neither
trust us, nor give to us, we must make it out as we can."

"How the cursed dogs bark! I think we shall do very well this
time, Gascoigne; we do not look as if we were worth robbing, at all
events, and we have the pistols to defend ourselves with if we are
attacked. Depend upon it I will show no more gold. And now let us

make our arrangements. Take you one pistol and take half the gold—I have it all in my right-hand pocket—my dollars and pistarenes in my left. You shall take half of them too. We have silver enough to go on with till we are in a safe place."

Jack then divided the money in the dark, and also gave Gascoigne a pistol.

"Now, then, shall we knock for admittance?—Let's first walk through the village, and see if there's anything like an inn. Those yelping curs will soon be at our heels; they come nearer and nearer every time. There's a cart, and it's full of straw—suppose we go to bed till to-morrow morning—we shall be warm, at all events."

"Yes," replied Gascoigne, "and sleep much better than in any of the cottages. I have been in Sicily before, and you have no idea how the fleas bite."

Our two midshipmen climbed up into the cart, nestled themselves into the straw, or rather Indian corn leaves, and were soon fast asleep. As they had not slept for two nights, it is not to be wondered at that they slept soundly—so soundly, indeed, that about two hours after they had got into their comfortable bed, the peasant, who had brought to the village some casks of wine to be shipped and taken down the coast in a felucca, yoked his bullocks, and not being aware of his freight, drove off, without in any way disturbing their repose, although the roads in Sicily are not yet macadamised.

The jolting of the roads rather increased than disturbed the sleep of our adventurers; and, although there were some rude shocks, it only had the effect of making them fancy in their dreams that they were again in the boat, and that she was still dashing against the rocks. In about two hours, the cart arrived at its destination—the peasant unyoked his bullocks and led them away. The same cause will often produce contrary effects: the stopping of the motion of the cart disturbed the rest of our two midshipmen; they turned round in the straw, yawned, spread out their arms, and then awoke. Gascoigne, who felt considerable pain in his shoulder, was the first to recall his scattered senses.

"Easy," cried he, as he sat up and shook off the corn leaves.

"Port it is," said Jack, half dreaming.

"Come, Easy, you are not on board now. Rouse and bit."

Jack then sat up and looked at Gascoigne. The forage in the cart was so high round them that they could not see above it; they rubbed their eyes, yawned, and looked at each other.

"Have you any faith in dreams?" said Jack to Gascoigne, "because I had a very queer one last night."

"Well, so had I," replied Gascoigne. "I dreamt that the cart rolled by itself into the sea, and went away with us right in the wind's eye back to Malta; and considering that it never was built for such service, she behaved uncommonly well. Now, what was your dream?"

"Mine was, that we woke up and found ourselves in the very town from which the speronare had sailed, and that they had found the fore part of the speronare among the rocks, had recognised her, and picked up one of our pistols. That they had laid hold of us, and had insisted that we had been thrown on shore in the boat, and asked us what had become of the crew—they were just seizing us, when I awoke."

"Your dream is more likely to come true than mine, Easy; but still I think we need not fear that. At the same time, we had better not remain here any longer; and it occurs to me, that if we tore our clothes more, it would be advisable—we shall, in the first place, look more wretched; and, in the next place, can replace them with the dress of the country, and so travel without exciting suspicion. You know that I can speak Italian pretty well."

"I have no objection to tear my clothes if you wish," replied Jack; "at the same time give me your pistol; I will draw the charges and load them again. They must be wet."

Having reloaded the pistols and rent their garments, the two midshipmen stood up in the cart and looked about them.

"Halloo!—why how's this, Gascoigne? last night we were close to the beach, and among houses, and now—where the devil are we? You dreamt nearer the mark than I did, for the cart has certainly taken a cruise."

"We must have slept like midshipmen, then," replied Gascoigne: "surely it cannot have gone far."

"Here we are, surrounded by hills on every side, for at least a couple of miles. Surely some good genius has transported us into the interior, that we might escape from the relatives of the crew whom I dreamt about," said Jack, looking at Gascoigne.

As it afterwards was known to them, the speronare had sailed from the very seaport in which they had arrived that night, and where they had got into the cart. The wreck of the speronare had been found, and had been recognised, and it was considered by the inhabitants that the padrone and his crew had perished in the gale.

Had they found our two midshipmen and questioned them, it is not improbable that suspicion might have been excited, and the results have been such as our hero had conjured up in his dream. But, as we said before, there is a peculiar providence for midshipmen.

On a minute survey, they found that they were in an open space which, apparently, had been used for thrashing and winnowing maize, and that the cart was standing under a clump of trees in the shade.

"There ought to be a house hereabouts," said Gascoigne, "I should think that behind the trees we shall find one. Come, Jack, you are as hungry as I am, I'll answer for it: we must look out for a breakfast somewhere."

"If they won't give us something to eat, or sell it," replied Jack, who was ravenous, clutching his pistol, "I shall take it—I consider it no robbery. The fruits of the earth were made for us all, and it never was intended that one man should have a superfluity and another starve. The laws of equality—"

"May appear very good arguments to a starving man, I grant, but still won't prevent his fellow-creatures from hanging him," replied Gascoigne. "None of your confounded nonsense, Jack; no man starves with money in his pocket, and as long as you have that, leave those that have none to talk about equality and the rights of man."

"I should like to argue that point with you, Gascoigne."

"Tell me, do you prefer sitting down here to argue, or to look out for some breakfast, Jack?"

"Oh, the argument may be put off, but hunger cannot."

"That's very good philosophy, Jack, so let's go on."

They went through the copse of wood, which was very thick, and soon discovered the wall of a large house on the other side.

"All right," said Jack; "but still let us reconnoitre. It's not a farmhouse; it must belong to a person of some consequence—all the better—they will see that we are gentlemen, notwithstanding our tattered dress. I suppose we are to stick to the story of the sea-mews at Gozo?"

"Yes," replied Gascoigne; "I can think of nothing better. But the English are well received in this island; we have troops at Palermo."

"Have we? I wish I was sitting down at the mess-table—but what's that? a woman screaming? Yes, by heavens!—come along, Ned." And away dashed Jack towards the house followed by Gascoigne. As they advanced the screams redoubled; they entered the porch, burst into the room from whence they proceeded, and found an elderly gentleman defending himself against two young men, who were held back by an elderly and a young lady. Our hero and his comrade had both drawn their pistols, and just as they burst open the door, the old gentleman who defended himself against such odds had fallen down. The two others burst from the women, and were about to pierce him with their swords, when Jack seized one by the collar of his coat and held him fast, pointing the muzzle of the pistol to his ear: Gascoigne did the same to the other. It was a very dramatic tableau. The two women flew to the elderly gentleman and raised him up; the two assailants being held just as dogs hold pigs by the ear, trembling with fright, with the points of their rapiers dropped, looked at the midshipmen and the muzzles of their pistols with equal dismay; at the same time, the astonishment of the elderly gentleman and the women, at such an unexpected deliverance, was equally great. There was a silence for a few seconds.

"Ned," at last said Jack, "tell these chaps to drop their swords, or we fire."

Gascoigne gave the order in Italian, and it was complied with. The midshipmen then possessed themselves of the rapiers, and gave the young men their liberty.

The elderly gentleman at last broke the silence.

"It would appear, signors, that there was a special interference of Providence, to prevent you from committing a foul and unjust murder. Who these are who have so opportunely come to my rescue, I know not, but thanking them as I do now, I think that you will your-selves, when you are calm, also thank them for having prevented you from committing an act which would have loaded you with remorse, and embittered your future existence. Gentleman, you are free to depart: you, Don Silvio, have indeed disappointed me; your grati-tude should have rendered you incapable of such conduct: as for you, Don Scipio, you have been misled; but you both have, in one point, disgraced yourselves. Ten days back my sons were both here,—why did you not come then? If you sought revenge on me, you could not have inflicted it deeper than through my children, and at least you would not have acted the part of assassins in attacking an old man. Take your swords, gentlemen, and use them better henceforth. Against future attacks I shall be well prepared."

Gascoigne, who perfectly understood what was said, presented the sword to the young gentleman from whom he had taken it—our hero did the same. The two young men returned them to their sheaths, and quitted the room without saying a word.

"Whoever you are, I owe to you and thank you for my life," said the elderly gentleman, scanning the outward appearance of our two midshipmen.

"We are," replied Gascoigne, "officers in the English navy, and gentlemen; we were wrecked in our boat last night, and have wandered here in the dark, seeking for assistance, and food, and some conveyance to Palermo, where we shall find friends, and the means of appearing like gentlemen."

"Was your ship wrecked, gentlemen?" inquired the Sicilian, "and many lives lost?"

"No, our ship is at Malta; we were in a boat on a party of pleasure, were caught by a gale, and driven on the coast. To satisfy you of the truth, observe that our pistols have the king's mark, and that we are not paupers we show you gold."

Gascoigne pulled out his doubloons—and Jack did the same, coolly observing,—

"I thought we were only to show silver, Ned!"

"It needed not that," replied the gentleman; "your conduct in this affair, your manners and address, fully convince me that you are what you represent; but were you common peasants, I am equally indebted to you for my life, and you may command me. Tell me in what way I can be of service."

"In giving us something to eat, for we have had nothing for many, many hours. After that we may, perhaps, trespass a little more upon your kind offices."

"You must, of course, be surprised at what has passed, and curious to know the occasion," said the gentleman; "you have a right to be informed of it, and shall be, as soon as you are more comfortable; in the meantime, allow me to introduce myself as Don Rebiera de Silva."

"I wish," said Jack, who, from his knowledge of Spanish, could understand the whole of the last part of the Don's speech, "that he would introduce us to his breakfast."

"So do I," said Gascoigne; "but we must wait a little—he ordered the ladies to prepare something instantly."

"Your friend does not speak Italian," said Don Rebiera.

"No, Don Rebiera, he speaks French and Spanish."

"If he speaks Spanish, my daughter can converse with him; she has but shortly arrived from Spain. We are closely united with a noble house in that country."

Don Rebiera then led the way to another room, and in a short time there was a repast brought in, to which our midshipmen did great justice.

"I will now," said the Don, "relate to you, sir, for the information of yourself and friend, the causes which produced this scene of violence, which you so opportunely defeated. But first, as it must be very tedious to your friend, I will send for Donna Clara and my daughter Agnes to talk to him; my wife understands a little Spanish, and my daughter, as I said before, has but just left the country, where, from circumstances, she remained some years."

As soon as Donna Clara and Donna Agnes made their appearance and were introduced, Jack, who had not before paid attention to them, said to himself, "I have seen a face like that girl's before." If so, he had never seen many like it, for it was the quintessence of brunette beauty, and her figure was equally perfect; although, not having yet completed her fifteenth year, it required still a little more development.

Donna Clara was extremely gracious, and as, perhaps, she was aware that her voice would drown that of her husband, she proposed to our hero to walk in the garden, and in a few minutes they took their seats in a pavilion at the end of it. The old lady did not talk much Spanish, but when at a loss for a word, she put in an Italian one, and Jack understood her perfectly well. She told him her sister had married a Spanish nobleman many years since, and that before the war broke out between the Spanish and the English they had gone over with all their children to see her; that when they wished to return, her daughter Agnes, then a child, was suffering under a lingering complaint, and it was thought advisable, as she was very weak, to leave her under the charge of her aunt, who had a little girl of nearly the same age; that they were educated together at a convent, near Tarragona, and that she had only returned two months ago; that she had a very narrow escape, as the ship in which her uncle, and aunt, and cousins, as well as herself, were on board, returning from Genoa, where her brother-in-law had been obliged to go to secure a succession to some property bequeathed to him, had been captured in the night by the English; but the officer, who was very polite, had allowed them to go away next day, and very handsomely permitted them to take all their effects.

"Oh, oh," thought Jack; "I thought I had seen her face before; this then was one of the girls in the corner of the cabin—now I'll have some fun."

During the conversation with the mother, Donna Agnes had remained some paces behind, picking now and then a flower, and not attending to what passed.

When our hero and her mother sat down in the pavilion she joined then, when Jack addressed her with his usual politeness.

"I am almost ashamed to be sitting by you, Donna Agnes, in this ragged dress—but the rocks of your coast have no respect for persons."

"We are under great obligations, signor, and do not regard such trifles."

"You are all kindness, signora," replied Jack; "I little thought this morning of my good fortune,—I can tell the fortunes of others, but not my own."

"You can tell fortunes!" replied the old lady.

"Yes, madame, I am famous for it—shall I tell your daughter hers?"

Donna Agnes looked at our hero, and smiled.

"I perceive that the young lady does not believe me; I must prove my art, by telling her of what has already happened to her. The signora will then give me credit."

"Certainly, if you do that," replied Agnes.

"Oblige me, by showing me the palm of your hand."

Agnes extended her little hand, and Jack felt so very polite, that he was nearly kissing it. However, he restrained himself, and examining the lines—

"That you were educated in Spain—that you arrived here but two months ago—that you were captured and released by the English, your mother has already told me; but to prove to you that I knew all that, I must now be more particular. You were in a ship mounting fourteen guns—was it not so?"

Donna Agnes nodded her head.

"I never told the signor that," cried Donna Clara.

"She was taken by surprise in the night, and there was no fighting. The next morning the English burst open the cabin-door; your uncle and your cousin fired their pistols."

"Holy Virgin!" cried Agnes, with surprise.

"The English officer was a young man, not very good-looking."

"There you are wrong, signor—he was very handsome."

"There is no accounting for taste, signora. You were frightened out of your wits, and with your cousin you crouched down in the corner of the cabin. Let me examine that little line closer. You had— yes, it's no mistake—you had very little clothes on."

Agnes tore away her hand and covered her face.

"È vero, è vero;* Holy Jesus! how could you know that?"

Of a sudden Agnes looked at our hero, and after a minute appeared to recognise him.

"Oh, mother, 'tis he—I recollect now, 'tis he!"

"Who, my child?" replied Donna Clara, who had been struck dumb with Jack's astonishing power of fortune-telling.

"The officer who captured us and was so kind."

Jack burst out into a laughter not to be controlled for some minutes, and then acknowledged that she had discovered him.

"At all events, Donna Agnes," said he at last, "acknowledge that, ragged as I am, I have seen you in a much greater dishabille."

Agnes sprang up, and took to her heels, that she might hide her confusion, and at the same time go to her father and tell him who he had as his guest.

Although Don Rebiera had not yet finished his narrative, this announcement of Agnes, who ran in breathless to communicate it, immediately brought all the parties together, and Jack received their thanks.

"I little thought," said the Don, "that I should have been so doubly indebted to you, sir. Command my services as you please, both of you. My sons are at Palermo, and I trust you will allow them the pleasure of your friendship when you are tired of remaining with us."

Jack made his politest bow, and then with a shrug of his shoulders looked down upon his habiliments, which, to please Gascoigne, he had torn into ribands, as much as to say, "We are not provided for a lengthened stay."

"My brothers' clothes will fit them, I think," said Agnes to her father; "they have left plenty in their wardrobes."

"If the signors will condescend to wear them till they can replace their own."

Midshipmen are very condescending. They followed Don Rebiera, and condescended to put on clean shirts belonging to Don Philip and Don Martin. Also to put on their trousers, to select their

---

* È vero: It is true.

best waistcoats and coats; in short, they condescended to have a regular fit-out—and it so happened that the fit-out was not far from a regular *fit*.

Having condescended, they then descended, and the intimacy between all parties became so great that it appeared as if they not only wore the young men's clothes but also stood in their shoes. Having thus made themselves presentable, Jack presented his hand to both ladies and led them into the garden, that Don Rebiera might finish his long story to Gascoigne without further interruption, and resuming their seats in the pavilion, he entertained the ladies with a history of his cruise in the ship after her capture. Agnes soon recovered from her reserve, and Jack had the forbearance not to allude again to the scene in the cabin, which was the only thing she dreaded. After dinner, when the family, according to custom, had retired for the siesta, Gascoigne and Jack, who had slept enough in the cart to last for a week, went out together in the garden.

"Well, Ned," said Jack, "do you wish yourself on board the *Harpy* again?"

"No," replied Gascoigne, "we have fallen on our feet at last, but still not without first being knocked about like peas in a rattle. What a lovely little creature that Agnes is! How strange that you should fall in with her again! How odd that we should come here!"

"My good fellow, we did not come here. Destiny brought us in a cart. She may take us to Tyburn in the same way."

"Yes, if you sport your philosophy as you did when we awoke this morning."

"Nevertheless, I'll be hanged if I'm not right. Suppose we argue the point?"

"Right or wrong, you will be hanged, Jack; so instead of arguing the point, suppose I tell you what the Don made such a long story about."

"With all my heart—let us go to the pavilion."

Our hero and his friend took their seats, and Gascoigne then communicated the history of Don Rebiera, to which we shall dedicate the ensuing chapter.

CHAPTER XX

A long story, which the reader must listen to, as well as our hero.

I HAVE already made you acquainted with my name, and I have only to add that it is one of the most noble in Sicily, and that there are few families who possess such large estates. My father was a man who had no pleasure in the pursuits of most of the young men of his age; he was of a weakly constitution, and was with difficulty reared to manhood. When his studies were completed he retired to his country seat belonging to our family, which is about twenty miles from Palermo, and shutting himself up, devoted himself wholly to literary pursuits.

"As he was an only son, his parents were naturally very anxious that he should marry; the more so as his health did not promise him a very extended existence. Had he consulted his own inclinations he would have declined, but he felt that it was his duty to comply with their wishes; but he did not trouble himself with the choice, leaving it wholly to them. They selected a young lady of high family and certainly of most exquisite beauty. I only wish I could say more in her favour—for she was my mother—but it is impossible to narrate the history without exposing her conduct. The marriage took place, and my father—having woke up, as it were, at the celebration—again returned to his closet, to occupy himself in abstruse studies—the results of which have been published, and have fully established his reputation as a man of superior talent and deep research. But, however much the public may appreciate the works of a man of genius, whether they be written to instruct or to amuse, certain it is that a literary man requires in his wife either a mind congenial to his own, or that pride in her husband's talents which induces her to sacrifice much of her own domestic enjoyment to the satisfaction of having his name extolled abroad. I mention this point as some extenuation of my mother's conduct. She was neglected most certainly, but not neglected for frivolous amusements, or because another form had captivated his fancy; but in his desire to instruct others, and I may add his ambition for renown, he applied himself to his literary pursuits, became abstracted, answered without hearing, and left his wife to amuse herself in any way she might please. A literary husband is, without exception—although always at home—the least domestic husband in the world, and must try the best of tempers—not by unkindness, for my father was kind and indulgent to excess, but by that state of perfect abstraction and indifference which he showed to everything except the favourite pursuit which absorbed him. My mother had but to speak, and every wish was granted—a refusal was unknown. You may say, what could she want more? I reply, that anything to a woman is preferable to indifference. The immediate consent to every wish took away, in her opinion, all merit in the grant—the value of everything is only relative, and in proportion to the difficulty of obtaining it. The immediate assent to every opinion was tantamount to insult—it implied that he did not choose to argue with her.

"It is true that women like to have their own way—but they like at the same time to have difficulties to surmount and to conquer; otherwise half the gratification is lost. Although tempests are to be deplored, still a certain degree of oscillation and motion are requisite to keep fresh and clear the lake of matrimony, the waters of which otherwise soon stagnate and become foul, and without some contrary currents of opinion between a married couple such a stagnation must take place.

"A woman permitted always and invariably to have her own way without control is much in the same situation as the child who insists upon a whole instead of half a holiday, and before the evening closes is tired of himself and everything about him. In short, a little contradiction, like salt at dinner, seasons and appetises the repast; but too much, like the condiment in question, spoils the whole, and it becomes unpalatable in proportion to its excess.

"My mother was a vain woman in every sense of the word—vain of her birth and of her beauty, and accustomed to receive that homage to which she considered herself entitled. She had been spoiled in her infancy, and as she grew up had learnt nothing, because she was permitted to do as she pleased; she was therefore frivolous, and could not appreciate what she could not comprehend. There never was a more ill-assorted union."

"I have always thought that such must be the case," replied Gascoigne, "in Catholic countries, where a young person is taken out of a convent and mated according to what her family or her wealth may consider as the most eligible connection."

"On that subject there are many opinions, my friend," replied Don Rebiera. "It is true, that when a marriage of convenience is

arranged by the parents, the dispositions of the parties are made a
secondary point; but then, again, it must be remembered, that when
a choice is left to the parties themselves, it is at an age at which there
is little worldly consideration: and, led away, in the first place, by
their passions, they form connections with those inferior in their station which are attended with eventual unhappiness; or, in the other,
allowing that they do choose in their own rank of life, they make
quite as bad or often a worse choice than if their partners were selected for them."

"I cannot understand that," replied Gascoigne.

"The reason is, because there are no means, or, if means, no wish,
to study each other's disposition. A young man is attracted by person, and he admires; the young woman is flattered by the admiration, and is agreeable; if she has any faults she is not likely to display
them—not concealing them from hypocrisy, but because they are not
called out. The young man falls in love, so does the young woman:
and when once in love, they can no longer see faults; they marry,
imagining that they have found perfection. In the blindness of love
each raises the other to a standard of perfection which human nature
can never attain, and each becomes equally annoyed on finding, by
degrees, that they were in error. The re-action takes place, and they
then under-rate, as much as before they had over-rated, each other.
Now, if two young people marry without this violence of passion,
they do not expect to find each other perfect, and perhaps have a better chance of happiness."

"I don't agree with you," thought Gascoigne; "but as you appear
to be as fond of argument as my friend Jack, I shall make no reply,
lest there be no end to the story."

Don Rebiera proceeded.

"My mother, finding that my father preferred his closet and his
books to gaiety and dissipation, soon left him to himself, and amused
herself after her own fashion, but not until I was born, which was ten
months after their marriage. My father was confiding, and, pleased
that my mother should be amused, he indulged her in everything.
Time flew on, and I had arrived at my fifteenth year, and came home
from my studies, it being intended that I should enter the army,
which you are aware is generally the only profession embraced in
this country by the heirs of noble families. Of course, I knew little of
what had passed at home, but still I had occasionally heard my
mother spoken lightly of, when I was not supposed to be present,

and I always heard my father's name mentioned with compassion, as if an ill-used man, but I knew nothing more: still this was quite sufficient for a young man, whose blood boiled at the idea of anything like a stigma being cast upon his family. I arrived at my father's—I found him at his books; I paid my respects to my mother,—I found her with her confessor. I disliked the man at first sight; he was handsome, certainly: his forehead was high and white, his eyes large and fiery, and his figure commanding; but there was a dangerous, proud look about him which disgusted me,—nothing like humility or devotion. I might have admired him as an officer commanding a regiment of cavalry, but as a churchman he appeared to be most misplaced. She named me with kindness, but he appeared to treat me with disdain; he spoke authoritatively to my mother, who appeared to yield implicitly, and I discovered that he was lord of the whole household. My mother, too, it was said, had given up gaieties and become devout. I soon perceived more than a common intelligence between them, and before I had been two months at home I had certain proofs of my father's dishonour; and, what was still more unfortunate for me, they were aware that such was the case. My first impulse was to acquaint my father; but, on consideration, I thought it better to say nothing, provided I could persuade my mother to dismiss Father Ignatio. I took an opportunity when she was alone to express my indignation at her conduct, and to demand his immediate dismissal, as a condition of my not divulging her crime. She appeared frightened, and gave her consent; but I soon found that her confessor had more power with her than I had, and he remained. I now resolved to acquaint my father, and I roused him from his studies that he might listen to his shame. I imagined that he would have acted calmly and discreetly; but, on the contrary, his violence was without bounds, and I had the greatest difficulty from preventing his rushing with his sword to sacrifice them both. At last he contented himself by turning Father Ignatio out of the house in the most ignominious manner, and desiring my mother to prepare for seclusion in a convent for the remainder of her days.—But he fell their victim; three days afterwards, as my mother was, by his directions, about to be removed, he was seized with convulsions, and died. I need hardly say that he was carried off by poison; this, however, could not be established till long afterwards. Before he died he seemed to be almost supernaturally prepared for an event which never came into my thoughts. He sent for another confessor, who drew up his confession in writing at his own request, and afterwards inserted it in his will. My mother remained in the house, and Father Ignatio had the insolence to return. I ordered him away, and he resisted. He was turned out by the servants. I had an interview with my mother, who defied me, and told me that I should soon have a brother to share in the succession. I felt that, if so, it would be the illegitimate progeny of her adultery, and told her my opinion. She expressed her rage in the bitterest curses, and I left her. Shortly afterwards she quitted the house and retired to another of our country seats, where she lived with Father Ignatio as before. About four months afterwards, formal notice was sent to me of the birth of a brother; but as when my father's will was opened, he there had inserted his confession, or the substance of it, in which he stated, that aware of my mother's guilt, and supposing that consequences might ensue, he solemnly declared before God that he had for years lived apart, I cared little for this communication. I contented myself with replying that as the child belonged to the church, it had better be dedicated to its service.

"I had, however, soon reason to acknowledge the vengeance of my mother and her paramour. One night I was attacked by bravos;* and had I not fortunately received assistance, I should have forfeited my life; as it was, I received a severe wound.

"Against attempts of that kind I took every precaution in future, but still every attempt was made to ruin my character, as well as to take my life. A young sister disappeared from a convent in my neighbourhood, and on the ground near the window from which she descended was found a hat, recognised to be mine. I was proceeded against, and notwithstanding the strongest interest, it was with difficulty that the affair was arranged, although I had incontestably proved an *alibi*.

"A young man of rank was found murdered, with a stiletto, known to be mine, buried in his bosom, and it was with difficulty that I could establish my innocence.

"Part of a banditti had been seized, and on being asked the name of their chief, when they received absolution, they confessed that I was the chief of the band.

"Everything that could be attempted was put into practice; and if I did not lose my life, at all events I was avoided by almost everybody as a dangerous and doubtful character.

* Bravos: Assassins.

"At last a nobleman of rank, the father of Don Scipio, whom you disarmed, was assassinated; the bravos were taken, and they acknowledged that I was the person who hired them. I defended myself, but the king imposed upon me a heavy fine and banishment. I had just received the order, and was crying out against the injustice, and lamenting my hard fate, as I sat down to dinner. Latterly, aware of what my enemies would attempt, I had been accustomed to live much alone. My faithful valet Pedro was my only attendant. I was eating my dinner with little appetite, and had asked for some wine. Pedro went to the buffet behind him to give me what I required. Accidentally I lifted up my head, and there being a large pier-glass opposite to me, I saw the figure of my valet, and that he was pouring a powder in the flagon of wine which he was about to present to me. I recollected the hat being found at the nunnery, and also the stiletto in the body of the young man.

"Like lightning it occurred to me, that I had been fostering the viper who had assisted to destroy me. He brought me the flagon. I rose, locked the door, and drawing my sword, I addressed him—

" 'Villain! I know thee; down on your knees, for your life is forfeited.'

"He turned pale, trembled, and sank upon his knees.

" 'Now, then,' continued I, 'you have but one chance—either drink off this flagon of wine, or I pass my sword through your body.—He hesitated, and I put the point to his breast,—even pierced the flesh a quarter of an inch.

" 'Drink,' cried I—'is it so very unjust an order to tell you to drink old wine? Drink,' continued I, 'or my sword does its duty.'

"He drank, and would then have quitted the room. 'No, no,' said I, 'you remain here, and the wine must have its effect. If I have wronged you I will make amends to you—but I am suspicious.'

"In about a quarter of an hour, during which time I paced up and down the room, with my sword drawn, my servant fell down, and cried in mercy to let him have a priest. I sent for my own confessor, and he then acknowledged that he was an agent of my mother and Father Ignatio, and had been the means of making it appear that I was the committer of all the crimes and murders which had been perpetrated by them, with a view to my destruction. A strong emetic having been administered to him, he partially revived, and was taken to Palermo, where he gave his evidence before he expired.

"When this was made known, the king revoked his sentence,

apologised to me, and I found that once more I was visited and courted by everybody. My mother was ordered to be shut up in a convent, where she died, I trust, in grace; and Father Ignatio fled to Italy, and I have been informed is since dead.

"Having thus rid myself of my principal enemies, I considered myself safe. I married the lady whom you have just seen, and before my eldest son was born, Don Silvio, for such was the name given to my asserted legitimate brother, came of age, and demanded his succession. Had he asked me for a proper support, as my uterine brother, I should not have refused; but that the son of Friar Ignatio, who had so often attempted my life, should, in case of my decease, succeed to the title and estates, was not to be borne. A lawsuit was immediately commenced, which lasted four or five years, during which Don Silvio married, and had a son, that young man whom you heard me address by the same name; but after much litigation, it was decided that my father's confessor and will had proved his illegitimacy, and the suit was in my favour. From that time to this, there has been a constant enmity. Don Silvio refused all my offers of assistance, and followed me with a pertinacity which often endangered my life. At last he fell by the hands of his own agents, who mistook him for me. Don Silvio died without leaving any provision for his family; his widow I pensioned, and his son I have had carefully brought up, and have indeed treated most liberally, but he appears to have imbibed the spirit of his father, and no kindness has been able to embue him with gratitude.

"He had lately been placed by me in the army, where he found out my two sons, and quarrelled with them both upon slight pretence; but, in both instances, he was wounded and carried off the field.

"My two sons have been staying with me these last two months, and did not leave till yesterday. This morning Don Silvio, accompanied by Don Scipio, came to the house, and after accusing me of being the murderer of both their parents, drew their rapiers to assassinate me. My wife and child, hearing the noise, came down to my assistance—you know the rest."

CHAPTER XXI

In which our hero is brought up all standing under a press of sail.

OUR LIMITS will not permit us to relate all that passed during our hero's stay of a fortnight at Don Rebiera's. He and Gascoigne were treated as if they were his own sons, and the kindness of the female part of the family was equally remarkable. Agnes, naturally perhaps, showed a preference or partiality for Jack: to which Gascoigne willingly submitted, as he felt that our hero had a prior and stronger claim, and during the time that they remained a feeling of attachment was created between Agnes and the philosopher, which, if not love, was at least something very near akin to it; but the fact was, that they were both much too young to think of marriage; and, although they walked and talked, and laughed, and played together, they were always at home in time for their dinner. Still, the young lady thought she preferred our hero, even to her brothers, and Jack thought that the young lady was the prettiest and kindest girl that he had ever met with. At the end of the fortnight, our two midshipmen took their leave, furnished with letters of recommendation to many of the first nobility in Palermo, and mounted on two fine mules with bell bridles. The old Donna kissed them both— the Don showered down his blessings of good wishes, and Donna Agnes' lips trembled as she bade them adieu; and, as soon as they were gone, she went up to her chamber and wept. Jack also was very grave, and his eyes moistened at the thoughts of leaving Agnes. Neither of them were aware, until the hour of parting, how much they had wound themselves together.

The first quarter of an hour our two midshipmen followed their guide in silence. Jack wished to be left to his own thoughts, and Gascoigne perceived it.

"Well, Easy," said Gascoigne, at last, "if I had been in your place, constantly in company of, and loved by, that charming girl, I could never have torn myself away."

"Loved by her, Ned!" replied Jack, "what makes you say that?"

"Because I am sure it was the case; she lived but in your presence. Why, if you were out of the room, she never spoke a word, but sat there as melancholy as a sick monkey—the moment you came in again, she beamed out as glorious as the sun, and was all life and spirit."

"I thought people were always melancholy when they were in love," replied Jack.

"When those that they love are out of their presence."

"Well, then, I am out of her presence, and I feel very melancholy, so I suppose, by your argument, I am in love. Can a man be in love without knowing it?"

"I really cannot say, Jack; I never was in love myself, but I've seen many others *spoony*. My time will come, I suppose, by-and-bye. They say, that for every man made, there is a woman also made to fit him, if he could only find her. Now, it's my opinion that you have found yours—I'll lay my life she's crying at this moment."

"Do you really think so, Ned? let's go back—poor little Agnes—let's go back; I feel I do love her, and I'll tell her so."

"Pooh, nonsense! it's too late now; you should have told her that before, when you walked with her in the garden."

"But I did not know it, Ned. However, as you say, it would be foolish to turn back, so I'll write to her from Palermo."

Here an argument ensued upon love, which we shall not trouble the reader with, as it was not very profound, both sides knowing very little on the subject. It did, however, end with our hero being convinced that he was desperately in love, and he talked about giving up the service as soon as he arrived at Malta. It is astonishing what sacrifices midshipmen will make for the objects of their adoration.

It was not until late in the evening that our adventurers arrived at Palermo. As soon as they were lodged at the hotel, Gascoigne sat down and wrote a letter in their joint names to Don Rebiera, returning him many thanks for his great kindness, informing him of their safe arrival, and trusting that they should soon meet again: and Jack took up his pen, and indited a letter in Spanish to Agnes, in which he swore that neither tide nor time, nor water, nor air, nor heaven, nor earth, nor the first lieutenant, nor his father, nor absence, nor death itself, should prevent him from coming back and marrying her, the first convenient opportunity, begging her to refuse a thousand offers, as come back he would, although there was no saying when. It was a perfect love letter, that is to say, it was the essence of nonsense; but that made it perfect, for the greater the love the greater the folly.

These letters were consigned to the man who was sent as their guide, and also had to return with the mules. He was liberally rewarded; and, as Jack told him to be very careful of his letter, the Italian naturally concluded that it was to be delivered clandestinely, and he delivered it accordingly, at a time when Agnes was walking in the garden thinking of our hero. Nothing was more opportune than the arrival of the letter; Agnes ran to the pavilion, read it over twenty times, kissed it twenty times, and hid it in her bosom; sat for a few minutes in deep and placid thought, took the letter out of its receptacle, and read it over and over again. It was very bad Spanish, and very absurd, but she thought it delightful, poetical, classical, sentimental, argumentative, convincing, incontrovertible, imaginative and even grammatical; for if it was not good Spanish, there was no Spanish half so good. Alas! Agnes was indeed unsophisticated, to be in such ecstacies with a midshipman's love letter. Once more she hastened to her room to weep, but it was from excess of joy and delight. The reader may think Agnes silly, but he must take into consideration the climate, and that she was not yet fifteen.

Our young gentlemen sent for a tailor, and each ordered a new suit of clothes; they delivered their letters of recommendation, and went to the banker to whom they were addressed by Don Rebiera.

"I shall draw for ten pounds, Jack," said Gascoigne, "on the strength of the shipwreck; I shall tell the truth, all except that we forgot to ask for leave, which I shall leave out; and I am sure the story will be worth ten pounds. What shall you draw for, Jack?"

"I shall draw for two hundred pounds," replied Jack; "I mean to have a good cruise while I can."

"But will your governor stand that, Easy?"

"To be sure he will."

"Then you're right—he is a philosopher—I wish he'd teach mine, for he hates the sight of a bill."

"Then don't you draw, Ned—I have plenty for both. If every man had his equal share and rights in the world, you would be as able to draw as much as I; and as you cannot, upon the principles of equality you shall have half."

"I really shall become a convert to your philosophy, Jack; it does not appear to be so nonsensical as I thought it. At all events, it has saved my old governor ten pounds, which he can ill afford, as a colonel on half-pay."

On their return to the inn, they found Don Philip and Don Martin, to whom Don Rebiera had written, who welcomed them with open arms. They were two very fine young men of eighteen and nineteen, who were finishing their education in the army. Jack asked them to dinner, and they and our hero soon became inseparable. They took him to all the theatres, the conversaziones of all the nobility, and as Jack lost his money with good humour, and was a very handsome fellow, he was everywhere well received and was made much of: many ladies made love to him, but Jack was only very polite, because he thought more and more of Agnes every day. Three weeks passed away like lightning, and neither Jack nor Gascoigne thought of going back. At last, one fine day H.M. frigate *Aurora* anchored in the bay, and Jack and Gascoigne, who were at a party at the Duke of Pentaro's, met with the captain of the *Aurora,* who was also invited. The Duchess introduced them to Captain Tartar,* who imagining them, from their being in plain clothes, to be young Englishmen of fortune on their travels, was very gracious and condescending. Jack was so pleased with his urbanity that he requested the pleasure of his company to dinner the next day: Captain Tartar accepted the invitation, and they parted shaking hands, with many expressions of pleasure in having made his acquaintance. Jack's party was rather large, and the dinner sumptuous. The Sicilian gentlemen did not drink much wine: but Captain Tartar liked his bottle, and although the rest of the company quitted the table to go to a ball given that evening by the Marquesa Novara, Jack was too polite not to sit it out with the captain: Gascoigne closed his chair to Jack's, who, he was afraid, being a little affected with the wine, would "let the cat out of the bag."

The captain was amazingly entertaining. Jack told him how happy he should be to see him at Forest Hill, which property the captain discovered to contain six thousand acres of land, and also that Jack was an only son; and Captain Tartar was quite respectful when he found that he was in such very excellent company. The captain of the frigate inquired of Jack what brought him out here, and Jack, whose prudence was departing, told him that he came in his Majesty's ship *Harpy.* Gascoigne gave Jack a nudge, but it was of no use, for as the wine got into Jack's brain, so did his notions of equality.

"Oh! Wilson gave you a passage; he's an old friend of mine."

"So he is of ours," replied Jack; "he's a devilish good sort of a fellow, Wilson."

"But where have you been since you came out?" inquired Captain Tartar.

---

* Captain Tartar: A tartar was thought to be a violent, irritable person.

"In the *Harpy*," replied Jack; "to be sure, I belong to her."

"You belong to her! in what capacity, may I ask?" inquired Captain Tartar in a much less respectful and confidential tone.

"Midshipman," replied Jack; "so is Mr Gascoigne."

"Umph! you are on leave then?"

"No, indeed," replied Jack; "I'll tell you how it is, my dear fellow."

"Excuse me for one moment," replied Captain Tartar, rising up; "I must give some directions to my servant which I forgot."

Captain Tartar hailed his coxswain out of the window, gave orders just outside of the door, and then returned to the table. In the meantime, Gascoigne, who expected a breeze, had been cautioning Jack, in a low tone, at intervals, when Captain Tartar's back was turned: but it was useless; the extra quantity of wine had got into Jack's head, and he cared nothing for Gascoigne's remonstrance. When the captain resumed his seat at the table, Jack gave him the true narrative of all that had passed, to which his guest paid the greatest attention. Jack wound up his confidence by saying, that in a week or so he should go back to Don Rebiera and propose for Donna Agnes.

"Ah!" exclaimed Captain Tartar, drawing his breath with astonishment, and compressing his lip.

"Tartar, the wine stands with you," said Jack, "allow me to help you."

Captain Tartar threw himself back in his chair, and let all the air out of his chest with a sort of whistle, as if he could hardly contain himself.

"Have you had wine enough?" said Jack, very politely; "if so, we will go to the Marquesa's."

The coxswain came to the door, touched his hat to the captain, and looked significantly.

"And so, sir," cried Captain Tartar, in a voice of thunder, rising from his chair, "you're a d——d runaway midshipman, who, if you belonged to my ship, instead of marrying Donna Agnes, I would marry you to the gunner's daughter, by G——d; two midshipmen sporting plain clothes in the best society in Palermo, and having the impudence to ask a post-captain to dine with them! To ask me and address me as '*Tartar*,' and '*my dear fellow!*' you infernal young scamps!" continued Captain Tartar, now boiling with rage, and striking his fist on the table so as to set all the glasses waltzing.

"Allow me to observe, sir," said Jack, who was completely

sobered by the address, "that we do not belong to your ship, and that we are in plain clothes."

"In plain clothes—midshipmen in mufti—yes, you are so: a couple of young swindlers, without a sixpence in your pocket, passing yourselves off as young men of fortune, and walking off through the window without paying your bill."

"Do you mean to call me a swindler, sir," replied Jack.

"Yes, sir, you—"

"Then you lie!" exclaimed our hero in a rage. "I am a gentleman, sir—I am sorry I cannot pay you the same compliment."

The astonishment and rage of Captain Tartar took away his breath. He tried to speak, but could not—he gasped, and gasped, and then sat or almost fell down in his chair—at last he recovered himself.

"Matthews—Matthews!"

"Sir," replied the coxswain, who had remained at the door.

"The sergeant of marines."

"Here he is, sir."

The sergeant entered, and raised the back of his hand to his hat.

"Bring your marines in—take charge of these two. Directly you are on board, put them both legs in irons."

The marines with their bayonets walked in and took possession of our hero and Gascoigne.

"Perhaps, sir," replied Jack, who was now cool again, "you will permit us to pay our bill before we go on board. We are no swindlers, and it is rather a heavy one—or, as you have taken possession of our persons, you will, perhaps, do us the favour to discharge it yourself"; and Jack threw on the table a heavy purse of dollars. "I have only to observe, Captain Tartar, that I wish to be very liberal to the waiters."

"Sergeant, let them pay their bill," said Captain Tartar in a more subdued tone, taking his hat and sword, and walking out of the room.

"By heavens, Easy, what have you done?—you will be tried by a court-martial, and turned out of the service."

"I hope so," replied Jack; "I was a fool to come into it. But he called me a swindler, and I would give the same answer to-morrow."

"If you are ready, gentlemen," said the sergeant who had been long enough with Captain Tartar to be aware that to be punished by him was no proof of fault having been committed.

"I will go and pack up our things, Easy, while you pay the bill," said Gascoigne. "Marine, you had better come with me."

In less than half an hour, our hero and his comrade, instead of finding themselves at the Marquesa's ball, found themselves very comfortably in irons under the half-deck of his Majesty's frigate, *Aurora*.

We shall leave them, and return to Captain Tartar, who had proceeded to the ball, to which he had been invited. On his entering he was accosted by Don Martin and Don Philip, who inquired what had become of our hero and his friend. Captain Tartar who was in no very good humour, replied briskly, "that they were on board his ship in irons."

"In irons! for what?" exclaimed Don Philip.

"Because, sir, they are a couple of young scamps who have introduced themselves into the best company, passing themselves off as people of consequence, when they are only a couple of midshipmen who have run away from their ship."

Now the Rebieras knew very well that Jack and his friend were midshipmen; but this did not appear to them any reason why they should not be considered as gentlemen, and treated accordingly.

"Do you mean to say, signor," said Don Philip, "that you have accepted their hospitality, laughed, talked, walked arm-in-arm with them, pledged them in wine, as we have seen you this evening, and after they have confided in you that you have put them in irons?"

"Yes, sir, I do," replied Captain Tartar.

"Then, by Heaven, you have my defiance, and you are no gentleman!" replied Don Philip, the elder.

"And I repeat my brother's words, sir," cried Don Martin.

The two brothers felt so much attachment for our hero, who had twice rendered such signal service to their family, that their anger was without bounds.

In every other service but the English navy there is not that power of grossly insulting and then sheltering yourself under your rank; nor is it necessary for the discipline of any service. To these young officers, if the power did exist, the use of such power under such circumstances appeared monstrous, and they were determined, at all events, to show to Captain Tartar that in society, at least, it could be resented. They collected their friends, told them what had passed, and begged them to circulate it through the room. This was soon done, and Captain Tartar found himself avoided. He went up to the Marquesa and spoke to her, she turned her head the other way. He addressed a count he had been conversing with the night before—he turned short round upon his heel, while Don Philip and Don Martin walked up and down talking, so that he might hear what they said, and looking at him with eyes flashing with indignation. Captain Tartar left the ball-room and returned to the inn, more indignant than ever. When he rose the next morning he was informed that a gentleman wished to speak with him; he sent up his card as Don Ignatio Verez, colonel commanding the fourth regiment of infantry. On being admitted, he informed Captain Tartar that Don Philip de Rebiera wished to have the pleasure of crossing swords with him, and requested to know when it would be convenient for Captain Tartar to meet him.

It was not in Captain Tartar's nature to refuse a challenge; his courage was unquestionable, but he felt indignant that a midshipman should be the cause of his getting into such a scrape. He accepted the challenge, but having no knowledge of the small sword, refused to fight unless with pistols. To this the colonel raised no objections, and Captain Tartar despatched his coxswain with a note to his second lieutenant, for he was not on good terms with his first. The meeting took place—at the first fire the ball of Don Philip passed through Captain Tartar's brain, and he instantly fell dead. The second lieutenant hastened on board to report the fatal result of the meeting, and shortly after, Don Philip and his brother, with many of their friends, went off in the governor's barge to condole with our hero.

The first lieutenant, now captain *"pro tempore,"* received them graciously, and listened to their remonstrances relative to our hero and Gascoigne.

"I have never been informed by the captain of the grounds of complaint against the young gentlemen," replied he, "and have therefore no charge to prefer against them. I shall therefore order them to be liberated. But as I learn that they are officers belonging to one of his Majesty's ships lying at Malta, I feel it my duty, as I sail immediately, to take them there and send them on board of their own ship."

Jack and Gascoigne were then taken out of irons and permitted to see Don Philip, who informed them that he had revenged the insult, but Jack and Gascoigne did not wish to go on shore again after what had passed. After an hour's conversation, and assurances of continued friendship, Don Philip, his brother, and their friends, took leave of our two midshipmen, and rowed on shore.

And now we must be serious.

We do not write these novels merely to amuse,—we have always had it in our view to instruct, and it must not be supposed that we have no other end in view than to make the reader laugh. If we were to write an elaborate work, telling truths, and plain truths, confining ourselves only to point out errors and to demand reform, it would not be read; we have therefore selected this light and trifling species of writing, as it is by many denominated, as a channel through which we may convey wholesome advice in a palatable shape. If we would point out an error, we draw a character, and although that character appears to weave naturally into the tale of fiction, it becomes as much a beacon as it is a vehicle of amusement. We consider this to be the true art of novel writing, and that crime and folly and error can be as severely lashed as virtue and morality can be upheld, by a series of amusing causes and effects, that entice the reader to take a medicine, which, although rendered agreeable to the palate, still produces the same internal benefit, as if it had been presented to him in its crude state, in which it would either be refused or nauseated.

In our naval novels, we have often pointed out the errors which have existed, and still do exist, in a service which is an honour to its country; for what institution is there on earth that is perfect, or into which, if it once was perfect, abuses will not creep? Unfortunately, others have written to decry the service, and many have raised up their voices against our writings, because they felt that, in exposing error, we were exposing them. But to this we have been indifferent; we felt that we were doing good, and we have continued. To prove that we are correct in asserting that we have done good, we will, out of several, state one single case.

In "The King's Own,"* a captain, when requested to punish a man *instanter* for a fault committed, replies that he never has and never will punish a man until twenty-four hours after the offence, that he may not be induced by the anger of the moment to award a severer punishment than in his cooler moments he might think commensurate—and that he wished that the Admiralty would give out an order to that effect.

Some time after the publication of that work, the order was given by the Admiralty, forbidding the punishment until a certain time had elapsed after the offence; and we had the pleasure of knowing from the first lord of the Admiralty of the time, that it was in consequence of the suggestion in the novel.

* "The King's Own": Marryat's second novel (1830).

If our writings had effected nothing else, we might still lay down our pen with pride and satisfaction: but they have done more, much more; and while they have amused the reader, they have improved the service: they have held up in their characters a mirror, in which those who have been in error may see their own deformity, and many hints which have been given have afterwards returned to the thoughts of those who have had an influence, have been considered as their own ideas, and have been acted upon. The conduct of Captain Tartar may be considered as a libel on the service—is it not? The fault of Captain Tartar was not in sending them on board, or even putting them in irons as deserters, although, under the circumstances, he might have shown more delicacy. The fault was in stigmatising a young man as a swindler, and the punishment awarded to the error is intended to point out the moral, that such an abuse of power should be severely visited. The greatest error now in our service, is the disregard shown to the feelings of the junior officers in the language of their superiors: that an improvement has taken place I grant, but that it still exists, to a degree injurious to the service, I know too well. The articles of war, as our hero was informed by his captain, were equally binding on officers and crew; but what a dead letter do they become if officers are permitted to break them with impunity! The captain of a ship will turn the hands up to punishment, read the article of war for the transgressing of which the punishment is inflicted, and to show at that time their high respect for the articles of war, the captain and every officer take off their hats. The moment the hands are piped down, the second article of war, which forbids all swearing, &c., in derogation of God's honour is immediately disregarded. We are not strait-laced,—we care little about an oath as a mere *expletive*; we refer now to swearing at *others*, to insulting their feelings grossly by coarse and intemperate language. We would never interfere with a man for d——g his *own* eyes, but we deny the right of his d——g those of *another*.

The rank of a master in the service is above that of a midshipman, but still the midshipman is a gentleman by birth, and the master, generally speaking, is not. Even at this moment, in the service, if the master were to d——n the eyes of a midshipman, and tell him that he was a liar, would there be any redress, or if so, would it be commensurate to the insult? If a midshipman were to request a court-martial, would it be granted? certainly not: and yet this is a point of more importance than may be conceived. Our service has been wonderfully improved since the peace, and those who are now permitted to enter it must be gentlemen. We know that even now there are many who cry out against this as dangerous, and injurious to the service; as if education spoilt an officer, and the scion of an illustrious house would not be more careful to uphold an escutcheon without blemish for centuries than one who has little more than brute courage; but those who argue thus are the very people who are injurious to the service, for they can have no other reason, except that they wish that the juniors may be tyrannised over with impunity.

Be it remembered that these are not the observations of a junior officer, smarting under insult—they are the result of deep and calm reflection. We have arrived to that grade, that, although we have the power to inflict, we are too high to receive insult, but we have not forgotten how our young blood has boiled when wanton, reckless, and cruel torture has been heaped upon our feelings, merely because, as a junior officer, we were not in a position to retaliate, or even to reply. And another evil is, that this *great error* is *disseminated*. In observing on it, in one of our works, called "Peter Simple," we have put the following true observation in the mouth of O'Brien. Peter observes, in his simple, right-minded way—

"I should think, O'Brien, that the very circumstance of having had your feelings so often wounded by such language when you were a junior officer would make you doubly careful not to use it towards others, when you had advanced in the service."

"Peter, that's just the first feeling, which wears away after a time, till at last your own sense of indignation becomes blunted, and becomes indifferent to it: you forget, also, that you wound the feelings of others, and carry the habit with you, to the great injury and disgrace of the service."

Let it not be supposed that in making these remarks we want to cause litigation, or insubordination. On the contrary, we assert that this error is the cause, and eventually will be much more the cause, of insubordination; for as the junior officers who enter the service are improved, so will they resist it. The complaint here is more against the officers than the captains, whose power has been perhaps already too much curtailed by late regulations: that power must remain, for although there may be some few who are so perverted as to make those whom they command uncomfortable, in justice to the service we are proud to assert, that the majority acknowledge, by their conduct, that the greatest charm attached to power is to be able to make so many people happy.

CHAPTER XXII

Our hero is sick with the service, but recovers with proper medicine. An argument, ending, as most do, in a blow up. Mesty lectures upon craniology.

THE DAY after the funeral, H.M. ship *Aurora* sailed for Malta, and on her arrival the acting captain sent our two midshipmen on board the *Harpy* without any remark, except "victualled the day discharged," as they had been borne on the ship's books as supernumeraries.*

Mr James, who was acting in the *Aurora*, was anxious to join the Admiral at Toulon, and intended to sail the next day. He met Captain Wilson at the governor's table, and stated that Jack and Gascoigne had been put in irons by order of Captain Tartar; his suspicions, and the report, that the duel had in consequence taken place; but Gascoigne and Jack had both agreed that they would not communicate the events of their cruise to anybody on board of the *Aurora*; and therefore nothing else was known, except that they must have made powerful friends somehow or another; and there appeared in the conduct of Captain Tartar, as well as in the whole transaction, somewhat of a mystery.

"I should like to know what happened to my friend Jack, who fought the duel," said the governor, who had laughed at it till he held his sides; "Wilson, do bring him here to-morrow morning, and let us have his story,"

"I am afraid of encouraging him, Sir Thomas, he is much too wild already. I told you of his first cruise. He has nothing but adventures, and they all end too favourably."

---

* Supernumeraries: Sailors in excess of the crew's company.

"Well, but you can send for him here and blow him up just as well as in your own cabin, and then we will have the truth out of him."

"That you certainly will," replied Captain Wilson, "for he tells it plainly enough."

"Well, to oblige me, send for him. I don't see he was much to blame in absconding, as it appears he thought he would be hung. I want to see the lad."

"Well, governor, if you wish it," replied Captain Wilson, who wrote a note to Mr Sawbridge, requesting he would send Mr Easy to him at the governor's house at ten o'clock in the morning.

Jack made his appearance in his uniform—he did not much care for what was said to him, as he was resolved to leave the service. He had been put in irons, and the iron had *entered into his soul.*

Mr Sawbridge had gone on shore about an hour before Jack had been sent on board, and he had remained on shore all the night. He did not therefore see Jack but for a few minutes, and thinking it his duty to say nothing to him at first, or to express his displeasure, he merely observed to him that the captain would speak to him as soon as he came on board. As Gascoigne and our hero did not know how far it might be safe, even at Malta, to acknowledge to what occurred on board the speronare, which might get wind, they did not even tell their messmates, resolving only to confide it to the captain.

When Jack was ushered into the presence of the captain, he found him sitting with the governor, and the breakfast on the table ready for them. Jack walked in with courage, but respectfully. He was fond of Captain Wilson, and wished to show him respect. Captain Wilson addressed him, pointed out that he had committed a great error in fighting a duel—a greater error in demeaning himself by fighting the purser's steward, and still greater in running away from his ship. Jack looked respectfully to Captain Wilson, acknowledged that he had done wrong, and promised to be more careful another time, if Captain Wilson would look over it.

"Captain Wilson, allow me to plead for the young gentleman," said the governor; "I am convinced that it has only been an error in judgment."

"Well, Mr Easy, as you express your contrition, and the governor interferes in your behalf, I shall take no more notice of this. But recollect, Mr Easy, that you have occasioned me a great deal of anxiety by your mad pranks, and I trust another time you will remember that

I am too anxious for your welfare not to be uncomfortable when you run such risks. You may now go on board to your duty, and tell Mr. Gascoigne to do the same; and pray let us hear of no more duels or running away."

Jack, whose heart softened at this kind treatment, did not venture to speak; he made his bow and was about to quit the room, when the governor said—

"Mr Easy, you have not breakfasted?"

"I have, sir," replied Jack, "before I came on shore."

"But a midshipman can always eat two breakfasts, particularly when his own comes first; so sit down and breakfast with us—it's all over now."

"Even if it was not," replied Captain Wilson, laughing, "I doubt whether it would spoil Mr Easy's breakfast. Come, Mr Easy, sit down."

Jack bowed, and took his chair, and proved that his lecture had not taken away his appetite. When breakfast was over, Captain Wilson observed—

"Mr Easy, you have generally a few adventures to speak of when you return, will you tell the governor and me what has taken place since you left us?"

"Certainly, sir," replied Jack; "but I venture to request that it may be under the promise of secrecy, for it's rather important to me and Gascoigne."

"Yes, if secrecy is really necessary, my boy; but I'm the best judge of that," replied the governor.

Jack then entered into a detail of his adventures, which we have already described, much to the astonishment of the governor and his captain, and concluded his narration by stating that he wanted to leave the service; he hoped that Captain Wilson would discharge him and send him home.

"Pooh, nonsense!" said the governor, "you shan't leave the Mediterranean while I am here. No, no—you must have more adventures, and come back and tell them to me. And recollect, my lad, that whenever you come to Malta, there is a bed at the governor's house, and a seat at his table, always ready for you."

"You are very kind, Sir Thomas," replied Jack, "but—"

"No buts at all, sir—you shan't leave the service! Besides, recollect that I can ask for leave of absence for you to go and see Donna Agnes. Ay, and send you there, too."

Captain Wilson also remonstrated with our hero, and he gave up the point. It was harsh treatment which made him form the resolution—it was kindness which overcame it.

"With your permission, Captain Wilson, Mr Easy shall dine with us to-day, and bring Gascoigne with him. You shall first scold him, and I'll console him with a good dinner. And, boy, don't be afraid to tell your story everywhere. Sit down and tell it at Nix Mangare stairs, if you please. I'm governor here!"

Jack made his obeisance, and departed.

"The lad must be treated kindly, Captain Wilson," said the governor; "he would be a loss to the service. Good heavens, what adventures, and how honestly he tells everything! I shall ask him to stay with me for the time you are here, if you will allow me: I want to make friends with him—he must not leave the service."

Captain Wilson, who felt that kindness and attention would be more effectual with our hero than any other measures, gave his consent to the governor's proposition. So Jack ate at the governor's table, and took lessons in Spanish and Italian until the *Harpy* had been refitted, after heaving down. Before she was ready a vessel arrived from the fleet, directing Captain Wilson to repair to Mahon* and send a transport, lying there, to procure live bullocks for the fleet. Jack did not join his ship very willingly, but he had promised the governor to remain in the service, and he went on board the evening before she sailed. He had been living so well that he had, at first, a horror of midshipman's fare, but a good appetite seasons everything, and Jack soon complained that there was not enough. He was delighted to see Jolliffe and Mesty after so long an absence; he laughed at the boatswain's cheeks, inquired after the purser's steward's shot-holes, shook hands with Gascoigne and his other messmates, gave Vigors a thrashing, and then sat down to supper.

"Ah, Massa Easy, why you take a cruise without me?" said Mesty; "dat very shabby. By de power, but I wish I was there. You ab too much danger, Massa Easy, without Mesty, anyhow."

The next day the *Harpy* sailed, and Jack went to his duty. Mr Asper borrowed ten pounds, and our hero kept as much watch as he pleased, which, as watching did not please him, was very little. Mr Sawbridge had long conversations with our hero, pointing out to

---

* Mahon: Puerto de Mahon, the chief town and port on the island of Minorca, in the western Mediterranean off the coast of Spain.

him the necessity of discipline and obedience in the service, and that there was no such thing as equality, and that the rights of man secured to everyone the property which he held in possession.

"According to your ideas, Mr Easy, a man has no more right to his wife than anything else, and any other man may claim her."

Jack thought of Agnes, and he made matrimony an exception, as he continued to argue the point; but although he argued, still his philosophy was almost upset at the idea of any one disputing with him the rights of man, with respect to Agnes.

The *Harpy* made the African coast, the wind continued contrary, and they were baffled for many days; at last they espied a brig under the land, about sixteen miles off; her rig and appearance made Captain Wilson suspect that she was a privateer of some description or another, but it was calm, and they could not approach her. Nevertheless Captain Wilson thought it his duty to examine her; so at ten o'clock at night the boats were hoisted out: as this was merely intended for a reconnoitre, for there was no saying what she might be, Mr Sawbridge did not go. Mr Asper was in the sick list, so Mr Smallsole the master had the command of the expedition. Jack asked Mr Sawbridge to let him have charge of one of the boats. Mr Jolliffe and Mr Vigors went in the pinnace with the master. The gunner had the charge of one cutter, and our hero had the command of the other. Jack, although not much more than seventeen, was very strong and tall for his age; indeed he was a man grown, and shaved twice a-week. His only object in going was to have a yarn for the governor when he returned to Malta. Mesty went with him, and, as the boat shoved off, Gascoigne slipped in, telling Jack that he was come to take care of him, for which considerate kindness Jack expressed his warmest thanks. The orders to the master were very explicit; he was to reconnoitre the vessel, and if she proved heavily armed not to attack, for she was embayed, and could not escape the *Harpy* as soon as there was wind. If not armed he was to board her, but he was to do nothing till the morning: the reason for sending the boats away so soon was, that the men might not suffer from the heat of the sun during the daytime, which was excessive, and had already put many men on the sick list. The boats were to pull to the bottom of the bay, not to go so near as to be discovered, and then drop their grapnels*

---

* Grapnels: Iron-clawed instruments used as anchors for small vessels and as grappling hooks for boarding enemy ships.

till daylight. The orders were given to Mr Smallsole in presence of the other officers who were appointed to the boats, that there might be no mistake, and the boats then shoved off. After a three hours' pull, they arrived to where the brig lay becalmed, and as they saw no lights moving on board, they supposed they were not seen. They dropped their grapnels in about seven fathoms water and waited for daylight. When Jack heard Captain Wilson's orders that they were to lie at anchor till daylight, he had sent down Mesty for fishing-lines, as fresh fish is always agreeable in a midshipman's berth: he and Gascoigne amused themselves this way, and as they pulled up the fish they entered into an argument, and Mr Smallsole ordered them to be silent. The point which they discussed was relative to boat service; Gascoigne insisted that the boats should all board at once— while our hero took it into his head that it was better they should come up one after another; a novel idea, but Jack's ideas on most points were singular.

"If you throw your whole force upon the decks at once, you over-power them," observed Gascoigne; "if you do not you are beaten in detail."

"Very true," replied Jack, "supposing that you have an overpow-ering force, or they are not prepared; but recollect, that if they are, the case is altered; for instance, as to fire-arms—they fire theirs at the first boat, and they have not time to re-load, when the second comes up with its fire reserved; every fresh boat arriving adds to the courage of those who have boarded, and to the alarm of those who defend; the men come on fresh and fresh. Depend upon it, Gascoigne, there is nothing like a 'corps de reserve.' "

"Will you keep silence in your boat, Mr Easy, or will you not?" cried the master; "you're a disgrace to the service, sir."

"Thank ye, sir," replied Jack, in a low tone. "I've another bite, Ned."

Jack and his comrade continued to fish in silence till the day broke. The mist rolled off the stagnant water, and discovered the brig, who, as soon as she perceived the boats, threw out the French tricolour, and fired a gun of defiance.

Mr Smallsole was undecided; the gun fired was not a heavy one, and so Mr Jolliffe remarked; the men, as usual, anxious for the attack, asserted the same, and Mr Smallsole, afraid of retreating from the enemy and being afterwards despised by the ship's company, ordered the boats to weigh their grapnels.

"Stop a moment, my lads," said Jack to his men, "I've got a bite." The men laughed at Jack's taking it so easy, but he was their pet; and they did stop for him to pull up his fish, intending to pull up to the other boats and recover their loss of a few seconds.

"I've hooked him now," said Jack; "you may up with the grapnel while I up with the fish." But this delay gave the other boats a start of a dozen strokes of their oars, which was a distance not easy to be regained.

"They will be aboard before us, sir," said the coxswain.

"Never mind that," replied Jack; "someone must be last."

"But not the boat I am in," replied Gascoigne; "if I could help it."

"I tell you," replied Jack, "we shall be the *'corps de reserve,'* and have the honour of turning the scale in our favour."

"Give way, my lads," cried Gascoigne, perceiving the other boats still kept their distance ahead of them, which was about a cable's length.

"Gascoigne, I command the boat," said Jack, "and I do not wish my men to board without any breath in their bodies—that's a very unwise plan. A steady pull, my lads, and not too much exertion."

"By heavens, they'll take the vessel before we get alongside."

"Even if they should, I am right, am I not, Mesty?"

"Yes, Massa Easy, you very right—suppose they take vessel without you, they no want you—suppose they want you, you come." And the negro, who had thrown his jacket off, bared his arm, as if he intended mischief.

The first cutter, commanded by the gunner, now gained upon the launch, and was three boat's-lengths ahead of her when she came alongside. The brig poured in her broadside—it was well directed, and down went the boat.

"Cutter's sunk," exclaimed Gascoigne; "by heavens! give way, my men."

"Now, don't you observe, that had we all three been pulling up together, the broadside would have sunk us all?" said Jack, very composedly.

"There's board in the launch—give way, my men, give way," said Gascoigne, stamping with impatience.

The reception was evidently warm; by the time that the launch had poured in her men, the second cutter was close under the brig's quarter—two more strokes and she was alongside; when of a sudden, a tremendous explosion took place on the deck of the vessel, and bodies and fragments were hurled up in the air. So tremendous was the explosion, that the men of the second cutter, as if transfixed, simultaneously stopped pulling, their eyes directed to the volumes of smoke which poured through the ports, and hid the whole of the masts and rigging of the vessel.

"Now's your time, my lads, give way, and alongside," cried our hero.

The men, reminded by his voice, obeyed—but the impetus already given to the boat was sufficient. Before they could drop their oars in the water they grazed against the vessel's sides, and, following Jack, were in a few seconds on the quarter-deck of the vessel. A dreadful sight presented itself—the whole deck was black, and corpses lay strewed; their clothes on them still burning, and among the bodies lay fragments of what once were men.

The capstern was unshipped and turned over on its side—the binnacles were in remnants, and many of the ropes ignited. There was not one person left on deck to oppose them.

As they afterwards learned from some of the men who had saved their lives by remaining below, the French captain had seen the boats before they anchored, and had made every preparation; he had filled a large ammunition chest with cartridges for the guns, that they might not have to hand them up. The conflict between the men of the pinnace and the crew of the vessel was carried on near the capstern, and a pistol fired had accidentally communicated with the powder, which blew up in the very centre of the dense and desperate struggle.

The first object was to draw water and extinguish the flames, which were spreading over the vessel; as soon as that was accomplished, our hero went aft to the taffrail, and looked for the cutter which had been sunk.—"Gascoigne, jump into the boat with four men—I see the cutter floats a quarter of a mile astern: there may be someone alive yet. I think now I see a head or two."

Gascoigne hastened away, and soon returned with three of the cutter's men; the rest had sunk, probably killed or wounded by the discharge of the broadside.

"Thank God, there's three saved!" said Jack, "for we have lost too many. We must now see if any of these poor fellows are yet alive, and clear the decks of the remnants of those who have been blown to pieces. I say, Ned, where should we have been if we had boarded with the pinnace?"

"You always fall upon your feet, Easy," replied Gascoigne; "but that does not prove that you are right."

"I see there's no convincing you, Ned, you are so confoundedly fond of argument. However, I've no time to argue now—we must look to these poor fellows; some are still alive."

Body after body was thrown through the ports, the habiliments, in most cases, enabling them to distinguish whether it was that of a departed friend or foe.

Jack turned round, and observed Mesty with his foot on a head which had been blown from the trunk.

"What are you about, Mesty?"

"Massa Easy, I look at dis, and I tink it Massa Vigors' head, and den I tink dis skull of his enemy nice present make to little Massa Gossett; and den I tink again, and I say, no, he dead and nebber thrash any more—so let him go overboard."

Jack turned away, forgiving Vigors in his heart; he thought of the petty animosities of a midshipman's berth, as he looked at the blackened portion of a body half an hour before possessing intellect.

"Massa Easy," said Mesty, "I tink you say right, anyhow, when you say forgive: den, Massa Vigors," continued Mesty, taking up the head by the singed hair, and tossing it out of the port; "you really very bad man—but Ashantee forgive you."

"Here's somebody alive," said Gascoigne to Jack, examining a body, the face of which was black as a cinder and not to be recognised, "and he is one of our men, too, by his dress."

Our hero went up to examine, and to assist Gascoigne in disengaging the body from a heap of ropes and half-burnt tarpaulings with which it was entangled. Mesty followed, and looking at the lower extremities said, "Massa Easy, dat Massa Jolliffe; I know him trousers; marine tailor say he patch um for ever, and so old dat de thread no hold; yesterday he had dis patch put in, and marine tailor say he be d——n if he patch anymore, please nobody."

Mesty was right; it was poor Jolliffe, whose face was burnt as black as a coal by the explosion. He had also lost three fingers of the left hand, but as soon as he was brought out on the deck he appeared to recover, and pointed to his mouth for water, which was instantly procured.

"Mesty," said Jack, "I leave you in charge of Mr Jolliffe; take every care of him till I can come back."

The investigation was then continued, and four English sailors found who might be expected to recover, as well as about the same number of Frenchmen; the remainder of the bodies were then thrown overboard. The hat only of the master was picked up between the guns, and there were but eleven Frenchmen found below.

The vessel was the *Franklin,* a French privateer of ten guns and sixty-five men, of which, eight men were away in prizes. The loss on the part of the vessel was forty-six killed and wounded. On that of the *Harpy,* it was five drowned in the cutter, and eighteen blown up belonging to the pinnace, out of which total of twenty-three, they had only Mr Jolliffe and five seamen alive.

"The *Harpy* is standing in with a breeze from the offing," said Gascoigne to Easy.

"So much the better, for I am sick of this, Ned; there is something so horrible in it, and I wish I was on board again. I have just been to Jolliffe; he can speak a little; I think he will recover. I hope so, poor fellow; he will then obtain his promotion, for he is the commanding officer of all us who are left."

"And if he does," replied Gascoigne, "he can swear that it was by having been blown up which spoilt his beauty—but here comes the *Harpy.* I have been looking for an English ensign to hoist over the French, but cannot find one; so I hoist a wheft* over it,—that will do."

The *Harpy* was soon hove-to close to the brig, and Jack went on board in the cutter to report what had taken place. Captain Wilson was much vexed and grieved at the loss of so many men: fresh hands were put in the cutter to man the pinnace, and he and Sawbridge both went on board to witness the horrible effects of the explosion as described by our hero.

Jolliffe and the wounded men were taken on board, and all of them recovered. We have before stated how disfigured the countenance of poor Mr Jolliffe had been by the small-pox—so severely was it burned that the whole of the countenance came off in three weeks like a mask, and every one declared that, seamed as it still was, Mr Jolliffe was better looking than he was before. It may be as well here to state, that Mr Jolliffe not only obtained his promotion, but a pension for his wounds, and retired from the service. He was still very plain, but as it was known that he had been blown up, the loss of his eye as well as the scars on his face were all put down to the same accident, and he excited interest as a gallant and

* Wheft (also waft): A signal flag.

maimed officer. He married, and lived contented and happy to a good old age.

The *Harpy* proceeded with her prize to Mahon. Jack, as usual, obtained a great deal of credit; whether he deserved it, or whether, as Gascoigne observed, he always fell upon his feet, the reader may decide from our narrative; perhaps there was a little of both. The seamen of the *Harpy*, if summoned in a hurry, used very often to reply, "Stop a minute, I've got a bite": as for Jack, he often said to himself, "I have a famous good yarn for the governor."

CHAPTER XXIII

Jack goes on another cruise—Love and diplomacy—Jack proves himself as clever for three, and upsets all the arrangements of the high contracting powers.

A FEW DAYS after the arrival of the *Harpy* at Port Mahon a cutter came in with despatches from the admiral. Captain Wilson found that he was posted into the *Aurora* frigate, in which a vacancy had been made by the result of our hero's transgressions.

Mr Sawbridge was raised to the rank of commander, and appointed to the command of the *Harpy*. The admiral informed Captain Wilson that he must detain the *Aurora* until the arrival of another frigate, hourly expected, and then she would be sent down to Mahon for him to take the command of her. Further, he intimated that a supply of live bullocks would be very agreeable, and begged that he would send to Tetuan* immediately.

Captain Wilson had lost so many officers that he knew not whom to send: indeed, now he was no longer in command of the *Harpy*, and there was but one lieutenant and no master or master's mate. Gascoigne and Jack were the only two serviceable midshipmen, and he was afraid to trust them on any expedition in which expedition was required.

"What shall we do, Sawbridge? shall we send Easy or Gascoigne, or both, or neither?—for if the bullocks are not forthcoming, the admiral will not let them off as we do."

* Tetuan: A coastal town, now called Tetouan, of northwestern Morocco. Often used by British blockaders for resupply.

"We must send somebody, Wilson," replied Captain Sawbridge, "and it is the custom to send two officers, as one receives the bullocks on board, while the other attends to the embarkation."

"Well, then send both, Sawbridge, but lecture them well first."

"I don't think they can get into any mischief there," replied Sawbridge; "and it's such a hole that they will be glad to get away from it."

Easy and Gascoigne were summoned, listened very respectfully to all Captain Sawbridge said, promised to conduct themselves with the utmost propriety, received a letter to the vice-consul, and were sent with their hammocks and chests in the cabin on board the *Eliza Ann,* brig, of two hundred and sixteen tons, chartered by government—the master and crew of which were all busy forward heaving up their anchors.

The master of the transport came aft to receive them: he was a short, red-haired young man, with hands as broad as the flappers of a turtle; he was broad-faced, broad-shouldered, well freckled, and pug-nosed; but if not very handsome he was remarkably good-humoured. As soon as the chests and hammocks were on deck, he told them that when he could get the anchor up and make sail, he would give them some bottled porter. Jack proposed that he should get the porter up, and they would drink it while he got the anchor up, as it would save time.

"It may save time, mayhap, but it won't save porter," replied the master; "however, you shall have it."

He called the boy, ordered him to bring up the porter, and then went forward. Jack made the boy bring up two chairs, put the porter on the companion hatch, and he and Gascoigne sat down. The anchor was weighed, and the transport ran out under her fore-topsail, as they were light-handed, and had to secure the anchor. The transport passed within ten yards of the *Harpy,* and Captain Sawbridge, when he perceived the two midshipmen taking it so very easy, sitting in their chairs with their legs crossed, arms folded, and their porter before them, had a very great mind to order the transport to heave-to, but he could spare no other officer, so he walked away, saying to himself, "There'll be another yarn for the governor, or I'm mistaken."

As soon as sail was made on the transport, the master, whose name was Hogg, came up to our hero, and asked him how he found the porter. Jack declared that he never could venture an opinion upon

the first bottle—"So, Captain Hogg, we'll trouble you for a second"—
after which they troubled him for a third—begged for a fourth—
must drink his health in a fifth—and finally pointed out the propriety of making up the half-dozen. By this time they found themselves
rather light-headed; so, desiring Captain Hogg to keep a sharp look-
out, and not to call them on any account whatever, they retired to
their hammocks.

The next morning they awoke late; the breeze was fresh and fair:
they requested Captain Hogg not to consider the expense, as they
would pay for all they ate and drank, and all he did, into the bargain,
and promised him a fit-out when they got to Tetuan.

What with this promise and calling him captain, our hero and
Gascoigne won the master's heart, and being a very good tempered
fellow, they did what they pleased. Jack also tossed a doubloon to the
men for them to drink on their arrival, and all the men of the transport were in a transport at Jack's coming to "reign over them." It
must be acknowledged that Jack's reign was, for the most part of it,
"happy and glorious." At last they arrived at Tetuan, and our
Pylades and Orestes* went on shore to call upon the vice-consul,
accompanied by Captain Hogg. They produced their credentials, and
demanded bullocks. The vice-consul was a very young man, short
and thin, and light-haired; his father had held the situation before
him, and he had been appointed his successor because nobody else
had thought the situation worth applying for. Nevertheless, Mr
Hicks was impressed with the immense responsibility of his office. It
was, however, a place of some little emolument at this moment, and
Mr Hicks had plenty on his hands besides his sister, who, being the
only English lady there, set the fashion of the place, and usurped all
the attention of the gentlemen mariners who occasionally came for
bullocks. But Miss Hicks knew her own importance, and had successively refused three midshipmen, one master's mate, and an acting
purser. African bullocks were plentiful at Tetuan, but English ladies
were scarce; moreover, she had a pretty little fortune of her own, to
wit, three hundred dollars in a canvas bag, left her by her father, and
entirely at her own disposal. Miss Hicks was very like her brother,
except that she was more dumpling in her figure, with flaxen hair;
her features were rather pretty, and her skin very fair. As soon as the
preliminaries had been entered into, and arrangements made in a

---

* Pylades and Orestes: Loyal friends in Greek mythology.

small room with bare walls, which Mr Hicks denominated his office, they were asked to walk into the parlour to be introduced to the vice-consul's sister. Miss Hicks tossed her head at the two midshipmen, but smiled most graciously at Captain Hogg. She knew the relative ranks of midshipman and captain. After a short time she requested the honour of Captain Hogg's company to dinner, and begged that he would bring his midshipmen with him, at which Jack and Gascoigne looked at each other and burst out in a laugh, and Miss Hicks was very near rescinding the latter part of her invitation. As soon as they were out of the house, they told the captain to go on board and get all ready whilst they walked round the town. Having peeped into every part of it, and stared at Arabs, Moors, and Jews, till they were tired, they proceeded to the landing-place, where they met the captain, who informed them that he had done nothing, because the men were all drunk with Jack's doubloon. Jack replied that a doubloon would not last for ever, and that the sooner they drank it out the better. They then returned to the vice-consul's, whom they requested to procure for them fifty dozen of fowls, twenty sheep, and a great many other articles which might be obtained at the place; for, as Jack said, they would live well going up to Toulon, and if there were any of the stock left they would give them to the admiral, for Jack had taken the precaution to put his *father's philosophy* once more to the proof before he quitted Mahon. As Jack gave such a liberal order, and the vice-consul cheated him out of at least one-third of what he paid, Mr Hicks thought he could do no less than offer beds to our midshipmen as well as to Captain Hogg; so, as soon as dinner was over, they ordered Captain Hogg to go on board and bring their things on shore, which he did. As the time usual for transports remaining at Tetuan before they could be completed with bullocks was three weeks, our midshipmen decided upon staying at least so long if they could find anything to do; or if they could not, doing nothing was infinitely preferable to doing duty. So they took up their quarters at the vice-consul's, sending for porter and other things which were not to be had but from the transport; and Jack, to prove that he was not a swindler, as Captain Tartar had called him, gave Captain Hogg a hundred dollars on account, for Captain Hogg had a large stock of porter and English luxuries, which he had brought out as a venture, and of which he had still a considerable portion left. As, therefore, our midshipmen not only were cheated by the vice-consul, but they also supplied his table. Mr Hicks was very hospitable, and everything was at their service except Miss Julia, who turned up her nose at a midshipman, even upon full pay; but she made great advances to the captain, who, on his part, was desperately in love: so the mate and the men made all ready for the bullocks, Jack and Gascoigne made themselves comfortable, and Captain Hogg made love, and thus passed the first week.

The chamber of Easy and Gascoigne was at the top of the house, and finding it excessively warm, Gascoigne had forced his way up to the flat roof above (for the houses are all built in that way in most Mahomedan countries, to enable the occupants to enjoy the cool of the evening, and sometimes to sleep there). Those roofs, where houses are built next to each other, are divided by a wall of several feet, to insure that privacy which the Mahomedan customs demand.

Gascoigne had not been long up there before he heard the voice of a female, singing a plaintive air in a low tone, on the other side of the wall. Gascoigne sang well himself, and having a very fine ear, he was pleased with the correctness of the notes, although he had never heard the air before. He leant against the wall, smoked his cigar, and listened. It was repeated again and again at intervals; Gascoigne soon caught the notes, which sounded so clear and pure in the silence of the night.

At last they ceased, and having waited another half-hour in vain, our midshipman returned to his bed, humming the air which had so pleased his ear. It haunted him during his sleep, and rang in his ears when he awoke, as it is well known any new air that pleases us will do. Before breakfast was ready, Gascoigne had put English words to it, and sang them over and over again. He inquired of the vice-consul who lived in the next house, and was answered, that it was an old Moor, who was reported to be wealthy, and to have a daughter, whom many of the people had asked in marriage, but whether for her wealth or for her beauty he could not tell; he had, however, heard that she was very handsome. Gascoigne made no further inquiries, but went out with Jack and Captain Hogg, and on board to see the water got in for the bullocks.

"Where did you pick up that air, Gascoigne? It is very pretty, but I never heard you sing it before."

Gascoigne told him, and also what he had heard from Mr Hicks.

"I am determined, Jack, to see that girl if I can. Hicks can talk Arabic fast enough; just ask him the Arabic for these words—'Don't be afraid—I love you—I cannot speak your tongue,'—and put them down on paper as they are pronounced."

Jack rallied Gascoigne upon his fancy, which could end in nothing.

"Perhaps not," replied Gascoigne; "and I should have cared nothing about it, if she had not sung so well. I really believe the way to my heart is through my ear;—however, I shall try to-night, and soon find if she has the feeling which I think she has. Now let us go back; I'm tired of looking at women in garments up to their eyes, and men in dirt up to their foreheads."

As they entered the house they heard an altercation between Mr and Miss Hicks.

"I shall never give my consent, Julia; one of those midshipmen you turn your nose up at is worth a dozen Hoggs."

"Now, if we only knew the price of a hog in this country," observed Easy, "we should be able to calculate our exact value, Ned."

"A hog, being an unclean animal, is not—"

"Hush," said Jack.

"Mr Hicks," replied Miss Julia, "I am mistress of myself and my fortune, and I shall do as I please."

"Depend upon it, you shall not, Julia. I consider it my duty to prevent you from making an improper match: and, as his Majesty's representative here, I cannot allow you to marry this young man."

"Mercy on us!" said Gascoigne, "his Majesty's representative!"

"I shall not ask your consent," replied the lady.

"Yes, but you shall not marry without my consent. I have, as you know, Julia, from my situation here, as one of his Majesty's 'corps diplomatick,' great power, and I shall forbid the banns; in fact, it is only I who can marry you."

"Then I'll marry elsewhere."

"And what will you do on board of the transport until you are able to be married?"

"I shall do as I think proper," replied the lady; "and I'll thank you for none of your indelicate insinuations." So saying, the lady bounced out of the room into her own, and our midshipmen then made a noise in the passage to intimate that they had come in. They found Mr Hicks looking very red and vice-consular indeed, but he recovered himself; and Captain Hogg making *his* appearance, they went to dinner; but Miss Julia would not make *her* appearance, and

Mr Hicks was barely civil to the captain, but he was soon afterwards called out, and our midshipmen went into the office to enable the two lovers to meet. They were heard then talking together, and after a time they said less, and their language was more tender.

"Let us see what's going on, Jack," said Gascoigne; and they walked softly, so as to perceive the two lovers, who were too busy to be on the look-out.

Captain Hogg was requesting a lock of his mistress's hair. The plump Julia could deny him nothing; she let fall her flaxen tresses, and taking out the scissors cut off a thick bunch from her hair behind, which she presented to the captain; it was at least a foot and a half long, and an inch in circumference. The captain took it in his immense hand, and thrust it into his coat-pocket behind, but one thrust down to the bottom would not get it in, so he thrust again and again until it was all coiled away like a cable in a tier.

"That's a liberal girl," whispered Jack, "she gives by *wholesale* what it will take some time to *retail*. But here comes Mr Hicks, let's give them warning; I like Hogg, and as she fancies pork, she shall have it, if I can contrive to help them."

That night Gascoigne went again on the roof, and after waiting some time heard the same air repeated: he waited until it was concluded, and then, in a very low tone, sung it himself to the words he had arranged for it. For some time all was silent, and then the singing recommenced, but it was not to the same air. Gascoigne waited until the new air had been repeated several times, and then, giving full scope to his fine tenor voice, sang the first air again. It echoed through the silence of the night air, and then he waited, but in vain; the soft voice of the female was heard no more, and Gascoigne retired to rest.

This continued for three or four nights, Gascoigne singing the same airs the ensuing night that he had heard the preceding, until at last it appeared that the female had no longer any fear, but changed the airs so as to be amused with the repetition of them next evening. On the fifth night she sang the first air, and our midshipman responding, she then sang another, until she had sung them all, waiting each time for the response. The wall was not more than eight feet high, and Gascoigne now determined, with the assistance of Jack, to have a sight of his unknown songstress. He asked Captain Hogg to bring on shore some inch line, and he contrived to make a ladder with three or four poles which were upstairs, used for drying linen. He fixed them against the wall without noise, all ready for the evening. It was a beautiful, clear moonlight night, when he went up, accompanied by Jack. The air was again sung, and repeated by Gascoigne, who then softly mounted the ladder, held by Jack, and raised his head above the wall; he perceived a young Moorish girl, splendidly dressed, half-lying on an ottoman, with her eyes fixed upon the moon, whose rays enabled him to observe that she was indeed beautiful. She appeared lost in contemplation; and Gascoigne would have given the world to have divined her thoughts. Satisfied with what he had seen, he descended, and singing one of the airs, he then repeated the words, "Do not be afraid—I love you—I cannot speak your language." He then sang another of the airs, and after he had finished he again repeated the words in Arabic; but there was no reply. He sang the third air, and again repeated the words, when, to his delight, he heard an answer in Lingua Franca.

"Can you speak in this tongue?"

"Yes," replied Gascoigne, "I can, Allah be praised! Be not afraid—I love you."

"I know you not; who are you? you are not of my people."

"No, but I will be anything that you wish. I am a Frank, and an English officer."

At this reply of Gascoigne there was a pause.

"Am I then despised?" said Gascoigne.

"No, not despised; but you are not of my people, or of my land; speak no more, or you will be heard."

"I obey," replied Gascoigne, "since you wish it; but I shall pine till to-morrow's moon. I go to dream of you. Allah protect you!"

"How amazingly poetical you were in your language, Ned," said Easy, when they went down into their room.

"To be sure, Jack, I've read the *Arabian Nights*. You never saw such eyes in your life; what a houri she is!"

"Is she as handsome as Agnes, Ned?"

"Twice as handsome by moonlight."

"That's all moonshine, and so will be your courting, for it will come to nothing."

"Not if I can help it."

"Why, Gascoigne, what would you do with a wife?"

"Just exactly what you would do, Jack."

"I mean, my dear Ned, can you afford to marry?"

"Not while the old governor lives, but I know he has some money in the funds. He told me one day that I could not expect more than three thousand pounds. You know I have sisters."

"And before you come into that you'll have three thousand children."

"That's a large family, Jack," replied Gascoigne, bursting out into laughter, in which our hero joined.

"Well, you know I only wanted to argue the point with you."

"I know that, Jack. But I think we're counting our chickens before they are hatched, which is foolish."

"In every other case except when we venture upon matrimony."

"Why, Jack, you're becoming quite sensible."

"My wisdom is for my friends, my folly for myself. Good-night."

But Jack did not go to sleep.

"I must not allow Gascoigne to do such a foolish thing," thought he. "Marry a dark girl on midshipman's pay, if he succeeds—get his throat cut if he does not."

As Jack said, his wisdom was for his friends, and he was so generous that he reserved none for his own occasions.

Miss Julia Hicks, as we before observed, set the fashions at Tetuan, and her style of dress was not unbecoming. The Moorish women wore large veils, or they may be called what you will, for their head-dresses descend to their heels at times and cover the whole body, leaving an eye to peep with, and hiding everything else. Now Miss Hicks found this much more convenient than the bonnet, as she might walk out in the heat of the sun without burning her fair skin, and stare at everybody and everything without being stared at in return. She therefore never went out without one of these overalls, composed of several yards of fine muslin. Her dress in the house was usually of coloured sarcenet, for a small vessel came into the port one day during her father's lifetime, unloaded a great quantity of bales of goods with English marks, and, as the vessel had gone out in ballast, there was a surmise on his part by what means they came into the captain's possession. He therefore cited the captain up to the governor, but the affair was amicably arranged by the vice-consul receiving about one quarter of the cargo in bales of silks and muslins. Miss Hicks had therefore all her dresses of blue, green, and yellow sarcenet, which, with the white muslin overall, made her as conspicuous as the only Frankish lady in the town had a right to be, and there was not a dog which barked in Tetuan which did not know the sister of the vice-consul, although few had seen her face.

Now it occurred to Jack, as Gascoigne was determined to carry on his amour, that in case of surprise it would be as well if he dressed himself as Miss Hicks. He proposed it to Gascoigne the next morning, who approved of the idea, and in the course of the day, when Miss Hicks was busy with Captain Hogg, he contrived to abstract one of her dresses and muslin overalls, which he could do in safety, as there were plenty of them, for Miss Hicks was not troubled with mantua-makers' bills.

When Gascoigne went up on the roof the ensuing night, he put on the apparel of Miss Hicks, and looked very like her as far as figure went, although a little taller. He waited for the Moorish girl to sing, but she did not; so he crept up the ladder and looked over the wall, when he observed that she was reclining as before in deep thought. His head, covered with the muslin, caught her eye, and she gave a faint scream.

"Fear not, lady," said Gascoigne, "it is not the first time that I have beheld that sweet face. I sigh for a companion. What would I not give to be sitting by your side! I am not of your creed, 'tis true, but does it therefore follow that we should not love each other?"

The Moorish girl was about to reply, when Gascoigne received an answer from a quarter whence he little expected it. It was from the Moor himself, who, hearing his daughter's scream, had come swiftly up to the roof.

"Does the Frankish lily wish to mingle her perfumes with the dark violet?" said he; for he had often seen the sister of the vice-consul, and he imagined it was she who had come on the roof and ascended the wall to speak with his daughter.

Gascoigne had presence of mind to avail himself of this fortunate mistake.

"I am alone, worthy Moor," replied he, pulling the muslin over his face, "and I pine for a companion. I have been charmed by the nightingale on the roof of your dwelling; but I thought not to meet the face of a man when I took courage to climb this ladder."

"If the Frankish lily will have courage to descend, she can sit by the side of the dark violet."

Gascoigne thought it advisable to make no reply.

"Fear not," said the old Moor; "what is an old man but a woman!" and the Moor brought a ladder, which he placed against the wall.

After a pause Gascoigne said, "It is my fate"; and he then descended, and was led by the Moor to the mattress upon which his daughter reclined. The Moor then took his seat near them, and they entered into conversation. Gascoigne knew quite enough of the vice-consul and his sister to play his part, and he thought proper to tell the Moor that her brother wished to give her as wife to the captain of the ship, whom she abhorred, and would take her to a cold and foggy climate; that she had been born here, and wished to live and die here, and would prefer passing her life in his women's apartments to leaving this country. At which, Abdel Faza, for such was his name, felt very amorous. He put his hand to his forehead, salaamed, and told Gascoigne that his zenana,* and all that were in it, were hers, as well as his house and himself. After an hour's conversation, in which Azar, his daughter, did not join, the old Moor asked Gascoigne to descend into the women's apartment; and observing his daughter's silence, said to her—

"Azar, you are angry that this Frankish houri should come to the apartments of which you have hitherto been sole mistress. Fear not, you will soon be another's, for Osman Ali has asked thee for his wife, and I have listened to his request."

Now Osman Ali was as old as her father, and Azar hated him. She offered her hand tremblingly, and led Gascoigne into the zenana. The Moor attended them to the threshold, bowed, and left them.

That Gascoigne had time to press his suit, and that he did not lose such a golden opportunity, may easily be imagined, and her father's communication relative to Osman Ali very much assisted our midshipman's cause.

He left the zenana, like most midshipmen, in love; that is, a little above quicksilver boiling heat. Jack, who had remained in a state of some suspense all this time, was not sorry to hear voices in an amicable tone, and in a few minutes afterwards he perceived that Gascoigne was ascending the ladder. It occurred to our hero that it was perhaps advisable that he should not be seen, as the Moor in his gallantry might come up the ladder with his supposed lady. He was right, for Abdel Faza not only followed her up the ladder on his side but assisted her to descend on the other, and with great ceremony took his leave.

Gascoigne hastened to Jack, who had been peeping, and gave him a detail of what had passed, describing Azar as the most beautiful, fascinating, and fond creature that ever was created. After half an

---

* Zenana: Part of a house set aside for women.

hour's relation he stopped short, because he discovered that Jack was fast asleep.

The visits of Gascoigne were repeated every night; old Abdel Faza became every time more gallant, and our midshipman was under the necessity of assuming a virtue if he had it not. He pretended to be very modest.

In the meantime Captain Hogg continued his attentions to the real Miss Hicks. The mate proceeded to get the bullocks on board, and as more than three weeks had already passed away, it was time to think of departing for Toulon; but Captain Hogg was too much in love; and as for Gascoigne, he intended, like all midshipmen in love, to give up the service. Jack reasoned with the captain, who appeared to listen to reason, because Miss Hicks had agreed to follow his fortunes, and crown his transports in the transport *Mary Ann*.* He therefore proposed that they should get away as fast as they could, and as soon as they had weighed the anchor he would come on shore, take off Miss Hicks, and make all sail for Toulon.

Jack might have suffered this; the difficulty was with Gascoigne, who would not hear of going away without his lovely Azar. At last Jack planned a scheme which he thought would succeed, and which would be a good joke to tell the governor. He therefore appeared to consent to Gascoigne's carrying off his little Moor, and they canvassed how it was to be managed. Jack then told Gascoigne that he had hit upon a plan which would succeed. "I find," said he, "from Captain Hogg, that he has an intention of carrying off Miss Hicks, and when I sounded him as to his having a lady with him, he objected to it immediately, saying, that he must have all the cabin to himself and his intended. Now, in the first place, I have no notion of giving up the cabin to Miss Hicks or Mrs Hogg. It will be very uncomfortable to be shut out, because he wishes to make love; I therefore am determined that he shall not take off Miss Hicks. He has proposed to me that he shall go on board, and get the brig under way, leaving me with a boat on shore to sign the vouchers, and that Miss Hicks shall slip into the boat when I go off at dusk. Now I will not bring off Miss Hicks; if he wants to marry her, let him do it when I am not on board. I have paid for everything, and I consider the cabin as mine.

"Look you, Ned, if you wish to carry off your little Moor, there is

---

* *Mary Ann:* The same vessel Marryat called *Eliza Ann* on page 191.

but one way, and that is a very simple one; leave her a dress of Miss Hicks's when you go there to-morrow night, and tell her to slip down at dusk, and come out of the house: all the danger will be in her own house, for as soon as she is out, she will be supposed to be the vice-consul's sister, and will not be observed or questioned. I will look out for and bring her on board instead of Miss Hicks. Hogg will have the brig under way, and will be too happy to make all sail, and she shall lock the cabin inside, so that the mistake shall not be discovered till the next morning, and we shall have a good laugh at Captain Hogg."

Gascoigne pronounced that Jack's scheme was capital, and agreed to it, thanking him, and declaring that he was the best friend that he ever had. "So I will be," thought Jack, "but you will not acknowledge it at first." Jack then went to Captain Hogg, and appeared to enter warmly into his views, but told him that Hicks suspected what was going on, and had told him so, at the same time declaring that he would not lose sight of his sister until after Hogg was on board.

"Now," says Jack, "you know you cannot do the thing by main force; so the best plan will be for you to go on board and get under way, leaving me to bring off Miss Hicks, when her brother will imagine all danger to be over."

"Many thanks, Mr Easy," replied Captain Hogg; "it will be capital, and I'll arrange it all with my Sophy. How very kind of you!"

"But, Hogg, will you promise me secrecy?"

"Yes," replied the captain.

"That Gascoigne is a very silly fellow, and wants to run away with a girl he has made acquaintance with here; and what do you think he has proposed? that after the ship was under way, that I shall carry her off in the boat; and he has borrowed one of the dresses of Miss Hicks, that it may appear to be her. I have agreed to it, but as I am determined that he shall not commit such a folly, I shall bring off Miss Hicks instead; and, observe, Hogg, he is that sort of wild fellow, that if he was to find that I had cheated him, he would immediately go on shore and be left behind; therefore we must hand Miss Hicks down in the cabin, and she will lock the door all night, so that he may not observe the trick till the next morning, and then we shall have a fine laugh at him."

Captain Hogg replied it would be an excellent joke, as Gascoigne did before him.

Now it must be observed, that the water and the bullocks, and the sheep and fowls, were all on board; and Mr Hicks, having received his money from Jack, had very much altered his manner; he was barely civil, for as he had got all he could out of our hero, he was anxious to get rid of him as well as of Captain Hogg. Our hero was very indignant at this, but as it would not suit his present views, pretended not to notice it—on the contrary, he professed the warmest friendship for the vice-consul, and took an opportunity of saying that he could not return his kindness in a better way than by informing him of the plot which had been arranged. He then told him of the intended escape of his sister, and that he was the person intended to bring her off.

"Infamous, by heavens!" cried the vice-consul; "I shall write to the foreign office on the subject."

"I think," said Jack, "it will be much better to do what I shall propose, which will end in a hearty laugh, and to the confusion of Captain Hogg. Do you dress yourself in your sister's clothes, and I will bring you off instead of her. Let him imagine that he has your sister secure; I will hand you down to the cabin, and do you lock yourself in. He cannot sail without my orders, and I will not sign the vouchers. The next morning we will open the cabin-door and have a good laugh at him. Desire your boat to be off at daylight to take you on shore, and I will then make him proceed to Toulon forthwith. It will be a capital joke."

So thought the vice-consul, as well as Gascoigne and Captain Hogg. He shook hands with Jack, and was as civil to him as before.

That night Gascoigne left one of Miss Hicks's many dresses with Azar, who agreed to follow his fortunes, and who packed up all the jewels and money she could lay her hands upon. Poor little child, she trembled with fear and delight. Miss Hicks smuggled, as she thought, a box of clothes on board, and in the box was her fortune of three hundred dollars. Mr Hicks laughed in his sleeve, so did Jack; and every one went to bed with expectations that their wishes would be realised. After an early dinner, Captain Hogg and Gascoigne went on board, both squeezing Jack's hand as if they were never to see him again, and looks of intelligence passed between all the parties.

As soon as they were out of the door the vice-consul chuckled, and Miss Hicks, who thought he chuckled at the idea of having rid himself of Captain Hogg, chuckled still more as she looked at our hero, who was her confidant; and our hero, for reasons known to the reader, chuckled more than either of them.

A little before dark, the boat was sent on shore from the brig, which was now under way, and Mr Hicks, as had been agreed, said that he should go into the office and prepare the vouchers—that is, put on his sister's clothes. Miss Hicks immediately rose, and wishing our hero a pleasant voyage, as had been agreed, said that she should retire for the night, as she had a bad headache—she wished her brother good-night, and went into her room to wait another hour, when our hero, having shoved off the boat to deceive the vice-consul, was to return, meet her in the garden, and take her off to the brig. Our hero then went into the office and assisted the vice-consul, who took off all his own clothes and tied them up in a handkerchief, intending to resume them after he had gone into the cabin.

As soon as he was ready, Jack carried his bundle and led the supposed Miss Hicks down to the boat. They shoved off in a great hurry, and Jack took an opportunity of dropping Mr Hicks's bundle overboard. As soon as they arrived alongside, Mr Hicks ascended, and was handed by Jack down into the cabin: he squeezed Jack's hand as he entered, saying in a whisper, "To-morrow morning what a laugh we shall have!" and then he locked the door. In the meantime the boat was hooked on and hoisted up, and Jack took the precaution to have the dead lights lowered, that Mr Hicks might not be able to ascertain what was going on. Gascoigne came up to our hero and squeezed his hand.

"I'm so much obliged to you, Jack. I say, to-morrow morning what a laugh we shall have!"

As soon as the boat was up, and the mainyard filled, Captain Hogg also came up to our hero, shaking him by the hand and thanking him; and he too concluded by saying, "I say, Mr Easy, to-morrow morning what a laugh we shall have!"

"Let those laugh who win," thought Jack.

The wind was fair, the watch was set, the course was steered, and all went down to their hammocks, and went to sleep, waiting for to-morrow morning. Mr Hicks, also, having nothing better to do, went to sleep, and by the morning dawn, the transport *Mary Ann* was more than a hundred miles from the African shore.

CHAPTER XXIV

Our hero plays the very devil.

W E MUST leave the reader to imagine the effect of the next morning's dénouement. Everyone was in a fury except Jack, who did nothing but laugh. The captain wanted to return to obtain Miss Hicks, Gascoigne to obtain Azar, and the vice-consul to obtain his liberty—but the wind was foul for their return, and Jack soon gained the captain on his side. He pointed out to him that, in the first place, if he presumed to return, he would forfeit his charter bond; in the second, he would have to pay for all the bullocks that died; in the third, that if he wished to take Miss Hicks as his wife, he must not first injure her character by having her on board before the solemnity; and lastly, that he could always go and marry her whenever he pleased; the brother could not prevent him. All this was very good advice, and the captain became quite calm and rational, and set his studding-sails below and aloft.

As for Gascoigne, it was no use reasoning with him, so it was agreed that he should have satisfaction as soon as they could get on shore again. Mr Hicks was the most violent; he insisted that the vessel should return, while both Jack and the captain refused, although he threatened them with the whole foreign office. He insisted upon having his clothes, but Jack replied that they had tumbled overboard as they pulled from the shore. He then commanded the mate and men to take the vessel back, but they laughed at him and his woman's clothes. "At all events, I'll have you turned out of the service," said he to our hero in his fury. "I shall be extremely obliged to you," said Jack—and Captain Hogg was so much amused with the vice-consul's appearance in his sister's clothes, that he quite forgot his own disappointment in laughing at his intended brother-in-law. He made friends again with Jack, who regained his ascendancy, and ordered out the porter on the capstern-head. They had an excellent dinner, but Mr Hicks refused to join them, which however did not spoil the appetite of Jack or the captain: as for Gascoigne, he could not eat a mouthful, but he drank to excess, looking over the rim of his tumbler, as if he could devour our hero, who only laughed the more. Mr Hicks had applied to the men to lend him some clothes, but Jack had foreseen that, and he was omnipotent. There was not a jacket or a pair of trousers to be had for love or money. Mr Hicks then considered it advisable to lower his tone, and he applied to Captain Hogg, who begged to be excused without he consented to his marriage with his sister, to which Mr Hicks gave an indignant negative. He then applied to Gascoigne, who told him in a very surly tone to go to h——ll. At last he applied to our hero, who laughed, and said that he would see him d——d first. So Mr Hicks sat down in his petticoats and vowed revenge. Gascoigne, who had drunk much and eaten nothing, turned in and went to sleep—while Captain Hogg and our hero drank porter on the capstern. Thus passed the first day, and the wind was famously fair—the bullocks lowed, the cocks crew, the sheep baa'd, and the *Mary Ann* made upwards of two hundred miles. Jack took possession of the other berth in the cabin, and his Majesty's representative was obliged to lie down in his petticoats upon a topsail which lay between decks, with a bullock on each side of him, who every now and then made a dart at him with their horns, as if they knew that it was to him that they were indebted for their embarkation and being destined to drive the scurvy out of the Toulon fleet.

We cannot enter into the details of the passage, which, as the wind was fair, was accomplished in ten days without the loss of a bullock. During this time Mr Hicks condescended to eat without speaking, imagining that the hour of retribution would come when they joined the admiral. Gascoigne gradually recovered himself, but did not speak to our hero, who continued to laugh and drink porter. On the eleventh morning they were in the midst of the Toulon fleet, and Mr Hicks smiled exultingly as he passed our hero in his petticoats, and wondered that Jack showed no signs of trepidation.

The fleet hove-to, Jack ran under the admiral's stern, lowered down his boat, and went on board, showed his credentials, and reported his bullocks. The general signal was made, there was a fair division of the spoil, and then the admiral asked our hero whether the master of the transport had any other stock on board. Jack replied that he had not; but that, having been told by the governor of Malta that they might be acceptable, he had bought a few sheep and some dozen of fowls, which were much at his service, if he would accept of them. The admiral was much obliged to the governor, and also to Jack, for thinking of him, but would not, of course, accept of the stock without paying for them. He requested him to send all of them on board that he could spare, and then asked Jack to dine with him, for Jack had put on his best attire, and looked very much of a gentleman.

"Mr Easy," said the flag-captain, who had been looking at the transport with his glass, "is that the master's wife on board?"

"No, sir," replied Jack; "it's the vice-consul."

"What, in petticoats! the vice-consul?"

"Yes, the vice-consul of Tetuan. He came on board in that dress when the brig was under way, and I considered it my duty not to delay, being aware how very important it was that the fleet should be provided with fresh beef."

"What is all this, Mr Easy?" said the admiral; "there has been some trick here. You will oblige me by coming into the cabin."

Easy followed the admiral and flag-captain into the cabin, and then boldly told the whole story how he tricked them all. It was impossible for either of them to help laughing, and when they began to laugh, it was almost as impossible to stop.

"Mr Easy," said the admiral at last, "I do not altogether blame you; it appears that the captain of the transport would have delayed sailing because he was in love—and that Mr Gascoigne would have stayed behind because he was infatuated, independent of the ill-will against the English which would have been excited by the abduction of the girl. But I think you might have contrived to manage all that without putting the vice-consul in petticoats."

"I acted to the best of my judgment, sir," replied Jack, very humbly.

"And altogether you have done well. Captain Malcolm, send a boat for the vice-consul."

Mr Hicks was too impatient to tell his wrongs to care for his being in his sister's clothes: he came on board, and although the tittering was great, he imagined that it would soon be all in his favour, when it was known that he was a diplomatic. He told his story, and waited for the decision of the admiral, which was to crush our hero, who stood with the midshipmen on the lee side of the deck; but the admiral replied, "Mr Hicks, in the first place, this appears to me to be a family affair concerning the marriage of your sister, with which I have nothing to do. You went on board of your own free will in woman's clothes. Mr Easy's orders were positive, and he obeyed them. It was his duty to sail as soon as the transport was ready. You may forward your complaint if you please, but, as a friend, I tell you that it will probably occasion your dismissal; for these kind of pranks are not understood at the foreign office. You may return to the transport, which, after she has touched at Mahon, will proceed again to Tetuan. The boat is alongside, sir."

Mr Hicks, astonished at the want of respect paid to a vice-consul, shoved his petticoats between his legs, and went down the side amidst the laughter of the whole of the ship's company. Our hero dined with the admiral, and was well received. He got his orders to sail that night for Minorca, and as soon as dinner was over he returned on board, where he found Captain Hogg very busy selling his porter—Gascoigne walking the deck in a brown study*—and Mr Hicks solus abaft, sulking in his petticoats.

As soon as they were clear of the boats, the *Mary Ann* hoisted her ensign and made sail, and as all the porter was not yet sold, Jack ordered up a bottle.

Jack was much pleased with the result of his explanation with the admiral, and he felt that, for once, he had not only got into no scrape himself, but that he had prevented others. Gascoigne walked the deck gloomily; the fact was, that he was very unhappy: he had had time to reflect, and now that the first violence had subsided, he felt that our hero had done him a real service, and had prevented him from committing an act of egregious folly; and yet he had summoned this friend to meet him in the field—and such had been his gratitude. He would have given the world to recall what had passed, and to make friends, but he felt ashamed, as most people do, to acknowledge his error; he had, however, almost made up his mind to it, and was walking up and down thinking in what manner he might contrive it, when Jack, who was sitting, as usual, in a chair by the capstern, with his porter by him, said to himself, "Now I'll lay my life that Ned wants to make friends, and is ashamed to speak first; I may be mistaken, and he may fly off at a tangent; but even if I am, at all events it will not be I who am wrong—I'll try him." Jack waited till Gascoigne passed him again, and then said, looking kindly and knowingly in his face,—

"I say, Ned, will you have a glass of porter?"

Gascoigne smiled, and Jack held out his hand; the reconciliation was effected in a moment, and the subject of quarrel was not canvassed by either party.

* A brown study: Lost in melancholy thoughts.

"We shall be at Minorca in a day or two," observed Jack, after a while; "now I shall be glad to get there. Do you know, Ned, that I feel very much satisfied with myself; I have got into no scrape this time, and I shall, notwithstanding, have a good story to tell the governor when I go to Malta."

"Partly at my expense," replied Gascoigne.

"Why, you will figure a little in it, but others will figure much more."

"I wonder what has become of that poor girl," observed Gascoigne, who could not refrain from mentioning her; "what hurts me most is, that she must think me such a brute."

"No doubt of that, Ned,—take another glass of porter."

"Her father gave me this large diamond."

"The old goat—sell it, and drink his health with it."

"No, I'll keep it in memory of his daughter."

Here Gascoigne fell into a melancholy reverie, and Jack thought of Agnes.

In two days they arrived at Mahon, and found the *Aurora* already there, in the command of Captain Wilson. Mr Hicks had persuaded Captain Hogg to furnish him with clothes, Jack having taken off the injunction as soon as he had quitted the admiral. Mr Hicks was aware, that if the admiral would not listen to his complaint, it was no use speaking to a captain: so he remained on board a pensioner upon Captain Hogg, and after our midshipmen quitted the transport they became very good friends. Mr Hicks consented to the match, and Captain Hogg was made happy. As for poor Azar, she had wandered about until she was tired, in Miss Hicks's dress, and at last returned broken-hearted to her father's, and was admitted by Abdel Faza himself; he imagined it was Miss Hicks, and was in transports—he discovered it was his daughter, and he was in a fury. The next day she went to the zenana of Osman Ali.

When Jack reported himself he did not tell the history of the elopements, that he might not hurt the feelings of Gascoigne. Captain Wilson was satisfied with the manner in which he had executed his orders, and asked him, "whether he preferred staying in the *Harpy*, or following him into the *Aurora*."

Jack hesitated.

"Speak frankly, Mr Easy; if you prefer Captain Sawbridge to me, I shall not be affronted."

"No, sir," replied Easy, "I do not prefer Captain Sawbridge to you; you have both been equally kind to me, but I prefer you. But the fact is, sir, that I do not much like to part with Gascoigne or—"

"Or who?" said the captain, smiling.

"With Mesty, sir; you may think me very foolish, but I should not be alive at this moment, if it had not been for him."

"I do not consider gratitude to be foolish, Mr Easy," replied Captain Wilson. "Mr Gascoigne I intend to take with me, if he chooses to come, as I have a great respect for his father, and no fault to find with him, that is, generally speaking; but as for Mesty—why he is a good man, and as you have behaved yourself very well, perhaps I may think of it."

The next day Mesty was included among the boat's crew taken with him by Captain Wilson, according to the regulations of the service, and appointed to the same situation under the master at arms of the *Aurora*. Gascoigne and our hero were also discharged into the frigate.

As our hero never has shown any remarkable predilection for duty, the reader will not be surprised at his requesting from Captain Wilson a few days on shore, previous to his going on board of the *Aurora*. Captain Wilson allowed the same licence to Gascoigne, as they had both been cooped up for some time on board of a transport. Our hero took up his quarters at the only respectable hotel in the town, and whenever he could meet an officer of the *Aurora*, he very politely begged the pleasure of his company to dinner. Jack's reputation had gone before him, and the midshipmen drank his wine and swore he was a trump. Not that Jack was to be deceived, but, upon the principles of equality, he argued that it was the duty of those who could afford dinners to give them to those who could not. This was a sad error on Jack's part; but he had not yet learnt the value of money; he was such a fool as to think that the only real use of it was to make other people happy. It must, however, be offered in his extenuation that he was a midshipman and a philosopher, and not yet eighteen.

At last Jack had remained so long on shore, keeping open house, and the first lieutenant of the *Aurora* found the officers so much more anxious for leave, now that they were at little or no expense, that he sent him a very polite message, requesting the pleasure of his company on board that evening. Jack returned an equally polite answer, informing the first lieutenant that not being aware that he wished to see him, he had promised to accompany some friends to a masquerade that night, but that he would not fail to pay his respects to him the next day. The first lieutenant admitted the excuse, and our hero, after having entertained half-a-dozen of the *Auroras,* for the *Harpy* had sailed two days before, dressed himself for the masquerade, which was held in a church about two miles and a half from Mahon.

Jack had selected the costume of the *devil,* as being the most appropriate, and mounting a jackass, he rode down in his dress to the masquerade. But, as Jack was just going in, he perceived a yellow carriage, with two footmen in gaudy liveries, draw up, and with his usual politeness, when the footmen opened the door, offered his arm to hand out a fat old dowager covered with diamonds; the lady looked up, and perceiving Jack covered with hair, with his trident and his horns, and long tail, gave a loud scream, and would have fallen had it not been for Captain Wilson, who, in his full uniform, was coming in, and caught her in his arms: while the old lady thanked him, and Captain Wilson bowed, Jack hastily retreated. "I shall make no conquests to-night," thought he; so he entered the church, and joined the crowd; but it was so dense that it was hardly possible to move, and our hero soon got tired of flourishing his trident, and sticking it into people, who wondered what the devil he meant.

"This is stupid work," thought Jack, "I may have more fun out-side": so Jack put on his cloak, left the masquerade, and went out in search of adventures. He walked into the open country, about half a mile, until he came to a splendid house, standing in a garden of orange-trees, which he determined to reconnoitre. He observed that a window was open and lights were in the room; and he climbed up to the window, and just opened the white curtain and looked in. On a bed lay an elderly person, evidently dying, and by the side of the bed were three priests, one of whom held the crucifix in his hand, another the censer, and a third was sitting at a table with a paper, pen, and ink. As Jack understood Spanish, he listened, and heard one of the priests say,—

"Your sins have been enormous, my son, and I cannot give you extreme unction or absolution unless you make some amends."

"I have," answered the moribund, "left money for ten thousand masses to be said for my soul."

"Five hundred thousand masses are not sufficient: how have you gained your enormous wealth? by usury and robbing the poor."

"I have left a thousand dollars to be distributed among the poor on the day of my funeral."

"One thousand dollars is nothing—you must leave all your property to holy church."

"And my children!" replied the dying man, faintly.

"What are your children compared to your salvation? reply not: either consent, or not only do I refuse you the consolation of the dying, but I excommunicate—"

"Mercy, holy father—mercy!" said the old man, in a dying voice.

"There is no mercy, you are damned for ever and ever. Amen. Now hear: *excommunicabo te*—"

"Stop—stop—have you the paper ready?"

"'Tis here, all ready, by which you revoke all former wills, and endow the holy church with your property. We will read it, for God forbid that it should be said that the holy church received an involuntary gift."

"I will sign it," replied the dying man, "but my sight fails me; be quick, absolve me." And the paper was signed, with difficulty, as the priests supported the dying man. "And now—absolve me."

"I do absolve thee," replied the priest, who then went through the ceremony.

"Now this is a confounded rascally business,"* said Jack to himself; who then dropped his cloak, jumped upon the window-sill, opened wide the window-curtains with both hands, and uttered a yelling kind of "ha! ha! ha! ha!"

The priests turned round, saw the demon as they imagined—dropped the paper on the table, and threw themselves with their faces on the floor.

"*Exorciso te*," stammered one.

"Ha! ha! ha! ha!" repeated Jack, entering the room, and taking up the paper which he burnt by the flame of the candle. Our hero looked at the old man on the bed; his jaw had fallen, his eyes were turned. He was dead. Jack then gave one more "ha! ha! ha! ha!" to keep the priests in their places, blew out the candles, made a spring out of the window, caught up his cloak, and disappeared as fast as his legs could carry him.

Jack ran until he was out of breath, and then he stopped, and sat down by the side of the road. It was broad moonlight, and Jack knew not where he was: "but Minorca has not many high roads," thought

---

* "A confounded rascally business": Marryat has conflicting views of Catholics in his works, but here he plays on a number of anti-Catholic stereotypes. Legislation opposed to long-established discrimination against Catholics was passed in 1829.

Jack, "and I shall find my way home. Now, let me see,—I have done some good this evening. I have prevented those rogues from disinheriting a family. I wonder who they are; they ought to be infinitely obliged to me. But if the priests find me out, what shall I do? I never dare come on shore again—they'd have me in the Inquisition. I wonder where I am," said Jack; "I will get on that hill, and see if I can take a departure."

The hill was formed by the road being cut perpendicularly almost through it, and was perhaps some twelve or fourteen feet high. Jack ascended it, and looked about him. "There is the sea, at all events, with the full moon silvering the waves," said Jack, turning from the road, "and here is the road; then that must be the way to Port Mahon. But what comes here?—it's a carriage. Why, it's the yellow carriage of that old lady with her diamonds, and her two splashy footmen!" Jack was watching it as it passed the road under him, when of a sudden, he perceived about a dozen men rush out, and seize the horses' heads,—a discharge of firearms, the coachman dropped off the box, and the two footmen dropped from behind. The robbers then opened the door, and were hauling out the fat old lady covered with diamonds. Jack thought a second—it occurred to him, that although he could not cope with so many, he might frighten them, as he had frightened one set of robbers already that night. The old lady had just been tumbled out of the carriage-door, like a large bundle of clothes tied up for the wash, when Jack, throwing off his cloak, and advancing to the edge of the precipice, with the full moon behind him throwing out his figure in strong relief, raised his trident, and just as they were raising their knives, yelled a most unearthly "ha, ha, ha, ha!" The robbers looked up, and forgetting the masquerade, for there is a double tremor in guilt, screamed with fear; most of them ran away, and dropped after a hundred yards; others remained paralysed and insensible. Jack descended the hill, went to the assistance of the old lady, who had swooned, and had to put her into the carriage; but although our hero was very strong, this was a work of no small difficulty. After one or two attempts, he lowered down the steps and contrived to bump her on the first, from the first he purchased her on the second, and from the second he at last seated her at the door of the carriage. Jack had no time to be over-polite. He then threw her back into the bottom of the carriage, her heels went up to the top, Jack shoved in her petticoats as fast as he could, for decency, and then shutting the door seized the reins, and jumped upon the box. "I don't know the way," thought Jack, "but we must needs go when the *devil drives*"; so sticking his trident into the horses, they set off at a rattling pace, passing over the bodies of the two robbers, who had held the reins, and who both lay before him in a swoon. As soon as he had brought the horses into a trot, he slackened the reins, for, as Jack wisely argued, they will be certain to go home if I let them have their own way. The horses, before they arrived at the town, turned off, and stopped at a large country house. That he might not frighten the people, Jack had put on his cloak, and taken off his mask and head-piece, which he had laid beside him on the box. At the sound of the carriage-wheels the servants came out, when Jack, in few words, told them what had happened. Some of the servants ran in, and a young lady made her appearance, while the others were helping the old lady out of the carriage, who had recovered her senses, but had been so much frightened that she had remained in the posture in which Jack had put her.

As soon as she was out, Jack descended from the coach-box and entered the house. He stated to the young lady what had taken place, and how opportunely he had frightened away the robbers, just as they were about to murder her relation; and also suggested the propriety of sending after the servants who had fallen in the attack; which was immediately done by a strong and well-armed party collected for the occasion. Jack, having made his speech, made a very polite bow and took his leave, stating that he was an English officer belonging to a frigate in the harbour. He knew his way back, and in half an hour was again at the inn, and found his comrades. Jack thought it advisable to keep his own secret, and therefore merely said, that he had taken a long walk in the country; and soon afterwards went to bed.

The next morning our hero, who was always a man of his word, packed up his portmanteau, and paid his bill. He had just completed this heavy operation, when somebody wanted to speak to him, and a sort of half-clerical, half-legal sort of looking gentleman was introduced, who, with a starched face and prim air, said that he came to request in writing the name of the officer who was dressed as a devil, in the masquerade of the night before.

Jack looked at his interrogator, and thought of the priests and the Inquisition. "No, no," thought he, "that won't do; a name I must give, but it shall be one that you dare not meddle with. A midshipman you might get hold of, but it's more than the whole island dare to touch a post-captain of one of his Majesty's frigates." So Jack took the paper and wrote Captain Henry Wilson, of his Majesty's ship *Aurora*.

The prim man made a prim bow, folded up the paper and left the room.

Jack threw the waiter half a doubloon, lighted his cigar, and went on board.

CHAPTER XXV

In which the old proverb is illustrated, "That you must not count your chickens before they are hatched."

THE FIRST LIEUTENANT of the *Aurora* was a very good officer in many respects, but, as a midshipman, he had contracted the habit of putting his hands in his pockets, and could never keep them out, even when the ship was in a gale of wind; and hands are of some use in a heavy lurch. He had more than once received serious injury from falling on these occasions, but habit was too powerful; and, although he had once broken his leg by falling down the hatchway, and had moreover a large scar on his forehead, received from being thrown to leeward against one of the guns, he still continued the practice; indeed, it was said that once when it was necessary for him to go aloft, he had actually taken the two first rounds of the Jacob's ladder without withdrawing them, until, losing his balance, he discovered that it was not quite so easy to go aloft with his hands in his pockets. In fact, there was no getting up his hands, even when all hands were turned up. He had another peculiarity, which was, that he had taken a peculiar fancy to a quack medicine, called Enouy's Universal Medicine for all Mankind; and Mr Pottyfar was convinced in his own mind that the label was no libel, except from the greatness of its truth. In his opinion, it cured everything, and he spent one of his quarterly bills every year in bottles of this stuff; which he not only took himself every time he was unwell, but occasionally when quite well, to prevent his falling sick. He recommended it to everybody in the ship, and nothing pleased him so much as to give a dose of it to everyone who could be persuaded to take it. The officers laughed at him, but it was generally behind his back, for he became very angry if contradicted upon this one point, upon which he certainly might be considered to be a little cracked. He was indefatigable in making proselytes to his creed, and expatiated upon the virtues of the medicine for an hour running, proving the truth of his assertions by a pamphlet, which, with his hands, he always carried in his trousers' pocket.

Jack reported himself when he came on board, and Mr Pottyfar, who was on the quarter-deck at the time, expressed a hope that Mr Easy would take his share of the duty, now that he had had such a spell on shore; to which Jack very graciously acceded, and then went down below, where he found Gascoigne and his new messmates, with most of whom he was already acquainted.

"Well, Easy," said Gascoigne, "have you had enough of the shore?"

"Quite," replied Jack, recollecting that, after the events of the night before, he was just as well on board; "I don't intend to ask for any more leave."

"Perhaps it's quite as well, for Mr Pottyfar is not very liberal on that score, I can tell you; there is but one way of getting leave from him."

"Indeed!" replied Jack; "and what is that?"

"You must pretend that you are not well, take some of his quack medicine, and then he will allow you a run on shore to work it off."

"Oh! that's it, is it? well then, as soon as we anchor in Valette, I'll go through a regular course, but not till then."

"It ought to suit you, Jack; it's an equality medicine; cures one disorder just as well as the other."

"Or kills—which levels all the patients. You're right, Gascoigne, I must patronise that stuff—for more reasons than one. Who was that person on deck in mufti?"

"The mufti, Jack; in other words, the chaplain of the ship, but he's a prime sailor, nevertheless."

"How's that?"

"Why, he was brought up on the quarter-deck, served his time, was acting lieutenant for two years, and then, somehow or another, he bore up for the church."

"Indeed—what were his reasons?"

"No one knows—but they say he has been unhappy ever since."

"Why so?"

"Because he did a very foolish thing, which cannot now be remedied. He supposed at the time that he would make a good parson, and now that he has long got over his fit, he finds himself wholly unfit for it—he is still the officer in heart, and is always struggling with his natural bent, which is very contrary to what a parson should feel."

"Why don't they allow parsons to be broke by a court-martial, and turned out of the service, or to resign their commissions, like other people?"

"It won't do, Jack—they serve heaven—there's a difference between that and serving his Majesty."

"Well, I don't understand these things. When do we sail?"

"The day after to-morrow."

"To join the fleet of Toulon?"

"Yes: but I suppose we shall be driven on the Spanish coast going there. I never knew a man-of-war that was not."

"No; wind always blows from the south, going up the Mediterranean."

"Perhaps you'll take another prize, Jack—mind you don't go away without the articles of war."

"I won't go away without Mesty, if I can help it. O dear, how abominable a midshipman's berth is after a long run on shore! I positively must go on deck and look at the shore, if I can do nothing else."

"Why, ten minutes ago you had had enough of it?"

"Yes, but ten minutes here has made me feel quite sick. I shall go to the first lieutenant for a dose."

"I say, Easy, we must both be physicked on the same day."

"To be sure; but stop till we get to Malta."

Jack went on deck, made acquaintance with the chaplain and some of the officers whom he had not known, then climbed up into the maintop, where he took a seat on the armolest, and, as he looked at the shore, thought over the events that had passed, until Agnes came to his memory, and he thought only of her. When a mid is in love, he always goes aloft to think of the object of his affection; why, I don't know, except that his reverie is not so likely to be disturbed by an order from a superior officer.

The *Aurora* sailed on the second day, and, with a fine breeze, stood across, making as much northing as easting; the consequence was, that one fine morning they saw the Spanish coast before they saw the Toulon fleet. Mr Pottyfar took his hands out of his pockets, because he could not examine the coast through a telescope without so doing; but this, it is said, was the first time that he had done so on the quarter-deck from the day that the ship had sailed from Port Mahon. Captain Wilson was also occupied with his telescope, so were many of the officers and midshipmen, and the men at the mast-heads used their eyes, but there was nothing but a few small fishing-boats to be seen. So they all went down to breakfast, as the ship was hove-to close in with the land.

"What will Easy bet," said one of the midshipmen, "that we don't see a prize to-day?"

"I will not bet that we do not see a vessel—but I'll bet you what you please, that we do not take one before twelve o'clock at night."

"No, no, that won't do—just let the teapot travel over this way, for it's my forenoon watch."

"It's a fine morning," observed one of the mates, of the name of Martin; "but I've a notion it won't be a fine evening."

"Why not?" inquired another.

"I've now been eight years in the Mediterranean, and know something about the weather. There's a watery sky, and the wind is very steady. If we are not under double-reefed topsails to-night, say I'm no conjurer."

"That you will be, all the same, if we are under bare poles," said another.

"You're devilish free with your tongue, my youngster.—Easy, pull his ears for me."

"Pull them easy, Jack, then," said the boy, laughing.

"All hands make sail!" now resounded at the hatchways.

"There they are, depend upon it," cried Gascoigne, catching up his hat and bolting out of the berth, followed by all the others except Martin, who had just been relieved, and thought that his presence in the waist might be dispensed with for the short time, at least, which it took him to swallow a cup of tea.

It was very true; a galliot* and four lateen vessels had just made their appearance round the easternmost point, and as soon as they observed the frigate, had hauled their wind. In a minute the *Aurora* was under a press of canvas, and the telescopes were all directed to the vessels.

"All deeply laden, sir," observed Mr Hawkins, the chaplain; "how the topsail of the galliot is scored!"

* Galliot: A small galley, which is a low vessel propelled by oars.

"They have a fresh breeze just now," observed Captain Wilson to the first lieutenant.

"Yes, sir, and it's coming down fast."

"Hands by the royal halyards, there."

The *Aurora* careened with the canvas to the rapidly-increasing breeze.

"Top-gallant sheet and halyards."

"Luff* you may, quarter-master; luff, I tell you. A small pull of that weather maintop-gallant brace—that will do," said the master.

"Top-men aloft there;—stand by to clew up the royals†—and, Captain Wilson, shall we take them in?—I'm afraid of that pole—it bends now like a coach-whip," said Mr Pottyfar, looking up aloft, with his hands in both pockets.

"In royals—lower away."

"They are going about, sir," said the second lieutenant, Mr Haswell.

"Look out," observed the chaplain, "it's coming."

Again the breeze increased, and the frigate was borne down.

"Hands reef topsails in stays, Mr Pottyfar."

"Aye, aye, sir—'bout ship."

The helm was put down and the topsails lowered and reefed in stays.

"Very well, my lads, very well indeed," said Captain Wilson.

Again the topsails were hoisted and top-gallant sheets home.‡ It was a strong breeze, although the water was smooth, and the *Aurora* dashed through at the rate of eight miles an hour, with her weather leeches§ lifting.

"Didn't I tell you so?" said Martin to his messmates on the gangway; "but there's more yet, my boys."

"We must take the top-gallant sails off her," said Captain Wilson, looking aloft—for the frigate now careened to her bearings, and the wind was increasing and squally. "Try them a little longer"; but another squall came suddenly—the halyards were lowered, and the sails clewed up and furled.

In the meantime the frigate had rapidly gained upon the vessels,

---

* Luff: To steer or sail in the direction from which the wind is blowing.

† Clew up the royals: To clew up means to draw up a sail's lower ends in preparation for furling. A royal is a small sail used in light winds.

‡ Sheets home: To sheet home is to haul in a sail until it is as tight and straight as possible.

§ Weather leeches: The edges of the sail on the side on which the wind is blowing.

which still carried on every stitch of canvas, making short tacks in-shore. The *Aurora* was again put about with her head towards them, and they were not two points on her weather-bow. The sky, which had been clear in the morning, was now overcast, the sun was obscured with opaque white clouds, and the sea was rising fast. Another ten minutes, and then they were under double-reefed top-sails and the squalls were accompanied with heavy rain. The frigate now dashed through the waves, foaming in her course, and straining under the press of sail. The horizon was so thick that the vessels ahead were no longer to be seen.

"We shall have it, I expect," said Captain Wilson.

"Didn't I say so?" observed Martin to Gascoigne. "We take no prizes this day, depend upon it."

"We must have another hand to the wheel, sir, if you please," said the quarter-master, who was assisting the helmsman.

Mr Pottyfar, with his hands concealed as usual, stood by the cap-stern. "I fear, sir, we cannot carry the mainsail much longer."

"No," observed the chaplain, "I was thinking so."

"Captain Wilson, if you please, we are very close in," said the master; "don't you think we had better go about?"

"Yes, Mr Jones.—Hands about ship—and—yes, by heavens we must!—up mainsail."

The mainsail was taken off, and the frigate appeared to be imme-diately relieved. She no longer jerked and plunged as before.

"We're very near the land, Captain Wilson; thick as it is, I think I can make out the loom of it—shall we wear round, sir?" continued the master.

"Yes,—hands wear ship—put the helm up."

It was but just in time, for, as the frigate flew round, describing a circle, as she payed off* before the wind, they could perceive the breakers lashing the precipitous coast, not two cables' length from them.

"I had no idea we were so near," observed the captain, compress-ing his lips—"can they see anything of those vessels?"

"I have not seen them this quarter of an hour, sir," replied the signal-man, protecting his glass from the rain under his jacket.

"How's her head now, quarter-master?"

* Payed off: Turned away from the wind.

"South south-east, sir."

The sky now assumed a different appearance—the white clouds had been exchanged for others dark and murky, the wind roared at intervals, and the rain came down in torrents. Captain Wilson went down into the cabin to examine the barometer.

"The barometer has risen," said he on his return on deck. "Is the wind steady?"

"No, sir, she's up and off three points."

"This will end in a south-wester."

The wet and heavy sails now flapped from the shifting of the wind.

"Up with the helm, quarter-master."

"Up it is—she's off to south-by-west."

The wind lulled, the rain came down in a deluge—for a minute it was quite calm, and the frigate was on an even keel.

"Man the braces. We shall be taken aback, directly, depend upon it."

The braces were hardly stretched along before this was the case. The wind flew round to the south-west with a loud roar, and it was fortunate that they were prepared—the yards were braced round, and the master asked the captain, what course they were to steer.

"We must give it up," observed Captain Wilson, holding on by the belaying pin. "Shape our course for Cape Sicie,* Mr Jones."

And the *Aurora* flew before the gale, under her foresail and top-sails close reefed. The weather was now so thick that nothing could be observed twenty yards from the vessel; the thunder pealed, and the lightning darted in every direction over the dark expanse. The watch was called as soon as the sails were trimmed, and all who could went below, wet, uncomfortable, and disappointed.

"What an old Jonah you are, Martin," said Gascoigne.

"Yes, I am," replied he; "but we have the worst to come yet, in my opinion. I recollect, not two hundred miles from where we are now, we had just such a gale in the *Favourite,* and we as nearly went down, when—"

At this moment a tremendous noise was heard above, a shock was felt throughout the whole ship, which trembled fore and aft as if it was about to fall into pieces: loud shrieks were followed by

* Cape Sicie: Cap Sicié, west of Toulon.

plaintive cries, the lower deck was filled with smoke, and the frigate was down on her beam ends.* Without exchanging a word, the whole of the occupants of the berth flew out, and were up the hatchway, not knowing what to think, but convinced that some dreadful accident had taken place.

On their gaining the deck it was at once explained; the foremast of the frigate had been struck by lightning, had been riven into several pieces, and had fallen over the larboard bow, carrying with it the main-topmast and jib-boom. The jagged stump of the foremast was in flames, and burned brightly, notwithstanding the rain fell in torrents. The ship, as soon as the foremast and main topmast had gone overboard, broached-to furiously, throwing the men over the wheel and dashing them senseless against the carronades; the forecastle, the forepart of the main deck, and even the lower deck, were spread with men, either killed or seriously wounded, or insensible from the electric shock. The frigate was on her beam ends, and the sea broke furiously over her; all was dark as pitch, except the light from the blazing stump of the foremast, appearing like a torch, held up by the wild demons of the storm, or when occasionally the gleaming lightning cast a momentary glare, threatening every moment to repeat its attack upon the vessel, while the deafening thunder burst almost on their devoted heads. All was dismay and confusion for a minute or two: at last Captain Wilson, who had himself lost his sight for a short time, called for the carpenter and axes—they climbed up, that is, two or three of them, and he pointed to the mizen-mast; the master was also there, and he cut loose the axes for the seamen to use; in a few minutes the mizen-mast fell over the quarter, and the helm being put hard up, the frigate payed off and slowly righted. But the horror of the scene was not yet over. The boatswain, who had been on the forecastle, had been led below, for his vision was gone for ever. The men who lay scattered about had been examined, and they were assisting them down to the care of the surgeon, when the cry of "Fire!" issued from the lower deck. The ship had taken fire at the coal-hole and carpenter's store-room, and the smoke that now ascended was intense.

"Call the drummer," said Captain Wilson, "and let him beat to quarters—all hands to their stations—let the pumps be rigged and the buckets passed along. Mr Martin, see that the wounded men are

_____
* On her beam ends: The ship was lying on her side.

taken down below. Where's Mr Haswell? Mr Pottyfar, station the men to pass the water on by hand on the lower deck. I will go there myself. Mr Jones, take charge of the ship."

Pottyfar, who actually had taken his hands out of his pockets, hastened down to comply with the captain's orders on the main deck, as Captain Wilson descended to the deck below.

"I say, Jack, this is very different from this morning," observed Gascoigne.

"Yes," replied Jack, "so it is; but I say, Gascoigne, what's the best thing to do?—when the chimney's on fire on shore, they put a wet blanket over it."

"Yes," replied Gascoigne; "but when the coal-hole's on fire on board, they will not find that sufficient."

"At all events, wet blankets must be a good thing, Ned, so let us pull out the hammocks; cut the lanyards and get some out—we can but offer them, you know, and if they do no good, at least it will show our zeal."

"Yes, Jack, and I think when they turn in again, those whose blankets you take will agree with you, that zeal makes the service very uncomfortable. However, I think you are right."

The two midshipmen collected three or four hands, and in a very short time they had more blankets than they could carry—there was no trouble in wetting them, for the main deck was afloat—and followed by the men they had collected, Easy and Gascoigne went down with large bundles in their arms to where Captain Wilson was giving directions to the men.

"Excellent, Mr Easy, excellent, Mr Gascoigne!" said Captain Wilson. "Come, my lads, throw them over now, and stamp upon them well"; the men's jackets and the captain's coat had already been sacrificed to the same object.

Easy called the other midshipmen, and they went up for a further supply; but there was no occasion, the fire had been smothered: still the danger had been so great that the fore magazine had been floated. During all this, which lasted perhaps a quarter of an hour, the frigate had rolled gunwale* under, and many were the accidents which occurred. At last all danger from fire had ceased, and the men were ordered to return to their quarters, when three officers and forty-seven men were found absent—seven of them were dead, most of

* Gunwale: The upper edge of a vessel's side.

them were already under the care of the surgeon, but some were still lying in the scuppers.*

No one had been more active or more brave during this time of danger, than Mr Hawkins, the chaplain. He was everywhere, and when Captain Wilson went down to put out the fire he was there, encouraging the men and exerting himself most gallantly. He and Mesty came aft when all was over, one just as black as the other. The chaplain sat down and wrung his hands—"God forgive me!" said he, "God forgive me!"

"Why so, sir?" said Easy, who stood near. "I am sure you need not be ashamed of what you have done."

"No, no, not ashamed of what I've done; but, Mr Easy—I have sworn so, sworn such oaths at the men in haste—I, the chaplain! God forgive me!—I meant nothing." It was very true that Mr Hawkins had sworn a great deal during his exertions, but he was at that time the quarter-deck officer and not the chaplain; the example to the men and his gallantry had been most serviceable.

"Indeed, sir," said Easy, who saw the chaplain was in great tribulation, and hoped to pacify him, "I was certainly not there all the time, but I only heard you say, 'God bless you, my men! be smart,' and so on; surely, that is not swearing."

"Was it *that* I said, Mr Easy, are you sure? I really had an idea that I had d——d them all in heaps, as some of them deserved—no, no, not deserved. Did I really bless them—nothing but bless them?"

"Yes, sir," said Mesty, who perceived what Jack wanted: "it was nothing, I assure you, but 'God bless you, Captain Wilson!—Bless your heart, my good men!—Bless the king!' and so on. You do nothing but shower down blessing and wet blanket."

"I told you so," said Jack.

"Well, Mr Easy, you've made me very happy," replied the chaplain; "I was afraid it was otherwise."

So indeed it was, for the chaplain had sworn like a boatswain; but as Jack and Mesty had turned all his curses into blessings, the poor man gave himself absolution, and shaking hands with Jack, hoped he would come down into the gun-room and take a glass of grog; nor did he forget Mesty, who received a good allowance at the gun-room door, to which Jack gladly consented, as the rum in the middy's berth had all been exhausted after the rainy morning; but Jack was in-

* Scuppers: Drains opening in a ship's side allowing water to run into the sea.

terrupted in his third glass, by somebody telling him the captain wanted to speak with Mr Hawkins and with him.

Jack went up, and found the captain on the quarter-deck with the officers.

"Mr Easy," said Captain Wilson, "I have sent for you, Mr Hawkins, and Mr Gascoigne, to thank you on the quarter-deck, for your exertions and presence of mind on this trying occasion." Mr Hawkins made a bow. Gascoigne said nothing, but he thought of having extra leave when they arrived at Malta. Jack felt inclined to make a speech, and began something about when there was danger that it levelled every one to an equality even on board of a man-of-war.

"By no means, Mr Easy," replied Captain Wilson; "it does the very contrary; for it proves which is the best man, and those who are the best raise themselves at once above the rest."

Jack was very much inclined to argue the point, but he took the compliment and held his tongue, which was the wisest thing he could have done; so he made his bow, and was about to go down into the midshipmen's berth when the frigate was pooped* by a tremendous sea, which washed all those who did not hold on down into the waist.† Jack was among the number, and naturally catching at the first object which touched him, he caught hold of the chaplain by the leg, who commenced swearing most terribly: but before he could finish the oath, the water which had burst into the cabin through the windows—for the dead lights, in the confusion, had not yet been shipped—burst out of the cross bulk-heads, sweeping like a torrent the marine, the cabin-door, and everything else in its force, and floating Jack and the chaplain with several others down the main hatchway on to the lower deck. The lower deck being also full of water, men and chests were rolling and tossing about, and Jack was sometimes in company with the chaplain, and at other times separated; at last they both recovered their legs, and gained the midshipmen's berth, which, although afloat, was still a haven of security. Mr Hawkins spluttered and spit, and so did Jack, until he began to laugh.

"This is very trying, Mr Easy," said the chaplain; "very trying indeed to the temper. I hope I have not sworn—I hope not."

* Pooped: A dangerous situation in which the sea breaks over a vessel's stern.
† Waist: The middle part of the upper deck of a ship.

"Not a word," said Jack—"I was close to you all the time—you only said, 'God preserve us!' "

"Only that? I was afraid that I said 'God d——n it!' "

"Quite a mistake, Mr Hawkins. Let's go into the gun-room, and try to wash this salt water out of our mouths, and then I will tell you all you said, as far as I could hear it, word for word."

So Jack by this means got another glass of grog, which was very acceptable in his wet condition, and made himself very comfortable, while those on deck were putting on the dead lights, and very busy setting the goose-wings of the mainsail, to prevent the frigate from being pooped a second time.

CHAPTER XXVI

In which our hero becomes excessively unwell, and agrees to go through a course of medicine.

THE HAMMOCKS were not piped down that night: some were taken indiscriminately for the wounded, but the rest remained in the nettings, for all hands were busy preparing jury masts and jury rigging, and Mr Pottyfar was so well employed that for twelve hours his hands were not in his pockets. It was indeed a dreadful night: the waves were mountains high, and chased the frigate in their fury, cresting, breaking, and roaring at her taffrail. But she flew before them with the wings of the wind; four men at the helm, assisted by others at the relieving tackles below. Jack, having been thanked on and washed off the quarter-deck, thought that he had done quite enough: he was as deep as he could swim before he had satisfied all the scruples of the chaplain, and, stowing himself away on one of the lockers of the midshipmen's berth, was soon fast asleep, notwithstanding that the frigate rolled gunwale under. Gascoigne had done much better; he had taken down a hammock, as he said, for a poor wounded man, hung it up and turned in himself. The consequence was, that the next morning the surgeon, who saw him lying in the hammock, had put him down in the report, but as Gascoigne had got up as well as ever, he laughed and scratched his name out of the list of wounded.

Before morning the ship had been pumped out dry, and all below made as secure and safe as circumstances would permit; but the gale still continued its violence, and there was anything but comfort on board.

"I say, Martin, you ought to be thrown overboard!" said Gascoigne; "all this comes from your croaking—you're a Mother Cary's chicken."*

"I wish I had been anyone's chicken," replied Martin; "but the devil a thing to nestle under have I had since I can well remember."

"What a bore to have no galley-fire lighted," said one of the youngsters; "no tea, and not allowed any grog."

"The gale will last three days," replied Martin, "and by that time we shall not be far from the admiral; it won't blow home there."

"Well, then, we shall be ordered in directly, and I shall go on shore to-morrow," replied Easy.

"Yes, if you're ill," replied Gascoigne.

"Never fear, I shall be sick enough. We shall be there at least six weeks, and then we'll forget all this."

"Yes," replied Martin, "we may forget it, but will the poor fellows whose limbs are shrivelled forget it? and will poor Miles, the boatswain, who is blind forever?"

"Very true, Martin; we are thinking about ourselves, not thankful for our escape, and not feeling for others," replied Gascoigne.

"Give us your hand, Ned," said Jack Easy. "And, Martin, we ought to thank you for telling us the truth—we are a selfish set of fellows."

"Still we took our share with the others," replied one of the midshipmen.

"That's more reason for us to be grateful and to pity them," replied Jack; "suppose you had lost your arm or your eyesight—we should have pitied you; so now pity others."

"Well, so I do, now I think of it."

"Think oftener, youngster," observed Martin, going on deck.

What a change from the morning of the day before; but twenty-four hours had passed away, and the sea had been smooth; the frigate dashed through the blue water, proud in all her canvas, graceful as a swan. Since that there had been fire, tempest, lightning, disaster, danger, and death; her masts were tossed about on the snowy

---

* Mother Cary's chicken: A storm petrel, a bird whose presence was believed to presage a storm.

waves, hundreds of miles away from her, and she—a wreck—was rolling heavily, groaning and complaining in every timber, as she urged her impetuous race with the furious running sea.

How wrong are those on shore who assert that sailors are not religious!—how is it possible, supposing them to be possessed of feeling, to be otherwise? On shore, where you have nothing but the change of seasons, each in its own peculiar beauty—nothing but the blessings of the earth, its fruits, its flowers—nothing but the bounty, the comforts, the luxuries which have been invented, where you can rise in the morning in peace, and lay down your head at night in security—God may be neglected and forgotten for a long time; but at sea, when each gale is a warning, each disaster acts as a check, each escape as a homily upon the forbearance of Providence, that man must be indeed brutalised who does not feel that God is there. On shore we seldom view Him but in all His beauty and kindness; but at sea we are as often reminded how terrible He is in His wrath. Can it be supposed that the occurrences of the last twenty-four hours were lost upon the minds of any one man in that ship? No, no. In their courage and activity they might appear reckless, but in their hearts they acknowledged and bowed unto their God.

Before the day was over, a jury-foremast* had been got up, and sail having been put upon it, the ship was steered with greater ease and safety—the main brace had been spliced to cheer up the exhausted crew, and the hammocks were piped down.

As Gascoigne had observed, some of the men were not very much pleased to find that they were minus their blankets, but Captain Wilson ordered their losses to be supplied by the purser and expended by the master; this quite altered the case, as they obtained new blankets in most cases for old ones, but still it was impossible to light the galley fire, and the men sat on their chests and nibbled biscuit. By twelve o'clock that night the gale broke, and more sail was necessarily put on the scudding vessel,† for the sea still ran fast and mountains high. At daylight the sun burst out and shone brightly on them, the sea went gradually down, the fire was lighted, and Mr Pottyfar, whose hands were again in his pockets, at twelve o'clock gave the welcome order to pipe to dinner. As soon as

---

* Jury-foremast: A temporary mast put up to replace a damaged one (in this case, the mast closest to the bow).
† Scudding vessel: A vessel running before the wind.

the men had eaten their dinner, the frigate was once more brought to the wind, her jury-mast forward improved upon, and more sail made upon it. The next morning there was nothing of the gale left except the dire effects which it had produced, the black and riven stump of the foremast still holding up a terrific warning of the power and fury of the elements.

Three days more, and the *Aurora* joined the Toulon fleet. When she was first seen it was imagined by those on board of the other ships that she had been in action, but they soon learnt that the conflict had been against more direful weapons than any yet invented by mortal hands. Captain Wilson waited upon the admiral, and of course received immediate orders to repair to port and refit. In a few hours the *Aurora* had shaped her course for Malta, and by sunset the Toulon fleet were no longer in sight.

"By de holy poker, Massa Easy, but that terrible sort of gale the other day anyhow—I tink one time, we all go to Davy Joney's lacker."

"Very true, Mesty; I hope never to meet with such another."

"Den, Massa Easy, why you go to sea? when man ab no money, noting to eat, den he go to sea, but everybody say you ab plenty money—why you come to sea?"

"I'm sure I don't know," replied Jack, thoughtfully; "I came to sea on account of equality and the rights of man."

"Eh, Massa Easy, you come to wrong place anyhow; now I tink a good deal lately, and by all de power, I tink equality all stuff."

"All stuff, Mesty, why? You used to think otherwise."

"Yes, Massa Easy, but den I boil de kettle for all young gentleman. Now dat I ship's corporal and hab cane, I tink so no longer."

Jack made no reply, but he thought the more. The reader must have perceived that Jack's notions of equality were rapidly disappearing; he defended them more from habit, and perhaps a wilfulness which would not allow him to acknowledge himself wrong;—to which may be added his love of argument. Already he had accustomed himself to obedience of his superiors, and, notwithstanding his arguments, he would admit of no resistance from those below him; not that it was hardly ever attempted, for Jack was anything but a tyrant and was much beloved by all in the ship. Every day brought its lesson, and Captain Wilson was now satisfied that Jack had been almost cured of the effects of his father's ridiculous philosophy.

After a few minutes, Mesty tapped his cane on the funnel and recommenced.

"Then why you stay at sea, Massa Easy?"

"I don't know, Mesty, I don't dislike it."

"But, Massa Easy, why you stay in midshipman berth, eat hard biscuit, salt pig, salt horse, when you can go shore and live like gentleman? Dat very foolish! Why not be your own master? By all power! suppose I had money, catch me board ship. Little sea very good, Massa Easy, open one's eyes; but tink of the lightning t'other night. Poor massa boatswain he shut um eyes for ebber!"

"Very true, Mesty."

"Me hope you tink of this, sar, and when you go on shore you take Mesty wid you. He sarve you well, Massa Easy, long as he live, by de holy St Patrick. And den, Massa Easy, you marry wife—hab pickaninny—lib like gentleman. You tink of this, Massa Easy."

The mention of the word marriage turned the thoughts of our hero to his Agnes, and he made no reply. Mesty walked away leaving our hero in deep thought.

This conversation had more effect upon Jack than would have been imagined, and he very often found he was putting to himself the question of Mesty—"Why do you stay at sea?" He had not entered the service with any particular view, except to find equality, and he could not but acknowledge to himself that, as Mesty observed, he had come to the wrong place. He had never even thought of staying to serve his time, nor had he looked forward to promotion, and one day commanding a ship. He had only cared for the present, without indulging in a future anticipation of any reward, except in a union with Agnes. Mesty's observations occasioned Jack to reflect upon the future for the first time in his life; and he was always perplexed when he put the question of Mesty, and tried to answer to himself as to what were his intentions in remaining in the service.

Nevertheless Jack did his duty very much to the satisfaction of Mr Pottyfar; and after a tedious passage, from baffling and light winds, the *Aurora* arrived at Malta. Our hero had had some conversation with his friend Gascoigne, in which he canvassed his future plans; all of which, however, ended in one settled point, which was that he was to marry Agnes. As for the rest, Gascoigne was of opinion that Jack ought to follow up the service and become a captain. But there was plenty of time to think about that, as he observed; now all they had to consider was how to get on shore, for the refitting of the ship was an excuse for detaining them on board, which they knew Mr Pottyfar would avail himself of. Jack dined in the gun-room on the day of their arrival, and he resolved that he would ask that very evening. Captain Wilson was already on shore at the governor's. Now, there had been a little difference of opinion between Mr Pottyfar and Mr Hawkins, the chaplain, on a point of seamanship, and most of the officers sided with the chaplain, who, as we have before observed, was a first-rate seaman. It had ended in high words, for Mr Hawkins had forgotten himself so far as to tell the first lieutenant that he had a great deal to learn, not having even got over the midshipman's trick of keeping his hands in his pockets; and Mr Pottyfar had replied that it was very well for him as chaplain to insult others, knowing that his cassock protected him. This was a bitter reply to Mr Hawkins, who at the very time that the insinuation made his blood boil, was also reminded that his profession forbade a retort. He rushed into his cabin, poor fellow, having no other method left, vented his indignation in tears, and then consoled himself by degrees with prayer. In the meantime Mr Pottyfar had gone on deck, wroth with Hawkins and with his messmates, as well as displeased with himself. He was, indeed, in a humour to be pleased with nobody, and in a most unfortunate humour to be asked leave by a midshipman. Nevertheless, Jack politely took off his hat, and requested leave to go on shore and see his friend the governor. Upon which Mr Pottyfar turned round to him, with his feet spread wide open, and, thrusting his hands to the very bottom of his pockets, as if in determination, said:

"Mr Easy, you know the state of the ship. We have everything to do—new masts, new rigging, everything almost to refit—and yet you ask to go on shore! Now, sir, you may take this answer for yourself, and all the other midshipmen in the ship, that not one soul of you puts his foot on shore until we are again all a-taunto."*

"Allow me to observe, sir," said our hero, "that it is very true that all our services may be required when the duty commences, but this being Saturday night, and tomorrow Sunday, the frigate will not be even moved till Monday morning; and as the work cannot begin before that, I trust you will permit leave until that time."

"My opinion is different, sir," replied the first lieutenant.

"Perhaps, sir, you will allow me to argue the point," replied Jack.

"No, sir, I never allow argument; walk over to the other side of the deck, if you please."

* A-taunto (or ataunt): Shipshape, fully rigged.

"O certainly, sir," said Jack, "if you wish it."

Jack's first idea was to go on shore without leave, but from this he was persuaded by Gascoigne, who told him that it would displease Captain Wilson, and that old Tom, the governor, would not receive him. Jack agreed to this, and then, after a flourish about the rights of man, tyranny, oppression, and so forth, he walked forward to the forecastle, where he found his friend Mesty, who had heard all that had passed, and who insidiously said to him in a low tone—

"Why you stay at sea, Massa Easy?"

"Why, indeed," thought Jack, boiling with indignation; "to be cooped up here at the will of another? I am a fool—Mesty is right— I'll ask for my discharge to-morrow." Jack went down below, and told Gascoigne what he had determined to do.

"You'll do no such thing, Jack," replied Gascoigne; "depend upon it, you'll have plenty of leave in a day or two. Pottyfar was in a pet with the chaplain, who was too much for him. Captain Wilson will be on board by nine o'clock."

Nevertheless, Jack walked his first watch in the *magnificents*, as all middies do when they cannot go on shore, and turned in at twelve o'clock with the resolution of sticking to his purpose, and quitting his Majesty's service; in fact, of presenting his Majesty with his between two and three years' time, served as midshipman, all free, gratis, and for nothing, except his provisions and his pay, which some captains are bold enough to assert that they not only are not worth, but not even the salt that accompanies it; forgetting that they were once midshipmen themselves, and at the period were, of course, of about the same value.

The next morning Captain Wilson came off; the ship's company were mustered, the service read by Mr Hawkins, and Jack, as soon as all the official duties were over, was about to go up to the captain, when the captain said to him,—

"Mr Easy, the governor desired me to bring you on shore to dine with him, and he has a bed at your service."

Jack touched his hat and ran down below, to make his few preparations.

By the time that Mesty, who had taken charge of his chest, &c., had put his necessaries in the boat, Jack had almost made up his mind that his Majesty should not be deprived yet awhile of so valuable an officer. Jack returned on deck, and found that the captain was not yet ready; he went up to Mr Pottyfar, and told him that the captain had ordered him to go on shore with him; and Mr Pottyfar, who had quite got over his spleen, said,—

"Very well, Mr Easy—I wish you a great deal of pleasure."

"This is very different from yesterday," thought Jack; "suppose I try the medicine?"

"I am not very well, Mr Pottyfar, and those pills of the doctor's don't agree with me—I always am ill if I am long without air and exercise."

"Very true," said the first lieutenant, "people require air and exercise. I've no opinion of the doctor's remedies; the only thing that is worth a farthing is the universal medicine."

"I should so long to try it, sir," replied Jack; "I read the book one day, and it said that if you took it daily for a fortnight or three weeks, and with plenty of air and exercise, it would do wonders."

"And it's very true," replied Mr Pottyfar; "and if you'd like to try it you shall—I have plenty—shall I give you a dose now?"

"If you please, sir," replied Jack; "and tell me how often I am to take it, for my head aches all day."

Mr Pottyfar took Jack down, and putting into his hand three or four bottles of the preparation, told him that he was to take thirty drops at night, when he went to bed, not to drink more than two glasses of wine, and to avoid the heat of the sun.

"But, sir," replied Jack, who had put the bottles in his pocket, "I am afraid that I cannot take it long; for as the ship is ready for fitting, I shall be exposed to the sun all day."

"Yes, if you are wanted, Mr Easy; but we have plenty here without you; and when you are unwell you cannot be expected to work. Take care of your health; and I trust, indeed I am sure, that you will find this medicine wonderfully efficacious."

"I will begin to-night, sir, if you please," replied Jack, "and I am very much obliged to you. I sleep at the governor's—shall I come on board to-morrow morning?"

"No, no; take care of yourself, and get well; I shall be glad to hear that you get better. Send me word how it acts."

"I will, sir, send you word by the boat every day," replied Jack, delighted; "I am very much obliged to you, sir. Gascoigne and I were thinking of asking you, but did not like to do so: he, poor fellow, suffers from headaches almost as bad as I do, and the doctor's pills are of no use to him."

"He shall have some too, Mr Easy; I thought he looked pale. I'll see to it this afternoon. Recollect, moderate exercise, Mr Easy, and avoid the sun at midday."

"Yes, sir," replied Jack, "I'll not forget"; and off went Jack, delighted. He ordered Mesty to put up his whole portmanteau instead of the small bundle he put into the boat, and telling Gascoigne what a spoke he had put into his wheel, was soon in the boat with the captain, and went on shore, where he was cordially greeted by the governor.

⚮

CHAPTER XXVII

In which Captain Wilson is repaid with interest for Jack's borrowing his name; proving that a good name is as good as a legacy.

W ELL, Jack, my boy, have you any long story ready for me?" inquired the governor.

"Yes, sir," replied Jack, "I have one or two very good ones."

"Very well, we'll hear them after dinner," replied old Tom. "In the meantime find out your room and take possession."

"That must not be for very long, governor," observed Captain Wilson. "Mr Easy must learn his duty, and there is a good opportunity now."

"If you please, sir," replied Jack, "I'm on the sick list."

"Sick list," said Captain Wilson; "you were not in the report I was given this morning."

"No, I'm on Mr Pottyfar's list, and I'm going through a course of the universal medicine."

"What's all this, Jack, what's all this? There's some story here. Don't be afraid of the captain—you've me to back you," said the governor.

Jack was not at all afraid of the captain, so he told him how the first lieutenant had refused him leave the evening before, and how he had now given him permission to remain, and try the universal medicine, at which the governor laughed heartily, nor could Captain Wilson refrain from joining.

"But, Mr Easy," replied the captain, after a pause, "if Mr Pottyfar will allow you to stay on shore, I cannot—you have your duty to learn. You must be aware that now is your time, and you must not lose opportunities that do not occur every day. You must acknowledge the truth of what I say."

"Yes, sir," replied Jack, "I admit it all, provided I do intend to follow the profession"; and so saying our hero bowed, and left the veranda where they had been talking.

This hint of Jack's, thrown out by him, more with the intention of preventing his being sent on board than with any definite idea, was not lost upon either the captain or the governor.

"Does he jib, then?" observed the governor.

"On the contrary, I never knew him more attentive, and so entirely getting rid of his former notions. He has behaved most nobly in the gale, and there has not been one complaint against him—I never was more astonished—he must have meant something."

"I'll tell you what he means, Wilson—that he does not like to be sent on board, nothing more. He's not to be cooped up—you may lead him, but not drive him."

"Yes, but the service will not admit of it. I never could allow it—he must do his duty like the rest, and conform to the rules."

"Exactly, so he must; but look ye, Wilson, you must not lose him: it's all easily settled—appoint him your orderly midshipman to and from the ship; that will be employment, and he can always remain here at night. I will tell him that I have asked, as a favour, what I now do, and leave me to find out what he is thinking about."

"It may be done that way, certainly," replied Captain Wilson, musing; "and you are more likely to get his intentions from him than I am. I am afraid he has too great a command of money ever to be fond of the ship; it is the ruin of a junior officer to be so lavishly supplied."

"He's a long way from ruin yet, Wilson—he's a very fine fellow, even by your own acknowledgment. You humoured him out of gratitude to his father, when he first came into the service; humour him a little now to keep him in it. Besides, if your first lieutenant is such a fool with his universal medicine, can you wonder at a midshipman taking advantage of it?"

"No, but I ought not to allow him to do so with my eyes open."

"He has made it known to you upon honour, and you ought not to take advantage of his confidence: but still what I proposed would, I think, be the best, for then he will be at his duty in a way that will suit all parties. You, because you employ him on service—the first lieutenant, because Jack can take his medicine—and Jack, because he can dine with me every day."

"Well, I suppose it must be so," replied Captain Wilson, laughing; "but still, I trust, you will discover what is working in his mind to induce him to give me that answer, governor."

"Never fear, Jack shall confess, and lay his soul as bare as that of a Catholic bigot before his padre."

The party sat down to dinner, and what with the governor's aide-de-camp and those invited, it was pretty numerous. After the cloth had been removed, the governor called upon Jack for his stories, whereupon, much to the surprise of Captain Wilson, who had never heard one word of it, for the admiral had not mentioned anything about it to him during the short time the *Aurora* was with the Toulon fleet, our hero gave the governor and the company the narrative of all that happened in the *Mary Ann* transport—the loves of Captain Hogg and Miss Hicks—the adventures of Gascoigne—and his plan, by which he baulked them all. The governor was delighted, and Captain Wilson not a little astonished.

"You prevented a very foolish thing, Mr Easy, and behaved very well," observed the captain, laughing again at the idea; "but you never told me of all this."

"No, sir," replied Jack, "I have always reserved my stories for the governor's table, where I am sure to meet you, and then telling once does for all."

Jack received his appointment as orderly midshipman, and everything went on well; for, of his own accord, he stayed on board the major part of the day to learn his duty, which very much pleased the captain and Mr Pottyfar. In this Jack showed a great deal of good sense, and Captain Wilson did not repent of the indulgence he had shown him. Jack's health improved daily, much to Mr Pottyfar's satisfaction, who imagined that he took the universal medicine night and morning. Gascoigne also was a patient under the first lieutenant's hands, and often on shore with our hero, who thought no more of quitting the service.

For seven weeks they had now remained in harbour, for even the masts had to be made, when, one day, Captain Wilson opened a letter he received at breakfast-time, and having read it, laid it down with the greatest surprise depicted in his countenance. "Good heavens! what can this mean?" said he.

"What's the matter, Wilson?" said the governor.

"Just hear its contents, Sir Thomas."

Captain Wilson then read in Spanish as follows:—

"HONOURABLE SIR,

"It is my duty to advise you that the Honourable Lady Signora Alforgas de Guzman, now deceased, has, in her testament, bequeathed to you the sum of one thousand doubloons in gold as a testimony of your kind services on the night of the 12th of August. If you will authorise any merchant here to receive the money, it shall be paid forthwith, or remitted in any way you please to appoint. May you live a thousand years!

"Your most obedient servant,
"ALFONZO XEREZ."

Jack heard the letter read, rose quietly, whistled low, as if not attending to it, and then slipped out of the room, unperceived by the governor or Captain Wilson.

The fact was, that although Jack had longed to tell the governor about his adventures after the masquerade, he did not like yet awhile, until he was sure that there were no consequences—because he had given the captain's name instead of his own. As soon as he heard the letter read, he at once perceived that it had been the old lady, and not the priests, who had made the inquiry, and that by giving Captain Wilson's name, he had obtained for him this fine legacy. Jack was delighted, but still puzzled, so he walked out of the room to reflect a little.

"What can it mean?" said Captain Wilson. "I never rendered any services to anyone on the 12th of August or after it. It is some mistake—12th of August—that was the day of the grand masquerade."

"A lucky one for you, at all events—for you know, mistake or not, no one else can touch the legacy. It can only be paid to you."

"I never heard of anything taking place at the masquerade—I was there, but I left early, for I was not very well. Mr Easy," said Captain Wilson, turning round; but Jack was gone.

"Was he at the masquerade?" asked the governor.

"Yes, I know he was, for the first lieutenant told me that he requested not to come on board till the next day."

"Depend upon it," replied the governor, striking his fist upon the table, "that Jack's at the bottom of it."

"I should not be surprised at his being at the bottom of anything," replied Captain Wilson, laughing.

"Leave it to me, Wilson; I'll find it out."

After a little more conversation, Captain Wilson went on board, leaving Jack on purpose that the governor might pump him. But this Sir Thomas had no occasion to do, for Jack had made up his mind to make the governor his confidant, and he immediately told him the whole story. The governor held his sides at our hero's description, especially at his ruse of giving the captain's name instead of his own.

"You'll kill me, Jack, before you've done with me," said old Tom, at last; "but now, what is to be done?"

Our hero now became grave; he pointed out to the governor that he himself had plenty of money, and would come into a large fortune, and that Captain Wilson was poor, with a large family. All Jack wished the governor to manage was, that Captain Wilson might consent to accept the legacy.

"Right, boy, right! you're my own boy," replied the governor, "but we must think of this, for Wilson is the very soul of honour, and there may be some difficulty about it. You have told nobody?"

"Not a soul but you, Sir Thomas."

"It will never do to tell him all this, Jack, for he would insist that the legacy belonged to you."

"I have it, sir," replied Jack. "When I was going into the masquerade, I offered to hand this very old lady, who was covered with diamonds, out of her carriage, and she was so frightened at my dress of a devil, that she would have fallen down had it not been for Captain Wilson, who supported her, and she was very thankful to him."

"You are right, Jack," replied the governor, after a short pause: "that will, I think, do. I must tell him the story of the friars, because I swore you had something to do with it—but I'll tell him no more: leave it all to me."

Captain Wilson returned in the afternoon, and found the governor in the veranda.

"I have had some talk with young Easy," said the governor, "and he has told me a strange story about that night, which he was afraid to tell to everybody."

The governor then narrated the history of the friars and the will.

"Well, but," observed Captain Wilson, "the history of that will afford no clue to the legacy."

"No, it does not; but still, as I said, Jack had a hand in this. He frightened the old lady as a devil, and you caught her in your arms and saved her from falling, so he had a hand in it, you see."

"I do now remember that I did save a very dowager-like old personage from falling at the sight of a devil, who, of course, must have been our friend Easy."

"Well, and that accounts for the whole of it."

"A thousand doubloons for picking up an old lady!"

"Yes, why not?—have you not heard of a man having a fortune left him for merely opening the pew door of a church, to an old gentleman?"

"Yes, but it appears so strange."

"There's nothing strange in this world, Wilson, nothing at all— we may slave for years and get no reward, and do a trifle out of politeness and become independent. In my opinion, this mystery is unravelled. The old lady, for I knew the family, must have died immensely rich: she knew you in your full uniform, and she asked your name; a heavy fall would have been to one so fat a most serious affair; you saved her, and she has rewarded you handsomely."

"Well," replied Captain Wilson, "as I can give no other explanation, I suppose yours is the correct one; but it's hardly fair to take a thousand doubloons from her relations merely for an act of civility."

"You really are quite ridiculous; the old lady owned half Murcia,* to my knowledge. It is no more to them than anyone leaving you a suit of mourning in an English legacy. I wish you joy; it will help you with a large family, and in justice to them you are bound to take it. Everybody does as he pleases with his own money,—depend upon it, you saved her from breaking her leg short off at the hip joint."

"Upon that supposition I presume I must accept of the legacy," replied Captain Wilson, laughing.

"Of course; send for it at once. The rate of exchange is now high. I will give you government bills, which will make it nearly four thousand pounds."

"Four thousand pounds for preventing an old woman from falling," replied Captain Wilson.

"Devilish well paid, Wilson, and I congratulate you."

"For how much am I indebted to the father of young Easy!" observed Captain Wilson, after a silence of some minutes; "if he had not assisted me when I was appointed to a ship, I should not have

* Murcia: A city and province in the south of Spain.

gained my promotion—nor three thousand pounds I have made in prize-money—the command of a fine frigate—and now four thousand pounds in a windfall."

The governor thought that he was more indebted to Jack than to his father for some of these advantages, but he was careful not to point them out.

"It's very true," observed the governor, "that Mr Easy was of service to you when you were appointed; but allow me to observe, that for your ship, your prize-money, and for your windfall, you have been wholly indebted to your own gallantry, in both senses of the word; still Mr Easy is a fine generous fellow, and so is his son, I can tell you. By-the-bye, I had a long conversation with him the other day."

"About himself?"

"Yes, all about himself. He appears to me to have come into the service without any particular motive, and will be just as likely to leave it in the same way. He appears to be very much in love with that Sicilian nobleman's daughter. I find that he has written to her, and to her brother, since he has been here."

"That he came into the service in search of what he never will find in this world, I know very well; and I presume that he has found that out—and that he will follow up the service is also very doubtful; but I do not wish that he should leave it yet, it is doing him great good," replied Captain Wilson."

"I agree with you there—I have great influence with him, and he shall stay yet awhile. He is heir to a very large fortune, is he not?"

"A clear eight thousand pounds a year, if not more."

"If his father dies he must, of course, leave; a midshipman with eight thousand pounds a year would indeed be an anomaly."

"That the service could not permit. It would be as injurious to himself as it would to others about him. At present, he has almost, indeed I may say quite, an unlimited command of money."

"That's bad, very bad. I wonder he behaves so well as he does."

"And so do I: but he really is a very superior lad, with all his peculiarities, and a general favourite with those whose opinions and friendship are worth having."

"Well, don't curb him too tight—for really he does not require it. He goes very well in a snaffle."*

---

* Snaffle: A bridle bit loosely restraining the horse.

CHAPTER XXVIII

"Philosophy made Easy" upon agrarian principles, the subject of some uneasiness to our hero—The first appearance, but not the last, of an important personage.

THE CONVERSATION was here interrupted by a mail from England which they had been expecting. Captain Wilson retired with his letters; the governor remained equally occupied; and our hero received the first letter ever written to him by his father. It ran as follows:—

"MY DEAR SON,

"I have many times taken up my pen with the intention of letting you know how things went on in this country. But as I can perceive around but one dark horizon of evil, I have as often laid it down again without venturing to make you unhappy with such bad intelligence.

"The account of your death, and also of your unexpectedly being yet spared to us, were duly received, and I trust, I mourned and rejoiced on each occasion with all the moderation characteristic of a philosopher. In the first instance I consoled myself with the reflection that the world you had left was in a state of slavery, and pressed down by the iron arm of despotism, and that to die was gain, not only in all the parson tells us, but also in our liberty; and, at the second intelligence, I moderated my joy for nearly about the same reasons, resolving, notwithstanding what Dr Middleton may say, to die as I have lived, a true philosopher.

"The more I reflect the more am I convinced that there is nothing required to make this world happy but equality, and the rights of man being duly observed—in short, that everything and everybody should be reduced to one level. Do we not observe that it is the law of nature—do not brooks run into rivers—rivers into seas—mountains crumble down upon the plains?—are not the seasons contented to equalise the parts of the earth? Why does the sun run round the ecliptic,* instead of the equator, but to give an equal share of his heat to both sides of the world? Are we not all equally born in misery?

---

* Ecliptic: The apparent orbit of the sun.

does not death level us all *aequo pede,* as the poet hath? are we not all equally hungry, thirsty, and sleepy, and thus levelled by our natural wants? And such being the case, ought we not to have our equal share of good things in this world, to which we have undoubted equal right? Can any argument be more solid or more level than this, whatever nonsense Dr Middleton may talk?

"Yes, my son, if it were not that I still hope to see the sun of Justice arise, and disperse the manifold dark clouds which obscure the land—if I did not still hope, in my time, to see an equal distribution of property—an Agrarian law passed by the House of Commons, in which all should benefit alike—I would not care how soon I left this vale of tears, created by tyranny and injustice. At present, the same system is carried on; the nation is taxed for the benefit of the few, and it groans under oppression and despotism; but I still do think that there is, if I may fortunately express myself, a bright star in the west; and signs of the times which comfort me. Already we have had a good deal of incendiarism about the country, and some of the highest aristocracy have pledged themselves to raise the people above themselves, and have advised sedition and conspiracy; have shown to the debased and unenlightened multitude that their force is physically irresistible, and recommended them to make use of it, promising that if they hold in power, they will only use that power to the abolition of our farce of a constitution, of a church, and of a king; and that if the nation is to be governed at all, it shall only be governed by the many. This is cheering. Hail, patriot lords! all hail! I am in hopes yet that the great work will be achieved, in spite of the laughs and sneers and shakes of the head, which my arguments still meet with from that obstinate fellow, Dr Middleton.

"Your mother is in a quiet way; she has given over reading and working, and even her knitting, as useless; and she now sits all day long at the chimney corner twiddling her thumbs, and waiting, as she says, for the millennium. Poor thing! she is very foolish with her ideas upon this matter, but as usual I let her have her own way in everything, copying the philosopher of old, who was tied to his Xantippe.*

"I trust, my dear son, that your principles have strengthened with

---

* Xantippe: The wife of Socrates; she was said to be a nag.

your years and fortified with your growth, and that, if necessary, you will sacrifice all to obtain what in my opinion will prove to be the real millennium. Make all the converts you can, and believe me to be,

"Your affectionate father, and true guide,

"Nicodemus Easy."

Jack, who was alone, shook his head as he read this letter, and then laid it down with a pish! He did it involuntarily, and was surprised at himself when he found that he had so done. "I should like to argue the point," thought Jack, in spite of himself; and then he threw the letter on the table, and went into Gascoigne's room, displeased with his father and with himself. He asked Ned whether he had received any letters from England, and, it being near dinnertime, went back to dress. On his coming down into the receiving-room with Gascoigne, the governor said to them,—

"As you both speak Italian, you must take charge of a Sicilian officer, who has come here with letters of introduction to me, and who dines here to-day."

Before dinner they were introduced to the party in question, a slight-made, well-looking young man, but still there was an expression in his countenance which was not agreeable. In compliance with the wishes of the governor, Don Mathias, for so he was called, was placed between our two midshipmen, who immediately entered into conversation with him, being themselves anxious to make enquiries about their friends at Palermo. In the course of conversation, Jack enquired of him whether he was acquainted with Don Rebiera, to which the Sicilian answered in the affirmative, and they talked about the different members of the family. Don Mathias, towards the close of the dinner, enquired of Jack by what means he had become acquainted with Don Rebiera, and Jack, in reply, narrated how he and his friend Gascoigne had saved him from being murdered by two villains; after this reply the young officer appeared to be less inclined for conversation, but before the party broke up, requested to have the acquaintance of our two midshipmen. As soon as he was gone, Gascoigne observed in a reflective way, "I have seen that face before, but where I cannot exactly say; but you know, Jack, what a memory of people I have, and I have seen him before, I am sure."

"I can't recollect that ever I have," replied our hero, "but I never knew anyone who could recollect in that way as you do."

The conversation was then dropped between them, and Jack was for some time listening to the governor and Captain Wilson, for the whole party were gone away, when Gascoigne, who had been in deep thought since he had made the observation to Jack, sprang up.

"I have him at last!" cried he.

"Have who?" demanded Captain Wilson.

"That Sicilian officer—I could have sworn that I had seen him before."

"That Don Mathias?"

"No, Sir Thomas! He is not Don Mathias! He is the very Don Silvio who was murdering Don Rebiera, when we came to his assistance and saved him."

"I do believe you are right, Gascoigne."

"I'm positive of it," replied Gascoigne; "I never made a mistake in my life."

"Bring me those letters, Easy," said the governor, "and let us see what they say of him. Here it is—Don Mathias de Alayeres. You may be mistaken, Gascoigne; it is a heavy charge you are making against this young man."

"Well, Sir Thomas, if that is not Don Silvio, I'd forfeit my commission if I had it here in my hand. Besides, I observed the change in his countenance when we told him it was Easy and I who had come to Don Rebiera's assistance; and did you observe after that, Easy, that he hardly said a word."

"Very true," replied Jack.

"Well, well, we must see to this," observed the governor; "if so, this letter of introduction must be a forgery."

The party then retired to bed, and the next morning, while Easy was in Gascoigne's room talking over their suspicions, letters from Palermo were brought up to him. They were in answer to those written by Jack on his arrival at Malta: a few lines from Don Rebiera, a small note from Agnes, and a voluminous detail from his friend Don Philip, who informed him of the good health of all parties, and of their goodwill towards him; of Agnes being as partial as ever; of his having spoken plainly, as he had promised Jack, to his father and mother relative to the mutual attachment; of their consent being given, and then withheld, because Father Thomaso, their confessor, would not listen to the union of Agnes with a heretic; but nevertheless telling Jack that this would be got over through the medium of his brother and himself, who were determined that their sister and he should not be made unhappy about such a trifle. But the latter part of the letter contained intelligence equally important, which was, that Don Silvio had again attempted the life of their father, and would have succeeded, had not Father Thomaso, who happened to be there, thrown himself between them. That Don Silvio in his rage had actually stabbed the confessor, although the wound was not dangerous. That in consequence of this, all further lenity was denied to him, and the authorities were in search of him to award him the punishment due to murder and sacrilege. That up to the present they could not find him, and it was supposed that he had made his escape to Malta in one of the speronares.

Such were the contents of the letter, which were immediately communicated to the governor and Captain Wilson, upon their meeting at breakfast.

"Very well, we must see to this," observed the governor, who then made his enquiries as to the other intelligence contained in the letters.

Jack and Gascoigne were uneasy till the breakfast was over, when they made their escape: a few moments afterwards Captain Wilson rose to go on board, and sent for them, but they were not to be found.

"I understand it all, Wilson," said the governor; "leave them to me; go on board and make yourself quite easy."

In the meantime our two midshipmen had taken their hats and walked away to the parapet of the battery, where they would not be interrupted.

"Now, Gascoigne," observed Jack, "you guess what I'm about—I must shoot that rascal this very morning, and that's why I came out with you."

"But, Easy, the only difference is this, that I must shoot him, and not you; he is my property, for I found him out."

"We'll argue that point," replied Jack: "he has attempted the life of my is-to-be, please God, father-in-law, and therefore I have the best claim to him."

"I beg your pardon, Jack, he is mine, for I discovered him. Now let me put a case: suppose one man walking several yards before another, picks up a purse, what claim has the other to it? I found him, and not you."

"That's all very well, Gascoigne; but suppose the purse you picked up to be mine, then I have a right to it, although you found it; he is my bird by right, and not yours."

"But I have another observation to make, which is very important; he is a blood relation of Agnes, and if his blood is on your hands, however much he may deserve it, depend upon it, it will be raised as an obstacle to your union: think of that."

Jack paused in thought.

"And let me induce you by another remark—you will confer on me a most particular favour."

"It will be the greatest I ever could," replied Jack, "and you ought to be eternally indebted to me."

"I trust to make him *eternally* indebted to me," replied Gascoigne.

Sailors, if going into action, always begin to reckon what their share of the prize-money may be, before a shot is fired—our two midshipmen appear in this instance to be doing the same.

The point having been conceded to Gascoigne, Jack went to the inn where Don Silvio had mentioned that he had taken up his quarters, and sending up his card, followed the waiter up-stairs. The waiter opened the door, and presented the card.

"Very well," replied Don Silvio, "you can go down and show him up."

Jack hearing these words, did not wait, but walked in, where he found Don Silvio very busy removing a hone upon which he had been whetting a sharp double-edged stiletto. The Sicilian walked up to him, offering his hand with apparent cordiality; but Jack, with a look of defiance, said, "Don Silvio, we know you; my object now is to demand, on the part of my friend, the satisfaction which you do not deserve, but which our indignation at your second attempt upon Don Rebiera induces us to offer; for if you escape from him you will have to do with me. On the whole, Don Silvio, you may think yourself fortunate, for it is better to die by the hands of a gentleman than by the gibbet."

Don Silvio turned deadly pale—his hand sought his stiletto in his bosom, but it was remaining on the table; at last he replied, "Be it so—I will meet you when and where you please, in an hour from this."

Jack mentioned the place of meeting, and then walked out of the room. He and Gascoigne then hastened to the quarters of an officer they were intimate with, and having provided themselves with the necessary fire-arms, were at the spot before the time. They waited for him till the exact time, yet no Don Silvio made his appearance.

"He's off," observed Gascoigne; "the villain has escaped us."

Half an hour over the time had passed, and still there was no sign of Gascoigne's antagonist, but one of the governor's aides-de-camp was seen walking up to them.

"Here's Atkins," observed Jack; "that's unlucky, but he won't interfere."

"Gentlemen," said Atkins, taking off his hat with much solemnity, "the governor particularly wishes to speak to you both."

"We can't come just now—we'll be there in half an hour."

"You must be there in three minutes, both of you. Excuse me, my orders are positive—and to see them duly executed I have a corporal and a file of men behind that wall—of course, if you walk with me quietly there will be no occasion to send for their assistance."

"This is confounded tyranny," cried Jack. "Well may they call him 'King Tom.' "

"Yes," replied Atkins, "and he governs here in 'rey absoluto'*—so come along."

Jack and Gascoigne, having no choice, walked up to the government house, where they found Sir Thomas in the veranda, which commanded a view of the harbour and offing.

"Come here, young gentlemen," said the governor, in a severe tone; "do you see that vessel about two miles clear of the port? Don Silvio is in it, going back to Sicily under a guard. And now remember what I say as a maxim through life. Fight with gentlemen, if you must fight, but not with villains and murderers. By 'consenting' to fight with a 'blackguard,' you as much disparage your cloth and compromise your own characters, as by refusing to give satisfaction to a 'gentleman.' There, go away, for I'm angry with you, and don't let me see you till dinner-time."

---

* "Rey absoluto": As absolute king.

CHAPTER XXIX

In which our hero sees a little more service, and is better employed than in fighting Don Silvio.

BUT before they met the governor at his table, a sloop of war arrived from the fleet with despatches from the commander-in-chief. Those to Captain Wilson required him to make all possible haste in fitting, and then to proceed and cruise off Corsica, to fall in with a Russian frigate* which was on that coast; if not there, to obtain intelligence, and to follow her wherever she might be.

All was now bustle and activity on board of the *Aurora*. Captain Wilson, with our hero and Gascoigne, quitted the governor's house and repaired on board, where they remained day and night. On the third day the *Aurora* was complete and ready for sea, and about noon sailed out of Valette Harbour.

In a week the *Aurora* had gained the coast of Corsica, and there was no need of sending look-out men to the mast-head, for one of the officers or midshipmen was there from daylight to dark. She ran up the coast to the northward without seeing the object of her pursuit, or obtaining any intelligence.

Calms and light airs detained them for a few days, when a northerly breeze enabled them to run down the eastern side of the island. It was on the eighteenth day after they had quitted Malta, that a large vessel was seen ahead about eighteen miles off. The men were then at breakfast.

"A frigate, Captain Wilson, I'm sure of it," said Mr Hawkins, the chaplain, whose anxiety induced him to go to the mast-head.

"How is she steering?"

"The same way as we are."

The *Aurora* was under all possible sail, and when the hands were piped to dinner, it was thought that they had neared the chase about two miles.

"This will be a long chase; a stern chase always is," observed Martin to Gascoigne.

---

* Russian frigate: England was at war with Russia from 1807 until Napoleon invaded Russia in 1812.

"Yes, I'm afraid so—but I'm more afraid of her escaping."

"That's not unlikely either," replied the mate.

"You are one of Job's comforters, Martin," replied Gascoigne.

"Then I'm not so often disappointed," replied the mate. "There are two points to be ascertained; the first is, whether we shall come up with the vessel or lose her—the next is, if we do come up with her, whether she is the vessel we are looking for."

"You seem very indifferent about it."

"Indeed I am not: I am the oldest passed midshipman in the ship, and the taking of the frigate will, if I live, give me my promotion, and if I'm killed, I shan't want it. But I've been so often disappointed, that I now make sure of nothing until I have it."

"Well, for your sake, Martin, I will still hope that the vessel is the one we seek, that we shall not be killed, and that you will gain your promotion."

"I thank you, Easy—I wish I was one that dared hope as you do."

Poor Martin! he had long felt how bitter it was to meet disappointment upon disappointment. How true it is, that hope deferred maketh the heart sick! and his anticipations of early days, the buoyant calculations of youth, had been one by one crushed, and now, having served his time nearly three times over, the reaction had become too painful, and, as he truly said, he dared not hope: still his temper was not soured, but chastened.

"She has hauled her wind, sir," hailed the second lieutenant from the topmast cross-trees.

"What think you of that, Martin?" observed Jack.

"Either that she is an English frigate, or that she is a vessel commanded by a very brave fellow, and well-manned."

It was sunset before the *Aurora* had arrived within two miles of the vessel; the private signal had been thrown out, but had not been answered, either because it was too dark to make out the colours of the flags, or that these were unknown to an enemy. The stranger had hoisted the English colours, but that was no satisfactory proof of her being a friend; and just before dark she had put her head towards the *Aurora*, who had now come stem down to her. The ship's company of the *Aurora* were all at their quarters, as a few minutes would now decide whether they had to deal with a friend or foe.

There is no situation perhaps more difficult, and demanding so much caution, as the occasional meeting with a doubtful ship. On the one hand, it being necessary to be fully prepared, and not allow the enemy the advantage which may be derived from your inaction; and on the other, the necessity of prudence, that you may not assault your friends and countrymen. Captain Wilson had hoisted the private night-signal, but here again it was difficult, from his sails intervening, for the other ship to make it out. Before the two frigates were within three cables' length of each other, Captain Wilson, determined that there should be no mistake from any want of precaution on his part, hauled up his courses and brailed up his driver* that the night-signal might be clearly seen.

Lights were seen abaft on the quarter-deck of the other vessel, as if they were about to answer, but she continued to keep the *Aurora* to leeward at about half a cable's length, and as the foremost guns of each vessel were abreast of each other, hailed in English—

"Ship ahoy! what ship's that?"

"His Majesty's ship *Aurora*," replied Captain Wilson, who stood on the hammocks. "What ship's that?"

By this time the other frigate had passed half her length clear of the beam of the *Aurora*, and at the same time that a pretended reply of "His Majesty's ship———" was heard, a broadside from her guns, which had been trained aft on purpose, was poured into the *Aurora*, and at so short a distance, doing considerable execution. The crew of the *Aurora*, hearing the hailing in English, and the vessel passing them apparently without firing, had imagined that she had been one of their own cruisers. The captains of the guns had dropped their lanyards in disappointment, and the silence which had been maintained as the two vessels met was just breaking up in various ways of lamentation at their bad luck, when the broadside was poured in, thundering in their ears, and the ripping and tearing of the beams and planks astonished their senses. Many were carried down below, but it was difficult to say whether indignation at the enemy's ruse, or satisfaction at discovering that they were not called to quarters in vain, most predominated. At all events, it was answered by three voluntary cheers, which drowned the cries of those who were being assisted to the cockpit.

"Man the larboard guns and about ship!" cried Captain Wilson, leaping off the hammocks. "Look out, my lads, and rake her in

---

* Brailed up his driver: Brails are small ropes by which a sail can be hoisted.

stays!* We'll pay him off for that foul play before we've done with him. Look out, my lads, and take good aim as she pays round."

The *Aurora* was put about, and her broadside poured into the stern of the Russian frigate—for such she was. It was almost dark, but the enemy, who appeared as anxious as the *Aurora* to come to action, hauled up her courses to await her coming up. In five minutes the two vessels were alongside, exchanging murderous broadsides at little more than pistol-shot—running slowly in for the land, then not more than five miles distant. The skin-clad mountaineers of Corsica were aroused by the furious cannonading, watching the incessant flashes of the guns, and listening to their reverberating roar.

After half an hour's fierce combat, during which the fire of both vessels was kept up with undiminished vigour, Captain Wilson went down on the main deck, and himself separately pointed each gun after it was loaded; those amidships being direct for the main-channels of the enemy's ship, while those abaft the beam were gradually trained more and more forward, and those before the beam more and more aft, so as to throw all their shot nearly into one focus, giving directions that they were all to be fired at once, at the word of command. The enemy, not aware of the cause of the delay, imagined that the fire of the *Aurora* had slackened, and loudly cheered. At the word given, the broadside was poured in, and, dark as it was, the effects from it were evident. Two of the midship ports of the antagonist were blown into one, and her mainmast was seen to totter, and then to fall over the side. The *Aurora* then set her courses, which had been hauled up, and shooting ahead, took up a raking position, while the Russian was still hampered with her wreck, and poured in grape and cannister† from her upper deck carronades to impede their labours on deck, while she continued her destructive fire upon the hull of the enemy from the main deck battery.

The moon now burst out from a low bank of clouds, and enabled them to accomplish their work with more precision. In a quarter of an hour the Russian was totally dismasted, and Captain Wilson ordered half of his remaining ship's company to repair the damages, which had been most severe, whilst the larboard men at quarters

---

* Rake her in stays: To fire a deadly broadside at the enemy's stern, the weakest part of the ship, while she is maneuvering and coming about.
† Grape and cannister: Small iron balls shot from cannons when in close combat; the effects were devastating.

continued the fire from the main deck. The enemy continued to return the fire from four guns, two on each of her decks, which she could still make bear upon the *Aurora;* but after some time even these ceased, either from the men having deserted them, or from their being dismounted. Observing that the fire from her antagonist had ceased, the *Aurora* also discontinued, and the jolly-boat astern being still uninjured, the second lieutenant was deputed to pull alongside of the frigate to ascertain if she had struck.

The beams of the bright moon silvered the rippling water as the boat shoved off; and Captain Wilson and his officers, who were still unhurt, leant over the shattered sides of the *Aurora,* waiting for a reply: suddenly the silence of the night was broken upon by a loud splash from the bows of the Russian frigate, then about three cables' length distant.

"What could that be?" cried Captain Wilson. "Her anchor's down. Mr Jones, a lead over the side, and see what water we have."

Mr Jones had long been carried down below, severed in two with a round shot—but a man leaped into the chains, and lowering down the lead sounded in seven fathoms.

"Then I suspect he will give us more trouble yet," observed Captain Wilson; and so indeed it proved, for the Russian captain, in reply to the second lieutenant, had told him in English, "that he would answer that question with his broadside," and before the boat was dropped astern, he had warped round with the springs on his cable, and had recommenced his fire upon the *Aurora.*

Captain Wilson made sail upon his ship, and sailed round and round the anchored vessel, so as to give her two broadsides to her one, and from the slowness with which she worked at her springs upon her cables, it was evident that she must be now very weak-handed. Still the pertinacity and decided courage of the Russian captain convinced Captain Wilson, that, in all probability, he would sink at his anchor before he would haul down his colours; and not only would he lose more of the *Aurora's* men, but also the Russian vessel, without he took a more decided step. Captain Wilson, therefore, resolved to try her by the board. Having poured in a raking fire, he stood off for a few moments, during which he called the officers and men on deck, and stated his intention. He then went about, and himself conning* the *Aurora,* ran her on board the Russian, pouring in his

* Conning: Directing the steering.

reserved broadside as the vessels came into collision, and heading his men as they leaped on the enemy's decks.

Although, as Captain Wilson had imagined, the Russian frigate had not many men to oppose to the *Aurora's*, the deck was obstinately defended, the voice and the arm of the Russian captain were to be heard and seen everywhere, and his men, encouraged by him, were cut down by numbers where they stood.

Our hero, who had the good fortune to be still unhurt, was for a little while close to Captain Wilson when he boarded, and was about to oppose his unequal force against that of the Russian captain, when he was pulled back by the collar by Mr Hawkins, the chaplain, who rushed in advance with a sabre in his hand. The opponents were well matched, and it may be said that, with little interruption, a hand-to-hand conflict ensued, for the moon lighted up the scene of carnage, and they were well able to distinguish each other's faces. At last, the chaplain's sword broke: he rushed in, drove the hilt into his antagonist's face, closed with him, and they both fell down the hatchway together. After this, the deck was gained, or rather cleared, by the crew of the *Aurora*, for few could be said to have resisted, and in a minute or two the frigate was in their possession. The chaplain and the Russian captain were hoisted up, still clinging to each other, both senseless from the fall, but neither of them dead, although bleeding from several wounds.

As soon as the main deck had been cleared, Captain Wilson ordered the hatches to be put on, and left a party on board while he hastened to attend to the condition of his own ship and ship's company.

It was daylight before anything like order had been restored to the decks of the *Aurora*; the water was still smooth, and instead of letting go her own anchor, she had hung on with a hawser* to the prize, but her sails had been furled, her decks cleared, guns secured, and the buckets were dashing away the blood from her planks and the carriages of the guns, when the sun rose and shone upon them. The numerous wounded had, by this time, been put into their hammocks, although there were still one or two cases of amputation to be performed.

The carpenter had repaired all shot-holes under or too near to the water-line, and then had proceeded to sound the well of the prize;

---

* Hawser: A large rope or small cable.

but although her upper works had been dreadfully shattered, there was no reason to suppose that she had received any serious injury below, and therefore the hatches still remained on, although a few hands were put to the pumps to try if she made any water. It was not until the *Aurora* presented a more cheerful appearance that Captain Wilson went over to the other ship, whose deck, now that the light of heaven enabled them to witness all the horrors even to minuteness, presented a shocking spectacle of blood and carnage. Body after body was thrown over; the wounded were supplied with water and such assistance as could be rendered until the surgeons could attend them; the hatches were then taken off, and the remainder of her crew ordered on deck; about two hundred obeyed the summons, but the lower deck was as crowded with killed and wounded as was the upper. For the present the prisoners were handed over down into the fore-hold of the *Aurora*, which had been prepared for their reception, and the work of separation of the dead from the living then underwent. After this, such repairs as were immediately necessary were made, and a portion of the *Aurora*'s crew, under the orders of the second lieutenant, were sent on board to take charge of her. It was not till the evening of the day after this night conflict that the *Aurora* was in a situation to make sail. All hands were then sent on board of the *Trident*, for such was the name of the Russian frigate, to fit her out as soon as possible. Before morning,—for there was no relaxation from their fatigue, nor was there any wish for it,—all was completed, and the two frigates, although in a shattered condition, were prepared to meet any common conflict with the elements. The *Aurora* made sail with the *Trident* in tow; the hammocks were allowed to be taken down, and the watch below permitted to repose.

In this murderous conflict the *Trident* had more than two hundred men killed and wounded. The *Aurora*'s loss had not been so great, but still it was severe, having lost sixty-five men and officers. Among the fallen there were Mr Jones, the master, the third lieutenant Mr Arkwright, and two midshipmen killed. Mr Pottyfar, the first lieutenant, was severely wounded at the commencement of the action. Martin the master's mate, and Gascoigne, the first mortally, and the second badly, were wounded. Our hero had also received a slight cutlass wound, which obliged him to wear his arm, for a short time, in a sling.

Among the ship's company who were wounded was Mesty; he had been hurt with a splinter before the *Trident* was taken by the board, but had remained on deck, and had followed our hero, watching over him and protecting him as a father. He had done even more, for he had with Jack thrown himself before Captain Wilson, at a time that he had received such a blow with the flat of a sword as to stun him, and bring him down on his knee. And Jack had taken good care that Captain Wilson should not be ignorant, as he really would have been, of this timely service on the part of Mesty, who certainly, although with a great deal of 'sang froid' in his composition when in repose, was a fiend incarnate when his blood was up.

"But you must have been with Mesty," observed Captain Wilson, "when he did me the service."

"I was with him, sir," replied Jack, with great modesty; "but was of very little service."

"How is your friend Gascoigne this evening?"

"Oh, not very bad, sir—he wants a glass of grog."

"And Mr Martin?"

Jack shook his head.

"Why, the surgeon thinks he will do well."

"Yes, sir, and so I told Martin; but he said that it was very well to give him hope—but that he thought otherwise."

"You must manage him, Mr Easy; tell him that he is sure of his promotion."

"I have, sir, but he won't believe it. He never will believe it till he has his commission signed. I really think that an acting order would do more than the doctor can."

"Well, Mr Easy, he shall have one to-morrow morning. Have you seen Mr Pottyfar? he, I am afraid, is very bad."

"Very bad, sir; and they say is worse every day, and yet his wound is healthy, and ought to be doing well."

Such was the conversation between Jack and his captain, as they sat at breakfast on the third morning after the action.

The next day Easy took down an acting order for Martin, and put it into his hands. The mate read it over as he lay bandaged in his hammock.

"It's only an acting order, Jack," said he; "it may not be confirmed."

Jack swore, by all the articles of war, that it would be; but Martin replied that he was sure it never would.

"No, no," said the mate, "I knew very well that I never should be made. If it is not confirmed, I may live; but if it is, I am sure to die."

Everyone that went to Martin's hammock wished him joy of his promotion; but six days after the action, poor Martin's remains were consigned to the deep.

The next person who followed him was Mr Pottyfar, the first lieutenant, who had contrived, wounded as he was, to reach a packet of the universal medicine, and had taken so many bottles before he was found out, that he was one morning found dead in his bed, with more than two dozen empty phials under his pillow, and by the side of his mattress. He was not buried with his hands in his pockets, but when sewed up in his hammock, they were, at all events, laid in the right position.

CHAPTER XXX

Modern philanthropy, which, as usual, is the cause of much trouble and vexation.

IN THREE WEEKS the *Aurora*, with her prize in tow, arrived at Malta. The wounded were sent to the hospital, and the gallant Russian captain recovered from his wounds about the same time as Mr Hawkins, the chaplain.

Jack, who constantly called to see the chaplain, had a great deal to do to console him. He would shake his hands as he lay in his bed, exclaiming against himself. "Oh," would he say, "the spirit is willing, but the flesh is weak. That I, a man of God, as they term me, who ought to have been down with the surgeons, whispering comfort to the desponding, should have gone on deck (but I could not help it), and have mixed in such a scene of slaughter. What will become of me?"

Jack attempted to console him by pointing out, that not only chaplains, but bishops, have been known to fight in armour from time immemorial. But Mr Hawkins's recovery was long doubtful, from the agitation of his mind. When he was able to walk, Jack introduced to him the Russian captain, who was also just out of his bed.

"I am most happy to embrace so gallant an officer," said the Russian, who recognised his antagonist, throwing his arms round the chaplain, and giving him a kiss on both cheeks. "What is his rank?" continued he, addressing himself to Jack, who replied, very quietly, "that he was the ship's padre."

"The padre!" replied the captain, with surprise, as Hawkins turned away with confusion. "The padre—par exemple! Well, I always had a great respect for the church. Pray, sir," said he, turning to Easy, "do your padres always head your boarders?"

"Always, sir," replied Jack; "it's a rule of the service—and the duty of a padre to show the men the way to heaven. It's our ninety-ninth article of war."

"You are a fighting nation," replied the Russian, bowing to Hawkins, and continuing his walk, not exactly pleased that he had been floored by a parson.

Mr Hawkins continued very disconsolate for some time; he then invalided, and applied himself to his duties on shore, where he would not be exposed to such temptations from his former habits.

As the *Aurora*, when she was last at Malta, had nearly exhausted the dockyard for her repairs, she was even longer fitting out this time, during which Captain Wilson's despatches had been received by the admiral, and had been acknowledged by a brig sent to Malta. The admiral, in reply, after complimenting him upon his gallantry and success, desired that, as soon as he was ready, he should proceed to Palermo with communications of importance to the authorities, and having remained there for an answer, was again to return to Malta to pick up such of his men as might be fit to leave the hospital, and then join the Toulon fleet. This intelligence was soon known to our hero, who was in ecstasies at the idea of again seeing Agnes and her brothers. Once more the *Aurora* sailed away from the high-crowned rocks of Valette, and with a fine breeze dashed through the deep blue waves.

But towards the evening the breeze increased, and they were under double-reefed topsails. On the second day they made the coast of Sicily, not far from where Easy and Gascoigne had been driven on shore; the weather was then more moderate, and the sea had, to a great degree, subsided. They therefore stood in close to the coast, as they had not a leading wind to Palermo. As they stood in, the glasses, as usual, were directed to land; observing the villas with which the hills and valleys were studded, with their white fronts embowered in orange groves.

"What is that, Gascoigne," said Easy, "under that precipice?—it looks like a vessel."

Gascoigne turned his glass in the direction— "Yes, it is a vessel on the rocks: by her prow she looks like a galley."

"It is a galley, sir—one of the row galleys—I can make out her bank of oars," observed the signal-man.

This was reported to Captain Wilson, who also examined her.

"She is on the rocks, certainly," observed he; "and I think I see people on board. Keep her away a point, quarter-master."

The *Aurora* was now steered right for the vessel, and in the course of an hour was not more than a mile from her. Their suppositions were correct—it was one of the Sicilian government galleys bilged on the rocks, and they now perceived that there were people on board of her, making signals with their shirts and pieces of linen.

"They must be the galley-slaves; for I perceive that they do not one of them change their positions: the galley must have been abandoned by their officers and seamen, and the slaves left to perish."

"That's very hard," observed Jack to Gascoigne; "they were condemned to the galleys, but not to death."

"They will not have much mercy from the waves," replied Gascoigne; "they will all be in kingdom come to-morrow morning, if the breeze comes more on the land. We have already come up two points this forenoon."

Although Captain Wilson did not join in this conversation, which he overheard as he stood on the forecastle gun, with his glass over the hammocks, it appears he was of the same opinion: but he demurred: he had to choose between allowing so many of his fellow-creatures to perish miserably, or to let loose upon society a set of miscreants, who would again enter a course of crime until they were re-captured, and, by so doing, probably displease the Sicilian authorities. After some little reflection he resolved that he would take his chance of the latter. The *Aurora* was hove-to in stays, and the two cutters ordered to be lowered down, and the boat's crew to be armed.

"Mr Easy, do you take one cutter, and the armourers; pull on board of the galley, release those people, and land them in small divisions. Mr Gascoigne, you will take the other to assist Mr Easy, and when he lands them in his boat, you will pull by his side ready to act, in case of any hostile attempt on the part of the scoundrels; for we must not expect gratitude: of course, land them at the nearest safe spot for debarkation."

In pursuance of these orders, our two midshipmen pulled away to the vessel. They found her fixed hard upon the rocks, which had pierced her slight timbers, and, as they had supposed, the respectable part of her crew, with the commander, had taken to the boats, leaving the galley-slaves to their fate. She pulled fifty oars, but had only thirty-six manned. These oars were forty feet long, and ran in from the thole-pin with a loom six feet long, each manned by four slaves, who were chained to their seat before it, by a running chain made fast by a padlock in amidships. A plank, of two feet wide, ran fore and aft the vessel between the two banks of oars, for the boatswain to apply the lash to those who did not sufficiently exert themselves.

"Viva los Inglesos!" cried the galley-slaves, as Easy climbed up over the quarter of the vessel.

"I say, Ned, did you ever see such a precious set of villains?" observed Easy, as he surveyed the faces of the men who were chained.

"No," replied Gascoigne; "and I think if the captain had seen them as we have, that he would have left them where they were."

"I don't know—but, however, our orders are positive. Armourer, knock off all the padlocks, beginning aft; when we have a cargo we will land them. How many are there?—twelve dozen;—twelve dozen villains to let loose upon society. I have a great mind to go on board again and report my opinion to the captain—one hundred and forty-four villains, who all deserve hanging—for drowning is too good for them."

"Our orders are to liberate them, Jack."

"Yes; but I should like to argue this point with Captain Wilson."

"They'll send after them fast enough, Jack, and they'll all be in limbo again before long," replied Gascoigne.

"Well, I suppose we must obey orders; but it goes against my conscience to save such villainous-looking rascals. Armourer, hammer away."

The armourer, who with the seamen appeared very much of Jack's opinion, and had not commenced his work, now struck off the padlocks one by one with his sledgehammer. As soon as they were released the slaves were ordered into the cutter, and when it was sufficiently loaded Jack shoved off, followed by Gascoigne as guard, and landed them at the point about a cable's length distant. It required six trips before they were all landed; the last cargo were on shore, and Easy was desiring the men to shove off, when one of the galleriens turned round, and cried out to Jack in a mocking tone, "Addio, signor, a reveder la." Jack started, stared, and, in the squalid, naked wretch who addressed him, he recognised Don Silvio!

"I will acquaint Don Rebiera of your arrival, signor," said the miscreant, springing up the rocks, and mixing with the rest, who now commenced hooting and laughing at their preservers.

"Ned," observed Easy to Gascoigne, "we have let that rascal loose."

"More's the pity," replied Gascoigne; "but we have only obeyed orders."

"It can't be helped, but I've a notion there will be some mischief out of this."

"We obeyed orders," replied Gascoigne.

"We've let the rascals loose not ten miles from Don Rebiera's."

"Obeyed orders, Jack."

"With a whole gang to back him, if he goes there."

"Orders, Jack."

"Agnes at his mercy."

"Captain's orders, Jack."

"I shall argue this point when I go on board," replied Jack.

"Too late, Jack."

"Yes," replied Easy, sinking down on the stern sheets with a look of despair.

"Give way, my lads, give way."

Jack returned on board, and reported what he had done: also that Don Silvio was among those liberated; and he ventured to mention his fears of what might take place from their contiguity to the house of Don Rebiera. Captain Wilson bit his lips: he felt that his philanthropy had induced him to act without his usual prudence.

"I have done a rash thing, Mr Easy, I am afraid. I should have taken them all on board and delivered them up to the authorities. I wish I had thought of that before. We must get to Palermo as fast as we can, and have the troops sent after these miscreants. Hands 'bout ship, fill the main yard."

The wind had veered round, and the *Aurora* was now able to lay up clear of the island of Maritimo.* The next morning she anchored in Palermo Roads—gave immediate notice to the authorities, who, wishing Captain Wilson's philanthropy at the devil, immediately despatched a large body of troops in quest of the liberated malefactors. Captain Wilson, feeling for Jack's anxiety about his friends, called him over to him on deck, and gave him and Gascoigne permission to go on shore.

---

* Maritimo: The island of Marettimo, off the western coast of Sicily.

"Will you allow me to take Mesty with me, sir, if you please?" said Jack.

"Yes, Mr Easy; but recollect that, even with Mesty, you are no match for one hundred and fifty men; so be prudent. I send you to relieve your anxiety, not to run into danger."

"Of course, sir," replied Jack, touching his hat, and walking away quietly till he came to the hatchway, when he darted down like a shot, and was immediately occupied with his preparations.

In half an hour our two midshipmen, with Mesty, had landed, and proceeded to the inn where they had put up before: they were armed up to the teeth. Their first inquiries were for Don Philip and his brother.

"Both on leave of absence," replied the landlord, "and staying with Don Rebiera."

"That's some comfort," thought Jack. "Now we must get horses as fast as we can.—Mesty, can you ride?"

"By all de power, can I ride, Massa Easy; suppose you ride Kentucky horse, you ride anyting."

In half an hour four horses and a guide were procured, and at eight o'clock in the morning the party set off in the direction of Don Rebiera's country seat.

They had not ridden more than six miles when they came up with one of the detachments sent out in pursuit of the liberated criminals. Our hero recognised the commanding officer as an old acquaintance, and imparting to him the release of Don Silvio, and his fears upon Don Rebiera's account, begged him to direct his attention that way.

"Corpo di Bacco—you are right, Signor Mid," replied the officer, "but Don Philip is there, and his brother too, I believe. I will be there by ten o'clock to-morrow morning; we will march almost the whole night."

"They have no arms," observed Easy.

"No, but they will soon get them: they will go to some small town in a body, plunder it, and then seek the protection of the mountains. Your captain has given us a pretty job."

Jack exchanged a few more words, and then, excusing himself on account of his haste, put the spurs to his horse and regained his own party, who now proceeded at a rapid pace.

"O signor!" said the guide, "we shall kill the horses."

"I'll pay for them," said Jack.

"Yes, but we shall kill them before we get there, Jack," replied Gascoigne, "and have to walk the rest of the way."

"Very true, Ned; let's pull up, and give them their wind."

"By de holy poker, Massa Easy, but my shirt stick to my ribs," cried Mesty, whose black face was hung with dewdrops from their rapid course.

"Never mind, Mesty."

It was about five o'clock in the afternoon when they arrived at the seat of Don Rebiera. Jack threw himself off his jaded steed, and hastened into the house, followed by Gascoigne. They found the whole family collected in the large sitting-room, quite ignorant of any danger threatening them, and equally astonished and pleased at the arrival of their old friends. Jack flew to Agnes, who screamed when she saw him, and felt so giddy afterwards that he was obliged to support her. Having seated her again, he was kindly greeted by the old people and the two young officers. After a few minutes dedicated to mutual inquiries, our hero stated the cause of their expeditious arrival.

"Don Silvio with one hundred and fifty galleriens, let loose on the coast yesterday afternoon!" exclaimed Don Rebiera; "you are right, I only wonder they were not here last night. But I expect Pedro from the town; he has gone down with a load of wine: he will bring us intelligence."

"At all events, we must be prepared," said Don Philip; "the troops, you say, will be here to-morrow morning."

"Holy Virgin!" exclaimed the ladies, in a breath.

"How many can we muster?" said Gascoigne.

"We have five men here, or we shall have by the evening," replied Don Philip— "all, I think, good men—my father, my brother, and myself."

"We are three—four with the guide, whom I know nothing about."

"Twelve in all—not one too many; but I think that now we are prepared, if they attack, we can hold out till the morning."

"Had we not better send the ladies away?" said Jack.

"Who is to escort them?" replied Don Philip; "we shall only weaken our force; besides, they may fall into the miscreants' hands."

"Shall we all leave the house together? they can but plunder it," observed Don Rebiera.

"Still, we may be intercepted by them, and our whole force will be nothing against so many," observed Don Philip, "if we are without defence, whereas in the house we shall have an advantage."

"E' vero," replied Don Rebiera, thoughtfully; "then let us prepare, for depend upon it Don Silvio will not lose such an opportunity to wreak his vengeance. He will be here to-night: I only wonder he has not been here with his companions before. However, Pedro will arrive in two hours."

"We must now see what means we have of defence," said Philip. "Come, brother—will you come, sir?"

CHAPTER XXXI

A regular set-to, in which the parties beaten are not knocked down, but rise higher and higher at each discomfiture—Nothing but the troops could have prevented them from going up to heaven.

DON REBIERA and his two sons quitted the room, Gascoigne entered into conversation with the senora, while Easy took this opportunity of addressing Agnes. He had been too much occupied with the consultation to pay her much attention before. He had spoken, with his eyes fixed upon her, and had been surprised at the improvement which had taken place in less than a year. He now went to her, and asked her, in a low voice, "whether she had received his letter?"

"Oh, yes!" replied she, colouring.

"And were you angry with what I said, Agnes?" in a low tone.

"No," replied she, casting her eyes down on the floor.

"I repeat now what I said, Agnes—I have never forgotten you."

"But—"

"But what?"

"Father Thomaso."

"What of him?"

"He never will—"

"Will what?"

"You are a heretic, he says."

"Tell him to mind his own business."

"He has great influence with my father and mother."

"Your brothers are on our side."

"I know that, but there will be great difficulty. Our religion is not the same. He must talk to you—he will convert you."

"We'll argue that point, Agnes. I will convert him if he has common sense; if not, it's no use arguing with him. Where is he?"

"He will soon be at home."

"Tell me, Agnes, if you had your own will, would you marry me?"

"I don't know; I have never seen anyone I liked so well."

"Is that all?"

"Is it not enough for a maiden to say?" replied Agnes, raising her eyes, and looking reproachfully. "Signor, let me go, here comes my father."

Notwithstanding, Jack cast his eyes to the window where Gascoigne and the senora were in converse, and, perceiving that the old lady's back was turned, he pressed Agnes to his bosom before he released her. The gentlemen then returned with all the fire-arms and destructive weapons they could collect.

"We have enough," observed Don Philip, "to arm all the people we have with us."

"And we are well armed," replied Jack, who had left Agnes standing alone. "What now are your plans?"

"Those we must now consult about. It appears"—but at this moment the conversation was interrupted by the sudden entrance of Pedro, who had been despatched to the town with the load of wine. He rushed in, flurried and heated, with his red cap in his hand.

"How now, Pedro, back so early!"

"O signor!" exclaimed the man—"they have taken the cart and the wine, and have drawn it away, up to the mountains."

"Who?" inquired Don Rebiera.

"The galley-slaves who have been let loose—and by the body of our blessed saint, they have done pretty mischief—they have broken into the houses, robbed everything—murdered many—clothed themselves with the best—collected all the arms, provisions, and wine they could lay their hands on, and have marched away into the mountains. This took place last night. As I was coming down within a mile of the town, they met me with my loaded cart, and they turned the bullocks round and drove them away along with the rest. By the blessed Virgin! but they are stained with blood, but not altogether of men, for they have cut up some of the oxen. I heard this from one of the herdsmen, but he too fled, and could not tell me more. But, signor, I heard them mention your name."

"I have no doubt of it," replied Don Rebiera. "As for the wine, I only hope they will drink too much of it to-night. But, Pedro, they will be here, and we must defend ourselves—so call the men together; I must speak to them."

"We shall never see the bullocks again," observed Pedro, mournfully.

"No: but we shall never see one another again, if we do not take care. I have information they come here to-night."

"Holy Saint Francis! and they say there are a thousand of them."

"Not quite so many, to my knowledge," observed Jack.

"They told me that a great many were killed in their attack upon the town, before they mastered it."

"So much the better. Go now, Pedro, drink a cup of wine, and then call the other men."

The house was barricadoed as well as circumstances would permit; the first story was also made a fortress by loading the landing-place with armoires and chests of drawers. The upper story, or attic, if it might be so called, was defended in the same way, that they might retreat from one to the other if the doors were forced.

It was eight o'clock in the evening before all was ready, and they were still occupied with the last defence, under the superintendence of Mesty, who showed himself an able engineer, when they heard the sound of an approaching multitude. They looked out of one of the windows, and perceived the house surrounded by the galley-slaves, in number apparently about a hundred. They were all dressed in a most fantastic manner with whatever they could pick up: some had fire-arms, but the most of them were supplied with only swords or knives. With them came also their cortège of plunder: carts of various descriptions, loaded with provisions of all sorts, and wine; women lashed down with ropes, sails from the vessels and boats to supply them with covering in the mountains, hay and straw, and mattresses. Their plunder appeared to be well chosen for their exigencies. To the carts were tied a variety of cattle, intended to accompany them to their retreat. They all appeared to be under a leader, who was issuing directions—that leader was soon recognised by those in the house to be Don Silvio.

"Massa Easy, you show me dat man," said Mesty, when he heard the conversation between Easy and the Rebieras; "only let me know him."

"Do you see him there, Mesty, walking down in front of those men? He has a musket in his hand, a jacket with silver buttons, and white trousers."

"Yes, Massa Easy, me see him well—let me look little more—dat enough."

The galley-slaves appeared to be very anxious to surround the house that no one should escape, and Don Silvio was arranging the men.

"Ned," said Jack, "let us show him that we are here. He said that he would acquaint Don Rebiera with our arrival—let us prove to him that he is too late."

"It would not be a bad plan," replied Gascoigne; "if it were possible that these fellows had any gratitude among them, some of them might relent at the idea of attacking those who saved them."

"Not a bit; but it will prove to them that there are more in the house than they think for; and we can frighten some of them by telling them that the soldiers are near at hand."

Jack immediately threw up the casement, and called out in a loud voice, "Don Silvio! galley-slave! Don Silvio!"

The party hailed turned round, and beheld Jack, Gascoigne, and Mesty, standing at the window of the upper floor.

"We have saved you the trouble of announcing us," called out Gascoigne. "We are here to receive you."

"And in three hours the troops will be here, so you must be quick, Don Silvio," continued Jack.

"*A reveder la,*" continued Gascoigne, letting fly his pistol at Don Silvio.

The window was then immediately closed. The appearance of our heroes, and their communication of the speedy arrival of the troops, was not without effect. The criminals trembled at the idea; Don Silvio was mad with rage—he pointed out to the men the necessity of immediate attack—the improbability of the troops arriving so soon, and the wealth which he expected was locked up by Don Rebiera in his mansion. This rallied them, and they advanced to the doors, which they attempted to force without success, losing several men by the occasional fire from those within the house. Finding their efforts, after half an hour's repeated attempts, to be useless, they retreated, and then bringing up a long piece of timber, which required sixty men to carry it, they ran with it against the door, and the weight and impetus of the timber drove it off its hinges, and an entrance was obtained; by this time it was dark, the lower story had been abandoned, but the barricade at the head of the stairs opposed their progress. Convenient loop-holes had been prepared by the defenders, who now opened a smart fire upon the assailants, the latter having no means of returning it effectually, had they had ammunition for their muskets, which fortunately they had not been able to procure. The combat now became fierce, and the galley-slaves were several times repulsed with great loss during a contest of two hours; but, encouraged by Don Silvio, and refreshed by repeated draughts of wine, they continued by degrees removing the barriers opposed to them.

"We shall have to retreat," exclaimed Don Rebiero; "very soon they will have torn down all. What do you think, Signor Easy?"

"Hold this as long as we can. How are we off for ammunition?"

"Plenty as yet—plenty to last for six hours, I think."

"What do you say, Mesty?"

"By holy St Patrig, I say hold out here—they got no fire-arms—and we ab um at arm-length."

This decision was the occasion of the first defence being held for two hours more, an occasional relief being afforded by the retreat of the convicts to the covered carts.

At last it was evident that the barricade was no longer tenable, for the heavy pieces of furniture they had heaped up to oppose entrance, were completely hammered to fragments by poles brought up by the assailants, and used as battering-rams. The retreat was sounded; they all hastened to the other story, where the ladies were already placed, and the galley-slaves were soon in possession of the first floor—exasperated by the defence, mad with wine and victory, but finding nothing.

Again was the attack made upon the second landing, but, as the stairs were now narrower, and their defences stronger in proportion, they, for a long while, gained no advantage. On the contrary, many of their men were wounded, and taken down below.

The darkness of the night prevented both parties from seeing distinctly, which was rather in favour of the assailants. Many climbed over the fortress of piled-up furniture, and were killed as soon as they appeared on the other side, and, at last, the only ammunition used was against those who made this rash attempt. For four long hours did this assault and defence continue, until daylight came, and then the plan of assault was altered: they again brought up the poles, hammered the pieces of furniture into fragments, and gained ground. The defenders were worn out with fatigue, but flinched not; they knew that their lives, and the lives of those dearest to them, were at stake, and they never relaxed their exertions; still the criminals, with Silvio at their head, progressed, the distance between the parties gradually decreased, and there was but one massive chest of drawers now defending the landing-place, and over which there was a constant succession of blows from long poles and cutlasses, returned with the bullets from their pistols.

"We must now fight for our lives," exclaimed Gascoigne to Easy, "for what else can we do?"

"Do?—get on the roof and fight there, then," replied Jack.

"By-the-bye, that's well thought of, Jack, said Gascoigne. "Mesty, up and see if there is any place we can retreat to in case of need."

Mesty hastened to obey, and soon returned with a report that there was a trap-door leading into the loft under the roof, and that they could draw the ladder up after them.

"Then we may laugh at them," cried Jack. "Mesty, stay here while I and Gascoigne assist the ladies up," explaining to the Rebieras and to their domestics why they went.

Easy and Gascoigne hastened to the signora and Agnes, conducted them up the ladder into the loft, and requested them to have no fear; they then returned to the defences on the stairs, and joined their companions. They found them hard pressed, and that there was little chance of holding out much longer; but the stairs were narrow, and the assailants could not bring their force against them. But now, as the defences were nearly destroyed, although the convicts could not reach them with their knives, they brought up a large supply of heavy stones, which they threw with great force and execution. Two of Don Rebiera's men and Don Martin were struck down, and this new weapon proved most fatal.

"We must retreat, Jack," said Gascoigne; "the stones can do no harm where we are going to. What think you, Don Philip?"

"I agree with you; let those who are wounded be first carried up, and then we will follow."

This was effected, and as soon as the wounded men were carried up the ladder, and the arms taken up to prevent their falling into the hands of the assailants, for they were now of little use to them, the ammunition being exhausted, the whole body went into the large room which contained the trap-door of the loft, and, as soon as they were up, they drew the ladder after them. They had hardly effected this, when they were followed with the yells and shoutings of the galley-slaves, who had passed the last barriers, and thought themselves sure of their prey: but they were disappointed—they found them more secure than ever.

Nothing could exceed the rage of Don Silvio at the protracted resistance of the party, and the security of their retreat. To get at them was impossible, so he determined to set fire to the room, and suffocate them, if he could do no otherwise. He gave his directions to his men, who rushed down for straw, but in so doing, he carelessly passed under the trap-door, and Mesty, who had carried up with him two or three of the stones, dashed one down on the head of Don Silvio, who fell immediately. He was carried away, but his orders were put in execution; the room was filled with straw and fodder, and lighted. The effects were soon felt: the trap-door had been shut, but the heat and smoke burst through; after a time, the planks and rafters took fire, and their situation was terrible. A small trap-window in the roof, on the side of the house, was knocked open, and gave them a temporary relief; but now the rafters burned and crackled, and the smoke burst on them in thick columns. They could not see, and with difficulty could breathe. Fortunately the room below that which had been fired was but one out of four on the attics, and, as the loft they were in spread over the whole of the roof, they were able to remove far from it. The house was slated with massive slate of some hundred weights each, and it was not found possible to remove them so as to give air although frequent attempts were made. Donna Rebiera sank exhausted in the arms of her husband, and Agnes fell into those of our hero, who, enveloped in the smoke, kissed her again and again; and she, poor girl, thinking that they must all inevitably perish, made no scruple, in what she supposed her last moment, of returning these proofs of her ardent attachment.

"Massy Easy, help me here,—Massa Gascoigne come here. Now heab wid all your might: when we get one off we get plenty."

Summoned by Mesty, Jack and Gascoigne put their shoulders to one of the lower slates; it yielded, was disengaged, and slid down with a loud rattling below. The ladies were brought to it, and their heads put outside; they soon recovered; and now that they had removed one, they found no difficulty in removing others. In a few minutes they were all with their heads in the open air, but still the house was on fire below, and they had no chance of escape. It was while they were debating upon that point, and consulting as to their chance of safety, that a breeze of wind wafted the smoke that issued from the roof away from them, and they beheld the detachment of troops making up to the house; a loud cheer was given, and attracted the notice of the soldiers. They perceived Easy and his companions; the house was surrounded and entered in an instant.

The galley-slaves who were in the house, searching for the treasure reported by Don Silvio to be concealed, were captured or killed, and in five minutes the troops had possession. But how to assist those above was the difficulty. The room below was in flames, and burning fiercely. There were no ladders that could reach so high, and there were no means of getting to them. The commandant made signs from below, as if to ask what he was to do.

"I see no chance," observed Don Philip, mournfully. "Easy, my dear fellow, and you, Gascoigne, I am sorry that the feuds of our family should have brought you to such a dreadful death; but what can be done?"

"I don't know," replied Jack, "unless we could get ropes."

"You quite sure, Massy Easy, that all galley rascals below gone?" asked Mesty.

"Yes," replied Easy, "you may see that; look at some of them bound there, under charge of the soldiers."

"Den, sar, I tink it high time we go too."

"So do I, Mesty; but how?"

"How? stop a little. Come, help me, Massy Easy; dis board" (for the loft was floored) "is loose; come help, all of you."

They all went, and with united strength pulled up the board.

"Now strike like hell!—and drive down de plaster," said Mesty, commencing the operation.

In a few minutes they had beaten an opening into one of the rooms below not on fire, pulled up another board, and Mesty having fetched the ladder, they all descended in safety, and, to the astonishment of the commandant of the troops, walked out of the door of the house, those who had been stunned with the stones having so far recovered as to require little assistance.

The soldiers shouted as they saw them appear, supporting the females. The commanding officer, who was an intimate friend of Don Philip, flew to his arms. The prisoners were carefully examined by

Mesty, and Don Silvio was not among them. He might, however, be among the dead who were left in the house, which now began to burn furiously. The galley-slaves who were captured amounted in number to forty-seven. Their dead they could not count. The major part of the plunder, and the carts, were still where they had been drawn up.

As soon as the culprits had been secured, the attention of the troops was directed to putting out the flames, but their attempts were ineffectual; the mansion was burned to the bare walls, and but little of the furniture saved; indeed, the major part of it had been destroyed in the attack made by Don Silvio and his adherents.

Leaving directions with Pedro and his people, that the property collected by the miscreants should be restored to the owners, Don Rebiera ordered the horses, and with the whole party put himself under the protection of the troops, who, as soon as they had been refreshed, and taken some repose, bent their way back to Palermo with the galley-slaves, bound and linked together in a long double row.

They halted when they had gone half-way, and remained for the night. The next day at noon, Don Rebiera and his family were once more in their palazzo, and our two midshipmen and Mesty took their leave, and repaired on board to make themselves a little less like chimney-sweepers.

Captain Wilson was not out of the ship. Jack made his report, and then went down below, very much pleased at what had passed, especially as he would have another long yarn for the governor on his return to Malta.

CHAPTER XXXII

In which our hero and Gascoigne ought to be ashamed of themselves, and did feel what might be called midshipmite compunction.

THE *AURORA* continued three weeks at Palermo, during which the most active search had been made for the remainder of the galley-slaves, and some few had been captured, but still Don Silvio, and a considerable number, were at large; and it was said that they had retired to the fastnesses in the mountains. Our hero was constantly on shore at Don Rebiera's house, and, after what had passed, he was now looked upon as soon to become a member of the family. The difference of religion was overlooked by Don Rebiera and the relations—by all but the confessor, Father Thomaso, who now began to agitate and fulminate into the ears of the Donna Rebiera all the pains and penalties attending heretical connection, such as excommunication and utter damnation. The effects of his remonstrances were soon visible, and Jack found that there was constraint on the part of the old lady, tears on the part of Agnes, and all father confessors heartily wished at the devil ten times a day, on the part of Don Philip and his brother. At last he wormed the truth out of Agnes, who told her tale, and wept bitterly.

"Ned, I don't much like the appearance of things," observed Jack; "I must get rid of that Father Thomaso."

"You'll find that rather difficult," observed Gascoigne; "besides, if you were rid of him you would have his place filled up with another."

"He has frightened that poor old woman into the dismals, and she has the pains of purgatory on her already. I shall go and talk to Mesty."

"How can Mesty help you?"

"I don't know, but you can't; so, for want of better advice, I'll try the Ashantee."

Our hero went to Mesty, and laid the difficult affair open to him.

"I see," said Mesty, showing his filed teeth, "you want him skull."

"No, I don't, Mesty; but I want him out of the way."

"How that possible, Massy Easy?—ship sail day after to-morrow. Now 'pose I ab time, I soon manage all dat. Stop a little."

"Confound it! but there's no stopping," replied Jack.

"Suppose, Massy Easy, you get leave go on shore—not come off again."

"That will be deserting, Mesty."

"By holy poker, I ab it—you go on shore and break your leg."

"Break my leg!—break my leave, you mean?"

"No, Massy Easy—you break your leg—den captain leave you shore, and leave me to take care of you."

"But why should I break my leg, and how am I to break my leg?"

"Only pretend break leg, Massa Easy. Go talk Massa Don Philip, he manage all dat.—Suppose man break his leg in seven pieces, it is not possible to take him board."

"Seven pieces, Mesty! that's rather too many. However, I'll think of this."

Jack then went back and consulted Gascoigne, who approved of Mesty's advice, and thought the scheme feasible.

"If we could only pretend that we were thrown out of a caricola, you break your leg, a compound fracture of course—I break my arm—both left on shore at sick quarters, with Mesty to take care of us."

"Capital, indeed," replied Jack; "I really would not mind it if it really took place; at all events we'll overturn the caricola."

"But shall we get leave the last day?"

"Yes, it's two days since I have been on shore, for I have not liked to go to Don Rebiera's since what Agnes told me. Besides, my clothes are all on shore, and that will be an excuse for a few hours."

Our two midshipmen applied for leave the next morning to be off in the afternoon. The first lieutenant gave them permission. They hastened to the hotel, sent for Don Philip, and made him a party to their plan. He readily promised his assistance, for he had resolved that our hero should marry his sister, and was fearful of the effect of his absence, coupled with Friar Thomaso's influence over his mother. He went to the surgeon of his regiment, who immediately entered into the scheme.

Our two midshipmen got into a caricola, rattled up and down the streets, and perceiving Captain Wilson at his window, flogged the horse into a gallop; when abreast of the barracks Jack ran the wheel against a bank, and threw himself and Gascoigne out. Midshipmen are never hurt by these accidents, but fortunately for the success of the enterprise their faces were cut and bruised. Don Philip was standing by: he called the men to pick up our two scamps, carried them into the barracks, and sent for the surgeons, who undressed them, put Jack's left leg into a multitude of splints, and did the same to Gascoigne's arm. They were then put to bed, their contused faces, with the blood, left "in statu quo," while Don Philip sent an orderly, as from the commandant, to Captain Wilson, to acquaint him that two of his officers had been thrown out of a caricola, and were lying dangerously hurt at the barracks.

"Good heavens, it must be Mr Easy and Mr Gascoigne!" said Captain Wilson, when the intelligence was communicated; "I saw them galloping down the street like two madmen just now. Coxswain, take the gig on board and tell the surgeon to come on shore immediately, and bring him up to me at the barracks."

Captain Wilson then put on his hat, buckled on his sword, and hastened to ascertain the extent of the injury. Don Philip kept out of the way, but the captain was ushered into the room by one of the officers, where he found, in two beds, our two midshipmen stretched out, the surgeon of the forces and the regimental surgeon in consultation between them, while attendants were standing by each bed with restoratives. The medical gentlemen saluted Captain Wilson, and looked very grave, talked about fractures, contusions, injuries, in the most interminable manner—hoped that Mr Easy would recover—but had doubts. The other gentleman might do well with care; that is, so far as his arm was concerned, but there appeared to be a concussion of the brain. Captain Wilson looked at the cut and blood-smeared faces of the two young men, and waited with anxiety the arrival of his own surgeon, who came at last, puffing with the haste he had made, and received the report of the brothers of the faculty.

The leg of Mr Easy fractured in two places—had been set—bone protruding—impossible to move him. Gascoigne, arm, compound fracture—contusion of the brain not certain. Now that all this would have been discovered to be false if the surgeon had been able to examine, is true; but how could he not credit the surgeon of the forces and the regimental surgeon, and how could he put the young men to fresh tortures by removing splints and unsetting limbs? Politeness, if nothing else, prevented his so doing, for it would have been as much as to say that either he did not credit their report, or that he doubted their skill. He looked at our hero and his companion, who kept their eyes closed, and breathed heavily with their mouths open, put on a grave face, as well as his brothers in the art, and reported to Captain Wilson.

"But when can they be moved, Mr Daly?" inquired the latter; "I cannot wait; we must sail to-morrow, or the next day at the farthest."

The surgeon, as in duty bound, put the question to the others, who replied that there would be great risk in moving before the fever, which might be expected the next day, and which might last ten days; but that Captain Wilson had better not think of removing them, as they should have every care and attention where they were, and could rejoin the ship at Malta. Mr Daly, the surgeon, agreed that this would be the most prudent step, and Captain Wilson then gave his consent.

That being settled, he walked up to the bed of Gascoigne, and spoke to him; but Gascoigne knew that he was to have a concussion of the brain, and he made no reply, nor gave any signs of knowing that Captain Wilson was near him. He then went to our hero, who, at the sound of Captain Wilson's voice, slowly opened his eyes without moving his head, and appeared to recognise him.

"Are you in much pain, Easy?" said the captain, kindly.

Easy closed his eyes again, and murmured, "Mesty, Mesty!"

"He wants his servant, the ship's corporal, sir," said the surgeon.

"Well," replied Captain Wilson, "he had better have him: he is a faithful fellow, and will nurse him well. When you go on board, Mr Daly, desire the first lieutenant to send Mesty on shore with Mr Gascoigne's and Mr Easy's chests, and his own bag and hammock. Good heavens! I would not for a thousand pounds that this accident had occurred. Poor foolish boys—they run in couples, and if one's in a scrape the other is sure to share it. Gentlemen, I return you many thanks for your kindness, and I must accept of your promised care for my unfortunate officers. I sail to-morrow at daylight. You will oblige me by informing their friends, the Rebieras, of their mischance, as I am sure they will contribute all they can to their comfort." So saying, Captain Wilson bowed and quitted the room, followed by the surgeon.

As soon as the door was closed the two midshipmen turned their heads round and looked at each other, but they were afraid to speak at first, in case of the return of the surgeon. As soon as it was announced to them that Captain Wilson and Mr Daly were outside the barrack-gate, our hero commenced—"Do you know, Ned, that my conscience smites me, and if it had not been that I should have betrayed those who wish to oblige us, when poor Captain Wilson appeared so much hurt and annoyed at our accident, I was very near getting up and telling him of the imposition, to relieve his mind."

"I agree with you, Jack, and I felt much the same—but what's done cannot be undone. We must now keep up the imposition for the sake of those who, to help us, have deceived him."

"I don't think that you would find an English surgeon who would have consented to such an imposition."

"No, that is certain; but after all, it is an imposition that has hurt nobody."

"Oh, I do not wish to moralise—but I repent of my share in the deceit; and had it to be done over again I would not consent to it."

"Not even for———? but I won't mention her name in barracks."

"I don't know," replied Jack; "but let's say no more about it, and thank these gentlemen for their kindness."

"Yes, but we must keep it up until we see the *Aurora* under all sail."

"And longer too," replied Jack; "we must not let the affair get wind even on shore. We must not recover quickly, but still appear to recover. Don Rebiera and his wife must be deceived. I have a plot in my head, but I cannot work it out clear till I see Mesty."

Don Philip now came in. He had seen Captain Wilson, who had requested him to look after the two invalids, and stated his intention to sail the next morning. They consulted with him, and it was agreed that no one should be acquainted with the real fact but his brother Martin, and that all Palermo should be as much deceived as Captain Wilson, for if not, it would put Father Thomaso on the *"qui vive,"** and make him fulminate more than ever. Our midshipmen ate an excellent dinner, and then remained in bed conversing till it was time to go to sleep; but long before that, Mesty had made his appearance with their clothes. The eyes of the Ashantee said all that was necessary—he never spoke a word, but unlashed his hammock and lay down in a corner, and they were soon all three asleep.

The next morning Captain Wilson called to ascertain how our hero and his companion were, but the room had been darkened, and he could not see their faces plainly. Easy thanked him for his kindness in allowing Mesty to attend them, and having received his orders as to their joining the ship as soon as they recovered, and having promised to be very cautious in their behaviour and keep out of all scrapes, he wished them a speedy recovery, and departed.

In little more than half an hour afterwards, Mesty, who had been peeping out of the shutters, suddenly threw them open with a loud laugh.

The *Aurora* was under way, with studding sails below and aloft standing out of the roads. Jack and Gascoigne got up, threw off the splints, and danced about in their shirts. As soon as they were quiet again, Mesty said in a grave tone, "Den why you stay at sea, Massa Easy?"

"Very true, Mesty, I've asked myself that question often enough lately; because I'm a fool, I suppose."

* *"Qui vive"*: Alert.

"And I, because I can't help it," replied Gascoigne; "never mind, we are on shore now, and I look for a famous cruise."

"But first we must see what the ground is we are to cruise on," replied Jack; "so, Mesty, let us have a palaver, as they say in your country."

The two midshipmen got into their beds, and Mesty sat on the chest between them, looking as grave as a judge. The question was, how to get rid of the padre Thomaso. Was he to be thrown over the mole-head to the fishes—or his skull broke—was Mesty's knife to be resorted to—was he to be kidnapped or poisoned—or were fair means to be employed—persuasion, bribery? Every one knows how difficult it is to get rid of a priest.

As our hero and Gascoigne were not Italians, they thought that bribery would be the more English-like way of doing the thing; so they composed a letter, to be delivered by Mesty to the friar, in which Jack offered to Father Thomaso the moderate sum of one thousand dollars, provided he would allow the marriage to proceed, and not frighten the old lady with ecclesiastical squibs and crackers.

As Mesty was often on shore with Jack, and knew the friar very well by sight, it was agreed that the letter should be confided to his charge; but as it was not consistent that a person in such a state as our hero was represented to be should sit up and write letters, the delivery was deferred for a few days, when after waiting that time, Mesty delivered the letter to the friar, and made signs that he was to take back the answer. The friar beckoned him that he was to accompany him to his room, where he read the letter, and then again made signs to him to follow him. The friar led the way to his monastery, and as soon as Mesty was in his cell, he summoned another who could speak English to act as interpreter.

"Is your master recovering?"

"Yes," replied Mesty, "he is at present doing well."

"Have you served him long?"

"No," replied Mesty.

"Are you very fond of him? does he treat you well, give you plenty of money?"

At these questions, the artful black conceived that there was something in the wind, and he therefore very quietly replied, "I do not care much for him."

The friar fixed his keen eye upon Mesty, and perceived there was a savage look about the black, from which he augured that he was a man who would suit his purpose.

"Your master offers me a thousand dollars; would you wish to gain this money for yourself?"

Mesty grinned, and showed his sharp-filed teeth.

"It would make me a rich man in my own country."

"It would," replied the friar; "now, you shall have it, if you will only give your master a small powder."

"I understand," replied Mesty; "hab those things in my country."

"Well—do you consent?—if so, I will write the letter to get the money."

"Suppose they find me out?" replied Mesty.

"You will be safe, and you shall be sent away as soon as possible—say, will you consent?"

"The whole thousand dollars?"

"Every one of them."

"Den give me the powder!"

"Stay a little," replied the friar, who went out of the cell, and, in about ten minutes, returned with an answer to our hero's letter, and a paper containing a greyish powder.

"Give him this in his soup or anything—spread it on his meat, or mix it up with his sugar if he eats an orange."

"I see," replied Mesty.

"The dollars shall be yours, I swear it on the holy cross."

Mesty grinned horribly, took his credentials, and then asked, "When I come again?"

"As soon as you have received the money bring it to me at Don Rebiera's—then give the powder: as soon as it is given you must let me know, for you must not remain in Palermo. I will myself conduct you to a place of safety."

Mesty then quitted the cell, and was shown out of the monastery.

"By de holy poker, he one d——n rascal!" muttered Mesty, as he was once in the open air. "But stop a little."

The Ashantee soon arrived at the barracks, and repeated the whole of the conference between him and Friar Thomaso.

"It must be poison, of course," observed Gascoigne; "suppose we try it upon some animal?"

"No, Massa Gascoigne," replied Mesty, "I try it myself, by-and-bye. Now what we do?"

"I must give you the order for the thousand dollars, Mesty," replied Jack. "The rascal here writes to me that for that sum, he will consent not only not to oppose me, but agrees to assist my cause; but the great question is, whether he will keep his word with you, Mesty; if not, I shall lose my money. So therefore we must now have another palaver, and argue the point."

The point was argued between Jack and Gascoigne. A thousand dollars was a large sum, but Jack's father was a philosopher. After many *pros* and *cons*, it was at last decided that the money should be given to Mesty; but Mesty should state, when he took the money to the friar, that he had administered the powder, and claim it when he presented it.

The next day, the order for the money was given to Mesty, and he went to Friar Thomaso with it. The friar hastened with Mesty to the monastery, and sent for the interpreter.

"You have given it?" inquired the friar.

"Yes—not one hour ago. Here de order for de money."

"You must run for the money before he is dead, for the powder is very rapid."

"And me," replied Mesty, apparently much alarmed, "where am I to go?"

"As soon as you bring the money here, you must go back to the barracks. Remain there till he is dead, and then return here. I will have all ready, and take you, as soon as it is dusk, to a monastery of our order in the mountains, where no one will think of looking for you, till the affair is blown over; and then I will find you a passage in some vessel out of the island."

Mesty hastened for the money, and taking it in a large bag to the monastery, delivered it to the friar's charge, and then returned to the barracks to Easy and Gascoigne. It was agreed that he should go with the friar, who would probably remain away some time; indeed, Mesty insisted upon so doing. Mesty stayed two hours, and then returned about dusk to the monastery, and reported the death of our hero. He remained there until it was dark, and then the friar ordered him to tie the bag of dollars to his saddle-bow. They mounted two mules, which stood already caparisoned,* and quitted Palermo.

In the morning Don Philip, as usual, made his appearance, and told our hero that the friar had been summoned away by the abbot, and would not return for some time.

* Caparisoned: A caparison is a covering placed over a saddle.

"I came to tell you this news," said Don Philip, "as I thought it would please you; the sooner you are now well the better. I mean to propose your being both removed to my father's palazzo, and then you can recover your lost ground during the confessor's absence."

"And I have the means," replied Jack, showing the friar's letter. Don Philip read it with astonishment, but was still more surprised when he heard the whole story from Jack. He was for a time silent: at last he said,—

"I am sorry for your poor black."

"Why so?" replied Jack.

"You will never see him again, depend upon it. A thousand dollars would sign the death warrant of a thousand blacks; but there is another reason—they will put him out of the way, that he may not give evidence. Where is the powder?"

"Mesty has it; he would not part with it."

"He is a shrewd fellow, that black; he may be too much for the friar," replied Don Philip.

"He means mischief, I'm sure," replied Gascoigne.

"Still I feel a great deal of alarm about him," replied Easy; "I wish now that I had not let him go."

"Are you sure that he went?"

"No, I am not; but the friar told him that he should take him to the mountains as soon as it was dark."

"And probably he will," replied Don Philip, "as the best place to get rid of him. However, the whole of this story must be told both to my father and my mother; to the former, that he may take the right measures, and to my mother, that it may open her eyes. Give me the copy of the letter you wrote to the friar, and then I shall have it all."

The report of the accident which had occurred to Easy and Gascoigne had been spread and fully believed throughout Palermo. Indeed, as usual, it had been magnified, and asserted that they could not recover. To Agnes only had the case been imparted in confidence by Don Philip, for her distress at the first intelligence had been so great that her brother could not conceal it.

Two days after Don Philip had made his parents acquainted with the villany of the friar, the midshipmen were transported to the palazzo, much to the surprise of everybody, and much to the renown of the surgeons, who were indemnified for their duplicity and false-hood by an amazing extension of their credit as skilful men.

After their arrival at the palazzo, Don Rebiera was also entrusted with the secret, but it went no farther. As now there was no particular hurry for our hero to get well, he was contented and happy in the society of Agnes and her parents; the old lady, after she had been informed of the conduct of Friar Thomaso, having turned round in our hero's favour, and made a vow never to have a confessor in the house again. Jack and Gascoigne were now as happy as could be; all their alarm was about Mesty, for whose return they were most anxious.

To Don Rebiera, Jack made known formally his intentions with regard to Agnes. He fully satisfied him as to his qualifications and his property, and Don Rebiera was fully aware of his debt of gratitude to our hero. But all he required was the consent of Jack's father, and until this was obtained, he would not consent to the marriage taking place. Jack attempted to argue the point; his father, he said, had married without consulting him, and therefore he had a right to marry without consulting his father. But Don Rebiera, not having any acquaintance with the rights of man and equality, did not feel the full force of Jack's argument, and made it a *sine qua non* that his parents should write and consent to the alliance before it took place.

CHAPTER XXXIII

In which Mesty should be called throughout Mephistopheles, for it abounds in black cloaks, disguises, daggers, and dark deeds.

O N THE FOURTH EVENING after the removal of our two midshipmen to the palazzo of Don Rebiera, as they were sitting in company with Agnes and Don Philip in their own room, a friar made his appearance at the door. They all started, for by his height they imagined him to be Friar Thomaso, but no one addressed him. The friar shut the door without saying a word, and then lifting up his cowl, which had been drawn over it, discovered the black face of Mesty. Agnes screamed, and all sprang from their seats at this unusual and unexpected apparition. Mesty grinned, and there was that in his countenance which said that he had much to communicate.

"Where is the friar—Mesty?" inquired Easy.

"Stop a little, Massa—suppose we lock door first, and den I tell all."

Taking this precaution, Mesty threw off the friar's gown, and appeared in his own dress, with the bag of dollars slung round his body.

"Now, Massa Easy, I hab a long tory to tell—so I tink I better begin at the beginning."

"It is the most approved method," replied Jack, "but stop when I hold up my finger, that we may translate what you say to the lady and Don Philip."

"Dat all right, sar. Friar and I get on two mule as soon as it quite dark. He make me carry all tousand dollars—and we ride out of town. We go up mountain and mountain, but the moon get up shine and we go on cheek by jowl—he nebber say one word, and I nebber say one word, 'cause I no speak his lingo, and he no understand my English. About two o'clock in de morning, we stop at a house and stay dere till eight o'clock, and den we go on again all next day, up all mountain, only stop once, eat a bit bread and drink lilly wine. Second night come on, and den we stop again, and people bow very low to him, and woman bring in rabbit for make supper. I go in the kitchen, woman make stew smell very nice, so I nod my head, and I say very good, and she make a face, and throw on table black loaf of bread and garlic, and make sign dat for my supper; good enough for black fellow, and dat rabbit stew for friar. Den I say to myself, stop a little; suppose friar hab all de rabbit, I tink I give him a lilly powder."

"The powder, Mesty?" exclaimed Jack.

"What does he say?" inquired Don Philip.

Gascoigne translated all that Mesty had communicated. The interest of the narrative now became exciting. Mesty continued:—

"Well, Massa Easy, den woman she go for dish to put stew in, and I take de powder and drop it in de pot, and den I sit down again and eat black bread, she say good enough for black man. She tir up de stew once more, and den she pour it out into dish, and take it to friar. He lick um chops, by all de powers, and he like um so well he pick all de bones, and wipe up gravy with him bread. You tink it very nice, Massa Friar, tink I; but stop a little. After he drink a whole bottle of wine, he tell em bring mules to de door, and he put him hands on de woman head, and dat de way he pay for him supper.

"The moon shone bright, and we go up all mountain, always go up, and 'bout two hour, he get off him mule and he put him hand so, and set down on de rock. He twist, and he turn, and he groan, for half an hour, and den he look at me, as much as to say, you black villain, you do this? for he not able to speak, and den I pull out de paper of de powder, and I show him, and make him sign he swallow it: he look again, and I laugh at him—and he die."

"Oh, Mesty, Mesty," exclaimed our hero; "you should not have done that,—there will mischief come from it."

"Now he dead, Massa Easy, so much less mischief."

Gascoigne then interpreted to Don Philip and Agnes, the former of whom looked very grave, and the latter terrified.

"Let him go on," said Don Philip; "I am most anxious to hear what he did with the body."

Mesty, at the request of our hero, proceeded: "Den I thought what I should do, and I said I would hide him, and I tink I take his coat for myself—so I pull off him coat and I pull off all his oder clothes—he not wear many—and I take the body in my arm, and carry him where I find a great split in de rock above all road. I throw him in, and den I throw plenty large pieces rock on him till I no see him any more; den I take de two mules and get on mine wid de dollars, and lead de other three four mile, till I come to a large wood—take off him saddle and bridle, turn him adrift. Den I tear up all clothes all in lilly bits, hide one piece here, noder piece dere, and de saddle and bridle in de bush. All right, now I say; so I put on friar cloak, hide my face, get on my mule, and den I look where I shall go—so I say, I not be in dis road anyhow, I pass through wood till I find nother. I go 'bout two mile—moon go down, all dark, and five six men catch hold my bridle, and they all got arms, so I do noting—they speak to me, but I no answer, and nebber show my face. They find all dollars (d——n um) fast enough, and they lead me away through the wood. Last we come to a large fire in de wood, plenty of men lie 'bout, some eat and some drink. They pull me off, and I hold down my head and fold my arms, just like friar do. They bring me along to one man, and pour out all my dollar before him. He give some order, and they take me away, and I peep through the cloak, and I say to myself, he that d——n galley-slave rascal Don Silvio."

"Don Silvio!" cried Jack.

"What does he say of Don Silvio?" demanded Don Philip.

Mesty's narrative was again translated, and he continued.

"Dey led me away 'bout fifty yards, tie me to tree, and den they leave me, and dey all drink and make merry, nebber offer me anything, so I hab noting den to eat; I eat de ropes and gnaw them through and den I stay there two hour until all go asleep, and all quiet; for I say to myself, stop a little. Den when dey all fast asleep, I take out my knife and I crawl 'long de ground, as we do in our country sometime—and den I stop and look 'bout me; no man watch but two, and dey look out for squarl, not look in board where I was. I crawl 'gain till I lay down 'longside that d——n galley-slave Don Silvio. He lie fast asleep with my bag thousand dollars under him head. So I tink, 'you not hab dem long, you rascal.' I look round—all right, and I drive my knife good aim into him heart and press toder hand on him mouth, but he make no noise; he struggle little and look up, and den I throw off de head of de gown and show him my black face, and he look and he try to speak; but I stop dat, for down go my knife again, and de d——n galley-slave dead as herring."

"Stop, Mesty, we must tell this to Don Philip," said Gascoigne.

"Dead! Don Silvio dead! well, Mesty, we are eternally obliged to you, for there was no safety for my father while he was living. Let him go on."

"So when I put de knife through his body, I lie down by him as if noting had happened, for ten minutes, and den I take de bag of dollars from under him head, and den I feel him all over, and I find him pistols and him purse, which I hab here, all gold. So I take them and I look—all asleep, and I crawl back to de tree. Den I stay to tink a little; de man on watch come up and look at me, but he tink all right and he go away again. Lucky ting, by de power, dat I go back to tree. I wait again, and den I crawl and crawl till I clear of all, and den I take to my heel and run for um life, till daylight come, and den I so tired I lie down in bush; I stay in bush all day, and den I set off again back here, for I find road and know my way. I not eat den for one day and one night, and come to house where I put my head in and find woman there. I not able to speak, so I help myself, and not show my face. She not like dat and make a bobbery, but I lift up my cloak and show my black face and white teeth, and den she tink me de debil. She run out of de house and I help myself very quick, and den set off and come close here yesterday morning. I hide myself all day and come in at night, and now, Massa Easy, you ab all de whole truth—and you ab your tousand dollars—and you ab got rid of de rascal friar and de d——n galley-slave, Don Silvio."

"Tell them all this, Ned," said Jack, who, whilst Gascoigne was so employed, talked with Mesty.

"I was very much frightened for you, Mesty," said Jack; "but still I thought you quite as cunning as the friar, and so it has turned out; but the thousand dollars ought to be yours."

"No, sar," replied Mesty, "the dollars not mine; but I hab plenty of gold in Don Silvio's purse—plenty, plenty of gold. I keep my property, Massa Easy, and you keep yours."

"I'm afraid that this affair may be found out, Mesty; the woman will spread the report of having been attacked by a black friar, and that will lead to suspicion, as the other friars of the convent knew that you left with Friar Thomaso."

"So I tink dat, but when a man starve, he quite forget his thought."

"I don't blame you; but now I must talk to Don Philip."

"Suppose you no objection, while you talk I eat something from the table then, Massa Easy, for I hungry enough to eat de friar, mule and all."

"Eat, my good fellow, and drink as much as you please."

The consultation between our two midshipmen and Don Philip was not long: they perceived the immediate necessity for the departure of Mesty, and the suspicion which would attach to themselves. Don Philip and Agnes left them, to go to Don Rebiera, and make him acquainted with what had passed, and to ask his advice.

When they went into the room, Don Rebiera immediately accosted his son.

"Have you heard, Philip, that Friar Thomaso has returned at last?—so the servants tell me."

"The report may be fortunate," replied Don Philip; "but I have another story to tell you."

He then sat down and imparted to Don Rebiera all the adventures of Mesty. Don Rebiera was for some time in deep thought; at last he replied,—

"That Don Silvio is no more is fortunate, and the negro would be entitled to reward for his destruction—but for the friar, that is a bad business. The negro might remain and tell the whole story, and the facts might be proved by the evidence of Signor Easy, and the letters; but what then? we should raise the whole host of the clergy against our house, and we have suffered too much from them already; the best plan would be the immediate departure, not only of the negro but of our two young friends. The supposition of Friar Thomaso being here, and their departure with the negro servant to rejoin their ship, will remove much suspicion and destroy all inquiry. They must be off immediately. Go to them, Philip, and point out to them the absolute necessity of this measure, and tell our young friend that I rigidly adhere to my promise, and as soon as he has his father's sanction I will bestow upon him my daughter. In the meantime I will send down and see if a vessel can be chartered for Malta."

Our hero and Gascoigne fully admitted the wisdom of this measure, and prepared for their departure; indeed, now that Don Rebiera's resolution had been made known to our hero, he cared more for obtaining his father's consent than he did for remaining to enjoy himself at Palermo; and before noon of the next day all was ready, the vessel had been procured, Jack took his leave of Agnes and her mother, and, accompanied by Don Rebiera and Don Philip (for Don Martin was on duty a few miles from Palermo), went down to the beach, and, having bid them farewell, embarked with Gascoigne and Mesty on board of the two-masted lateen which had been engaged, and before sunset not a steeple of Palermo was to be seen.

"What are you thinking of, Jack?" said Gascoigne, after our hero had been silent half an hour.

"I have been thinking, Ned, that we are well out of it."

"So do I," replied Gascoigne; and here the conversation dropped for a time.

"What are you thinking of now, Jack?" said Gascoigne, after a long pause.

"I've been thinking that I've a good story for the old governor."

"Very true," replied Gascoigne; and both were again silent for some time.

"What are you thinking of now, Jack?" said Gascoigne, after another long interval.

"I've been thinking that I shall leave the service," replied Jack.

"I wish you would take me with you," replied Gascoigne, with a sigh; and again they were both in deep contemplation.

"What are you thinking of now, Jack?" said Gascoigne again.

"Of Agnes," replied our hero.

"Well, if that's the case, I'll call you when supper's ready. In the meantime I'll go and talk with Mesty."

CHAPTER XXXIV

Jack leaves the service, in which he had no business, and goes home to mind his own business.

ON THE FOURTH DAY they arrived at Malta, and our two midshipmen, as soon as they had settled with the padrone of the vessel, went up to the government house. They found the governor in the veranda, who held out both his hands, one to each.

"Glad to see you, my lads. Well, Jack, how's the leg—all right? don't limp? And your arm, Gascoigne?"

"All right, sir, and as sound as ever it was," replied they both.

"Then you're in luck, and have made more haste than you deserve, after your mad pranks: but now sit down, and I suppose, my friend Jack, you have a story to tell me."

"O yes, Sir Thomas, and a very long one."

"Then I won't have it now, for I expect people on business; we'll have it after dinner. Get your things up and take possession of your rooms. The *Aurora* sailed four days ago. You've had a wonderful recovery."

"Wonderful, sir!" replied our hero; "all Palermo rings with it."

"Well you may go now—I shall see you at dinner. Wilson will be delighted when he hears that you have got round again, for he was low-spirited about it, I can tell you, which is more than you deserve."

"He's right there," said our hero to Gascoigne, as they walked away.

When dinner was over, Jack narrated to the governor the adventures of Mesty, with which he was much interested; but when they were quite alone in the evening, the governor called our two midshipmen into the veranda, and said,—

"Now my lads, I'm not going to preach, as the saying is, but I've been long enough in the world to know that a compound fracture of the leg is not cured in fourteen or sixteen days. I ask you to tell me the truth. Did not you deceive Captain Wilson on this point?"

"I am ashamed to say that we did, sir," replied Easy.

"How did you manage that, and why?"

Jack then went into further details relative to himself and his amour, stating his wish to be left behind, and all that had passed.

"Well, there's some excuse for you, but none for the surgeons. If any surgeon here had played such a trick, I would have hung him, as sure as I'm governor. This affair of yours has become serious. Mr Easy, we must have some conversation on the matter to-morrow morning."

The next morning the packet from England was reported off the harbour's mouth. After breakfast the letters were brought on shore, and the governor sent for our hero.

"Mr Easy, here are two letters for you; I am sorry to say, with black seals. I trust that they do not bring the intelligence of the death of any very near relative."

Jack bowed without speaking, took the letters, and went to his room. The first he opened was from his father.

"MY DEAR JOHN,—You will be much grieved to hear that your poor mother, after sitting in the corner for nearly two years waiting for the millennium, appeared to pine away; whether from disappointment or not I do not know; but at last, in spite of all Dr Middleton could do, she departed this life; and, as the millennium would not come to her as she expected, it is to be hoped she is gone to the millennium. She was a good wife, and I always let her have her own way. Dr Middleton does not appear to be satisfied as to the cause of her death, and has wished to examine; but I said no, for I am a philosopher, and it is no use looking for causes after effects; but I have done since her death what she never would permit me to do during her life. I have had her head shaved, and examined it very carefully as a phrenologist, and most curiously has she proved the truth of the sublime science. I will give you the result. Determination, very prominent; Benevolence, small; Caution, extreme; Veneration, not very great; Philo-progenitiveness, strange to say, is very large, considering she has but one child; Imagination, very strong: you know, my dear boy, she was always imagining some nonsense or another. Her other organs were all moderate. Poor dear creature! she is gone, and we may well wail, for a better mother or a better wife never existed. And now, my dear boy, I must request that you call for your discharge, and come home as soon as possible. I cannot exist without you, and I require your assistance in the grand work I have in contemplation. The time is at hand, the cause of equality will soon triumph; the abject slaves now hold up their heads; I have electrified them with my speeches, but I am getting old and feeble; I require my son to leave my mantle to, as one prophet did to another, and then I will, like him, ascend in glory.*

> "Your affectionate Father,
> "Nicodemus Easy."

From this it would appear, thought Jack, that my mother is dead, and that my father is mad. For some time our hero remained in a melancholy mood; he dropped many tears to the memory of his mother, whom, if he had never respected, he had much loved: and it was not till half an hour had elapsed, that he thought of opening the other letter. It was from Dr Middleton.

"My dear Boy,—Although not a correspondent of yours, I take the right of having watched you through all your childhood, and from a knowledge of your disposition, to write you a few lines. That you have, by this time, discarded your father's foolish, nonsensical philosophy, I am very sure. It was I who advised your going away for that purpose, and I am sure, that, as a young man of sense, and the heir to a large property, you will before this have seen the fallacy of your father's doctrines. Your father tells me that he has requested you to come home, and allow me to add any weight I may have with you in persuading you to do the same. It is fortunate for you that the estate is entailed, or you might soon be a beggar, for there is no saying what debts he might, in his madness, be guilty of. He has already been dismissed from the magistracy by the lord-lieutenant, in consequence of his haranguing the discontented peasantry, and I may say, exciting them to acts of violence and insubordination. He has been seen dancing and hurrahing round a stack fired by an incendiary. He has turned away his keepers, and allowed all poachers to go over the manor. In short, he is not in his senses; and, although I am far from advising coercive measures, I do consider that it is absolutely necessary that you should immediately return home, and look after what will one day be your property. You have no occasion to follow the profession, with eight thousand pounds per annum. You have distinguished yourself,—now make room for those who require it for their subsistence. God bless you. I shall soon hope to shake hands with you.

> "Yours most truly,
> "G. Middleton."

---

* Ascend in glory: A reference to the prophet Elijah. Elijah, leaving his mantle for Elisha, was taken up to heaven in a whirlwind (2 Kings 2:11–15).

There was matter for deep reflection in these two letters, and Jack never felt before how much his father had been in the wrong. That he had gradually been weaned from his ideas was true, but still he had, to a certain degree, clung to them, as we do to a habit; but now he felt that his eyes were opened; the silly, almost unfeeling letter of his father upon the occasion of his mother's death, opened his eyes. For a long while Jack was in a melancholy meditation, and then casting his eyes upon his watch, he perceived that it was almost dinner-time. That he could eat his dinner was certain, and he scorned to pretend to feel what he did not. He therefore dressed himself and went down, grave, it is true, but not in tears. He spoke little at dinner, and retired as soon as it was over, presenting his two letters to the governor, and asking his advice for the next morning. Gascoigne followed him, and to him he confided his trouble; and Ned, finding that Jack was very low-spirited, consoled him to the best of his power, and brought a bottle of wine which he procured from the butler. Before they returned to bed, Jack had given his ideas to his friend, which were approved of, and wishing him a good-night, he threw himself into bed, and was soon fast asleep.

"One thing is certain, my good fellow," observed the governor to our hero, as he gave him back his letters at the breakfast table the next morning; "that your father is as mad as a March hare. I agree with that doctor, who appears a sensible man, that you had better go home immediately."

"And leave the service altogether, sir?" replied Jack.

"Why, I must say, that I do not think you exactly fitted for it. I shall be sorry to lose you, as you have a wonderful talent for adventure, and I shall have no more yarns to hear when you return; but, if I understand right from Captain Wilson, you were brought into the profession because he thought that the service might be of use in eradicating false notions, rather than from any intention or necessity of your following it up as a profession."

"I suspect that was the case, sir," replied Jack; "as, for my own part, I hardly know why I entered it."

"To find a mare's nest, my lad; I've heard all about it; but never mind that: the question is now about your leaving it, to look after your own property, and I think I may venture to say, that I can arrange all that matter at once, without referring to admiral or captain. I will be responsible for you, and you may go home in the packet, which sails on Wednesday for England."

"Thank you, Sir Thomas, I am much obliged to you," replied Jack.
"You, Mr Gascoigne, I shall, of course, send out by the first opportunity to rejoin your ship."

"Thank you, Sir Thomas, I am much obliged to you," replied
Gascoigne, making a bow.

"You'll break no more arms, if you please, sir," continued the governor; "a man in love may have some excuse in breaking his leg, but
you had none."

"I beg your pardon, sir; if Mr Easy was warranted in breaking his
leg out of love, I submit that I could do no less than break my arm
out of friendship."

"Hold your tongue, sir, or I'll break your head from the very
opposite feeling," replied the governor, good-humouredly. "But
observe, young man, I shall keep this affair secret, as in honour
bound; but let me advise you, as you have only your profession to
look to, to follow it up steadily. It is high time that you and Mr Easy
were separated. He is independent of the service, and you are not. A
young man possessing such ample means will never be fitted for the
duties of a junior officer. He can do no good for himself, and is certain to do much harm to others: a continuance of his friendship
would probably end in your ruin, Mr Gascoigne. You must be aware,
that if the greatest indulgence had not been shown to Mr Easy by his
captain and first lieutenant, he never could have remained in the service so long as he has done."

As the governor made the last remark in rather a severe tone, our
two midshipmen were silent for a minute. At last Jack observed, very
quietly,—

"And yet, sir, I think, considering all, I have behaved pretty well."

"You have behaved very well, my good lad, on all occasions in
which your courage and conduct, as an officer, have been called
forth. I admit it; and had you been sent to sea with a mind properly
regulated, and without such an unlimited command of money, I have
no doubt but that you would have proved an ornament to the service. Even now I think you would, if you were to remain in the service under proper guidance and necessary restrictions, for you have,
at least, learnt to obey, which is absolutely necessary before you are
fit to command. But recollect, what your conduct would have
brought upon you, if you had not been under the parental care of
Captain Wilson. But let us say no more about that: a midshipman
with the prospect of eight thousand pounds a-year is an anomaly

which the service cannot admit, especially when that midshipman is resolved to take to himself a wife."

"I hope that you approve of that step, sir."

"That entirely depends upon the merit of the party, which I know nothing of, except that she has a pretty face, and is of one of the best Sicilian families. I think the difference of religion a ground of objection."

"We will argue that point, sir," replied Jack.

"Perhaps it will be the cause of more argument than you think for, Mr Easy; but every man makes his own bed, and as he makes it, so must he lie down in it."

"What am I to do about Mesty, sir? I cannot bear the idea of parting with him."

"I am afraid that you must; I cannot well interfere there."

"He is of little use to the service, sir; he has been sent to sick quarters as my servant: if he may be permitted to go home with me, I will procure his discharge as soon as I arrive, and send him on board the guard-ship till I obtain it."

"I think that, on the whole, he is as well out of the service as in it, and therefore I will, on consideration, take upon myself the responsibility, provided you do as you say."

The conversation was here ended, as the governor had business to attend to, and Jack and Gascoigne went to their rooms to make their arrangements.

"The governor is right," observed Gascoigne; "it is better that we part, Jack. You have half unfitted me for the service already; I have a disgust of the midshipmen's berth; the very smell of pitch and tar has become odious to me. This is all wrong; I must forget you and all our pleasant cruises on shore, and once more swelter in my greasy jacket. When I think that, if our pretended accidents were discovered, I should be dismissed the service, and the misery which that would cause to my poor father, I tremble at my escape. The governor is right, Jack; we must part, but I hope you never will forget me."

"My hand upon it, Ned. Command my interest, if ever I have any—my money—what I have, and the house, whether it belongs to me or my father—as far as you are concerned at least, I adhere to my notions of perfect equality."

"And abjure them, I trust, Jack, as a universal principle."

"I admit, as the governor asserts, that my father is as mad as a March hare."

"That is sufficient; you don't know how glad it makes me to hear you say that."

The two friends were inseparable during the short time that they remained together. They talked over their future prospects, their hopes and anticipations, and when the conversation flagged, Gascoigne brought up the name of Agnes.

Mesty's delight at leaving the service, and going home with his patron was indescribable. He laid out a portion of his gold in a suit of plain clothes, white linen shirts, and in every respect the wardrobe of a man of fashion; in fact, he was now a complete gentleman's gentleman; was very particular in frizzing his woolly hair—wore a white neck-cloth, gloves, and cane. Every one felt inclined to laugh when he made his appearance; but there was something in Mesty's look, which, at all events, prevented their doing so before his face. The day for sailing arrived. Jack took leave of the governor, thanking him for his great kindness, and stating his intention of taking Malta in his way out to Palermo in a month or two. Gascoigne went on board with him, and did not go down the vessel's side till it was more than a mile clear of the harbour.

CHAPTER XXXV

Mr Easy's wonderful invention fully explained by himself—much to the satisfaction of our hero, and it is to be presumed to that also of the reader.

A T LAST the packet anchored in Falmouth Roads. Jack, accompanied by Mesty, was soon on shore with his luggage, threw himself into the mail, arrived in London, and, waiting there two or three days, to obtain what he considered necessary from a fashionable tailor, ordered a chaise to Forest Hill. He had not written to his father to announce his arrival, and it was late in the morning when the chaise drew up at his father's door.

Jack stepped out and rang the bell. The servants who opened the door did not know him; they were not the same as those he left.

"Where is Mr Easy?" demanded Jack.

"Who are you?" replied one of the men, in a gruff tone.

"By de powers, you very soon find out who he is," observed Mesty.

"Stay here, and I'll see if he is at home."

"Stay here? stay in the hall like a footman? What do you mean, you rascal?" cried Jack, attempting to push by the man.

"O, that won't do here, master; this is Equality Hall; one man's as good as another."

"Not always," replied Jack, knocking him down. "Take that for your insolence, pack up your traps, and walk out of the house to-morrow morning."

Mesty, in the meantime, had seized the other by the throat.

"What I do with this fellow, Massa Easy?"

"Leave him now, Mesty: we'll settle their account to-morrow morning. I presume I shall find my father in the library."

"His father!" said one of the men to the other; "he's not exactly a chip off the old block."

"We shall have a change, I expect," replied the other, as they walked away.

"Mesty," cried Jack, in an authoritative tone, "bring those two rascals back to take the luggage out of the chaise; pay the position, and tell the housekeeper to show you my room, and yours. Come to me for orders as soon as you have done this."

"Yes, sir," replied Mesty. "Now come here, you d——n black-guard, and take tings out of chaise, or by de holy poker I choak your luff, both of you."

The filed teeth, the savage look, and determination of Mesty, had the due effect. The men sullenly returned, and unloaded the chaise. In the meantime, Jack walked into his father's study; his father was there—the study was lighted up with argand lamps,* and Jack looked with astonishment. Mr Easy was busy with a plaster cast of a human head, which he pored over, so that he did not perceive the entrance of his son. The cast of the skull was divided into many com-partments, with writing on each; but what most astonished our hero was the alteration in the apartment. The book-cases and books had all been removed, and in the centre, suspended from the ceiling, was an apparatus which would have puzzled anyone, composed of rods in every direction, with screws at the end of them, and also tubes in equal number, one of which communicated with a large air-pump, which stood on a table. Jack took a short survey, and then walked up to his father and accosted him.

---

* Argand lamps: Oil-burning lamps using a cylindrical wick.

"What!" exclaimed Mr Easy, "is it possible?—yes, it is my son John! I'm glad to see you, John,—very glad, indeed," continued the old gentleman, shaking him by both hands—"very glad that you have come home; I wanted you—wanted your assistance in my great and glorious project, which, I thank Heaven, is now advancing rapidly. Very soon shall equality and the rights of man be proclaimed everywhere. The pressure from without is enormous, and the bulwarks of our ridiculous and tyrannical constitution must give way. King, lords, and aristocrats; landholders, tithe-collectors, church and state, thank God, will soon be overthrown, and the golden age revived—the millennium—the true millennium—not what your poor mother talked about. I am at the head of twenty-nine societies, and if my health lasts, you will see what I will accomplish now that I have your assistance, Jack"; and Mr Easy's eyes sparkled and flashed in all the brilliancy of incipient insanity.

Jack sighed, and to turn the conversation he observed, "You have made a great change in this room, sir. What may all this be for? Is it a machine to improve equality and the rights of man?"

"My dear son," replied Mr Easy, sitting down and crossing his legs complacently, with his two hands under his right thigh, according to his usual custom, when much pleased with himself,—"why, my dear son, that is not exactly the case, and yet you have shown some degree of perception even in your guess; for if my invention succeeds (and I have no doubt of it), I shall have discovered the great art of rectifying the mistakes of nature, and giving an equality of organisation to the whole species, of introducing all the finer organs of humanity, and of destroying the baser. It is a splendid invention, Jack, very splendid. They may talk of Gall and Spurzheim,* and all those; but what have they done? nothing but divided the brain into sections, classed the organs, and discovered where they reside; but what good result has been gained from that? the murderer by nature remained a murderer—the benevolent man a benevolent man—he could not alter his organisation. I have found out how to change all that."

"Surely, sir, you would not interfere with the organ of benevolence."

"But indeed I must, Jack. I, myself, am suffering from my organ

---

* Gall and Spurzheim: Franz Joseph Gall (1758–1828), Austrian anatomist and founder of phrenology; Johann Kaspar Spurzheim (1776–1832), German physician and phrenologist.

of benevolence being too large: I must reduce it, and then I shall be capable of greater things, shall not be so terrified by difficulties, shall overlook trifles, and only carry on great schemes for universal equality and the supreme rights of man. I have put myself into that machine every morning for two hours, for these last three months, and I feel now that I am daily losing a great portion."

"Will you do me the favour to explain an invention so extraordinary, sir?" said our hero.

"Most willingly, my boy. You observe that in the centre there is a frame to confine the human head, somewhat larger than the head itself, and that the head rests upon the iron collar beneath. When the head is thus firmly fixed, suppose I want to reduce the size of any particular organ, I take the boss corresponding to where that organ is situated in the cranium, and fix it on it. For you will observe that all the bosses inside of the top of the frame correspond to the organs as described in this plaster cast on the table. I then screw down pretty tight, and increase the pressure daily, until the organ disappears altogether, or is reduced to the size required."

"I comprehend that part perfectly, sir," replied Jack; "but now explain to me by what method you contrive to raise an organ which does not previously exist."

"That," replied Mr Easy, "is the greatest perfection of the whole invention, for without I could do that, I could have done little. I feel convinced that this invention of mine will immortalise me. Observe all these little bell-glasses which communicate with the air-pump; I shave my patient's head, grease it a little, and fix on the bell-glass, which is exactly shaped to fit the organ in length and breadth. I work the air-pump, and raise the organ by an exhausted receiver. It cannot fail. There is my butler, now; a man who escaped hanging last spring assizes on an undoubted charge of murder. I selected him on purpose; I have flattened down murder to nothing, and I have raised benevolence till it's like a wen."

"I am afraid my poor father's head is an exhausted receiver," thought Jack, who then replied, "Well, sir, if it succeeds it will be a good invention."

"If it succeeds!—why, it has succeeded—it cannot fail. It has cost me near two thousand pounds. By-the-bye, Jack, you have drawn very liberally lately, and I had some trouble, with my own expenses, to meet your bills; not that I complain—but what with societies, and my machine, and tenants refusing to pay their rents, on the principle that the farms are no more mine than theirs, which I admit to be true, I have had some difficulty in meeting all demands."

"The governor was right," thought Jack, who now inquired after Dr Middleton.

"Ah, poor silly man! he's alive yet—I believe doing well. He is one who will interfere with the business of others, complains of my servants—very silly man indeed—but I let him have his own way. So I did your poor mother. Silly woman, Mrs Easy—but never mind that."

"If you please, sir, I have also a complaint to make of the servants for their insolence to me: but we will adjourn, if you please, as I wish to have some refreshment."

"Certainly, Jack, if you are hungry; I will go with you. Complain of my servants, say you?—there must be some mistake—they are all shaved, and wear wigs, and I put them in the machine every other morning: but I mean to make an alteration in one respect. You observe, Jack, it requires more dignity: we must raise the whole machinery some feet, ascend it with state as a throne, for it is the throne of reason, the victory of mind over nature."

"As you please, sir; but I am really hungry just now."

Jack and his father went into the drawing-room and rang the bell; not being answered, Jack rose and rang again.

"My dear sir," observed Mr Easy, "you must not be in a hurry; every man naturally provides for his own wants first, and afterwards for those of others. Now my servants—"

"Are a set of insolent scoundrels, sir, and insolence I never permit. I knocked one down as I entered your house, and, with your permission, I will discharge two, at least, to-morrow."

"My dear son," exclaimed Mr Easy, "you knocked my servant down!—are you not aware, by the laws of equality—"

"I am aware of this, my dear father," replied Jack, "that by all the laws of society we have a right to expect civility and obedience from those we pay and feed."

"Pay and feed! Why, my dear son,—my dear Jack,—you must recollect—"

"I recollect, sir, very well; but if your servants do not come to their recollection in a very short time, either I or they must quit the house."

"But, my dear boy, have you forgotten the principles I instilled into you? Did you not go to sea to obtain that equality foiled by tyranny and despotism here on shore? Do you not acknowledge and support my philosophy?"

"We'll argue that point to-morrow, sir—at present I want to obtain my supper"; and Jack rang the bell furiously.

The butler made his appearance at this last summons, and he was followed by Mesty, who looked like a demon with anger.

"Mercy on me, whom have we here?"

"My servant, father," exclaimed Jack, starting up; "one that I can trust to, and who will obey me. Mesty, I wish some supper and wine to be brought immediately—see that scoundrel gets it ready in a moment. If he does not, throw him out of the door, and lock him out. You understand me."

"Yes, Massa," grinned Mesty; "now you hab supper very quick, or Mesty know the reason why. Follow me, sar," cried Mesty, in an imperative tone to the butler: "quick, sar, or by de holy poker, I show you what Mesty can do;" and Mesty grinned in his wrath.

"Bring supper and wine immediately," said Mr Easy, giving an order such as the butler had never heard since he had been in the house.

The butler quitted the room, followed by the Ashantee.

"My dear boy—my Jack—I can make every allowance for hunger, it is often the cause of theft and crime in the present unnatural state of society—but really you are too violent. The principles—"

"Your principles are all confounded nonsense, father," cried Jack, in a rage.

"What, Jack!—my son—what do I hear? This from you—nonsense! Why, Jack, what has Captain Wilson been doing with you?"

"Bringing me to my senses, sir."

"Oh dear! oh dear! my dear Jack, you will certainly make me lose mine."

"Gone already," thought Jack.

"That you, my child, so carefully brought up in the great and glorious school of philosophy, should behave this way—should be so violent—forget your sublime philosophy, and all—just like Esau, selling your birthright for a mess of pottage.* Oh, Jack, you'll kill me! and yet I love you, Jack—whom else have I to love in this world? Never mind, we'll argue the point, my boy—I'll convince you—in a week all will be right again."

"It shall, sir, if I can manage it," replied Jack.

---

* Just like Esau, selling your birthright for a mess of pottage: Esau sold his birthright to his younger brother, Jacob, for a bowl of porridge (Genesis 25:29–34).

"That's right, I love to hear you say so—that's consoling, very consoling—but I think now, I was wrong to let you go to sea, Jack."

"Indeed you were not, father."

"Well, I'm glad to hear you say so: I thought they had ruined you, destroyed all your philosophy—but it will be all right again—you shall come to our societies, Jack—I am president—you shall hear me speak, Jack—you shall hear me thunder like Demosthenes*—but here comes the tray."

The butler, followed by Mesty, who attended him as if he was his prisoner, now made his appearance with the tray, laid it down in a sulky manner and retired. Jack desired Mesty to remain.

"Well, Mesty, how are they getting on in the servants' hall?"

"Regular mutiny, sar—ab swear dat they no stand our nonsense, and dat we both leave the house to-morrow."

"Do you hear, sir? your servants declare that I shall leave your house to-morrow."

"You leave my house, Jack, after four years' absence!—no, no. I'll reason with them—I'll make them a speech. You don't know how I can speak, Jack."

"Look you, father, I cannot stand this; either give me a carte-blanche to arrange this household as I please, or I shall quit it myself to-morrow morning."

"Quit my house, Jack! no, no—shake hands and make friends with them; be civil, and they will serve you—but you know, upon the principles—"

"Principles of the devil!" cried Jack, in a rage.

"Of the devil, Jack; dear me! I wish you had never gone to sea."

"In one word, sir, do you consent, or am I to leave the house?"

"Leave the house! O no; not leave the house, Jack. I have no son but you. Then do as you please—but you must not send away my murderer, for I must have him cured, and shown as a proof of my wonderful invention."

"Mesty, get my pistols ready for to-morrow morning, and your own too—do ye hear?"

"All ready, massa," replied Mesty; "I tink dat right."

"Right!—pistols, Jack! What do you mean?"

"It is possible, father, that you may not have yet quite cured your

---

* Demosthenes: Generally considered the greatest of the Greek orators. He lived from 384–322 B.C.

murderer, and therefore it is as well to be prepared. I will now wish
you good-night; but, before I go, you will be pleased to summon one
of the servants, that he may inform the others that the household is
under my control for the future."

The bell was again rung, and was this time answered with more
expedition. Jack told the servant, in presence of his father, that, with
the consent of the latter, he should hereafter take the whole control of
the establishment, and that Mesty would be the major-domo from
whom they would receive their orders. The man stared, and cast an
appealing look to Mr Easy, who hesitated, and at last said—

"Yes, William; you'll apologise to all, and say that I have made the
arrangement."

"You apologise to none, sir," cried Jack; "but tell them that I will
arrange the whole business to-morrow morning. Tell the woman to
come here and show me my bed-room. Mesty, get your supper and
then come up to me; if they dare to refuse you, recollect who does,
and point them out to-morrow morning. That will do, sir; away with
you, and bring flat candlesticks."

CHAPTER XXXVI

In which Jack takes up the other side of the argument, and proves that he can argue as well
on one side as the other.

THIS SCENE may give some idea of the state of Mr Easy's household upon our hero's arrival. The poor lunatic, for such we must
call him, was at the mercy of his servants, who robbed, laughed at,
and neglected him. The waste and expense were enormous. Our
hero, who found how matters stood, went to bed, and lay the best
part of the night resolving what to do. He determined to send for Dr
Middleton, and consult him.

The next morning, Jack rose early; Mesty was in the room, with
warm water, as soon as he rang.

"By de power, Massa Easy, your fader very silly old man."

"I'm afraid so," replied Jack.

"He not right here," observed Mesty, putting his fingers to his
head.

Jack sighed, and desired Mesty to send one of the grooms up to the door. When the man knocked he desired him to mount a horse and ride over to Dr Middleton, and request his immediate attendance.

The man, who was really a good servant, replied, "Yes, sir," very respectfully, and hastened away.

Jack went down to breakfast, and found it all ready, but his father was not in the room: he went to his study, and found him occupied, with the carpenter, who was making a sort of a frame as the model of the platform or dais, to be raised under the wonderful invention. Mr Easy was so busy that he could not come to breakfast, so Jack took his alone. An hour after this, Dr Middleton's carriage drove up to the door. The Doctor heartily greeted our hero.

"My dear sir—for so I suppose I must now call you—I am heartily glad that you have returned. I can assure you that it is not a moment too soon."

"I have found out that already, Doctor," replied Jack; "sit down. Have you breakfasted?"

"No, I have not; for I was so anxious to see you, that I ordered my carriage at once."

"Then sit down, Doctor, and we will talk over matters quietly."

"You of course perceive the state of your father. He has been some time quite unfit to manage his own affairs."

"So I am afraid."

"What do you intend to do, then—put them in the hands of trustees?"

"I will be trustee for myself, Dr Middleton. I could not do the other without submitting my poor father to a process, and confinement, which I cannot think of."

"I can assure you, that there are not many in Bedlam* worse than he is; but I perfectly agree with you; that is, if he will consent to your taking charge of the property."

"A power of attorney will be all that is requisite," replied Jack; "that is, as soon as I have rid the house of the set of miscreants who are in it; and who are now in open mutiny."

"I think," replied the Doctor, "that you will have some trouble. You know the character of the butler."

"Yes, I have it from my father's own mouth. I really should take

* Bedlam: St. Mary of Bethlehem, a mental hospital in London.

it as a great favour, Dr Middleton, if you could stay here a day or two. I know that you have retired from practice."

"I would have made the same offer, my young friend. I will come here with two of my servants; for you must discharge these."

"I have one of my own who is worth his weight in gold—that will be sufficient. I will dismiss every man you think I ought; and as for the women, we can give them warning, and replace them at leisure."

"That is exactly what I should propose," replied the Doctor. "I will now go, if you please; procure the assistance of a couple of constables, and also of your father's former legal adviser, who shall prepare a power of attorney."

"Yes," replied Jack, "and we must then find out the tenants who refuse to pay upon the principles of equality, and he shall serve them with notice immediately."

"I am rejoiced, my dear young friend, to perceive that your father's absurd notions have not taken root."

"They lasted some time, nevertheless, Doctor," replied Jack, laughing.

"Well, then, I will only quit you for an hour or two, and then, as you wish it, will take up my quarters here as long as you find me useful."

In the forenoon, Dr Middleton again made his appearance, accompanied by Mr Hanson, the solicitor, bringing with him his portmanteau and his servants. Mr Easy had come into the parlour, and was at breakfast when they entered. He received them very coolly; but a little judicious praise of the wonderful invention had its due effect; and after Jack had reminded him of his promise that, in future, he was to control the household, he was easily persuaded to sign the order for his so doing—that is, the power of attorney.

Mr Easy also gave up to Jack the key of his escritoire, and Mr Hanson possessed himself of the books, papers, and receipts necessary to ascertain the state of his affairs, and the rents which had not yet been paid up. In the meantime the constables arrived. The servants were all summoned; Mr Hanson showed them the power of attorney, empowering Jack to act for his father, and, in less than half an hour afterwards, all the men-servants, but two grooms, were dismissed; the presence of the constables and Mesty prevented any resistance, but not without various threats on the part of the butler, whose name was O'Rourke. Thus, in twenty-four hours, Jack had made a reformation in the household.

Mr Easy took no notice of anything; he returned to his study and his wonderful invention. Mesty had received the keys of the cellar, and had now complete control over those who remained. Dr Middleton, Mr Hanson, Mr Easy, and Jack, sat down to dinner, and everything wore the appearance of order and comfort. Mr Easy ate very heartily, but said nothing till after dinner, when as was his usual custom, he commenced arguing upon the truth and soundness of his philosophy.

"By-the-bye, my dear son, if I recollect right, you told me last night that you were no longer of my opinion. Now, if you please, we will argue this point."

"I'll argue the point with all my heart, sir," replied Jack, "will you begin?"

"Let's fill our glasses," cried Mr Easy, triumphantly; "let's fill our glasses, and then I will bring Jack back to the proper way of thinking. Now then, my son, I trust you will not deny that we are all born equal."

"I do deny it, sir," replied Jack; "I deny it *in toto*—deny it from the evidence of our own senses, and from the authority of Scripture. To suppose all men were born equal, is to suppose that they are equally endowed with the same strength, and with the same capacity of mind, which we know is not the case. I deny it from Scripture, from which I could quote many passages; but I will restrict myself to one—the parable of the Talents: 'To one he gave five talents, to another but one,' holding them responsible for the trust reposed in them. We are all intended to fill various situations in society, and are provided by Heaven accordingly."

"That may be," replied Mr Easy; "but that does not prove that the earth was not intended to be equally distributed among all alike."

"I beg your pardon; the proof that that was not the intention of Providence, is that that equality, allowing it to be put in practice, could never be maintained."

"Not maintained!—no, because the strong oppress the weak, tyrants rise up and conquer—men combine to do wrong."

"Not so, my dear father; I say it could not be maintained without the organisation of each individual had been equalised, and several other points established. For instance, allowing that every man had, *ab origine*, a certain portion of ground. He who was the strongest or the cleverest would soon cause his to yield more than others would, and thus the equality be destroyed. Again, if one couple had ten children, and another had none, then again would equality be broken in upon, as the land that supports two in the one instance, would have to feed twelve in the other. You perceive, therefore, that without rapine or injustice, your equality could not be preserved."

"But, Jack, allowing that there might be some diversity from such causes, that would be a very different thing from the present monstrous state of society, in which we have kings and lords, and people, rolling in wealth, while others are in a state of pauperism, and obliged to steal for their daily bread."

"My dear father, I consider that it is to this inequality that society owes its firmest cementation—that we are enabled to live in peace and happiness, protected by just laws, each doing his duty in that state of life to which he is called, rising above or sinking in the scale of society according as he has been entrusted with the five talents or the one. Equality can and does exist nowhere. We are told that it does not exist in heaven itself—how can it exist upon earth?"

"But that is only asserted, Jack, and it is not proof that it ought not to exist."

"Let us argue the point, father, coolly. Let us examine a little what would be the effect if all was equality. Were all equal in beauty there would be no beauty, for beauty is only by comparison—were all equal in strength, conflicts would be interminable—were all equal in rank, and power, and possessions, the greatest charms of existence would be destroyed—generosity, gratitude, and half the finer virtues would be unknown. The first principle of our religion, charity, could not be practised—pity would never be called forth—benevolence, your great organ, would be useless, and self-denial a blank letter. Were all equal in ability, there would be no instruction, no talent, no genius—nothing to admire, nothing to copy, to respect—nothing to rouse emulation, or stimulate to praiseworthy ambition. Why, my dear father, what an idle, unprofitable, weary world would this be, if it were based on equality!"

"But, allowing all that, Jack," replied Mr Easy, "and I will say you argue well in a bad cause, why should the inequality be carried so far—king and lords, for instance?"

"The most lasting and imperishable form of building is that of the pyramid, which defies ages, and to that may the most perfect form of society be compared. It is based upon the many, and rising by degrees, it becomes less as wealth, talent, and rank increase in the individual, until it ends at the apex or monarch, above all. Yet each several stone from the apex to the base is necessary for the preservation of the structure, and fulfils its duty in its allotted place. Could you prove that those at the summit possess the greatest share of happiness in this world, then, indeed, you have a position to argue on; but it is well known that such is not the case; and provided he is of a contented mind, the peasant is more happy than the king, surrounded as the latter is by cares and anxiety."

"Very well argued, indeed, my dear sir," observed Dr Middleton.

"But, my dear boy, there are other states of society than monarchy; we have republics and despotisms."

"We have, but how long do they last compared to the first? There is a cycle in the changes which never varies. A monarchy may be overthrown by a revolution, and republicanism succeed, but that is shortly followed by despotism, till, after a time, monarchy succeeds again by unanimous consent, as the most legitimate and equitable form of government; but in none of these do you find a single advance to equality. In a republic, those who govern are more powerful than the rulers in a restricted monarchy—a president is greater than a king, and next to a despot, whose will is law. Even in small societies you find, that some will naturally take the lead and assume domination. We commence the system at school, when we are first thrown into society, and there we are taught systems of petty tyranny. There are some few points in which we obtain equality in this world, and that equality can only be obtained under a well-regulated form of society, and consists in an equal administration of justice and of laws, to which we have agreed to submit for the benefit of the whole—the equal right to live and not be permitted to starve, which has been obtained in this country. And when we are called to account, we shall have equal justice. Now my dear father, you have my opinion."

"Yes, my dear, this is all very well in the abstract; but how does it work?"

"It works well. The luxury, the pampered state, the idleness—if you please, the wickedness—of the rich, all contribute to the support, the comfort, and employment of the poor. You may behold extravagance—it is a vice; but that very extravagance circulates money, and the vice of one contributes to the happiness of many. The only vice which is not redeemed by producing commensurate good, is avarice. If all were equal, there would be no arts, no manufactures, no industry, no employment. As it is, the inequality of the distribution of wealth may be compared to the heart, pouring forth the blood like a steam-engine through the human frame, the same blood returning from the extremities by the veins, to be again propelled, and keep up a healthy and vigorous circulation."

"Bravo, Jack!" said Dr Middleton. "Have you anything to reply, sir?" continued he, addressing Mr Easy.

"To reply, sir?" replied Mr Easy, with scorn; "why, he has not given me half an argument yet: why that black servant even laughs at him—look at him there showing his teeth. Can he forget the horrors of slavery? can he forget the base unfeeling lash? No, sir, he has suffered, and he can estimate the divine right of equality. Ask him now, ask him, if you dare, Jack, whether he will admit the truth of your argument."

"Well, I'll ask him," replied Jack, "and I tell you candidly that he was once one of your disciples. Mesty, what's your opinion of equality?"

"Equality, Massa Easy?" replied Mesty, pulling up his cravat; "I say d——n equality, now I major-domo."

"The rascal deserves to be a slave all his life."

"True, I ab been slave—but I a prince in my own country. Massa Easy tell how many skulls I have."

"Skulls—skulls—do you know anything of the sublime science? Are you a phrenologist?"

"I know man's skull very well in Ashantee country, anyhow."

"Then if you know that, you must be one. I had no idea that the science had extended so far—maybe it was brought from thence. I will have some talk with you to-morrow. This is very curious. Dr Middleton, is it not?"

"Very, indeed, Mr Easy."

"I shall feel his head to-morrow after breakfast, and if there is anything wrong, I shall correct it with my machine. By-the-bye, I have quite forgot, gentlemen; you will excuse me, but I wish to see what the carpenter has done for me, and after that I shall attend the meeting of the society. Jack, my boy, won't you come and hear my speech?"

"Thank you, sir, but I cannot well leave your friends."

Mr Easy quitted the room.

"Are you aware, my dear sir, that your father has opened his preserves to all the poachers?" said Mr Hanson.

"The devil he has!"

"Yes, he has allowed several gangs of gipsies to locate themselves in his woods much to the annoyance of the neighbourhood, who suffer from their depredations," continued Dr Middleton.

"I find, by the receipts and books, that there is nearly two years' rental of the estate due; some tenants have paid up in full, others not for four years. I reckon fourteen thousand pounds still in arrear."

"You will oblige me by taking immediate steps, Mr Hanson, for the recovery of the sums due."

"Most certainly, Mr John. I trust your father will not commit himself to-night as he has done lately."

When they rose to retire, Dr Middleton took our hero by the hand. "You do not know, my dear fellow, what pleasure it gives me to find that, in spite of the doating of your mother and the madness of your father, you have turned out so well. It is very fortunate that you have come home; I trust you will now give up the profession."

"I have given it up, sir; which, by-the-bye, reminds me that I have not applied for either my discharge or that of my servant; but I cannot spare time yet, so I shall not report myself."

CHAPTER XXXVII

In which our hero finds himself an orphan, and resolves to go to sea again without the smallest idea of equality.

T HE NEXT MORNING, when they met at breakfast, Mr Easy did not make his appearance, and Jack inquired of Mesty where he was.

"They say down below that the old gentleman not come home last night."

"Did not come home!" said Dr Middleton; "this must be looked to."

"He great rascal, dat butler man," said Mesty to Jack; "but de old gentleman not sleep in his bed, dat for sure."

"Make enquiries when he went out," said Jack.

"I hope no accident has happened," observed Mr Hanson; "but his company has lately been very strange."

"Nobody see him go out, sar, last night," reported Mesty.

"Very likely he is in his study," observed Dr Middleton; "he may have remained all night, fast asleep, by his wonderful invention."

"I'll go and see," replied Jack.

Dr Middleton accompanied him, and Mesty followed. They opened the door, and beheld a spectacle which made them recoil with horror. There was Mr Easy, with his head in the machine, the platform below fallen from under him, hanging, with his toes just touching the ground. Dr Middleton hastened to him, and, assisted by Mesty and our hero, took him out of the steel collar which was round his neck: but life had been extinct for many hours, and, on examination, it was found that the poor old gentleman's neck was dislocated.

It was surmised that the accident must have taken place the evening before, and it was easy to account for it. Mr Easy, who had had the machine raised four feet higher, for the platform and steps to be placed underneath, must have mounted on the frame modelled by the carpenter for his work, and have fixed his head in, for the knob was pressed on his bump of benevolence. The framework, hastily put together with a few short nails, had given way with his weight, and the sudden fall had dislocated his neck.

Mr Hanson led away our hero, who was much shocked at this unfortunate and tragical end of his poor father, while Dr Middleton ordered the body to be taken up into a bedroom, and immediately despatched a messenger to the coroner of the county. Poor Mr Easy had told his son but the day before, that he felt convinced that this wonderful invention would immortalise him, and so it had, although not exactly in the sense that he anticipated.

We must pass over the few days of sorrow, and closed shutters, which always are given to these scenes. The coroner's inquest and the funeral over, daylight was again admitted, our hero's spirits revived, and he found himself in possession of a splendid property, and his own master.

He was not of age, it is true, for he wanted nine months; but on opening the will of his father, he found that Dr Middleton was his sole guardian. Mr Hanson, on examining and collecting the papers, which were in the greatest confusion, discovered bank-notes in different corners, and huddled up with bills and receipts, to the amount of two thousand pounds, and further, a cheque signed by Captain Wilson on his banker, for the thousand pounds advanced by Mr Easy, dated more than fifteen months back.

Dr Middleton wrote to the Admiralty, informing them that family affairs necessitated Mr John Easy, who had been left at sick quarters, to leave his Majesty's service, requesting his discharge from it forthwith. The Admiralty were graciously pleased to grant the request, and lose the services of a midshipman. The Admiralty were also pleased to grant the discharge of Mesty, on the sum required for a substitute being paid in.

The gipsies were routed out of their abodes, and sent once more to wander. The gamekeepers were restored, the preserves cleared of all poachers, and the gentry of the country were not a little pleased at Jack's succession, for they had wished that Mr Easy's neck had been broken long ago. The societies were dissolved, since, now that Mr Easy no longer paid for the beer, there was nothing to meet for. Cards and compliments were sent from all parts of the county, and every one was anxious that our hero should come of age, as then he would be able to marry, to give dinners, subscribe to the foxhounds, and live as a gentleman ought to do.

But during all these speculations, Jack had made Dr Middleton acquainted with the history of his amour with Agnes de Rebiera, and all particulars connected therewith, also with his determination to go out to bring her home as his wife. Dr Middleton saw no objection to the match, and he perceived that our hero was sincere. And Jack had made inquiries when the packet would sail for Malta, when Mesty, who stood behind his chair, observed,—

"Packet bad vessel, Massa Easy. Why not go out in man-of-war?"

"Very true," replied Jack; "but you know, Mesty, that is not so easy."

"And den how come home, sar? Suppose you and Missy Agnes taken prisoner—put in prison?"

"Very true," replied Jack; "and as for a passage home in a man-of-war, that will be more difficult still."

"Den I tink, sar, suppose you buy one fine vessel—plenty of guns—take out letter of marque*—plenty of men, and bring Missy Agnes home like a lady. You captain of your own ship."

"That deserves consideration, Mesty," replied Jack, who thought of it during that night: and the next day resolved to follow Mesty's advice. The Portsmouth paper lay on the breakfast-table. Jack took it up, and his eye was caught by an advertisement for the sale of the *Joan d'Arc*, prize to H.M. ship *Thetis*, brigantine of 278 tons, copper-bottomed, armed, *'en flute,'*† with all her stores, spars, sails, running

---

* Letter of marque: A license from a sovereign authorizing the captain of a privately owned ship to seek reprisal against a hostile state.

† *"En flute"*: Said of a warship that is not carrying all its armament so that it can be used in transport.

and standing rigging, then lying in the harbour of Portsmouth, to take place on the following Wednesday.

Jack rang the bell, and ordered post-horses.

"Where are you going, my dear boy?" inquired Dr Middleton.

"To Portsmouth, Doctor."

"And pray what for, if not an impertinent question?"

Jack then gave Dr Middleton an insight into his plan, and requested that he would allow him to do so, as there was plenty of ready money.

"But the expense will be enormous."

"It will be heavy, sir, I grant; but I have calculated it pretty nearly, and I shall not spend at the rate of more than my income. Besides, as letter of marque, I shall have the right of capture; in fact, I mean to take out a privateer's regular licence."

"But not to remain there and cruise?"

"No, upon my honour; I am too anxious to get home again. You must not refuse me, my dear guardian."

"As a lady is in the case, I will not, my dear boy; but be careful what you are about."

"Never fear, sir, I will be back in four months, at the farthest; but I must now set off and ascertain if the vessel answers the description given in the advertisement."

Jack threw himself into the chariot. Mesty mounted into the rumble, and in two hours they were at Portsmouth; went to the agent, viewed the vessel, which proved to be a very fine fast-sailing craft, well found, with six brass carronades on each side. The cabins were handsome, fitted up with bird's-eye maple, and gilt mouldings.

This will do, thought Jack: a couple of long brass nines, forty men and six boys, and she will be just the thing we require. So Mesty and Jack went on shore again, and returned to Forest Hill to dinner, when he desired Mr Hanson to set off for Portsmouth, and bid at the sale for the vessel, as he wished to purchase her. This was Monday, and on Wednesday Mr Hanson purchased her, as she stood, for £1750, which was considered about half her value.

Dr Middleton had, in the meantime, been thinking very seriously of Jack's project. He could see no objection to it, provided that he was steady and prudent, but in both these qualities Jack had not exactly been tried. He therefore determined to look out for some steady naval lieutenant, and make it a *sine qua non* that our hero should be accompanied by him, and that he should go out as sailing-master.

Now that the vessel was purchased, he informed Jack of his wish; indeed, as Dr Middleton observed, his duty as guardian demanded this precaution, and our hero, who felt very grateful to Dr Middleton, immediately acquiesced.

"And, by-the-bye, Doctor, see that he is a good navigator; for although I can fudge a day's work pretty well, latterly I have been out of practice."

Everyone was now busy: Jack and Mesty at Portsmouth, fitting out the vessel, and offering three guineas ahead to the crimps for every good able seaman—Mr Hanson obtaining the English register, and the letters of licence, and Dr Middleton in search of a good naval dry-nurse. Jack found time to write to Don Philip and Agnes, apprising them of the death of his father, and his intentions.

In about six weeks all was ready, and the brigantine, which had taken out her British register and licence under the name of the *Rebiera*, went out of harbour, and anchored at Spithead. Dr Middleton had procured, as he thought, a very fit person to sail with Jack, and our hero and Mesty embarked, wishing the Doctor and Solicitor good-bye, and leaving them nothing to do but to pay the bills.

The person selected by Dr Middleton, by the advice of an old friend of his, a purser in the navy, who lived at Southsea, was a Lieutenant Oxbelly, who, with the ship's company, which had been collected, received our hero as their captain and owner upon his arrival on board. There certainly was no small contrast between our hero's active slight figure and handsome person, set off with a blue coat, something like the present yacht-club uniform, and that of his second in command, who waddled to the side to receive him. He was a very short man, with an uncommon protuberance of stomach, with shoulders and arms too short for his body, and hands much too large, more like the paws of a Polar bear than anything else. He wore trousers, shoes, and buckles. On his head was a foraging cap, which, when he took it off, showed that he was quite bald. His age might be about fifty-five or sixty; his complexion florid, no whiskers, and little beard, nose straight, lips thin, teeth black with chewing, and always a little brown dribble from the left corner of his mouth (there was a leak there, he said). Altogether his countenance was prepossessing, for it was honest and manly, but his waist was preposterous.

"Steady enough," thought Jack, as he returned Mr Oxbelly's salute.

"How do you do, sir?" said Jack; "I trust we shall be good ship-mates," for Jack had not seen him before.

"Mr Easy," replied the lieutenant, "I never quarrel with anyone, except (I won't tell a story) with my wife."

"I am sorry that you have ever domestic dissensions, Mr Oxbelly."

"And I only quarrel with her at night, sir. She will take up more than her share of the bed, and won't allow me to sleep single; but never mind that, sir; now will you please to muster the men?"

"If you please, Mr Oxbelly."

The men were mustered, and Jack made them a long speech upon subordination, discipline, activity, duty, and so forth.

"A very good speech, Mr Easy," said Mr Oxbelly, as the men went forward; "I wish my wife had heard it. But, sir, if you please, we'll now get under way as fast as we can, for there is a Channel cruiser working up at St Helen's,* and we may give him the go-by by running through the Needles."

"But what need we care for the Channel cruiser?"

"You forget, sir, that as soon as she drops her anchor she will come on board and take a fancy to at least ten of our men."

"But they are protected."†

"Yes, sir, but that's no protection, now-a-days. I have sailed in a privateer at least three years, and I know that they have no respect for letters of marque or for privateers."

"I believe you are right, Mr Oxbelly; so, if you please, we will up with the anchor at once."

The crew of the *Ribiera* had been well chosen; they were prime men-of-war's men, most of whom had deserted from the various ships on the station, and, of course, were most anxious to be off. In a few minutes the *Ribiera* was under way with all sail set below and aloft. She was in excellent trim and flew through the water; the wind was fair, and by night they had passed Portland Lights, and the next morning were steering a course for the Bay of Biscay without having encountered what they feared more than an enemy,—a British cruiser to overhaul them.

---

* St. Helen's: Village on the Isle of Wight. Also the name given to the roadstead between the Isle of Wight and Portsmouth, on the mainland.

† Protected: From impressment. The Navy was so desperate for men that few were spared from the dreaded press. Marryat was opposed to the practice except under dire conditions and wrote a pamphlet against it in 1822 that angered the Admiralty.

"I think we shall do now, sir," observed Mr Oxbelly to our hero; "we have made a famous run. It's twelve o'clock, and if you please I'll work the latitude, and let you know what it is. We must shape our course so as not to run in with the Brest squadron. A little more westing, sir. I'll be up in one minute. My wife—but I'll tell you about that when I come up."

"Latitude 41° 12′, sir. I was about to say that my wife, when she was on board of the privateer that I commanded—"

"Board of the privateer, Mr Oxbelly?"

"Yes, sir, would go; told her it was impossible, but she wouldn't listen to reason—came on board, flopped herself into the standing bed-place, and said that there she was for the cruise,—little Billy with her—"

"What! your child, too?"

"Yes, two years old—fine boy—always laughed when the guns were fired, while his mother stood on the ladder and held him on the top of the booby-hatch."

"I wonder that Mrs Oxbelly let you come here now?"

"So you would, sir, but I'll explain that—she thinks I'm in London about my half-pay. She knows all by this time, and frets, I don't doubt; but that will make her thin, and then there will be more room in the bed. Mrs Oxbelly is a very stout woman."

"Why, you are not a little man!"

"No, not little—tending to be lusty, as the saying is—that is, in good condition. It's very strange that Mrs Oxbelly has an idea that she is not large. I cannot persuade her to it. That's the reason we always spar in bed. She says it is I, and I know that it is she who takes the largest share of it."

"Perhaps you may both be right."

"No, no; it is she who creates all the disturbance. If I get nearer to the wall she jams me up till I am as thin as a thread-paper. If I put her inside and stay outside, she cuts me out as you do a cask, by the chime, till I tumble out of bed."

"Why don't you make your bed larger, Mr Oxbelly?"

"Sir, I have proposed it, but my wife will have it that the bed is large enough if I would not toss in my sleep. I can't convince her. However, she'll have it all to herself now. I slept well last night, for the first time since I left the *Boadicea*."

"The *Boadicea*?"

"Yes, sir, I was second lieutenant of the *Boadicea* for three years."

"She's a fine frigate, I'm told."

"On the contrary, such a pinched-up little craft below I never saw. Why, Mr Easy, I could hardly get into the door of my cabin—and yet, as you must see, I'm not a large man."

"Good heavens! is it possible," thought Jack, "that this man does not really know that he is monstrous?"

Yet such was the case. Mr Oxbelly had no idea that he was otherwise than in good condition, although he had probably not seen his knees for years. It was his obesity that was the great objection to him, for in every other point there was nothing against him. He had, upon one pretence and another, been shifted, by the manœuvres of the captains, out of different ships, until he went up to the Admiralty to know if there was any charge against him. The first lord at once perceived the charge to be preferred, and made a mark against his name as not fit for anything but harbour duty. Out of employment, he had taken the command of a privateer cutter, when his wife, who was excessively fond, would, as he said, follow him with little Billy. He was sober, steady, knew his duty well; but he weighed twenty-six stone,* and his weight had swamped him in the service.

His wish, long indulged, had become, as Shakespeare says, the father of his thought,† and he had really at last brought himself to think that he was not by any means what could be considered a fat man. His wife, as he said, was also a very stout woman, and this exuberance of flesh on both sides, was the only, but continual, ground of dispute.

* Twenty-six stone: 364 pounds.
† As Shakespeare says: The reference is to King Henry's words to Prince Hal: "Thy wish was father, Harry, to that thought" (Henry IV, Part 2 4.5.93).

CHAPTER XXXVIII

In which our hero, as usual, gets into the very middle of it.

O N THE ELEVENTH DAY the *Rebiera* entered the straits, and the rock of Gibraltar was in sight as the sun went down; after which the wind fell light, and about midnight it became calm, and they drifted up. At sunrise they were roused by the report of heavy guns, and perceived an English frigate about eight miles further up the straits, and more in the mid-channel, engaging nine or ten Spanish gun-boats, which had come out from Algesiras to attack her. It still continued a dead calm, and the boats of the frigate were all ahead towing her, so as to bring her broadside to bear upon the Spanish flotilla. The reverberating of the heavy cannon on both sides over the placid surface of the water—the white smoke ascending as the sun rose in brilliancy in a clear blue sky—the distant echoes repeated from the high hills—had a very beautiful effect for those who are partial to the picturesque. But Jack thought it advisable to prepare for action instead of watching for tints—and, in a short time, all was ready.

"They'll not come to us, Mr Easy, as long as they have the frigate to hammer at; but still we had better be prepared, for we cannot well pass them without having a few shot. When I came up the straits in the privateer we were attacked by two and fought them for three hours; their shot dashed the water over our decks till they were wet fore and aft, but somehow or another they never hit us—we were as low as they were. I'll be bound but they'll hull the frigate though. Mrs Oxbelly and Billy were on deck the whole time—and Billy was quite delighted, and cried when they took him down to breakfast."

"Why, Mrs Oxbelly must be very courageous."

"Cares neither for shot nor shell, sir—laughs when they whiz over her head, and tells Billy to hark. But, sir, it's not surprising; her father is a major, and her two brothers are lieutenants in the bombardiers."

"That, indeed," replied Jack—"but, see, there is a breeze springing up from the westward."

"Very true, Mr Easy, and a steady one it will be, for it comes up dark and slow; so much the better for the frigate, for she'll get little honour and plenty of mauling at this work."

"I hope we shall take it up with us," observed Jack; "how far do you reckon the gun-boats from the shore?"

"I should think about five miles, or rather less."

"Trim sails, Mr Oxbelly—perhaps we may cut one or two of these off—steer in-shore of them."

"Exactly. Up there, my lads, set top-gallant studding sails, topmast studdings to hand—rig out the booms—keep as you go now, my lad—we shall be well in-shore of them, and out of the range of the batteries."

The breeze came down fresh, and all sail was set upon the *Rebiera*. She took the wind down with her, and it passed her but little—half a mile ahead of them all was still and smooth as a glass mirror, and they neared and gained in-shore at the same time. The gun-boats were still engaging the frigate, and did not appear to pay any attention to the *Rebiera* coming down. At last the breeze reached them and the frigate, light at first and then gradually increasing, while the *Rebiera* foamed through the water, and had now every chance of cutting off some of the gun-boats. The frigate trimmed her sails and steered towards the flotilla, which now thought proper to haul off and put their heads in-shore, followed by the frigate firing her bow-chasers. But the *Rebiera* was now within half gun-shot in-shore, and steering so as to intercept them. As she rapidly closed, the flotilla scarcely knew how to act; to attack her would be to lose time, and allow the frigate to come up and occasion their own capture; so they satisfied themselves with firing at her as she continued to run down between them and the land. As they neared, Jack opened his fire with his eighteen-pound carronades and long nines. The gun-boats returned his fire, and they were within a quarter of a mile, when Jack shortened sail to his topsails, and a warm engagement took place, which ended in one of the gun-boats being, in a few minutes, dismasted. The frigate, under all canvas, came rapidly up, and her shot now fell thick. The flotilla then ceased firing, passing about two cables' length ahead of the *Rebiera*, and making all possible sail for the land. Jack now fired at the flotilla as they passed, with his larboard broadside, while with his starboard he poured in grape and canister upon the unfortunate gun-boat which was dismasted, and which soon hauled down her colours. In a few minutes more the remainder were too far distant for the carronades, and, as they did not fire, Jack turned his attention to take possession of his prize, sending a boat with ten men on board, and heaving-to close to her to take her in tow. Ten minutes more and the frigate was also hove-to a cable's length from the *Rebiera,* and our hero lowered down his other quarter-boat to go on board.

"Have we any men hurt, Mr Oxbelly?" inquired Jack.

"Only two; Spearling has lost his thumb with a piece of langrage,* and James has a bad wound in the thigh."

"Very well; I will ask for the surgeon to come on board."

Jack pulled to the frigate, and went up the side, touched his hat in due form, and was introduced by the midshipmen to the other side, where the captain stood.

"Mr Easy!" exclaimed the captain.

"Captain Sawbridge!" replied our hero, with surprise.

"Good heavens! what brought you here?" said the captain; "and what vessel is that?"

"The *Rebiera,* letter of marque, commanded and owned by Mr Easy," replied Jack, laughing.

Captain Sawbridge gave him his hand. "Come down with me into the cabin, Mr Easy; I am very glad to see you. Give you great credit for your conduct, and am still more anxious to know what has induced you to come out again. I knew that you had left the service."

Jack, in a very few words, told his object in fitting out the *Rebiera;* "but," continued Jack, "allow me to congratulate you upon your promotion, which I was not aware of. May I ask where you left the *Harpy,* and what is the name of your frigate?"

"The *Latona.* I have only been appointed to her one month, after an action in which the *Harpy* took a large corvette, and am ordered home with despatches to England. We sailed yesterday evening from Gibraltar, were becalmed the whole night, and attacked this morning by the gun-boats."

"How is Captain Wilson, sir?"

"I believe he is very well, but I have not seen him."

"How did you know, then, that I had left the service, Captain Sawbridge?"

"From Mr Gascoigne, who is now on board."

"Gascoigne!" exclaimed our hero.

"Yes, he was sent up to join the *Aurora* by the governor, but she had left the fleet, and having served his time, and a passing day

* Langrage (or langrel, langrace, or langridge): A type of cannister shot with jagged pieces of iron often used by privateers to cut up rigging and spare the hull of a vessel, preserving its value.

being ordered, he passed, and thought he might as well go home with me and see if he could make any interest for his promotion."

"Pray, Captain Sawbridge, is the gun-boat our prize or yours?"

"It ought to be wholly yours; but the fact is, by the regulations, we share."

"With all my heart, sir. Will you send an assistant-surgeon on board to look after two of my men who are hurt?"

"Yes, directly; now send your boat away, Easy, with directions to your officer in command. We must go back to Gibraltar, for we have received some injury, and, I am sorry to say, lost some men. You are going then, I presume, to stay on board and dine with me: we shall be at anchor before night."

"I will with pleasure, sir. But now I will send my boat away and shake hands with Gascoigne."

Gascoigne was under the half-deck waiting to receive his friend, for he had seen him come up the side from his station on the forecastle. A hurried conversation took place, after our hero had dismissed his boat with the assistant-surgeon in it to dress the two wounded men. Jack then went on deck, talked with the officers, looked with pleasure at the *Rebiera* with the gun-boat in tow, keeping company with the frigate, although only under the same canvas—promised Gascoigne to spend the next day with him either on shore or on board the *Rebiera,* and then returned to the cabin, where he had a long conference with Captain Sawbridge.

"When you first entered the service, Easy," said Captain Sawbridge, "I thought that the sooner the service was rid of you the better: now that you have left it, I feel that it has lost one who, in all probability, would have proved a credit to it."

"Many thanks, sir," replied Jack; "but how can I be a midshipman with eight thousand pounds a-year?"

"I agree with you that it is impossible:—but dinner is serving: go into the after-cabin and the steward will give you all you require."

Our hero, whose face and hands were not a little grimed with the gunpowder, washed himself, combed out his curly black hair, and found all the party in the fore-cabin. Gascoigne, who had not been asked in the forenoon, was, by the consideration of Captain Sawbridge, added to the number. Before dinner was long off the table, the first lieutenant reported that it was necessary to turn the hands up, as they were close to the anchorage. The party, therefore, broke up sooner than otherwise would have been the case; and as soon as the *Latona's* sails were furled, Captain Sawbridge went on shore to acquaint the governor with the results of the action. He asked Jack to accompany him, but our hero, wishing to be with Gascoigne, excused himself until the next day.

"And now, Easy," said Gascoigne, as soon as the captain had gone over the side, "I will ask permission to go on board with you—or will you ask?"

"I will ask," replied Jack; "a gentleman of fortune has more weight with a first lieutenant than a midshipman."

So Jack went up to the first lieutenant, and with one of his polite bows, hoped, "if duty would permit, he would honour him by coming on board that evening with some of his officers, to see the *Rebiera* and to drink a bottle or two of champagne."

The first lieutenant, as the *Rebiera* was anchored not two cables' lengths from him, replied, "that as soon as he had shifted the prisoners and secured the gun-boat, he would be very glad": so did three or four more of the officers, and then Jack begged as a favour, that his old friend, Mr Gascoigne, might be permitted to go with him now, as he had important packages to entrust to his care to England. The first lieutenant was very willing, and Gascoigne and our hero jumped into the boat, and were once more in all the confidence of tried and deserved friendship.

"Jack, I've been thinking of it, and I've made up my mind," said Gascoigne. "I shall gain little or nothing by going home for my promotion: I may as well stay here, and as I have served my time and passed, my pay is now of little consequence. Will you take me with you?"

"It was exactly what I was thinking of, Ned. Do you think that Captain Sawbridge will consent?"

"I do: he knows how I am circumstanced, and that my going home was merely because I was tired of looking after the *Aurora*."

"We'll go together and ask him to-morrow," replied Jack.

"At all events, you'll have a more gentlemanly companion than Mr Oxbelly."

"But not so steady, Ned."

The first lieutenant and officers came on board, and passed a merry evening. There's nothing passes time more agreeably away than champagne, and if you do not affront this regal wine by mixing him with any other, he never punishes you the next morning.

CHAPTER XXXIX

A council of war, in which Jack decides that he will have one more cruise.

A S CAPTAIN SAWBRIDGE did not return on board that evening, Easy went on shore and called upon him at the governor's, to whom he was introduced, and received an invitation to dine with him. As Gascoigne could not come on shore, our hero took this opportunity of making his request to Captain Sawbridge, stating that the person he had with him was not such as he wished and could confide everything to; that is, not one to whom he could talk about Agnes. Jack, as he found that Captain Sawbridge did not immediately assent, pressed the matter hard: at last Captain Sawbridge, who reflected that Gascoigne's interest hereafter would be much greater through his friend Easy, than any other quarter, and that the more the friendship was cemented the more advantageous it might prove to Gascoigne, gave his consent to our hero's wish, who called on board of the *Latona* to acquaint Gascoigne and the first lieutenant of Captain Sawbridge's intentions, and then went on board of the *Rebiera* and ordered Mesty to come with his portmanteau on shore to the inn, that he might dress for dinner. Gascoigne, now considered as not belonging to the *Latona*, was permitted to accompany him: and Jack found himself looking out of the window at which he had hung out his trousers upon the memorable occasion when the boatswain had to follow his own precept, of duty before decency.

"What scenes of adventures I have passed through since that," thought Jack; "not much more than four years ago, then not three weeks in the service." Whereupon Jack fell into a deep reverie, and thought of the baboon and of Agnes.

The repairs of the *Latona* were all made good by the next day, and Gascoigne, having received his discharge ticket, went on board of the *Rebiera*. The gun-boat was put into the hands of the agent, and shortly afterwards purchased by government. The *Rebiera*'s crew did not, however, obtain their prize-money and share of the head-money, for she had seventy men on board, until their return, but, as they said, they had broken the ice and that was everything. Moreover, it gave them confidence in themselves, in their vessel, and in their commander. Our hero weighed a short time after the *Latona*, having first taken leave of Captain Sawbridge, and committed to his care a letter to Dr Middleton.

Once more behold the trio together,—the two midshipmen hanging over the taffrail, and Mesty standing by them. They had rounded Europa Point, and, with a fine breeze off the land, were lying close-hauled along the Spanish shore. Mr Oxbelly was also walking near them.

"When I was cruising here it was very different," observed Jack: "I had a vessel which I did not know how to manage, a crew which I could not command, and had it not been for Mesty, what would have become of me!"

"Massa Easy, you know very well how to get out of scrapes, anyhow."

"Yes, and how to get into them," continued Gascoigne.

"And how to get others out of them, too, Ned."

" 'No more of that, Hal, an thou lovest me,' "* quoted Gascoigne. "I have often wondered what has been the lot of poor Azar."

"The lot of most women, Ned, in every country—prized at first, neglected afterwards—the lot she might have had with you."

"Perhaps so," replied Ned, with a sigh.

"Massa Easy, you get eberybody out of scrape; you get me out of scrape."

"I do not recollect how, Mesty."

"You get me out from boil kettle for young gentlemen—dat devil of a scrape."

"And I'm sure I've got you out of a scrape, Mr Oxbelly."

"How so, Mr Easy?"

"How so!—have I not prevented your quarrelling with your wife every night?"

"Certainly, sir, you have been the means. But do you know when we were engaging the other day, I could not help saying to myself, 'I wish my wife was here now, holding little Billy at the hatchway.' "

"But at night, Mr Oxbelly."

"At night!—why, then I'm afraid I should have wished her home again—it's astonishing how comfortable I sleep now every night.

---

* "No more of that, Hal, an thou lovest me": Falstaff speaking to Prince Hal (*Henry IV, Part 1* 2.4.264).

Besides, in this climate it would be intolerable. Mrs Oxbelly is a very large woman—very large indeed."

"Well, but now we must hold a council of war. Are we to run up the coast, or to shape a course direct for Palermo?"

"Course direct, and we shall take nothing, that is certain," said Gascoigne.

"If we take nothing we shall make no prize-money," continued Oxbelly.

"If we make no prize-money the men will be discontented," said Easy.

"If no ab noting to do—it will be d——d 'tupid," continued Mesty.

"Now then the other side of the question. If we steer for Palermo, we shall be sooner there and sooner home."

"To which I reply," said Gascoigne, "that the shorter the cruise is, the less I shall have of your company."

"And I shall have to sleep with Mrs Oxbelly," continued Oxbelly.

"Hab fine ship, fine gun, fine men, and do noting," cried Mesty. "By de power, I no like dat, Massa Easy."

"You want eight months of coming of age, Jack," observed Gascoigne.

"It won't make a difference of more than three or four weeks," said Mr Oxbelly; "and the expenses have been very great."

"But—"

"But what, Jack?"

"Agnes."

"Agnes will be better defended going home by men who have been accustomed to be in action. And, as for her waiting a little longer, it will only make her love you a little more."

"Sleep single a little longer, Mr Easy, it's very pleasant," said Mr Oxbelly.

"That's not very bad advice of yours," observed Gascoigne.

"*Stop a little*, Massa Easy," said Mesty, "you know dat very good advice."

"Well, then," replied Jack, "I will, as I am quite in the minority. We will work up the whole coast—up to Toulon. After all, there's something very pleasant in commanding your own ship, and I'm not in a hurry to resign it—so that point's decided."

The *Rebiera* was steered into the land, and at sunset they were not four miles from the lofty blue mountains which overhang the town of Malaga.* There were many vessels lying at the bottom of the bay, close in with the town; the wind now fell light, and the *Rebiera,* as she could not fetch the town, tacked as if she were a merchant vessel standing in, and showed American colours, a hint which they took from perceiving three or four large vessels lying in the outer roads, with the colours of that nation hoisted at the peak.

"What is your intention, Jack?" said Gascoigne.

"I'll be hanged if I know yet. I think of working up to the outer roads, and anchoring at night—boarding the American vessels, and gaining intelligence."

"Not a bad idea; we shall then learn if there is anything to be done, and if not, we may be off at daylight."

"The pratique† boat will not come off after sunset."

"And if they did, we could pass for an American, bound to Barcelona or anywhere else—the outer roads where the vessels lie are hardly within gun-shot."

Mesty, who had resumed his sailor's clothes, now observed, "What we do, Massa Easy, we do quickly—time for all ting, time for show face and fight—time for hide face, crawl, and steal."

"Very true, Mesty, we'll crawl this time, and steal if we can. It's not the warfare I like best of the two."

"Both good, Massa Easy; suppose you no steal board of polacca ship, you not see Missy Agnes."

"Very true, Mesty. 'Bout ship, Mr Oxbelly."

"Mr Oxbelly not good for boat service," observed Mesty, showing his teeth.

It was dark before the *Rebiera* was anchored in the outer roads, a cable's length astern of the outermost American vessel. One of her quarter-boats was lowered down, and Gascoigne and our hero pulled alongside, and, lying on their oars, hailed, and asked the name of the vessel.

"So help me Gad, just now I forget her name," replied a negro, looking over the gangway.

"Who's the captain?"

"So help me Gad, he gone on shore."

"Is the mate on board?"

"No, so help me Gad—he gone shore, too."

---

* Malaga (Málaga): A town in southern Spain.
† Pratique: Permission, after having been cleared by the health authorities, for a vessel to enter a port.

"Who is aboard then?"

"So help me Gad, nobody on board but Pompey—and dat me."

"Good ship-keepers, at all events," said Jack. "A ship in the outer roads, with only a black fellow on board! I say, Pompey, do they always leave you in charge of the vessel?"

"No, sar; but to-night great pleasure on shore. Eberybody dance and sing, get drunk, kick up bobbery, and all dat."

"What, is it a festival?"

"So help me Gad, I no know, sar."

"Is there anyone on board of the other vessels?"

"Eberybody gone on shore. Suppose they have black man, he stay on board."

"Good-night, Pompey."

"Good-night, sar. Who I say call when captain come on board?"

"Captain Easy."

"Captain He-see, very well, sar."

Our hero pulled to another ship, and found it equally deserted; but at the third he found the second mate with his arm in a sling, and from him they gained the information that it was a great festival, being the last day of the carnival; and that everyone was thinking of nothing but amusement.

"I've a notion," said the mate, in reply, "that you're American."

"You've guessed right," replied Jack.

"What ship, and from what port?"

"Rhode Island, the *Susan and Mary*," replied Gascoigne.

"I thought you were north. We're of New York. What news do you bring?"

"Nothing," replied he, "we are from Liverpool last."

A succession of questions was now put by the American mate, and answered very skilfully by Gascoigne, who then inquired how the market was?

It was necessary to make and reply to all these enquiries before they could ask apparently indifferent questions of American traders; at last, Gascoigne enquired,—

"Do you think they would allow us to go on shore? the pratique boat has not been on board."

"They'll never find you out if you are off before daylight; I doubt if they know that you are anchored. Besides, from Liverpool you would have a clean bill of health, and if they found it out, they would not say much; they're not over particular, I've a notion."

"What are those vessels lying in-shore?"

"I guess they have olive oil on board, the chief on 'em. But there are two double lateens come in from Valparaiso the day before yesterday, with hides and copper. How they 'scaped the British, I can't tell, but they did, that's sure enough."

"Good-night, then."

"You won't take a glass of sling* this fine night with a countryman?"

"To-morrow, my good fellow, to-morrow; we must go on shore now."

Our hero and Gascoigne returned on board the *Rebiera,* consulted with Oxbelly and Mesty, and then manned and armed the two quarter and stern boats. They thought it advisable not to hoist out their long-boat; no fire-arms were permitted to be taken, lest, going off by accident or otherwise, an alarm should be given. Our hero and Mesty proceeded in the first boat, and pulled in for the town; Gascoigne shortly after in the second, and the boatswain in the jolly-boat, followed at some distance.

There was no notice taken of them; they pulled gently down to the landing-place, which was deserted. There was a blaze of light, and the sounds of revelry in every quarter on shore; but the vessels appeared equally deserted as the American ones in the offing.

Finding themselves unobserved, for they had taken the precaution to pull only two oars in each boat, they dropped gently alongside one of the double-masted lateen vessels, and Mesty stepped on board. He peeped down in the cabin, and perceived a man lying on the lockers; he came up in his stealthy manner, closed the hatch softly, and said, "All right." Jack left Gascoigne to take out this vessel, which he did very successfully, for it was very dark; and although there were sentries posted not far off, their eyes and ears were turned towards the town, listening to the music.

A second vessel, her consort, was boarded in the same way, but here they found a man on deck whom they were obliged to seize and gag. They put him down in the cabin, and Mesty, with another boat's crew, cut her cables, and swept her gently out towards the American vessels. One more vessel was required, and Jack, pulling two oars as usual, saluted a galliot heavily laden, but of what her cargo consisted was not known. In this vessel they found two men

---

* Sling: A drink made from thick cane syrup and alcoholic liquor.

in the cabin playing cards, whom they seized and bound, and, cutting her cables, were obliged to make sail upon her, as she was much too large to sweep out. As they were making sail they, however, met with an interruption which they did not expect. The crew belonging to the vessel, having had enough amusement for the evening, and intending to sail the next morning, had thought it right to come off sooner than the others: it was then about midnight or a little later, and while some of Jack's men were aloft, for he had six with him, Jack, to his annoyance, heard a boat coming off from the shore, the men in her singing a chorus. The galliot was at that time just under steerage way, her topsails had been loosed and her jib hoisted, but the former had not been sheeted home, for the three men below could not, in the dark, find the ropes. The other three men were on the fore-yard loosing the foresail, and Jack was undetermined whether to call them down immediately, or to allow them to loose the sail, and thus get good way on the vessel, so as to prevent the boat, which was loaded with men, from overtaking them. The boat was not more than twenty yards from the galliot, when, not finding her where they left her, they pulled to the right, and lay on their oars. This gave a moment of time, but they very soon spied her out. "Carambo!" was the exclamation—and the head of the boat was pulled round.

"Down, my lads, in a moment by the swifters," cried Jack. "Here's a boat on board of us."

The men were in a few seconds on deck, and the others, who had now sheeted home the topsails, hastened aft. The vessel soon gathered way, but before that her way was sufficient, the boat had pulled under the counter, and the Spaniards, letting their oars swing fore and aft, were climbing up, their knives in their teeth. A scuffle ensued, and they were thrown down again, but they renewed their attempt. Our hero, perceiving a small water or wine cask lashed to the gunwale, cut it loose with his cutlass, and with one of the men, who was by his side, pushed it over, and dropped it into the boat. It struck the gunwale, stove a plank, and the boat began to fill rapidly; in the meantime the galliot had gained way—the boat could not longer be held on, from its weight, and dropped astern with the men in it. Those who were half in and half out were left clinging to the gunwale of the vessel, and as they climbed up were secured, and put down in the cabin. Fortunately, no fire-arms having been used on either side, the alarm was not given generally, but the sentry reported fighting on board one of the vessels, and the people of the guard-boat were collected, and pulled out; but they only arrived in time to see that the galliot was under way, and that the two other vessels from Valparaiso were not in their berths.

They hastened on shore, gave the alarm: the gun-boats, of which there were three at the mole,* were ordered out, but half the crew and all the officers were on shore, some at balls, others drinking at taverns or posadas;† before they could be collected, all three vessels were alongside of the *Rebiera:* and not aware that anything had been discovered, our hero and his crew were lulled in security. Jack had gone on board, leaving fourteen of his men on board the galliot— Gascoigne had done the same—Mesty still remained on board his vessel; and they were congratulating themselves, and ordering the men on board to the windlass, when they heard the sound of oars.

"Silence!—what is that?" exclaimed Oxbelly. "The gun-boats or row-boats, as sure as I'm alive!"

At this moment Mesty jumped up the side.

"Massa Easy, I hear row-boat not far off."

"So do we, Mesty. Gascoigne, jump into the boat—tell the men in the prizes to make all sail right out, and leave us to defend their retreat—stay on board of one and divide your men."

"Dat all right, Massa Easy.—Mr Gascoigne, be smart—and now, sar, cut cable and make sail; no time get up anchor."

This order was given, but although the men were aloft in a moment, and very expeditious, as the *Rebiera* payed her head round and the jib was hoisted, they could perceive the boom of the three gun-boats pulling and sailing not five cables' length from them. Although rather short-handed, topsails, courses and top-gallant sails were soon set, the men down to their quarters, and the guns cast loose, before the gun-boats were close under their stern. Then Jack rounded to, braced up, and the *Rebiera* stood across them to the westward.

"Why the devil don't they fire?" said Jack.

"I tink because they no ab powder," said Mesty.

Mesty was right—the ammunition chests of the gun-boats were always landed when they were at the mole, in case of accidents, which might arise from the crew being continually with cigars in

---

* Mole: A large pier or junction.
† Posadas: Boardinghouses.

their mouths, and in the hurry they had quite forgotten to put them on board.

"At all events, we have powder," said Jack, "and now we'll prove it. Grape and canister, my lads, and take good aim."

The commanders of the gun-boats had hailed each other, and agreed to board the *Rebiera,* but she now had good way on her, and sailed faster than they pulled. A well-directed broadside astonished them—they had no idea of her force; and the execution done was so great, that they first lay on their oars and then pulled back to the mole with all speed, leaving the *Rebiera* in quiet possession of her prizes, which had already gained two miles in the offing.

The *Rebiera,* as soon as Jack perceived that the gun-boats had retreated, was put before the wind, and soon closed with her captures, when she was hove-to till daylight with the three vessels in company. Gascoigne returned on board, prize-masters were selected, and Jack determined to keep them all with him, and take them to Palermo.

CHAPTER XL

In which there is another slight difference of opinion between those who should be friends.

THE TWO lateen vessels proved of considerable value, being laden with copper, hides, and cochineal. The galliot was laden with sweet-oil, and was also no despicable prize. At daylight they were all ready, and, to the mortification of the good people of Malaga, sailed away to the eastward without interruption.

"Me tink we do dat job pretty well, Massa Easy," observed Mesty, as he laid the breakfast table.

"Nothing like trying," replied Gascoigne; "I'm sure when we stood into the bay I would have sold all my prize-money for a doubloon. How do I share, Jack?"

"Only as one of the crew, Ned, for you are a supernumerary, and our articles and agreement for prize-money were signed previous to our sailing."

"I ought to share with Mr Oxbelly's class by rights," replied Gascoigne.

"That would be to take half my prize-money away. I shall want it all, Mr Gascoigne, to pacify my wife for giving her the slip."

"Ah, very well; I'll get all I can."

For ten days they ran down the coast, going much too fast for the wishes of the crew, who were anxious to make more money. They seized a fishing-boat and put on board of her the four prisoners, which they had found in the vessels, and arrived off Barcelona, without falling in with friend or foe. The next morning, the wind being very light, they discovered a large vessel at daylight astern of them to the westward, and soon made her out to be a frigate. She made all sail in chase, but that gave them very little uneasiness, as they felt assured that she was a British cruiser. One fear, however, came over them, that she would, if she came up with them, impress a portion of their men.

"As certain as I'm here, and Mrs Oxbelly's at Southsea," said Oxbelly, "they'll take some of the men—the more so as, supposing us to be a Spanish convoy, they will be disappointed."

"They will hardly take them out of the prizes," observed Easy.

"I don't know that; men must be had for his Majesty's service somehow. It's not their fault, Mr Easy—the navy must be manned, and as things are so, so things must be. It's the king's prerogative, Mr Easy, and we cannot fight the battles of the country without it."

"Yes," replied Gascoigne, "and although, as soon as the services of seamen are no longer wanted, you find that there are demagogues on shore who exclaim against impressment, they are quiet enough on the point when they know that their lives and property depend upon sailors' exertions."

"Very true, Mr Gascoigne, but it's not our fault if we are obliged to take men by force; it's the fault of those who do not legislate so as to prevent the necessity. Mrs Oxbelly used to say that she would easily manage the matter if she were Chancellor of the Exchequer."

"I dare say Mrs Oxbelly would make a very good Chancellor of the Exchequer," replied Gascoigne, smiling; "one thing is certain, that if they gave the subject half the consideration they have others of less magnitude, an arrangement might be made by which his Majesty's navy would never be short of men."

"No doubt, no doubt, Mr Gascoigne; but, nevertheless, the king's prerogative must never be given up."

"There I agree with you, Mr Oxbelly; it *must be held* in case of sudden emergency and absolute need."

"We'll argue that point by-and-bye," replied Jack; "now let us consult as to our measures. My opinion is, that if I made more sail we should beat the frigate, but she would come up with the prizes."

"That's the best thing we can do, Mr Easy; but let us send a boat on board of them, and take out all the men that can possibly be spared, that there may be no excuse for impressing them."

"Yes," replied Gascoigne; "and as the wind is falling it is possible it may fall calm, and they may send their boats; suppose we separate a mile or two from each other."

"Dat very good advice, Massa Gascoigne," observed Mesty.

This plan was acted upon; only three men were left in the lateens, and four in the galliot, and the vessels, in obedience to the orders, sheered off on both sides of the *Rebiera,* who made all sail and started ahead of the prizes. This manœuvre was perceived on board of the frigate, and made them sure that it was a Spanish convoy attempting to escape. The fire-engine was got on deck, sails wetted, and every exertion made to come up. But about four o'clock in the afternoon, when the frigate was eight or nine miles off, it fell calm, as Gascoigne had predicted, and the heads of all the vessels, as well as the frigate, were now round the compass.

"There's out boats," said Mr Oxbelly; "they will have a long pull, and all for nothing."

"How savage they will be!" observed Gascoigne.

"Never mind that," replied Jack; "Mesty says that dinner is ready."

After dinner, they all went on deck, and found that the boats had separated, one pulling for each of the prizes, and two for the *Rebiera.* In less than an hour, they would probably be alongside.

"And now let us decide how we are to act. We must not resist, if they attempt to impress the men?"

"I've been thinking upon that matter, Mr Easy, and it appears to me that the men must be permitted to act as they please, and that we must be neuter. I, as a lieutenant in his Majesty's service, cannot of course act, neither can Mr Gascoigne. You are not in the service, but I should recommend you to do the same. That the men have a right to resist, if possible, is admitted; they always do so, and never are punished for so doing. Under the guns of the frigate, of course we should only have to submit; but those two boats do not contain more than twenty-five men, I should think, and our men are the stronger party. We had better leave it to them, and stand neuter."

"Dat very good advice," said Mesty; "leab it to us": and Mesty walked away forward where the seamen were already in consultation.

Jack also agreed to the prudence of this measure, and he perceived that the seamen, after a consultation with Mesty, were all arming themselves for resistance.

The boats were now close on board, and English colours were hoisted at the gaff. This did not, however, check the impetus of the boats, who, with their ensigns trailing in the still water astern of them, dashed alongside, and an officer leaped on board, cutlass in hand, followed by the seamen of the frigate. The men of the *Rebiera* remained collected forward—Easy, Gascoigne, and Oxbelly aft.

"What vessel is this?" cried the lieutenant who commanded the boats.

Jack, with the greatest politeness, took off his hat, and told him that it was the *Rebiera* letter of marque, and that the papers were ready for his inspection.

"And the other vessels?"

"Prizes to the *Rebiera,* cut out of Malaga Bay," replied Jack.

"Then you are a privateer," observed the disappointed officer. "Where are your papers?"

"Mr Oxbelly, oblige me by bringing them up," said Jack.

"Fat Jack of the bone house," observed the lieutenant, looking at Oxbelly.

"A lieutenant in his Majesty's service, of longer standing than yourself, young man," replied Oxbelly, firmly;—"and who, if he ever meets you in any other situation, will make you answer for your insolent remark."

"Indeed!" observed the lieutenant, ironically; "now, if you had said you were once a boatswain or gunner."

"Consider yourself kicked," roared Oxbelly, losing his temper.

"Heyday! why, you old porpoise!"

"Sir," observed Jack, who listened with indignation, "Mr Oxbelly is a lieutenant in his Majesty's service, and you have no right to insult him, even if he were not."

"I presume you are all officers," replied the lieutenant.

"I am, sir," retorted Gascoigne, "an officer in his Majesty's service, and on board of this vessel by permission of Captain Sawbridge of the *Latona.*"

"And I was, until a few months ago, sir," continued Jack; "at present I am captain and owner of this vessel—but here are the papers. You will have no obstruction from us in the execution of your duty—at the same time, I call upon the two young gentlemen by your side, and your own men, to bear witness to what takes place."

"O very well, sir—just as you please. Your papers, I perceive, are all right. Now you will oblige me by mustering your men."

"Certainly, sir," replied Jack: "send all the men aft to muster, Mr Oxbelly."

The men came aft to the mainmast, with Mesty at their head, and answered to their names. As the men passed over, the lieutenant made a pencil-mark against ten of them, who appeared the finest seamen; and, when the roll had been called, he ordered those men to get their bags and go into the boat.

"Sir, as you must observe, I am short-handed, with my men away in prizes; and I, as commander of this vessel, protest against this proceeding: if you insist upon taking them, of course I can do nothing," observed Jack.

"I do insist, sir; I'm not going on board empty-handed, at all events."

"Well, sir, I can say no more," said Jack, walking aft to the taffrail, to which Oxbelly and Gascoigne had retreated.

"Come, my lads, get those men in the boat," said the lieutenant.

But the men had all retreated forward in a body, with Mesty at their head, and had armed themselves. Some of the seamen of the frigate had gone forward, in obedience to their officer, to lead the men selected into the boat; but they were immediately desired to keep back. The scuffle forward attracted the notice of the lieutenant, who immediately summoned all his men out of the boats.

"Mutiny, by heavens! Come up all of you, my lads."

Mesty then came forward, with a sabre in one hand and a pistol in the other, and then addressed the seamen of the frigate:—

"I tell you dis, my lads—you not so strong as we—you not got better arms—we not under gun of frigate now, and ab determination not to go board. 'Pose you want us, come take us—'pose you can. By all de power, but we make mince-meat of you, anyhow."

The seamen paused—they were ready to fight for their country, but not to be killed by or kill those who were their own countrymen, and who were doing exactly what they would have done themselves. The lieutenant thought otherwise; he was exasperated at this sensation.

"You black scoundrel, I left you out because I thought you not worth having, but now I'll add you to the number."

"Stop a little," replied Mesty.

The lieutenant would not take the Ashantee's very prudent advice; he flew forward to seize Mesty, who, striking him a blow with the flat of his sabre, almost levelled him to the deck. At this the men and other officers of the frigate darted forward; but after a short scuffle, in which a few wounds were received, were beaten back into the boats. The lieutenant was thrown in after them, by the nervous arm of Mesty—and assailed by cold shot and other missiles, they sheered off with precipitation, and pulled back in the direction of the frigate.

"There will be a row about this," said Oxbelly, "as soon as they come clear of the vessel. If the frigate gets hold of us she will show us no mercy. There is a breeze coming from the north-west. How fortunate! we shall be three leagues to windward, and may escape."

"I doubt if she could catch us. At any point of sailing they may come up with the prizes, but can do nothing with them."

"No, the boats which boarded them are already returned to the frigate; she must wait for them, and that will give us a start, and it will be night before they can make sail."

"Fire a gun for the prizes to close," said Jack; "we will put the men on board again, and then be off to Palermo as fast as we can."

"We can do no better," said Oxbelly. "If ever I chance to meet that fellow again, I will trouble him to repeat his words. Trim the sails, my lads."

"His language was unpardonable," observed Jack.

"Since I've been in the service, Mr Easy, I have always observed that some officers appear to imagine, that because they are under the king's pennant, they are warranted in insulting and tyrannising over all those who have not the honour to hoist it; whereas, the very fact of their being king's officers should be an inducement to them to show an example of courtesy and gentlemanly conduct in the execution of their duty, however unpleasant it may be."

"It is only those who, insignificant themselves, want to make themselves of importance by the pennant they serve under," replied our hero.

"Very true, Mr Easy; but you are not aware that a great part of the ill-will shown to the service is owing to the insolence of those young men in office. The king's name is a warrant for every species of tyranny and unwarrantable conduct. I remember Mrs Oxbelly telling one of them, when—"

"I beg your pardon, Mr Oxbelly," interrupted Jack, "but we have no time to chat now; the breeze is coming down fast, and I perceive the prizes are closing. Let us lower down the boat, send the men on board again, and give them their orders—which I will do in writing, in case they part company."

"Very true, sir. It will be dark in half an hour, and as we are now standing in-shore, they will think that we intend to remain on the coast. As soon as it is quite dark we will shape our course for Palermo. I will go down and look at the chart."

CHAPTER XLI

Which winds up the nautical adventures of Mr Midshipman Easy.

IN HALF AN HOUR the prizes were again alongside, the men put on board, and the boat hoisted up. The frigate still remained becalmed to leeward, and hoisted in her boats. They watched until she was hid by the shades of night, and then wearing round stood away, with the wind two points free, for the coast of Sicily. The next morning when the sun rose there was nothing in sight. Strange anomaly, in a state of high civilisation, where you find your own countrymen avoided and more dreaded than even your foes!

The run was prosperous, the weather was fine, and the prizes did not part company.

On the sixteenth day the *Rebiera* and her convoy anchored in Palermo Bay. The wind was light in the morning that they stood in, and as Jack had a large blue flag with *Rebiera* in white letters hoisted at the main, Don Philip and Don Martin were on board and greeting our hero, before the *Rebiera*'s anchor had plunged into the clear blue water.

The information which our hero received, after having been assured of the health of Agnes and her parents, was satisfactory. The disappearance of the friar had, at first, occasioned much surprise; but as the servants of Don Rebiera swore to his return without the black, and the letter of Don Rebiera, sent to the convent, requesting his presence, was opened and read, there was no suspicion against the family. A hundred conjectures had been afloat, but gradually they had subsided, and it was at last supposed that he had been carried off by the banditti, some of whom had been taken, and acknowledged that they had seized a friar, on a day which they could not recollect. The reader will remember that it was Mesty.

The *Rebiera* received pratique, and Jack hastened on shore with Don Philip and his brother, and was once more in company of Agnes, who, in our hero's opinion, had improved since his departure. Most young men in love think the same after an absence, provided it is not too long. The prizes were sold and the money distributed, and every man was satisfied, as the cargoes fetched a larger sum than they had anticipated.

We must pass over the *pros* and *cons* of Don Rebiera and his lady, the pleading of Jack for immediate nuptials, the unwillingness of the mother to part with her only daughter, the family consultation, the dowry, and all these particulars. A month after his arrival Jack was married, and was, of course, as happy as the day was long.

A few days afterwards, Mr Oxbelly advised departure, as the expenses of the vessel were heavy, and it was his duty so to do. Don Philip and Don Martin obtained leave to go to England, with their sister and her husband. Nevertheless, Jack, who found Palermo a very pleasant residence, was persuaded by the Don and his wife to remain there a month, and then there was crying and sobbing, and embracing, and embarking; and at last the *Rebiera,* whose cabins had been arranged for the reception of the party, weighed and made sail for Malta, Jack having promised to call upon the governor.

In four days they anchored in Valette Harbour, and Jack paid his respects to his old friend, who was very glad to see him. The governor sent his own barge for Mrs Easy, and she was installed in the state apartments, which were acknowledged to be very comfortable. Our hero had, as usual, a long story to tell the governor, and the governor listened to it very attentively, probably because he thought it would be the last, which opportunity Jack employed to narrate the unfortunate end of his father.

"I would not have said so at the time, Mr Easy, but now the wound is healed, I tell you, that it is the best thing that could have happened—poor old gentleman! he was mad indeed."

Our hero remained a fortnight at Malta, and then Signora Easy was re-embarked, and once more the *Rebiera* made sail.

"Fare you well, my lad; what I have seen of your brothers-in-law pleases me much; and as for your wife, it will be your own fault if she is not all that you would wish. If ever I come to England again, I will pay my first visit to Forest Hill. God bless you!"

But Sir Thomas never did go back to England, and this was their final adieu. Once more the *Rebiera* pursued her course, stopped a day or two at Gibraltar, shared the proceeds of the captured gun-boat, and then made sail for England, where she arrived without adventure or accident in three weeks. Thus ended the last cruise of Mr Midshipman Easy. As soon as their quarantine at the Motherbank was over, they disembarked, and found Dr Middleton and Mr Hanson waiting for them at the George Hotel. Our hero scarcely had time to introduce his wife, when the waiter said, that a lady wished to speak to him. She did not wait to know if Jack was visible, but forced her way past him. Jack looked at her large proportions, and decided at once that it must be Mrs Oxbelly, in which conjecture he was right.

"Pray, sir, what do you mean by carrying off my husband in that way?" exclaimed the lady, red with anger.

"God forbid that I should have to carry your husband, Mrs Oxbelly, he is rather too heavy."

"Yes, sir, but it's little better than kidnapping, and there's a law for kidnapping children at all events. I shall send my lawyer to you, that you may depend upon."

"You hardly can consider your husband as a child, Mrs Oxbelly," replied Jack, laughing.

"Very well, sir, we shall see. Pray, where is he now?"

"He is on board, Mrs Oxbelly, and will be delighted to see you."

"I'm not quite so sure of that."

"He's very anxious to see little Billy," said Gascoigne.

"What do you know of little Billy, young man?"

"And more than anxious to be on shore again. He's quite tired of sleeping single, Mrs Oxbelly."

"Ah, very well, he has been talking, has he? very well," exclaimed the lady, in a rage.

"But," said Easy, "I am happy to say, that with pay and prize-money, during his short absence, he has brought home nearly five hundred pounds."

"Five hundred pounds!—you don't say so, sir?" exclaimed Mrs Oxbelly; "are you sure of that?"

"Quite sure," rejoined Gascoigne.

"Five hundred pounds!—Well, that is comfortable—dear me! how glad I shall be to see him! Well, Mr Easy, it was hard to part with him in so unhandsome a way—but all's for the best in this world. What a dear nice lady your wife is, Mr Easy—but I won't intrude—I beg pardon. Where is the brig, Mr Easy?"

"Now coming into harbour," replied Gascoigne; "if you bargain, you can get off for twopence."

"Five hundred pounds!" exclaimed Mrs Oxbelly, whose wrath was now appeased.

"By all power, she no fool of a woman dat," said Mesty, as she retreated curtseying. "I tink Mr Oxbelly very right sleep tingle."

We have now come to the end of our hero's adventures: that afternoon they all started for Forest Hill, where everything was ready for their reception. The *Rebiera*'s men were paid off, and were soon distributed on board of his Majesty's ships; the vessel was sold, and Mr Oxbelly retired to Southsea, to the society of his wife and little Billy. Whether he obtained from his wife a divorce *de thoro* is not handed down.

OUR HERO, who was now of age, invited all within twenty miles of home to balls and dinners, became a great favourite, kept a pack of hounds, rode with the foremost, received a deputation to stand for the county, on the conservative interest, was elected without much expense, which was very wonderful, and took his seat in Parliament. Don Philip and Don Martin, after two months' stay, took their passage back to Palermo, fully satisfied with the prospects of their sister as to competence and happiness. Jack had no occasion to argue the point with Agnes; she conformed at once to the religion of her husband, proved an excellent and affectionate wife, and eventually the mother of four children, three boys and a girl.

Mesty held his post with dignity, and proved himself trustworthy. Gascoigne, by the interest of the conservative member, soon obtained the rank of post-captain, and was always his devoted and sincere friend. And thus ends the history of Mr Midshipman Easy.

ABOUT THE EDITORS

The Heart of Oak Sea Classics book series is edited by DEAN KING, author of *A Sea of Words: A Lexicon and Companion for Patrick O'Brian's Seafaring Tales* (Henry Holt, 1995; second edition, 1997) and *Harbors and High Seas: An Atlas and Geographical Guide to the Aubrey-Maturin Novels of Patrick O'Brian* (Holt, 1996), and editor, with John B. Hattendorf, of *Every Man Will Do His Duty: An Anthology of Firsthand Accounts from the Age of Nelson, 1793–1815* (Holt, 1997).

Comments on or suggestions for the Heart of Oak Sea Classics series can be sent to Dean King c/o Henry Holt & Co., 115 West 18th St., New York, NY 10011 or E-mailed to him at DeanHKing@aol.com.

The series' scholarly advisors are JOHN B. HATTENDORF, Ernest J. King Professor of Maritime History at the U.S. Naval War College, and CHRISTOPHER MCKEE, Samuel R. and Marie-Louise Rosenthal Professor and Librarian of the College, Grinnell College, author of, most recently, *A Gentlemanly and Honorable Profession: The Creation of the U.S. Naval Officer Corps, 1794–1815* (Naval Institute Press, 1991).

LOUIS J. PARASCANDOLA is an Associate Professor of English at Long Island University's Brooklyn Campus where he teaches British and

African American literatures. He holds a Ph.D. in English from the CUNY Graduate School. His publications include *"Puzzled Which to Choose": Conflicting Sociopolitical Views in the Works of Captain Frederick Marryat* (Peter Lang Publishing Co., 1997) and *"Winds Can Wake Up the Dead": An Eric D. Walrond Reader* (Wayne State University Press, 1998).